His mouth covered hers with no hesitancy—as if he had every right to go deep.

His tongue was savage and demanding, holding nothing back and accepting no evasion. Nate tasted of loneliness, anger, and lust. Hard, needy, *demanding* lust.

The men at the door were watching.

But her body didn't care—instantly igniting instead of pushing away. Her heart thundered in her ears, and she fell into his heat, uncaring of whether or not he caught her. He wrapped around her, his unyielding body holding her upright. He caressed her with his tongue, and she met him thrust for thrust, fierce pleasure lighting her on fire.

Audrey forgot where they were, who they were, everything but the desperate need he created.

He broke the kiss, blatant male hunger crossing his face. His breath panted out even as he moved them in tune with the music.

She softened against him, allowing him to lead so she didn't collapse. Her mind whirled, and she shook her head to regain reality. "Nathan, what do you want?" The question emerged as a breathless plea she couldn't mask.

That quickly, all hints of desire slid from his face. His chin hardened. "Want? I want to know what happened to the child you were carrying five years ago when you ripped out my heart. Where's my baby, Audrey?"

Also by Rebecca Zanetti

Forgotten Sins
Sweet Revenge
Total Surrender

BLIND
FAITH

REBECCA ZANETTI

FOREVER

NEW YORK   BOSTON

Copyright © 2014 by Rebecca Zanetti
Excerpt from *Total Surrender* copyright © 2014 by Rebecca Zanetti
All rights reserved. In accordance with the U.S. Copyright Act of 1976, the scanning, uploading, and electronic sharing of any part of this book without the permission of the publisher constitute unlawful piracy and theft of the author's intellectual property. If you would like to use material from the book (other than for review purposes), prior written permission must be obtained by contacting the publisher at permissions@hbgusa.com. Thank you for your support of the author's rights.

Forever
Hachette Book Group
1290 Avenue of the Americas
New York, NY 10104

www.HachetteBookGroup.com

Printed in the United States of America

Originally published as an ebook

First mass-market edition: January 2015
10 9 8 7 6 5 4 3 2

OPM

Forever is an imprint of Grand Central Publishing.
The Forever name and logo are trademarks of Hachette Book Group, Inc.

The Hachette Speakers Bureau provides a wide range of authors for speaking events. To find out more, go to www.hachettespeakersbureau.com or call (866) 376-6591.

The publisher is not responsible for websites (or their content) that are not owned by the publisher.

To Kathy and Herb Zanetti, AKA Guga and Papa, who love and protect family with everything they are.

ACKNOWLEDGMENTS

Publishing a book requires both solitude to write and collaboration to make happen. BLIND FAITH wouldn't exist without the generosity and hard work from several amazing people. I'd first like to express my gratitude to my family and friends, especially Big Tone, for keeping me from becoming a hermit as I write.

A big thank-you to my editor, Michele Bidelspach, who is singularly one of the most insightful and intelligent women I've ever had the honor of working with.

To my agent, Caitlin Blasdell, who has provided much-needed guidance, humor, and protection in this wild publishing industry—my career and writing are where they are right now because of our mutual hard work. To Liza Dawson, thank you for the support and the fun dinners while at conferences!

Thanks to Megha Parekh for all the hard work and great communication, and thanks to copy editor Carrie Andrews and production editor Jamie Snider for the precise, excellent work. Thank you also to Diane Luger and Larry Rostant for the truly awesome book covers, and to everyone at Grand Central Publishing / Forever who work so tirelessly getting books to happy readers.

Finally, thanks to my street team, Rebecca's Realm Runners, for the incredible support and a fun place to play on Facebook.

BLIND FAITH

PROLOGUE

Southern Tennessee Hills
Twenty Years Ago

NATHAN'S BOOTS ECHOED on the hard tiles, the deep sound thrown back by the cinder blocks lining the wall. He'd wiped the snow off the bottom of his boots before heading inside, but the soles were still slippery. His eleven-year-old gut churned, and his mind spun. His older brother, Mattie, was out on a mission, and shit was about to hit the fan.

The situation was totally Nate's fault, but he couldn't be taken from the facility. If he was forced out, Matt would blame himself. And who would take care of the two younger brothers when Matt went out on assignment? At around twelve years old, Matt often went out on a job, and somebody had to protect Shane and Jory. Nate had taken on the duty years ago.

He paused outside of the office doorway and took several deep breaths. Centering himself, he smoothed his face into innocent lines and knocked on the door.

"Come in," came the low baritone of the commander.

Sweat dripped down Nate's back. He shoved open the door and hurried inside to stand at attention. The scents of bleach and gunpowder nauseated him.

The commander studied him with black, fathomless eyes while sitting behind a metal desk. He wore a soldier's uniform, his hair in a buzz cut, his body lean and hard. Behind him sat a woman furiously scribbling in a notebook on a small table. Dr. Madison, the head scientist who studied the cadets at the facility, liked to scribble.

"We seem to have a situation, Cadet Nathan," the commander said.

Nate's spit dried up. "Yes, sir." God, please make the situation be about what he'd done wrong and not about Matt's mission. Matt was invincible. Nothing could happen to him.

"We found your stash of tree, decorations, and cookies," Dr. Madison said, her blue eyes narrowing in calculation.

Relief tickled down Nate's spine. Matt was all right. "Yes, ma'am." Damn it. He'd hidden those items carefully in a storage shack on the outskirts of one of the training fields. How had they found everything?

"Cadet Nathan, this is a military facility. You are a soldier created in a lab to follow orders and protect our organization." The commander pushed back from the desk and rose to his full height. "How in the world did you learn about Christmas?"

Nate tilted his head to look way up at the commander's face. Someday Nate would be taller and bigger. Even tougher. But now, not so much. "I can't remember, sir." In truth, he and his three brothers had snuck into computer rooms to watch television sitcoms via satellite. The idea of Christmas had struck a chord with all of them.

The brothers fought for freedom by following orders, and they fought for other people to have families and pretty trees with presents. Maybe someday Nate and his brothers could have that, too. If they were strong enough and good enough, maybe they'd get families who would love them. Christmas seemed to be about family and love, both of which intrigued Nate until his chest hurt.

"Humph." The commander clasped his hands behind his back. "I take it you were planning some sort of celebration with your brothers?"

Nate's knees wobbled, but he stayed upright. "Yes, sir. I thought the younger brothers should have good memories of their childhoods." It was too late for him, and that was all right. But he needed to give his younger brothers something good in their lives. Plus, seeing the younger kids happy cut down on Matt's guilt over how hard he trained them.

"How did you procure the items?" Dr. Madison asked, her pencil poised to write.

Nate shrugged. "I cut off the top of a tree and made the decorations from old weapons." The presents he'd either stolen throughout the compound or made himself, and those were hidden somewhere else. Hopefully safely. Jory would love the modified remote-control attack helicopter.

"I could have you hanged," the commander said thoughtfully.

Dread and fear heated Nate's lungs. Who would take care of Shane and Jory? "Yes, sir."

The commander scratched his chin and eyed Madison. "Well?" he asked her.

Nate gulped in air and looked toward the woman. Would she want him hanged?

Dr. Madison pursed her red lips. "I think we should give Cadet Nathan a choice."

Great. Another one of her crappy experiments. "A choice, ma'am?" Nate asked.

"Yes. The first choice is that you relinquish all of the Christmas items, and we'll forget this ever happened." She tapped her pencil on the paper. "The second choice is that you go ahead with Christmas for your brothers, and we'll forget this ever happened."

Nate swallowed. "What's the catch, ma'am?"

She smiled, revealing sharp white teeth. "A few days after your pseudo-Christmas, you go onto the training field with the three oldest Brown brothers."

The three oldest were all around fifteen, and although Nate was a hell of a fighter, he'd get hurt. Nobody could take on all three of them.

His mind reeled as he considered his options. A little bit of pain was worth giving Shane and Jory a small bit of happiness. Of thinking they were part of a real family with good times. Plus, Matt often came back from a mission angry and depressed. A happy memory would be good for him, too.

"I'll take the second choice—with one condition," Nate said, his chin lifting.

Dr. Madison giggled. "Listen to the boy, Commander. He's giving us conditions."

The commander lifted a dark eyebrow, his lip twisting. "What's the condition, Cadet?"

Nathan took a deep breath. Maybe the Brown brothers wouldn't break too many of his bones. "This deal is between us, and I don't go onto the field with the Browns until Matt is out on another mission." Jory and Shane would think Nate had gotten in trouble but wouldn't know why. Hopefully by the time Matt returned, Nate would be mostly healed, so he wouldn't figure it out. "Matt can't know the truth."

"Interesting." Madison smoothed back her black hair. "You don't want him to know you're sacrificing your health for your brothers?"

"No, ma'am." Definitely not. Matt would blame himself and maybe go off the deep end and finally challenge the commander. None of them were ready for that. Yet.

Dr. Madison nodded. "You intrigue me, young man. How far would you go for family? For love?"

Nate frowned. "I don't understand the question, ma'am."

She smiled, her eyes lighting up. "You have a deal, Cadet Nathan. Have a very merry Christmas."

CHAPTER
1

Washington, DC
Present Day

T HE GLITTERING HOTEL ballroom teemed with rep-
tiles and predators more dangerous than any snake
or rebel fighter Nate had killed in humid jungles far from
home. These masked their true natures with designer
suits and red lipstick as they used the sword of power in
another typical fund-raiser for some useless cause. He
could put them all down within seconds.

Or maybe he just needed to follow his younger
brother's advice and stay the hell away from people for
a while.

Unfortunately, he didn't have time to seek solitude.

The kill chip implanted near his spine pulsed as his
heart rate sped up, forcing blood quickly through his
veins. Veins much too close to the abnormal killing
device. So he counted evenly to control his heart, eyeing the exits from the opulent ballroom, estimating how
many security guards stood at watch. At least seven had

been provided by the hotel, while several more, dressed in Armani, chatted with partygoers as if they belonged.

They didn't belong amid the rich and powerful any more than Nate did.

The difference was that Nate liked it that way.

Even so, he'd donned a Brioni tuxedo that had earned him more than one come-hither glance since he'd arrived at the fund-raiser—from women and a couple of men. A fake beard covered his jaw, while brown contacts masked his eye color. But there was no way to hide his height or the breadth of his chest, so he used them to his advantage in the sleek suit.

Even with his size, hiding in plain sight was one of his specialties.

His heart rate slowed, and he tuned in to the mundane conversations around him. With his enhanced hearing, he often had to filter most noise or he'd go insane. But tonight he listened for one woman, opening up his senses. Heart and respiratory rates had signatures—tempo, rhythm, and something too difficult to explain—and right now he hunted for one he'd once known well.

She didn't seem to be in the large ballroom.

A group of lobbyists argued to his left, while two women in glittering sheaths spoke over champagne glasses to his right. The men argued about the next Super Bowl, and the women disagreed over international relations with China.

He bit back a grin and maneuvered between tables, once again shoving the bombarding sounds into a box.

While the ability to hear a penny hit the ground outside the raucous gathering gave him the edge he needed, now he required a clear head. This might be the most difficult job he'd ever taken, but if he or his brothers were to survive, he needed to find the one woman he'd never thought he'd seek.

Only to save his brothers from their kill chips would he even attempt to speak with her again. She'd broken his heart once, and once was enough. He had never believed in second chances—for himself or for anybody else.

But his one true job in life, the reason he had purpose, was to protect his brothers. So he'd storm hell once again to do what he needed to do.

"Excuse me." A petite blonde in sparkling red brushed her breasts against his arm. "Do I know you?"

"No." He fell back on training and pasted on a charming smile. "Much to my dismay."

She twittered, and bloodred lips curved in a smile. Even in the four-inch spiked heels, she had to tip back her head to meet his gaze. She licked her lips. "I'm sure we've met."

He had the oddest urge to back away from her voracious smile. What did she want? His supersenses allowed him to pay attention to the security patrolling the room while also monitoring her eye movements so he could discern the truth. As a liar, she wasn't bad. But they didn't know each other. "I'm afraid we haven't met."

"Let's remedy that situation." She stepped closer, and the scent of strong floral perfume gathered around them.

From her breathing and the slight dilation of her pupils, he could tell she'd probably imbibed at least three glasses of champagne. If he'd needed a companion to use as cover, she would've been perfect. But this was a solo mission.

A heartbeat echoed in his head, shoving away all other sounds. *Thump. Thump. Thump.* Familiar and once dear—he knew that beat. Slowly, he turned toward the doorway to the smaller room.

Audrey.

This was the closest he'd been to her in five years. His

focus remained on the stunning woman across the room. His entire body tensed, and adrenaline flooded his system. He'd been gifted the genetic ability to control his bodily responses, and usually he was the best. But at the moment, he might as well be a robot on the fritz and not a trained, unfeeling assassin.

She'd thinned out in the five years they'd been apart, shedding the last vestiges of her teenage years. Nicely muscled arms showed health, while faint circles under her eyes hinted that she worked too hard.

He already knew how hard she worked, considering he'd been tailing her for a week. From a distance. Hoping to get a glimpse of her child. Their child.

Even after seven whole days, one look at her and his body short-circuited. That had to end.

Her dress covered her breasts in a way that was both alluring and modest, while the high heels accented toned legs. Those legs had felt amazing wrapped around his hips, and sometimes, when dreams intruded, he could still feel her. Smell her. Taste her.

She smiled at a man gesturing wildly to another man. Nate idly tuned in to the conversation, noting it centered around tort reform.

"Well." The blonde in front of him spun on a heel and huffed off.

He'd forgotten all about her. If she had been a threat, she could've stabbed him in the gut. He wouldn't have seen it coming.

Yet another example of why he needed to stay away from Audrey Madison.

Even so, he slid his champagne glass onto a table and strode toward the smaller ballroom. It was time to find the truth—whether Audrey liked it or not.

• • •

Somebody was watching her. Audrey Madison glanced around the opulent ballroom, her face remaining calm while her heart roared into overdrive. She'd navigated a lonely childhood, surviving with finely honed instincts. The need to fight or flee lived in her daily moments.

Now was the time to flee.

Elegant and sexy, her black cocktail dress wrapped tightly around her fit form and wouldn't hinder her escape. Unfortunately, the three-inch Jimmy Choo heels needed to be kicked off, a necessity made nearly impossible by the two U.S. senators currently debating tort reform to her left.

She automatically smiled at a pun from her boss, Senator Nash. He'd slicked back his gray hair and trimmed his mustache, making him look more like a rancher playing dress-up than ever before.

She turned and took a sip of champagne while searching unobtrusively for the threat.

Men in tuxedos and women in stunning dresses scattered throughout the most prestigious hotel ballroom in Washington, DC. Tension rode high in the party atmosphere due to the hint of power threading through the air. The attendees of the political fund-raiser either had power and were desperate to hold on to it, or they were filching at tendrils and grappling to claim more.

Her reason for being there differed. Somewhat.

In fact, she'd give her seven-hundred-dollar shoes away in a nanosecond for the opportunity to curl up with comfy socks and *Little Women*. Sure, it was a classic, but it was about siblings and a nicer time. She owned several dog-eared copies.

The idea that people in real life could have families and make homes was as much fiction as the novels she read. Audrey's talent lay in subterfuge and not in home-making, unfortunately. She'd love to have kids and make the world a fun place for them—from birthday parties to the everyday cutting of crusts off sandwiches. Carol Brady from *The Brady Bunch* had the best job around, in Audrey's opinion. Not only did Carol have a safe life, but she had a family. A real one.

Audrey took another sip of champagne, searching for the source of her unease. Where was the threat?

Her gaze swept past the two imposing soldiers dressed in suits standing by the outside exit, pretending to chat. They'd been following her for weeks, and they were certainly owned by the commander. He'd been having her followed, and the only explanation she could come up with was that he'd lost trust in her. If he'd ever had any.

He'd put her in the political world as an aide to a powerful senator to further the commander's agenda, and if he discovered her own agenda, he'd have her killed.

But the two guys watching her proved that the commander wasn't sure yet—she was still standing.

No, a stronger predator stood near. She *felt* him.

As if drawn by a magnet, her focus landed on a man leaning casually against the doorway leading to the dance floor. He looked familiar, but she couldn't quite place him until recognition slammed into her, heating her ears and weakening her knees. It couldn't be. It *really* couldn't be.

Her fingers lightened their hold around the champagne flute, and she clutched tight to keep from dropping the delicate crystal.

How could Nathan be here? Heat flowed through her so quickly her lungs seized. Panic flared into her veins, and furious tears pricked the backs of her eyes. In a nanosecond, her entire central nervous system snapped like a live wire.

His gaze held hers captive as he lifted one lip in a mocking grin.

That one minor, sarcastic move dashed any silly dream she'd harbored of his finding her. Rescuing her. Declaring he still loved her and offering her a chance at a life with him.

At the realization, a very welcomed anger swept away her panic. She lifted her flute and silently toasted him, taking a deep drink and keeping his gaze, no matter how much the contact stung. Then, with a gentle smile, she turned to the men and excused herself.

Slowly, as if she had all the time in the world, she maneuvered around people, her hips nearly swaying. After five years of physical therapy, she almost walked without a limp. The high heels were in celebration of her doctor's visit two weeks earlier, where the doctor proclaimed her leg was as good as it was going to get.

Now all she needed was a confirmation that her last surgery three months ago had repaired her internally and she could finally relax. Concentrating on walking smoothly, she made her way toward the dance floor and to him.

Even as she kept up a calm façade, her mind raced. He had to get out of there. Didn't he realize the commander still hunted him? For years she'd figured she'd be the bait to bring Nathan back, but she hadn't thought he was stupid enough to seek her out. Especially in public.

The commander would have no problem causing a scene if it meant reclaiming one of the Gray brothers.

She reached Nate's side and almost recoiled from the heat and familiar scent of the man. Male and spice, something undeniably dangerous—Nathan. All Nathan.

Instead, she held out a hand as if they'd never met. As if he didn't still occupy every dream she had after falling into an exhausted sleep. "Hello. I'm Audrey."

Nathan's hand engulfed hers in a touch so familiar her heart broke all over again, even while desire unfurled inside her abdomen. "Jason McGovern. I work for the Neoland Corporation as a lobbyist."

Ah. Good choice. Several executives from flush technology firms were in attendance at the ball. Audrey extracted her hand and forced an interested smile as she studied him. He had inserted brown contacts to mask his unusual gray eyes, but the longer brown hair seemed to be his. She had wondered if he would grow it out after escaping the military group that had raised him. A shadow lined his jaw, also looking natural. He'd definitely hardened even more in the five years they'd been apart. "Your disguise doesn't hide much," she whispered.

He lifted a muscled shoulder that revealed the true predator lurking beneath the classic jacket. "I'm done hiding."

Those three innocuous words flared her neurons awake in terror. He had to stay underground, away from the commander and his men. "You can't beat them." Nobody could beat them. "Leave now, Nathan. Please." She needed him alive, even if he hated her. The world had to keep him in it.

"Now, Audrey, you actually sound like you care." He claimed her flute and finished the remaining champagne in two drinks, his lips covering the same spot she'd used. The hard cords of his neck flexed.

Feminine awareness zinged through her body and pebbled her nipples. The man had always been dangerous, yet an edge lived in him now that was as appealing as it was deadly. That edge tempted her on a primal level she'd hoped had disappeared when he had. Apparently not.

To mask her unwelcome desire, she moved to go. "Well, enjoy your night." She expected him to stop her retreat and wasn't surprised when his calloused hand

wrapped around her bare upper arm, but she hadn't antici-
pated his next words.

"Let's dance." He turned her toward the dance floor.

She balked. "No." She couldn't dance with him,
couldn't be touched by him.

"Yes." His hold slid down to the back of her elbow, and
he ushered her toward where the orchestra was playing
"I Will Wait for You" by Michel Legrand. The warmth
in Nate's touch flared her nerves to life in an erotic need
she'd worked hard to overcome.

She could either cause a scene or go along with him.
Didn't he understand if she protested, he'd be a dead man?

He turned and pulled her into his arms.

The bittersweet moment her body met his stole her
breath away, while memories of passion and love assailed
her. For the briefest of times, she'd belonged in the safe
circle of his arms. The only time in her life she'd been
truly happy and not alone. Ah, the dreams she'd spun,
even though she'd known better.

Happily-ever-after didn't exist for her. Hell, it didn't
exist for anybody.

The music wound around them, through them, pro-
claiming a romance that couldn't really exist. His heated
palm settled at the small of her waist.

Every instinct she had tempted her to slide against
him, to burrow into his warmth. Her mind fought to keep
her body calm, but her brain had never triumphed when
dealing with Nathan. Her heart had ruled and in the end
had been shattered.

Not again.

"Nate—"

"Shhh." He tightened his hold and drew her into an
impressive erection.

She gasped, her face heating, her sex convulsing. Blinking, she glanced up to see if the contact affected him, and stilled at the look in his eyes.

Furious. The man was truly furious. Even with the contacts masking his eyes, his anger shone bright.

She tried to step back, but he kept her where he wanted her. Yeah, she knew she'd hurt him when she'd ended their relationship, but after nearly five years, he shouldn't still be so mad. He'd had freedom for five years, which was a heck of a lot better than she'd had. She'd had pain and fear and uncertainty. She blinked. "What is wrong with you?"

His impossibly hard jaw somehow hardened even more. "Oh, we'll discuss that shortly." Threat lived strongly in the calm words. "For now, we're going to finish this dance. Then you'll take the north exit and meet me in my car so we can talk."

"If I don't?" she asked quietly, awareness quickening her breath.

His hands flexed. "I know where you live, I know your daily routine in working for Senator Nash, and I know where you go when you need time alone. You can't hide, you can't outrun me—and you know it."

The hairs on the back of her neck rose. "How long have you been watching me?" More importantly, why hadn't she noticed?

"A week. Long enough to know the two apes near the doorway are following you, too. What's up with that?" His hold tightened just enough to show his strength.

She shrugged. "They haven't made a move, so I'm not worrying about it." Not true, and by the narrowing of Nate's eyes, she knew he could still smell a lie a mile away. "The commander is having me followed."

Nate's jaw clenched. "Why?"

"Dunno." They didn't have time to discuss it. "You should go now."

"No." He spun her, easily controlling their movements. Her leg hitched, and she stumbled against him.

He frowned. "What's wrong?"

"Nothing." None of his business, that was. "What do you want to talk about?"

His gaze narrowed, and he spun her again. She tripped again. Her stupid leg didn't move that way. She glanced toward the doorway and the two soldiers watching her. They'd straightened to alert stances. She tried to look normal.

"What's wrong with your leg?" Nate asked, brows furrowing.

Oh, they were so not going into her injuries on the dance floor. "You almost sound like you care." She threw his words back at him, gratified when his nostrils flared.

His gaze probed deep, wandering down her neck. He blinked several times, his chest moving with a harsh intake of breath. "I like your dress," he rumbled, his voice a low whisper.

With his tight hold, she had no doubt the tops of her breasts were visible. "Nathan, don't—"

"Don't what?" His gaze rose to her lips. A light of a different sort percolated through his angry eyes. She knew that look. Her body heated and her thighs softened. His erection jumped against her, and she bit down a groan.

"One kiss, Audrey."

Her eyes widened to let in more light. "No," she breathed. One of his hands held hers, the other pressed against her back. Thank goodness. He couldn't grab her and kiss her, no matter how appealing the thought. "Bad idea."

"I know." Nate didn't need hands. His lips met hers so quickly, she never saw him move.

His mouth covered hers with no hesitancy, no question—as if he had every right to go deep. His tongue was savage and demanding, holding nothing back and accepting no evasion. He tasted of loneliness, anger, and lust. Hard, needy, *demanding* lust.

The men at the door were watching.

But her body didn't care—instantly igniting instead of bolting. Her heart thundered in her ears, and she fell into his heat, uncaring of whether he caught her. He wrapped around her, his unyielding body holding her upright. He caressed her with his tongue, and she met him thrust for thrust, fierce pleasure lighting her on fire.

She forgot where they were, who they were, everything but the desperate need he created.

He broke the kiss, blatant male hunger crossing his face. His breath panted out even as he moved them in tune with the music.

She softened against him, allowing him to lead so she didn't collapse. Her mind whirled, and she shook her head to regain reality. "Nathan, what do you want?" The question emerged as a breathless plea she failed to mask.

That quickly, all hints of desire slid from his face. His chin hardened. "Want? I want to know what happened to the child you were carrying five years ago when you ripped out my heart. Where's my baby, Audrey?"

CHAPTER
2

NATHAN SETTLED AGAINST the leather seat in the SUV, his gaze on the side entrance to the ballroom as rain smashed down on the windshield. Even though he'd expected some kind of reaction, the slam to the gut upon touching Audrey again had stolen his breath away. For a few moments he was a lovesick kid again who had hopes for a future with the girl beyond his dreams. After the song had ended, he'd had to walk away to pull himself together. Now, waiting outside for her, he settled himself.

He felt nothing.

She hadn't answered his direct question about the baby and had instead spun away from him. That time he'd let her go.

But the second he had her alone, she was going to tell him the truth.

Cold and purposeful, he'd follow his mission parameters and get the information he needed from Audrey. First, he'd find his kid. Less than a week ago, he and his brothers had found Audrey's mother's video diary where the woman claimed Audrey was pregnant with Nate's child.

It had been recorded five years ago, before he'd escaped from the military group that had created him.

He'd instantly set out to find Audrey. After a week of following her, he knew the kid didn't live with her. Had she actually given birth and left a child to the monsters who'd created Nate? That couldn't be possible.

The nearly desperate hope that filled him at the thought of a child ached somewhere deep in his gut, making a mockery of his lack of feelings. So badly, he wanted a kid. Wanted his brothers to have kids. Matt and Shane had found love, and they should be able to have families. Real ones like they'd all seen on television so long ago.

They could create families and have what they'd never experienced as kids. Could be part of something good, and maybe have their bloodlines live on. Sure, they'd been created by monsters, but if they created something good, couldn't that balance out their past?

Maybe someday that good would outshine all the bad they'd done.

But he wondered, since he hadn't seen a child this past week, had the video been wrong? Was there ever a child? If so, how could Audrey not tell him?

Yeah, he wasn't exactly a good guy, considering the missions he'd taken. He knew dozens of ways to kill somebody. But he'd let Audrey in, and she should've known he'd love a child. He would've protected that child with everything he was. A surprising loss flooded him, at both her lack of trust and the idea that maybe no kid existed. All he needed was the truth from Audrey either way. Once that was confirmed, Nate would gain her cooperation in obtaining access to the computer codes that would save his brothers' lives.

Rain continued beating down on the windshield, the

darkness swirling around outside. Of course, his senses were enhanced, and his vision rivaled a wild animal's. In fact, he heard Audrey's heels clicking toward the door right before she pushed it open. A slight hitch slowed her gait, and he wondered again how she'd hurt her leg.

Not that he cared. He couldn't care—not again. His brothers came first, and saving them was his only mission. Probably his last mission.

Yet when Audrey stepped out into the deluge, he instantly slipped out of the SUV and hurried to open the passenger side door, his large hand protecting her head from the rain. After she'd settled her legs into his front seat, he shut the door, senses tuned in to their surroundings. So far, nobody had followed her out.

Good.

Stretching back inside the vehicle, he paused. "Give me your phone."

She started and swung toward him. "I didn't bring one tonight."

He measured her breathing with his ears and listened for her steady heartbeat. She was telling the truth. "Why not?"

She shrugged. "GPS. Why make it easy for them?"

What in the world was she talking about? "Who?"

"Doesn't matter." She squinted out at the pouring rain. "Are we staying here?"

"No." He maneuvered into traffic and quickly drove away from the ballroom.

The vehicle filled with her scent of gardenias and woman. He'd seen her naked, he'd tasted her freshly washed skin, and he knew without a doubt that the scent was all her. No perfumes...all female. Once again, the sweetness threatened to drop him to his knees.

He'd loved her. Completely.

"Put on your seat belt," he said quietly, making a left turn.

"Yours isn't on."

Of course his wasn't on. If something happened, he needed access to his weapon and the availability to jump out of the car already firing. Yet the safest course for Audrey was to be belted in. "Now, Audrey."

From his peripheral vision, he could see her blink. Could almost feel her mind spinning as she decided whether to defy or humor him.

She hesitated one second too long.

Pulling to the side of the quiet street, he reached over her and grasped the belt. His forearm brushed her breasts, and his groin flared to life. A quick click of the buckle, and he drove the car back onto the road.

"Become a take-charge bully, have you?" she muttered, crossing her legs.

He cut a look at her that felt hard. "Yes. You might want to remember that." He'd been trained by the best in the world at intimidation.

So when she rolled her stunning blue eyes, he stilled. The woman knew how well he'd been trained, and she understood some of his heightened abilities. After she'd betrayed him, how could she not fear him? At least a little?

She cleared her throat. "Where are we going?"

"Somewhere to talk." He turned down a side street, heading for a motel across the Washington Bridge.

"We can talk here," she said, glancing at her watch. "It's late, and I have work tomorrow."

He gave a short nod. "How did you escape the men watching you?"

She lifted a creamy shoulder. "I just went out the back door. They weren't expecting the move because I haven't done anything unpredictable for the two weeks they've been tailing me."

Smart. Uncomfortably so. "Have you been planning something unpredictable?" he asked.

"No, but a girl likes to keep all options open."

Was she as calm as she appeared? Tuning in his senses, the ones beyond normal, he took note of her increased heart rate and rapid breathing. Though she looked calm, her body was rioting. Not as in control as she seemed, but he appreciated her nearly bored façade. His Audrey had grown up in the last five years. "I prefer you alone and contained when we speak," he said. Yeah, he meant to sound threatening.

Her sigh echoed with irritation. "Listen, Nate—"

"No. We'll talk in a few minutes."

"Fine." She turned to watch the streetlights brighten and then dim outside the car, effectively ignoring him.

Several minutes later, he turned into a dive of a motel, parking by the last room on the bottom floor. Audrey reached for her door, and he stopped her with a hand on her arm. "Stay in the vehicle." Jumping out, he shut his door and listened through the storm.

No close-by heartbeats, no sense of danger. Good.

Crossing in front of the car, he opened her door and held out a hand to assist her.

She glanced at his hand and gingerly slid her palm against his. A shiver wandered up her arm, and she stepped out of the car. Tentatively. Waiting for a moment, she tested her balance in those heels on the cracked concrete and released his hand.

"What's wrong with your leg?" he asked.

"Nothing." She hunched her bare shoulders against the rain, and he herded her toward the doorway to room 112.

Unlocking it, he stepped inside, holding out a hand for her to wait. A quick smell and listen proved nobody had been in the room. "Come in."

He ushered her inside and shut the door. Ratty orange shag carpet covered the floors, and a maroon flowered bedspread covered the king-sized bed. Two dented chairs perched next to a particleboard table. The television was circa 1980 and the prints on the walls were of dogs playing golf. Not poker...golf.

Audrey glanced around the room and at the bed before turning toward him. "It smells like death in here."

"Not even close." The room stank like smoke and sweat, not death. He'd been around enough death to know the difference. "Have a seat."

She swallowed and glanced at the rickety chairs but didn't move. "Okay."

"You won't need a tetanus shot," he said. "Probably." The woman was clearly used to much finer things. He glanced down at her form. The black dress hugged her body, revealing the tops of her incredible breasts. The heels elongated her legs in a way that made him want them wrapped around his hips. She'd tossed her dark hair up on her head, revealing a slender and vulnerable neck. High cheekbones, full mouth, and eyes that defied description as merely blue, Audrey had grown even more beautiful in the five years since he'd last touched her.

But he'd never really known her, now, had he?

"Sit." He pulled out a chair for her and dropped into the remaining one, hoping it held his weight. "Now talk."

She gingerly slid onto the chair, eyeing the dented table. Her gaze rose to meet his. "There's no child, Nate. I'm sorry."

The words cut into his heart like a spike. He studied

her face, her breathing, her movements, eye flickers, and changes in skin temperature to ensure he received the truth. "Were you pregnant?"

"Yes."

His gut heaved. He didn't need to ask the next question as to whose kid it was. Audrey had been a virgin when they'd gotten together. "What happened?"

"Miscarriage." Her voice remained calm, but a flash of pain lightened her eyes. "Eight weeks in, and I miscarried. It's common and not a reflection of your ability to have more children."

Sorrow wanted to choke him, so he numbed his feelings. "Did you know?"

"Know what?"

"That you were pregnant when we broke up?"

"No." She tapped pink nails on the table. "I found out a week later."

He eyed her closely. No signs of lying, and the truth ripped through him with painful blades. A kid. A real kid. "Were you going to tell me?"

"Yes." She lifted a shoulder. "I was trying to figure out a way to get to you without my mother knowing, and the world exploded. You disappeared, I lost the baby, and I thought that was the end of things. I always wanted you to find freedom, and you finally had a chance."

He leaned toward her. "Why didn't you leave?"

Her gaze dropped to her hands. "I didn't have anywhere else to go."

A lie. Or rather, an evasion. She wasn't telling him something. "This is the time that you tell me everything, Audrey. No secrets."

Her head jerked up, challenge firming her chin. "Or what?"

He lifted an eyebrow. Good question. "You know I can make you talk."

She smiled, unveiling a dimple he remembered well in her left cheek. "I know you're trained, Nate. But I also know that you don't torture women to get information. I'm not exactly scared here."

He reached for her hand, flattening it under his. Fire lanced up his arm, settling through his body. One touch. All it took was one touch for his body to light on fire. Yet he kept his voice calm and his face expressionless. "Who said anything about torture?"

She swallowed, a flush sliding from her chest up and over her face. "Get real."

He didn't speak, just kept his gaze on hers. Knowing and hard. The way she met his stare impressed him, but he wouldn't let her win the little contest of wills. Time was running short, and he required her cooperation.

She gave in first with a little huff. "Fine. What do you want?"

His gaze unwillingly shot to the bed before focusing back on her. "Information."

"About what?" A little frown settled between her arched eyebrows.

"Everything. Where's the commander, where's the headquarters, where's your mother, and more importantly, how do we defuse the chips?"

"What chips?" she asked.

Fury rushed through him so quickly his ears tingled. He grabbed her arms and hauled her up, stepping into her space and staring her down. "Don't ever play dumb with me, Audrey. I promise you won't like the result."

Sparks burst in her eyes, and she shoved him two-handed in the chest.

He didn't move.

"I've never played dumb, and I have no idea what you're talking about." Her hands remained on his chest, nails curling into his pecs.

The idea she couldn't help him was unthinkable, and he gripped her tighter. "The chips near our spines. Where's the computer program to defuse them, and who has the damn codes?" Only stubborn will kept him from shaking her.

She blinked and bit her lip. "I honestly have no idea what you're talking about."

"You're lying." She had to be.

She shook her head, pursing her lips. Soft, kissable lips he still tasted in his dreams. Far too tempting for any man to ignore. "I'm telling the truth."

The denial cut him deep, and he struggled to maintain clarity. The woman stood so close—touching him. Her nails bit into his skin, sending electrical zaps through his body. His mind shut down. He yanked her closer, and his mouth took hers.

Anger and desperation hinted on his kiss as he took her mouth. No finesse, no cajoling, just a furious taking.

Even so, she kissed him back, losing herself in his storm, her hands flattening across his hard chest. She'd missed him. Missed this. The feeling of being swept up, of being everything. His passion made her feel alive. Although the kiss was full of fury, her body ignited for the first time in five long years.

His tongue swept inside her mouth, tasting her, taking everything. One broad hand slipped to the small of her back, pressing her against a rock-hard erection full of demand.

Her cleft swelled, and her knees trembled. A cramp started in her bad leg, and she ignored it, caught up in the moment.

With a low growl, his free hand tugged down the top of her dress. Wrenching his lips free, he nipped her earlobe, wandering lower, taking one nipple into his mouth. Electricity shot from her breast to her clit. She bit her lip to stop from crying out.

Her legs gave out.

He swept her up, her legs straddling him, and pressed her against the wall.

This couldn't happen. She stilled, her hands sliding through his thick hair. "I wondered if you'd grow it out." Was this her voice? Husky and needy?

He scraped her nipple with sharp teeth.

Need zinged through her body to settle between her legs. She gasped. Nate had always been beyond gentle with her, and she'd wondered at the primal male she knew lived within him. But in their short time together, he'd treated her as something fragile and delicate.

Now the real Nate was unleashed.

At sensing the real man, her heart thumped. For so long, she'd wondered about him. Very few people in the world were allowed to see who he really was, and for the first time, she was on the *inside*. Where she'd always wanted to belong.

With a soft *pop*, he released her nipple to glance up. Even behind the contacts, those eyes darkened, glittering with hunger. His nostrils flared as he exhaled. As he regained control.

That cut jaw hardened. "Now tell me about the chips."

Vulnerability competed with the desire raging inside her. Her skirt had pooled up, and her legs were spread, his erection pressing against her panties. The top of the dress remained down, revealing her breasts. "Put me down, and we'll talk."

"Oh, we'll talk now." His hands clenched on her buttocks.

She began to struggle and only succeeded in brushing her breasts against his chest and her sex against his cock. Lust caught her breath in her throat. "Now, Nate."

"No." Determination lived in every line on his chiseled face. "This is a perfect position for you to tell me everything."

She couldn't physically take him, and she knew it. A punch to his eyes would result in an irritated smile from him—and she wasn't armed. She tried to harden her expression, but her leg cramped, and she winced.

His gaze narrowed. "What's wrong?"

She wanted to lie, but it was really starting to hurt. "Leg cramp."

He glanced down at her left leg and stilled. "What the fuck?" Moving quickly, he pivoted and deposited her on the bed, sliding the dress up farther. "What happened to you?"

She sighed and reached down to rub the area right above her knee. "My leg broke in several places and needed a few surgeries to repair."

"How?" he asked, his voice hoarse.

She'd give anything to be able to lie, but Nate was a human lie detector. "The day you escaped the military organization, I was at the facility."

"No." He shook his head and released her, stepping back. "I made sure you were off base when we blew it apart."

She nodded. "I started bleeding and went to the infirmary." They had the best medical facilities in the world, and she had hoped they'd be able to save the baby.

He coughed, going pale. "So I did this?"

"No." She shook her head. "The ceiling collapsed, and debris trapped me. You were right in that I wasn't supposed to be there."

He paled further. "D-did I kill the baby?"

"No." She swallowed, tears pricking the backs of her eyes. "I promise. You didn't." She'd done everything possible to protect the baby, but what if the stress and fear about the military organization had caused the miscarriage? Logically, she knew better. But emotion, not logic, kept her up at night anyway. She couldn't forgive herself, and there was no doubt Nate would ever forgive her. His world had to be black and white, and she had understood that from the beginning.

He rubbed his chin, his shoulders relaxing. "All right."

She wiped her nose. "I'd already seen an ultrasound, and the baby was gone. I promise, the explosion didn't harm the baby. It was already too late." Nate would never be able to live with having caused the miscarriage. "I'm sorry."

He ran a hand through his thick hair, looking more out of sorts than she'd ever seen him. "Promise me."

She nodded, her gaze meeting his. "I give you my word."

He blinked and dropped to his haunches. Wide hands settled on her knees. Dark sorrow and determination angled his features. "I don't want any more hurt between us, Audrey. I'm sorry about the baby, but I need to save my brothers."

"I understand." She'd been trying to save both him and his brothers since the beginning. "But the best thing for you is to stay hidden from the commander. He's looking for you."

Nate scowled. "I don't have a choice, and you know it. Tell me about the chips."

What in the heck was he talking about? "Again, I don't know about any chips." She placed her hands over his.

He frowned and studied her for several tension-filled moments. Then he closed his eyes on a strong exhale. "You really don't."

"No. What chips?"

His shoulders slumped. "The ones planted near our spines that are set to detonate in less than three weeks."

"Detonate?" Fear prickled her skin. "How did this happen?"

"During routine surgeries, the doctors implanted the devices near our spine." He rubbed his chin.

She gasped. "My mother had a part in this?"

"Yes." He stood and pushed away from the bed. "If we don't find the computer program and right codes, the chips will detonate, and we'll all be killed."

CHAPTER
3

NATE THREW HIS duffel bag on the bed in the rustic cabin. The dump where he'd taken Audrey was rented by the hour, and he'd had no intention of staying there. After their discussion, he had taken Audrey home before returning to his home base a few miles away. The commander's soldiers had remained out of sight, but he heard their hearts beating and their breath panting out. They were near her apartment, and he didn't like that at all.

He'd wanted to take them both out, but that would alert the commander he was in town. So, he'd headed back to his quaint cabin to get some work done.

His hands shook as he allowed himself one moment to feel. No child. For the briefest time, he'd almost been a father. Sorrow and anger roared through him, and he took several deep breaths, his chin dropping to his chest. What would his kid have been like? What would he and Audrey have been like as parents?

His brothers would've made wonderful uncles. Shane could've taught the kid sports, and Matt would've taught him hunting. Josie, Shane's wife, could've helped with his or her math homework, and Matt's love, Laney, would've helped with science.

The kid would've had a great life with a real family and love.

Plus, the proof of one kid would show Shane and Matt that they could have kids. Something they desperately wanted.

The families on television had parents, kids, and cousins, and that's all the Dean boys had ever wanted.

His lungs seized as the impossible picture of a family, of his child, faded into nothingness. For a very brief time, even though the kid hadn't made it, Nate had been a father. He'd deserved to know that at the time and to experience the reality of that miracle while there had still been hope.

Audrey had kept that from him. Sure, she'd said she had planned to tell him the truth, and he wanted to believe her. But even with his abilities, he wasn't sure. He was as damaged as a guy could get, so why would any mother want him near a child?

The life he'd lost threatened to consume him, so he slowly, bit by bit, stopped feeling anything. His head lifted.

He stalked over to the cut-off door perched on an old tree trunk that served as a table. One of the two green striped patio chairs creaked as he lowered his bulk to sit and booted up his laptop.

Five minutes passed while he typed in security codes until finally his oldest brother came into focus. "I made contact," he said.

Matt leaned forward, gray eyes concerned. "And?"

"She lost the baby." Nate kept his voice level as he gave his report.

Matt blinked and ran a hand over his face. "Jesus, Nate. I'm sorry."

Pain spiraled in Nate's gut, and he shoved emotion away. "And we hurt her. When we blew up the facility... Audrey was there." He didn't have the strength to keep his voice from cracking on the end.

Matt stilled. "Was she pregnant? I mean, did we—"

"No. She'd already miscarried when she was at the facility."

Matt shook his head. "But you made sure she wasn't there, that she was scheduled to be in DC."

Yeah. He'd thought he'd taken care of her, even though they were over. But he hadn't, and something had gone wrong. The woman definitely had a limp. His guilt angered him, and he fought to keep his expression stoic so his brother wouldn't see the turmoil. "Apparently Audrey was at the medical facility because the miscarriage had started."

"So she lost the baby." Matt swallowed. "How many experiments did the scientists put her through at that time? Just because a woman finally got pregnant by one of us?"

Nate sat back, his mind reeling. He hadn't even considered what the commander and his scientists had probably done to Audrey in testing after they'd finally found a female who could get pregnant with one of the Gray brothers' sperm.

The evil scientists had harvested the brothers' sperm during surgeries to repair injuries sustained while on missions, and then they had tried unsuccessfully to impregnate surrogate mothers. Even before this violation occurred, the brothers had fully intended to escape the group that had raised and trained them. Freedom mattered.

But the military group, led by the commander, had

made sure there was a brother out on mission at all times, and if he failed, his brothers would die back home.

Until they finally were at the base at the same time.

They'd blown it all to hell and escaped.

"When we finally got loose, Audrey stayed with the commander and her mother," Nate said slowly. "Her mother always had a hold on her I didn't understand, and now Audrey is working with them." Of course, he'd never had a mother, so he didn't understand the bond.

Anger blazed across Matt's face before he quickly banished it. "Maybe Audrey didn't have a choice?"

"No. She chose them, chose working with them over me, before she knew she'd become pregnant." Nate shook his head. "When she ended things between us almost five years ago, she even admitted her mother set us up from the start. I assume Dr. Madison wanted to see what I'd be like in love. If I could feel love for somebody who wasn't family." The thought that he'd been used by the one person he'd ever let in shot spikes into his gut, even after all of these years. When Audrey had confirmed her mother's involvement in their relationship, she'd been telling the truth.

"I know it was an experiment initially, but that doesn't mean she knew all the facts. Maybe she was supposed to befriend you," Matt said.

"I know." Nate stretched his neck, his shoulders settling. "We started as an experiment, but her feelings were real. Just not strong enough to trust me when things turned bad." And that was the crux of the matter.

Matt nodded, turned to the side, and glared. "Stop poking me."

"I'm not." Shane, Nate's younger brother, came into focus as he shoved a shoulder into Matt and scooted him over. "Are you in a secured place?"

"Yes." Nate glanced around at the two-room cabin. A bedroom took up one room, while a small kitchenette fronted the far wall near a rugged stone fireplace in the other room. "Nobody followed me from town."

"You didn't take Audrey there?" Shane asked.

"Of course not," Nate said. "I believe I taught you evasive maneuvers when you were eight years old."

Shane frowned, his eyes identical to Matt's in both gray color and deep concern. "Just wanted to make sure your head was on straight."

"I'm fine." Nate drew in a deep breath, calming his racing heart. Seeing Audrey again had taken a toll, but he was fine now. Reaching out, he widened the scope of his screen to better see. His brothers were both over six feet tall and broad with strong features, and their similar faces took up too much room on the screen. Matt had a square jaw, and Shane's features appeared more angular, but there was no doubt they shared a sperm donor. "Audrey is working for Senator Nash, who's on the appropriation's subcommittee for advanced defense spending."

"In other words, for top-secret, bullshit military experiments and funding," Shane muttered.

"Exactly," Nate said, glad to be on the topic of their enemies and not on Audrey.

Matt exhaled. "So, the commander maneuvered Audrey in place to gain more funding. I'm sorry, Nate."

"Why?" Nate kept his gaze level. "We knew she worked for them. Dr. Madison raised her, so why did we expect anything different?" Yeah, he felt for Audrey after having been raised by the psychopathic neurobiologist, but she'd made her choice. He'd offered her freedom, and she'd chosen dubious safety.

"What's your plan now?" Matt asked quietly.

Nate shrugged. "The commander has a base outside of DC in Virginia, and that's where we'll find the codes and computer system to defuse our chips. And I think that's where we'll find Jory."

Hope leaped across Shane's face while regret twisted Matt's lips. "You mean we'll find out about his death," Matt said.

Nat shook his head. His youngest brother had been missing for two years, and Nate had to find Jory. The chances were good that Jory was dead, but a small marble of hope lived in him that somehow, even after two years of no contact, Jory somehow still lived. Even after seeing a video showing Jory being shot and falling to the floor, Nate hoped. Hell, he even prayed in case a God existed who gave a shit. "I'll find out what happened to him."

The hope fled Shane's expression. "I can't be sure I saw him move in the other video."

Nate nodded. Shane had seen a video where he thought Jory had moved after being shot, but Shane had been suffering from a head injury resulting in amnesia, and the video had never been seen again. "I know," Nate said.

Matt cut his eyes at Shane and back at Nate. "I can take over this assignment, Nate."

"No." Nate's jaw hardened until it ached. He understood his brothers were worried about him, but he couldn't change that. Both Matt and Shane had somehow found love and the courage to stay with their women for the small amount of time they had left, and Nate would die trying to save them. They deserved happiness, if it were possible. Growing up, he'd been the bridge between Matt, who had to train them mercilessly, and the two younger brothers, Jory and Shane, who still needed hope and fun. Now that Jory was probably dead, and the other two had found love, Nate had nothing left—except to make sure his brothers survived.

He could live with that—what else possibly mattered?

Now that two of his brothers were happy, he could finally relax. His job was nearly done. Not once since Audrey had dumped him had he considered he'd find happiness—he'd known from early on that he'd end bloody and most likely alone.

While the thought brought some sadness, he'd become accustomed to it. Everyone had a destiny, and with his skills, the second he'd left the military, he'd become unnecessary after the last mission of deactivating the chips.

He should probably want the joy his brothers had found, and maybe deep down he did. But the reality was the reality, so why wish? If he managed to get into the right facility and send out the codes, there was little chance he'd make it out. Which was all right.

Matt shook his head. "Earth to Nate."

Nate blinked, his mind zeroing back on the conflict at hand. "I can get what we need from Audrey—you can't." He glanced at his watch, ignoring the innuendo in his words. "Though it's going to be more difficult than I'd hoped—she didn't know about the chips near our spines."

Matt's eyebrows rose. "You believe that?"

"Yes. The truth shocked her."

"So she'll help us?" Doubt clouded Shane's face. "Are you sure?"

"She'll help us." Nate nodded. The woman would help them whether she liked it or not.

Shane's jaw hardened. "Did you ask her about Jory?"

Nate breathed out. "Not yet. I want to catch her by surprise."

"Okay," Shane said. "Get the intel and get out, Nate."

Nate nodded. "We know the info isn't at the Colorado base after our last raid, and we blew Tennessee up. That leaves the new headquarters outside of DC, and Audrey is our way in to get info on the chips as well as Jory. I'll check in after phase two tomorrow." He shut the laptop before his brothers argued any more.

With a quick glance around the cabin, he fetched his jacket and headed back into the rain. He needed to see what Audrey did with the opening he'd given her. How loyal was she to the commander and her mother?

Time to find out. He'd watch her apartment through the night and make sure she went to work in the morning.

Every instinct he owned clamored that the woman was hiding something.

After a sleepless night, Audrey wore fashionable yet flat boots with her dress to work, just in case. She couldn't afford to be in heels if she needed to make a quick escape, and she knew without a doubt that day was coming.

A kill chip waited next to Nathan's spine. How was it possible Audrey's mother had never even hinted at the deadly device? For five years, Audrey had hoped and prayed Nate had found some sort of happiness. Freedom.

But no, his very survival had been threatened by Audrey's mother.

Why in the world did that make her feel guilty?

She reached the grand doorway of her office building and held the door open for a woman pushing a baby stroller. The baby, a little girl, gurgled up at Audrey with innocent and devastating sweetness.

Audrey bit back an instant slice of pain and tried to smile. Every baby she saw reminded her of the one she'd lost—even five years after the fact.

Drawing a deep breath, she paused to glance at the reflective windows. The hair on the back of her neck prickled, proving she was being followed.

But she couldn't find the soldiers this time. They blended into the crowd.

If they made a move, she wouldn't know until it happened.

Her breath hitched. Panic rippled through her, and she shoved inside the building, ducking through the metal detector and hurrying toward the elevator. She made it inside as the doors were closing.

Taking several more deep breaths, she calmed herself. Had she pissed off the commander by ditching his bulldogs the previous night? What if they made a move on her? Could she fight them off?

As the elevator doors opened to the plush office, she forced a smile and nodded to the receptionist before maneuvering down a hallway to her office. Setting her briefcase on one of the two leather guest chairs, she tried not to limp as she crossed around her desk to sit.

Life was spinning out of control. She could no longer identify the people following her, and now, Nate was going to die in three weeks.

Nausea filled her stomach. She was in the best position to find the codes, but that was by her own design. She'd schemed to put herself in a position of trust with the commander. For weeks, she'd felt the presence of the guards the commander had assigned to watch her. For days she'd feared he'd discovered the truth—that she was working against him. Wholeheartedly.

But no.

The commander had been waiting for Nate to make contact because of the kill chips.

Nate and his brothers were the best at tactical maneuvers, but even they weren't invincible. While Nate had avoided the guards the previous night, he couldn't take on the commander alone.

A rustle sounded by Audrey's doorway, and Senator Nash loped inside followed by Ernie Rastus, his chief of staff. "You disappeared quickly last night. Everything okay?" The senator dropped into the vacant chair and tugged at the red-striped tie fastened around his white dress shirt.

"I'm afraid I ate a bad shrimp," Audrey said, one eyebrow lifting.

Ernie grimaced. Small and lean, the brilliant man shoved wire-rimmed glasses up his nose. "That's why I never eat seafood."

"Good point." Audrey smiled and glanced at the senator. "That's a nice tie."

"I hate ties." He gave up the fight and smoothed long-boned hands down the faded dress pants that led to his customary black cowboy boots. "But we're meeting with those tech-genius folks today, and I figured I should dress up a little."

"Did you bring a suit jacket?" Audrey asked.

His bushy gray eyebrows rose to meet his gray hairline. "Do you think I need one?"

Probably. "No, I'm sure you're fine."

The senator shrugged a fit shoulder. "You can take the cowboy out of Wyoming, but—"

"The boots and hat go with him," Audrey finished with a smile. There were very few people in politics she actually liked, and the senator topped the list. A rancher, he'd been widowed a decade previous and had run for office to keep living, having been left with no family. Now he'd found his own mission.

One she shared. "I think I'm being followed."

The senator leaned forward. "Do you think the commander knows our agenda?"

"No." Audrey trusted her boss but wouldn't expose Nathan. "I'm sure that now my medical treatments are finally finished, they're worried I'll run for the hills."

Ernie coughed. "What if they find out the senator is actually playing them? Do you really think they're a threat to a United States senator?"

Oh, these men had no idea. "Yes. I don't think the commander would think twice at taking out either one of you." Audrey rubbed her thigh.

"Unbelievable," Ernie muttered. "Maybe we should close him down now."

"How and why?" the senator asked. "We don't have any proof that he's done anything wrong, and it's not like he'll just hand evidence to us."

Ernie frowned and focused back on Audrey. "I saw you dancing last night. How is your leg?" he asked, smoothing back his graying hair.

"Much better, but I'll always have the limp." More importantly, all of the internal damage had been repaired, and she might even be normal someday. In the distant future, when she ran far away from her mother and the commander.

But first, she had a job to do. "How close are we to shutting them down?"

"Soon." The senator rested muscular forearms on his legs. "I've gained the commander's trust, or what there is of it, and as soon as we get the information on the newest studies, we'll go public and end their reign."

Audrey swallowed. "Are you sure the commander has continued his experiments?"

"Yes. I'm fairly certain there's a brand-new crop of soldiers he's created that are training right now. We need to find out where before we shut him down." The senator's blue eyes sizzled with passion.

Audrey nodded, tempted to tell her friends about Nate. But only Nate could take that risk, and she wouldn't take it for him, although she trusted the senator and Ernie. The senator was no dummy. When the commander had begun buttering him up in order to get funding, Nash had hired investigators, who'd uncovered a little bit of the truth.

Not much, though.

However, they had discovered the commander's maneuvering to get Audrey the job with the senator.

Instead of turning her in or trying to manipulate her, the senator had approached her with his suspicions about the covert military group.

Just like an honorable man would.

He treated her with dignity and respect...and most important, trust. She couldn't envision any other angle he might have but honestly trying to destroy the covert group, and she wanted to help. "I'm glad you trusted me enough to tell me your real agenda," she said.

The senator nodded. "I'm thankful you agreed to help us after the commander sent you here undercover. Without your knowledge of the group, we wouldn't be so close to fixing everything." His clean-shaven jaw clenched. "I've insisted upon seeing the commander's training facility before I push for a vote for more funding. He'll have to show me."

Audrey's heart thumped. Hard. "You're sure there's a secondary facility besides the one right outside of DC?"

"Positive." The senator stretched his neck. "I've been to the Virginia compound, and while the security, computer, and medical facilities are impressive, after seeing the last budget report, I know there's another training compound. Somewhere."

Dread forced Audrey to sit up straighter. "I'd hoped the experiments had stopped."

"No." The senator shook his head.

An aide appeared around the doorway. "The group from the technology corporation is waiting in the conference room."

The senator stood. "Here we go."

Ernie stood as well, his head barely reaching the senator's chin. "I have to bow out of this one—meeting with Darian Hannah, the lobbyist for Red Force."

Audrey lifted an eyebrow. "I have a meeting with him coming up."

Ernie sighed. "I know. He's coming at us from every angle to gain funding. He works hard, and he's a good guy. Not sure about the group he represents."

"They're not as bad as the commander's organization," the senator muttered.

"Perhaps." Ernie shrugged a slim shoulder. "But how do we know for sure? Maybe his group is conducting the same asinine experiments as the commander."

"I hope not," the senator said on a strong exhale.

Ernie turned on a shiny Italian loafer and headed out.

The senator groaned. "Are you ready for this meeting, Audrey?"

"Of course." Audrey pushed to her feet and retrieved several manila folders. "TechnoZyn represents the biggest technology firm in the United States, and it wants military funding." She walked around the desk to follow the senator through the office and into the large conference room.

The senator paused before entering and turned toward her to speak quietly. "Computer companies now want military funding. Crazy. But they are willing to build factories in Wyoming, which will help my economy."

Brokering deals like this made her stomach hurt. It was so wrong on so many levels. Unfortunately, she needed the leverage to take down the commander. She comforted herself with the thought that the commander and her mother would never actually see the money, because the senator would shut them down first.

The senator popped his knuckles. "I hate this crap." Forcing on a down-home smile, he turned and headed into the conference room.

Audrey stifled a chuckle and followed him, smiling for the two men and one woman already seated at the table. They all stood as she and the senator entered the room. Her gait faltered as she took in the second man. *Nathan.*

Once again he wore the colored contacts and facial hair.

Recovering quickly, she nodded as introductions were made, a roar filling her ears. Was he crazy? How had he infiltrated the technology group? The fact that it was in competition with the commander was way too close to home for him.

He stood and leaned to take her hand in his much larger one. "I had the pleasure of meeting Ms. Madison at the ball last night."

She tugged her hand free. "Yes, but I thought Mr. McGovern worked as a lobbyist for the Neoland Corporation?"

The other man, George Fairbanks, a top executive at TechnoZyn, smirked. "He did. We acquired the Neoland Corporation three days ago but haven't gone public with the information yet."

Audrey lifted her chin. So Nate had somehow chosen a cover in a company a mere week ago, and then it had been bought out by TechnoZyn? Impressive contacts and information he had developed. How had he known about a secret industry takeover before it had happened? That was the only way he could've put himself into place so perfectly.

She glanced at him, and he had the gall to grin. That smile. Her body reacted as if the last five years of separation hadn't occurred. Heat flared between them and zinged through her body to settle between her legs.

How did he do that?

Digging deep, she yanked her gaze from him and focused on the senator.

The senator frowned at Fairbanks. "While I appreciate the plan to invest and make a fortune before going public, it's risky for you."

Fairbanks shrugged and sat. "Maybe, but it's not like you're going to turn us in, are you, Senator?"

"Of course not," the blonde sitting between Nathan and Fairbanks said with a smooth smile. She shook the senator's and then Audrey's hand. "I'm Lilith Mayes."

The woman had a surprisingly strong grip. "I've read your last income projection report—very impressive," Audrey said as she was released to sit. The creative blonde manipulated numbers to the point of committing fraud. But now was the time to deal with the lesser of two evils, and the commander was all evil.

"Thank you," Lilith said, sitting down close to Nathan as he also sat. Very close to Nathan. She patted his muscled arm. "I had help."

Audrey's teeth ground together, and a sharp spear sliced into her heart. What in the world? After all this time, jealousy decided to rear up? No. Her life had become a risk just to survive, and she didn't have time for anything else. "That's good to hear."

Nathan's upper lip quirked, and he kept his focus on her. "So. How can we do business together?"

CHAPTER
4

Nate ignored the blonde playing footsie with him under the table and focused on Audrey. She was good at hiding her feelings—but not good enough. The second she'd noticed him, her heart had sped up, and her rate of breathing had increased.

Good. He needed her off balance.

Her blue eyes shot sparks at him, and he hoped nobody else noticed the pretty flush covering her cheekbones. Tearing her gaze from his, she handed a bunch of manila folders to the senator.

The senator looked more like a farmhand than a powerful lawmaker. His background seemed clean, and he appeared to want to make things better for his state, even if he had to break a few rules to do it.

Nate respected him for that and had no problem breaking rules himself.

Unfortunately, even after all this time, he'd figured Audrey would be above such things. The thought that she'd break the law in order to gain more funding for the commander hurt. Shit, it pissed him off beyond belief.

The senator rubbed his shoulder. "If you build your two

newest factories in Wyoming, Audrey has outlined the tax breaks and subsidies for you." He pushed a file folder across to Nate, who slid it to Lilith and read along with her.

"This all works assuming we receive military funding." Finally, Nate lifted his head, his gut swirling. "The plan is very impressive. Where did you learn to move money around like this?" The proposal certainly violated several laws but would be hard to detect. Of course, he knew exactly where she'd learned her skills.

She met his gaze without flinching. "I learned from the best, Mr. McGovern."

"Not exactly something you can put on a résumé." He spoke with heat, instantly irritated with himself. Why did he care that she'd learned manipulation from the commander? Even so, aggravation ticked along his spine. Tension filled the room.

Lilith glanced at him and slid her hand along his thigh under the table. Her fingers were strong and not nearly as delicate as Audrey's. "We appreciate the senator and his staff working with us, don't we?" Lilith said smoothly, sharp nails digging in.

"Yes." He needed to get himself under control even as he covered his surprise at Lilith's forwardness. He'd met the woman only a week ago, and she decided to make a move now? In a business meeting?

He'd been trained to seduce women, to learn their needs and wants, and yet, he couldn't figure any of them out. It was like they played from a different game plan.

Audrey wasn't the person he'd thought, even five years ago. So he turned toward Lilith and smiled, wanting nothing more than to seize Audrey and tear her out of the room for an explanation. "You're the smart one here. What do you think about the proposal?"

Lilith preened under his compliment and turned back toward the graphs, her palm sliding toward his dick. "I think we have some negotiating to do, but this is a very nice start. And you're the smart one here."

She had no idea. He halted her hand before she could get even more inappropriate.

Audrey's breath hitched, and Nate turned to study her calm composure. The innocent girl he'd known had learned to mask her feelings too well. She obviously knew what was happening under the table, and for some reason, it bothered her.

An odd sadness filled him. When they'd first met, she'd held nothing back from him. Every thought, every feeling, every fear had lived freely on her expressive face. As tough as she'd become, the vulnerable and fragile woman inside still lived, and he ached with the need to see her safe enough to return.

But she wasn't his to save, and she wasn't his to protect—and never would be. That truth clawed through him with sharp blades.

Once again, he wondered if he should've taken her with him five years ago whether she liked it or not. At least she wouldn't have been caught in the explosion. Nor would she have learned how to mask her emotions so well. Maybe there was more of her mother in her than he'd feared, because without his abilities, he'd have no clue she was even affected right now.

He tore his gaze away and turned toward Lilith. Tall and willowy, the accountant had a sharpness to her that would've impressed him had she not been trying to commit fraud. The red designer suit she wore hugged a too-thin body. "What points would you like to discuss?" he asked.

She pursed ruby-tinted lips. "The property taxes are a nice place to start. We'd like them waived."

Audrey leaned forward, her voice level but her heart racing. "On page three of your report, you'll see a list of the counties that will forgo property taxes and can compare their requirements to see which ones you prefer."

Nate compared the two women. Audrey's nicely rounded form filled out her understated blue suit in a way that made him salivate. Even now, with so much time and distance between them, he wanted her, which did nothing but irritate him. "So you've bribed the county officials already?"

Sparks lit her blue eyes. "No. Individual counties can waive such taxes because jobs will be created by the company that will help the local economy. I'd assumed you would've known that, Mr. McGovern." She lifted her chin in challenge.

Damn, he'd love to meet that challenge. "I understand." His special abilities gave him the edge he needed, and it was time to use them. He turned toward the senator. "Are we getting funded or not?"

The senator tapped one file folder, his gaze remaining steady. "I haven't decided who to recommend yet."

Lie. Definite lie. The politician's heart rate sped up, and tiny facial muscles twitched. While the senator lied with skill, Nathan detected lies with hard-earned experience. Nate glanced at Audrey, who stared intently at him.

Yeah, she knew his skill.

She also knew he'd figured out the senator was lying. The smile that lifted Nathan's lips held a warning.

From the widening of her eyes, she read it correctly.

"Well now"—Nathan leaned forward—"I think we can start negotiating so you do decide who to recommend."

At that point, his wildcat flashed him a smile that held more menace than a panther eyeing dinner.

His cock instantly flared to life.

Challenge lit her eyes in a way that heated every nerve in his body. "Yes, let's start," she said.

Two hours later, Nate sat back in his chair, more impressed than ever with the blue-eyed, slick-tongued woman who'd once held his heart. "You drive a tough bargain."

The senator stretched his neck. "Audrey's the best."

Yes, she was. Enjoyment had illuminated her face during the entire talk, and Nate wondered if it was the nature of politics or the challenge of sparring with him that had brought her to life. While watching her the last week without her knowledge, he hadn't seen nearly the passion on her face for her job as he had in the last two hours.

Years ago, not once in their time together had Audrey expressed an interest in either politics or lobbying. In fact, she'd wanted to work with young kids, hadn't she?

The door opened, and a slightly graying head poked in. "Sorry to interrupt. Audrey, do you have a minute?"

Ernie Rastus, the senator's chief of staff, was thinner than Nate had expected from the background files he'd dug up.

Audrey excused herself and left the room, shutting the door quietly behind her.

That quickly, the fun of negotiating disappeared. Nate kept one ear on the conversation between Lilith and the senator, while listening intently to another conversation in the hallway. Had Audrey forgotten about his enhanced senses? Or did she not care if he eavesdropped on her conversation?

"How's the meeting going?" Ernie Rastus asked.

"Okay. This McGovern fellow isn't the sharpest tool in the shed," Audrey said dryly.

Laughter rippled through Nate, and he coughed into his hand to disguise it from the members in the conference room. The brat remembered his enhanced hearing just fine.

"In fact, he spent more time flirting with the senator than dealing with numbers." Pure glee filled Audrey's voice in the hallway.

Ernie snorted. "With the senator?"

"Yes. At one point, when the senator complimented him, McGovern actually purred." Audrey chuckled, and even through the closed doorway, the sound sprang Nate's cock to life. He'd show her *purring*.

"So much for you charming him," Ernie said, a smile in his voice.

"Oh, I don't know"—Audrey's voice lowered—"I bet I could still have McGovern eating out of my hand. He seems rather...simple."

Nate bit his lip to keep from smiling, considering the senator and Lilith had started arguing about state taxes. He'd love to eat out of Audrey's hand. Or navel.

Ernie cleared his throat. "So long as we get the money, I don't care what a moron TechnoZyn's lobbyist is."

Did that jackass call him a moron? Nate crossed his arms.

"Right, Jason?" Lilith asked, forcing Nate's attention back to the conference room.

"Absolutely," he answered automatically, his main focus still on the conversation outside the room. Lilith nodded and launched into another argument.

Outside, Ernie sighed. "I had a decent meeting with Darian Hannah. He said Red Force is willing to fight hard for the Senate military funding."

Audrey breathed out. "Isn't everybody?"

"Good point," Ernie said.

Who was Red Force? Nate pretended interest in Lilith's tirade and tilted his head to better hear the outside conversation. His gut rebelled. Audrey really was in place to obtain funding for the commander from the U.S. government through the senator's subcommittee. Nate had always feared that her pathological need to find some sort of connection with her mother would lead her into trouble.

Even so, the thought that the gentle woman he'd once fallen for would align herself with such a monster tilted Nate's world. His head pounded, and a stone dropped into his gut. How could he have been so wrong about her?

The sound of somebody patting somebody's arm reached Nate's ears.

"So, I guess maybe I'll go flirt with McGovern to help out?" Ernie asked with a chuckle.

Audrey laughed. "I think you're too nice for him. Seems like a guy who likes to take it rough."

Oh, she did not just say that. Nate pretended to purse his lips in thought to keep from smiling again.

Ernie snorted. "One of those guys who likes the feel of a whip, like that group who demonstrated outside last year? Remember? They had whips, leather, and some odd contraptions I'd never seen before, and they chanted something about freedom of expression."

"Definitely. That McGovern is a *bottom*, without question. Probably has a monstrous dom named Bubba who spanks him nightly." Audrey coughed delicately.

That was it. He'd never been able to refuse a gauntlet once it had been thrown down. Nate stood slowly. "If you'll excuse me for a moment, Senator. Where's the restroom?"

"Go left when you leave the room, and you won't miss it," the senator said, his gaze remaining on Lilith. "As I was saying, when you pay property taxes, you fund schools, roads, and land development."

"But, Senator—" Lilith started.

Nate opened the door, gratified when Audrey's eyes widened. He held out a hand to Ernie and shut the door behind him. "Jason McGovern."

"Ernie Rastus." The man's fingers were long, tapered, and calloused. His dossier noted he liked to build rocking chairs as a hobby.

Nate made sure to squeeze a bit too tightly. "Mr. Rastus, do you mind if I have a word with Miss Madison, here? We were in the middle of a conversation last night when I had to leave, and I'd like to finish up."

Ernie frowned, curiosity in his eyes. "All right. I'll catch up with you later, Audrey." He hastened down the hallway, his gaze on the papers in his hands.

"What are you doing?" Audrey hissed. "We can't know each other."

"Dom named Bubba?" Nate asked, raising one eyebrow.

Audrey snorted. "You shouldn't eavesdrop."

He stepped into her. "And you shouldn't challenge me by using words like *dom*, *rough*, and *spank*." His voice lowered to the tone of gravel in a cement mixer, and anger rushed through him at the blatant danger she'd sought with the commander and politics. How could he be so pissed at her for aligning with the commander and yet want her naked and bent over a table with a desire that pushed everything else to the side?

She blinked, her pupils dilating.

Layers upon layers upon layers. Nate lowered his face, keeping her gaze. He reached out and fingered a strand of her hair, shoving the fury down. "Or was that an invitation to explore a little bit? I never did spank you." Frankly, he'd love to make sure every time she sat down for the next week she thought a little harder about consequences. Her current path with the commander would get her killed. "Bare hand or belt, baby?"

She swallowed, pink flushing across her fine cheekbones. Desire glimmered in her luminous eyes, and she tried to blink it away.

Oh yeah. They hadn't had nearly enough time together.

"Knock it off, Nate," she hissed, slapping his hand. "Stop playing games."

He kept his hold on her hair, allowing the natural dominance he'd been born with to reflect in his smile. "You started the game. Too late to set the rules."

"There are no rules," she muttered.

"Exactly." Heat filtered through him in response to the rapid pounding of a small vein in her neck. More than ever, he'd kill to have her writhing beneath him, his name on her lips.

Memories assailed him, and he exhaled through the desperate need to taste her.

Footsteps penetrated through the heartbeat roaring between his ears, and Nate stepped back, releasing her hair. Two secretaries walked by behind them and kept on going.

They once again had the hallway to themselves.

Audrey cleared her throat. "Enough, Nate."

He lifted a shoulder while his brain bellowed for him to get the hell away from her before he broke cover. "Maybe not. We'll see." Raised voices echoed from the conference room, and he filed the sound into the nothingness he used to keep from hearing too much and going crazy. "Why do you work here? You don't like politics."

"I have a job to do." Her chin tilted at a stubborn angle that made him want to take a bite.

"No." His gaze dropped to her lips—so pink and ready for him. "You wanted to go back to school, maybe get a master's, and work in early childhood development. Work with little kids. What happened?"

"Life happened, and I grew up." Her gaze shuttered. "Now, if you're done playing with me, we really should get back to the meeting."

Playing with her? Nate inhaled her natural gardenia scent. "Ah, baby, I'm just getting started."

CHAPTER
5

After the disastrous meeting with Nathan, a luncheon with the senator, and three more meetings with special interest groups, Audrey wanted to head home for a hot bath and a stiff drink. The drive home took longer than usual because of traffic, and she finally sighed in relief when she walked into her quiet apartment in Virginia, rain dripping from her coat and umbrella.

She'd been unable to spot the men tailing her, but she felt their presence. These two or three were so much better than the last couple at disguising themselves. When would they make a move against her?

The door closed silently behind her, and she jumped. Turning, she took in the man lounging against the heavy oak. The scent of wild male filled her feminine apartment. "You have a death wish," she muttered.

Nathan lifted an eyebrow, muscled arms crossed. "You going to kill me?"

The man had no clue how tempting the thought suddenly became. "No, but I'm being watched, and maybe they're waiting for you to show up." She slipped her arms out of her coat. Lying to him kept her on full alert, while the guilt of doing so leavened her limbs.

"I saw the two men watching you," Nate said, rolling his eyes.

"Lucky you." Darn it. She'd been unable to spot them. "Get out of town, and I promise I'll find out what I can about the kill chips."

His eyes darkened to a dangerous gray. He'd ditched the contacts. "Your promise doesn't mean much to me."

Hurt chilled her throughout, partially because he was spot on. "I'm sure that's true." Lying to him about her plan with the senator was a mistake, but even so, she threw down the gauntlet. "But you don't have a choice."

"Don't I?" he asked, his voice lowering to a softness that was all the more deadly for the low tenor.

She shivered, and not from fear. The tone he used... she'd known it well. Southern promises and heated nights. Her nipples sprang alive, and her sex softened. "I'm telling you, the commander has people watching me."

"I know."

Was he crazy? "You won't be able to hide from them for long." Sure, he was trained, but so were the men watching her.

"Sure I will. Especially with this cover as Jason McGovern from the technology firm you're working with." His gaze warmed as it traveled from her feet to her face. "In fact, we'll be seeing a lot of each other."

"No, we won't." Panic awakened inside her on the heels of raw desire. "They might be waiting for you to show up, and I'm bait."

"Why would you be bait?" he asked, no expression crossing his chiseled face.

Not because he still loved her, obviously. Pain cut into

her, and she rubbed her stomach. "I'm your way in, and you know it. They know it. We all know it." She shook out her umbrella. "Now get out of my apartment."

"No." Curiosity glinted in his eyes.

Her hold tightened on the wood as she lifted the umbrella. "Don't push me, Nate."

His arms dropped to his sides. "Or what?" he drawled, male cockiness in full force.

She swung. God help her, she knew better, but she did it anyway. With all her strength, with all the emotion she was tamping down, she swung the umbrella full force at his face.

He caught it easily in one hand, pivoting and trapping her against the door. Over two hundred pounds of hard muscled male pinned her in place.

She'd forgotten how quickly he could move. Her breath panted out while her knees weakened.

He stared down at her, fury glinting in his eyes, a vein standing out along his neck. "What did I teach you?" he ground out.

She blinked. "What?"

"Self-defense. What's your first lesson?" Anger rode every word.

The door cooled her back while the warm male vibrating with temper heated her front. "Um, to aim for the neck or eyes?" What was his point?

"Exactly." He stepped into her, still glaring. "Swinging an umbrella at a guy like me? Never let temper put you in more danger."

Her mind swam. He was angry because she hadn't really tried to harm him? She couldn't deal with the confusion on top of everything else. "What do you want from me?"

"Answers." He tossed the umbrella to the floor.

There was no way to physically kick him out. Her shoulders slumped along with her spirit. "Fine. Do we have to talk here in the entryway?" she asked.

"No." He stepped back to allow her to hang her coat in the closet by the door. "I put noodles on."

She stilled. He cooked dinner? Almost in a dream, she followed him through the small apartment and into the kitchen.

"Sit." He gestured toward the petite mahogany circular table that had come with the apartment and then turned toward a pot sitting on the stovetop.

Her leg cramped, but she walked without a hitch to take one of the chairs, her mind fuzzing. Somehow Nate had found matching aqua placemats, ivory napkins, and pasta bowls. "I think I've entered the Twilight Zone," she muttered, unfolding her napkin.

Nate grinned, skirting the kitchen bar to dump aromatic pasta on her plate.

The smile warmed her heart and spread to unfurl desire in her abdomen. She shook her head to focus. "I didn't have fresh tomatoes and garlic." Or Parmesan cheese, for that matter.

"I hit the store first." He served pasta into his bowl before reaching for a bottle of wine breathing on the counter. "Shiraz, if I remember right." The light hit the dark red liquid as he filled two wineglasses.

"You remember right," she murmured, trying to find some sort of balance. The one man she'd ever loved, the only man she'd ever slept with, the one whose heart she had broken...had cooked her dinner. What in the holy heck was going on?

He sat and glanced at the tidy and quaint kitchen. "Your place doesn't reflect you much."

She looked around at sterile silver appliances and faded birch cabinets. No personal touches had been placed anywhere in the apartment, much less in the kitchen. "The apartment was furnished when I rented it, and I haven't had time to nest." In fact, she needed to be able to move in minutes if necessary.

He nodded and took a swallow of the wine. "I found your 'go bag' hidden behind the false cabinet in the bathroom."

Her hand stilled in reaching for the wineglass. "Nosy, aren't you?"

He took another drink of the wine. "Who are you planning to run from?"

She wrapped her fingers around the delicate stem. "You."

He didn't move, but tension instantly spiraled around them. "Don't lie to me, Audrey."

"Or what?" she asked, taking a sip of the potent wine, her breath speeding up.

He leaned toward her. "Do you really want to know?"

Hell, no. The scent of wild male, all Nathan, slammed into her, sending her system into overdrive. How could he be so sexy after all this time? Even with the new edge of danger riding him hard, he all but promised rough sex that would be worth it. "I'm not afraid of you, Nate." She took a bigger swallow, her stomach heating instantly from both the man and the drink.

His smile lacked humor. "Another lie. Knock it off."

Enough of this. She slid the wineglass to the side and leaned toward him, meeting his dark gaze. "Or. What?"

His gaze dropped to her lips. "I'd forgotten that about you," he mused, almost to himself.

"What?" she asked, her voice thickening.

His chin lifted, and he captured her gaze. "How you liked to push me to lose control."

There had been a time she would've loved to take his control. To prove she was special—the only woman to get past his training and the rigid rules he set for himself. "But you never did, did you?"

"No." He sat back. "I'm not lost and lovesick anymore. Believe me, after everything that has happened, you want me in control."

But did she? Nathan out of control, just for her? The imminent broken heart might be worth the pain. She twirled perfectly cooked angel hair pasta around her fork and took a bite, nearly humming at the explosion of flavors. She swallowed. "This is delicious. While I appreciate dinner, you need to leave afterward." Before the men watching her discovered him.

He smiled.

Her heart dropped.

Sampling his dinner, he swallowed before speaking. "I haven't been clear. This is what is going to happen. First, you're going to answer all of my questions, and then we're going to come up with a plausible plan for you to get me into the commander's base outside of DC. Finally, you're leaving town."

"No." She ate more of the pasta, wondering how far Nate would go. "I'll get the information for you, but the commander is probably waiting for you, and I can't leave DC yet."

"Why not?"

She shrugged. "I have business."

"Committing fraud to fund the commander and your mother?" Nate tossed his napkin down.

"Yes."

His gaze narrowed. The seconds ticked by, and Audrey struggled to remain still and unaffected as he studied her. She ate slowly, no longer tasting the delicious meal.

Finally, he cocked his head to the side. "You just lied."

"No, I didn't." Although her one little word skirted the truth, didn't it? "You've lost your touch."

"Think so?" he whispered, pushing back from the table.

Intrigue skittered down her back. "Yes." She placed her napkin over the nearly empty bowl.

"Interesting." For such a large man, Nate moved with surprising grace around the table, where he dropped to his haunches and reached for the zipper on her boot. "I didn't get a chance to study your leg when it was around my hip in the hotel room. Let's take a moment here."

"No." The word exploded from her, and she tried to scoot back in the chair. "Let go."

His grip remained strong and sure. "I want to see the damage I caused." While the words remained steady, his eyes swirled with a fatalistic regret.

"You didn't know I was at the compound when you detonated the explosives," she said softly, placing her hand over his and leaning toward him. He'd changed, and not just physically. The old Nate was full of fun and hope for the future. This one? Raw determination with no hope. The reality of that hurt something deep inside her.

She'd sacrificed for him to find a life, and how dare he give up? "We'll find the codes to save you."

He lifted a shoulder. "I promised my brothers I'd get the code to save them, and I will."

The words he left out said a lot more than the ones he'd used. She held him tighter. "What about you?"

His gaze fastened on their hands. "Let me see, Audrey."

"That wasn't an answer." She lifted his chin with her free hand, stubble scratching her palm. "You're not a coward. Stop acting like giving up is okay—I demand more from you than that."

"That's all you're getting." He jerked his head to the side as if her touch burned him.

Hurt and anger shoved her back in the chair. "Fine. You want answers? Ask the questions, but let my fucking leg go."

One dark eyebrow rose. "You've got quite the mouth on you now, don't you?"

"You have no idea." She needed space. On his haunches, he met her gaze evenly while trapping her in place. Her nipples peaked in interest. "Let's go into the living room."

"No." He remained in place. "Tell you what. I'll ask questions, and if you tell the truth, I won't move. If you lie to me again, I'm going to remove an article of your clothing, starting with this boot."

Alarm and fury threatened to choke her, so she forced a sarcastic smile. "I didn't know you were into sex games, soldier."

His smile beat hers in sarcasm, hands down. "There's a lot you don't know about me. Wanna learn?"

Man, she'd love to meet his bluff. Except, Nate didn't bluff. "If I scream, those men watching me will come running."

"You try to scream, and I'll be on you before one sound escapes." A tension of a different sort cascaded from him, all but dampening her panties. Sexual need filled the tiny apartment, leavening the very oxygen.

What in the world was wrong with her? "You're an ass."

"I'm glad we understand each other." He reached for the zipper of her leather boot. "Question number one. Where's the commander's new base?"

"Thirty miles outside of Dillwyn." Her free foot twitched with the need to kick him in the face.

"Kick me, and we'll do this naked," he said, eyes knowing. One of his gifts was to see beneath the surface, and by the darkening of those eyes, he saw exactly what he did to her.

Desire slammed into her abdomen. How did he do that? Her body remembered him well even though it had been five years since he'd taken her to unbelievable heights. A primal part of her wanted to jump right back into the fire with him. Desire feathered along her skin, raising goose bumps. "Threatening me is no way to gain my cooperation," she muttered.

"How well manned is the facility?" Nate asked, a flush crossing his cheekbones.

Yeah. Their closeness affected him as well. But while she tried to hide her reaction, he allowed his free rein.

He smiled, but it wasn't his usual cocky smirk. It was a baring of teeth. Primal and honest. Nate wanted her.

She paused, trying to focus on the question and not the desire uncoiling in her body. "Same as the place in Tennessee, I think. There's an infirmary, several labs, weapon caches, and offices."

"Any new trainees?" Nate's jaw hardened visibly.

"No." Audrey shook her head, trying to draw in fresh air. "Only adults, and I don't know how many are the commander's soldiers and how many are with the U.S. military. If any."

"Are you due there any time soon?" His finger slipped beneath the boot, caressing her bare skin.

"No," she whispered, her body rioting. Heat flared up from her chest, scalding her throat.

His eyes darkened, and he unzipped the boot. "A lie." With a sharp tug, he removed it to toss onto the ground. Amusement quirked his lip. "I like your sock."

Heat spun into her cheeks at the striped purple and green sock. "I need to do laundry." The boot had covered the fuzzy sock, and she hadn't figured anybody would see it.

"All right." His thick hand banded around her other calf as he eyed the zipper. "When are you due back at the commander's DC facility?"

His touch sent tingles up her leg right to her sex. She had to get away before she started shedding her clothing and jumped him. An ache pounded in her core, and she fought the urge to rub her thighs together. This should *not* be turning her on. "I'm due at the DC facility the day after tomorrow."

"Why?"

"For a checkup regarding my last surgery." She tried to tug her foot free, and he held tight. He always did have an unbreakable hold. Flutters cascaded down her back.

His gaze lifted to meet hers. "How many surgeries have there been?"

She frowned, thinking back. "Five on my leg and three internally to repair fallopian tubes and one ovary. I lost the other one." Why lie? She cleared her throat. "Where have you been for five years?"

"No." He glanced at her exposed knees and cleared his throat. "I ask the questions."

"You want answers? You provide them, too." If he insisted on interrogating her, she deserved to have her curiosity appeased.

He rubbed his whiskers. "I've been all over, undercover,

trying to take on the commander and get the kill chips. Can you have kids now?" His gaze remained down.

"Yes." She probably wouldn't get the chance to have kids, though. The idea that she'd once almost had his kid made her heart ache, and deep down she'd wondered at another chance with Nate. She didn't want hope with him—not again. Talk about impossible. "Well, I probably can have kids."

"I'm glad for you." His shoulders lowered, his gaze shuttering. "Who is the senator going to recommend funding this year? What military group?"

Her stomach undulated. When Nate shut her out like that, the entire world turned cold. But she couldn't tell him the truth, and he'd sense a half-truth. "I don't know."

Her zipper released in record time, and the second boot flew across the room.

"Hey! That wasn't a lie, damn it." She kicked out with the now revealed fuzzy pink sock.

"A refusal is the same as a lie." A frown settled between his brows, and he sat back, his gaze gentling. "Your socks don't match, Audrey." Bemusement and a softness coated his strong voice.

She hunched her shoulders. "I really need to do some laundry, like I said."

His grin reminded her of the younger Nathan as he ran a warm palm up the calf of her injured leg, caressing each scar, dimple, and pin. "How many breaks in your leg?"

The question caught her off guard. "Just four," she said. The sensation of his hand on her after so much time sent butterflies winging to life below her abdomen. While she wanted to pull away, memories of his touch scalded her body into electric need.

He massaged her leg, and she fought a low groan. "Stop."

"Am I hurting you?" he asked, decreasing the pressure, watching her closely, his gaze predatory and intent. Sexy as sin and twice as dangerous.

"No," she breathed out. But her muscles were quickly turning to mush, and she needed to be on high alert with him. Nate had changed, and he probably wasn't above using seduction to get what he wanted. Feminine need built inside her, and she took a deep breath to regain control. "How are your brothers?"

His fingers flexed in warning below her knee. "Off-limits."

Yeah, that hurt. "Fine. Then so is the senator."

"No." Nate removed the purple sock, his thumbs skimming her skin. "I like your toenails."

She shivered and glanced down at the sparkling pink polish. "Give me back my sock."

"No. How close have Nash and the commander become?" Nate asked, tucking his thumb into her remaining sock. Even while he remained gentle, his movements were controlling and dangerously sexual.

She'd often wondered about this side of him. Anger and need melded inside her, pooling at the apex of her thighs. "The commander doesn't confide in me," she whispered.

Her other sock flew across the room. "Knock it off, Nate."

He ran his palms up her knees. "You're misreading me if you think I won't take all your clothes, Aud."

The nickname. He used to whisper it in her ear, late at night, in stolen hours alone. Naked, panting, fully complete, he'd murmur in that low Southern drawl he usually masked.

She swallowed and fought the charm of sexy memories. "The commander hasn't told me anything."

"Yet you know something."

She had to protect him from her plan. "Nate, I—"

A knock sounded on the door.

Nate jumped up, drawing a gun from the back of his waist. "You expecting anybody?"

"No." She pushed out of her chair. Fear sizzled into her bloodstream. What would Nate do?

He cuffed her arm with strong fingers and led her through the apartment to the door, where he peered through the keyhole. Every muscle down his back visibly tightened, and his arms seemed to vibrate.

When he turned toward her, she involuntarily stepped back from the deadly rage glittering in his eyes. "What?" she asked.

Nate's face hardened until no expression lived in the dangerous hollows and cut lines. "I'll be in the other room. If you say a word about me, or if you try to leave with him, I'll shoot him dead. I mean it." Without another word, he released her, turned on his heel, and stalked into the lone bedroom.

Audrey took a deep breath, her lungs seizing. What in the world? One glance through the keyhole, and she stopped breathing completely. Oh. Her hand shook when she reached for the doorknob to open the door. Her biggest enemy and greatest fear stood before her in fatigues and combat boots. She disliked herself for lying to Nate, but she'd hate herself if she got him killed. Panic threatened to cut off her air even as she forced on a polite smile. She opened the door. "Good evening, Commander."

CHAPTER
6

T HE SCENT OF gardenias surrounded Nate in the sensual bedroom. While Audrey hadn't decorated the rest of the apartment, the lone bedroom whispered of her sensuality. A deep purple bedspread, dreamy paintings of storms over mountains, and antique furniture all showed class and femininity. Two open doors led to a walk-in closet and attached bath.

The closet looked as if a hurricane had passed through, and discarded clothing littered the floor around the bed.

He'd forgotten what a slob she was. At the memory, his lips twitched.

Then a voice from his biggest nightmares echoed from the other room. The commander—in the flesh and close enough to kill. Nate's system instantly shot into cold, deadly alertness.

He crept forward and cracked the bedroom door open to better see the man who'd ordered his creation. The bastard hadn't changed much in twenty years. Tall, lean, and muscular, the emotionless soldier even sat at attention on Audrey's floral sofa.

His black hair had turned a steel gray, shaped in a buzz cut as always.

The gun lay heavy against Nate's back, offering opportunity. His fingers twitched with the need to hold cold silver and end the man who'd created such a hellacious childhood for Nate's brothers. But now wasn't the time. Not until Nate found the codes to defuse the kill chips, and not until he discovered what had happened to his youngest brother.

But having the commander sit so close to Audrey heated the breath in Nate's lungs.

"So these are the other pseudo-military organizations currently vying for funding," the commander said, pointing at a series of papers laid out on Audrey's coffee table. "What do you know about them?"

Audrey leaned forward, her slender face pale. "The NSA decommissioned this one a day ago." She tapped her nails on a piece of paper. While she appeared calm, Nate could hear her heart racing and a stressed tenor in her voice.

Would the commander notice?

Apparently Audrey understood that being allies with the commander wouldn't guarantee her safety if she screwed up. So why would the woman align with him? Nate rubbed his chin, trying to make sense of the situation.

The commander glanced at her. "Why did the NSA get involved with that organization?"

She shrugged. "Failure to complete several covert operations that almost brought attention to the States."

A satisfied gleam filled the commander's eyes. "Good. Were they also operating outside of the U.S.'s military reach?"

"No. You're the only organization, as far as I know, that considers the United States as merely a client. Of course, our military and political leaders have no idea about that."

While she kept her expression bland, a bite echoed in her words.

The commander nodded as if he hadn't noticed the tone. "What about these other two groups?"

"They're in the running for funding from the subcommittee," Audrey said.

The commander anchored her arm. "We put you in place to prevent that."

Nate felt a growl low in his belly at the sight of the commander touching Audrey. Even now, he wanted her away from the sadistic monster. So when she patted the commander's arm, all feeling left Nate's legs.

Audrey chuckled. "The senator is on board with your plan and realizes your organization can accomplish much more than the other two. I believe he will be able to convince the remaining members of the subcommittee to earmark all of the funds for you. Don't worry, Franklin."

Franklin? She fucking called him by his first name? Who the hell was this woman, and how could Nate have been so wrong about her?

"Good." The commander brushed the papers into a pile and pointed to something on the top page. "The base out of North Carolina run by this group is going to experience a gas explosion late tomorrow that will put them out of commission, so they'll be out of the running."

Audrey pursed her lips and slid a paper from the bottom. "So that leaves TechnoZyn Corporation and the Red Force group that's headquartered in Florida."

The commander chuckled. "Such amateurs. A computer company and *Red Force*. Having a name is a bad idea, and choosing a stupid one is ridiculous."

Audrey nodded. "I have a dinner date with Darian Hannah tomorrow night, and I'll find out more about them."

Nate stilled.

The commander's gray eyebrow arched. "He's the newly hired lobbyist for the group?"

"We believe so," Audrey said.

"Who arranged the meeting?" the commander asked.

Audrey leaned back. "He's been asking me to dinner for about a month."

Approval lifted the commander's thin lips. "Smart to make him wait. Is the dinner a personal or business meeting?"

"I think he wants both."

"Sometimes you remind me so much of your mother," the commander said, his tone flat and factual, as if making a business observation.

Fury roared through Nate.

Regret tinged Audrey's smile. "Genetics do shape us."

"Absolutely. I'll report back to your mother what a wonderful job you're doing here. She advocated your assignment, while I had doubts. I'm pleased she was right." The commander gathered his papers together.

"Thank you." Audrey reached for a piece of paper that had fallen onto the floor. "I owed her and you."

"Yes, you did." The commander stood and tucked his papers at his side. "The doctors did an amazing job healing you. Sometimes I forget how badly you were injured when I see you thriving like this, working so hard for our cause."

His *cause*? Nate rubbed a hand through his hair. He shoved an image of Audrey, broken and hurt, down in his mind.

Audrey stood up. "I'll find out from Darian Hannah what he and Red Force have planned, and more importantly, what they know about you." She retrieved a pillow from a chair to replace on the sofa. "I'm sure they don't know a thing."

"Good. I'd hate to think they know about any of our experiments," the commander muttered.

Nate swallowed several times. The woman really was working with the commander. While Nate had suspected her complicity, deep down, he'd hoped he was wrong. That Audrey was an unwilling victim somehow. How had she become so lost in five years? Did she think Nate was just an *experiment*?

Only thoughtfulness colored Audrey's tone. "Don't worry, I'll find out what Darian knows."

Anger glinted in the commander's black eyes. "Do what you have to do and report back to me Thursday morning." He all but marched to the door.

"I have my last doctor's appointment on Thursday and will request to see you afterward." Audrey escorted him, her head barely coming to the commander's shoulder.

"Excellent." The commander paused and turned. "How was the fund-raiser the other night?"

Audrey's heartbeat increased in tempo, and Nate winced in the bedroom. "It was fine. Why?" she asked, her tone merely curious and in a direct contrast to the blood whooshing through her veins. But the commander couldn't hear that, now, could he?

"I had several friends there, and they said you disappeared. Where did you go?" The commander stepped slightly into her space.

Nate tensed, ready to leap.

Audrey chuckled. "The party became boring and I walked to ease the cramp in my leg. After the pain eased, I came home."

She was a damn good liar.

Nate's breath heated and his lungs seized. The sense of loss threatened to swamp him, so he welcomed the tide of hot, fierce anger rising in him. With anger came control, as only a bastard with no soul could manage. His fingers twitched with the need to kill the commander, so he placed a hand against the wall to keep himself inside the bedroom as he watched.

The commander studied Audrey and slowly nodded. "You are dedicated to our cause, right?"

The bastard wanted her afraid. Nate reached for the gun tucked at his waistband.

"Of course." She tilted her head to meet the commander's gaze.

Most trained men faltered when trying to do that. An unwelcome admiration welled in Nate, mingling with the anger. During their brief time together, nightmares had plagued him with the terror that he wouldn't be able to protect her. As Audrey plotted with the commander now, it became painfully obvious she learned to hold her own—even with evil.

Nate felt a loss of something he hadn't realized he had. His senses reeling, he backed up to sit on the bed before he did something that would get them both killed.

The outside door opened and closed, and the tension in the small apartment dissipated. Seconds later, Audrey strode barefoot into the room. "He's gone."

Nate nodded, his gut swirling, his mind finally settling on the sure fact that she'd never be who he'd fallen in love with. That woman didn't exist, and this one had used him. Deep down, he'd always hoped she'd be able to explain what had happened.

He truly was alone.

Fine. Reality sucked and bit like a hungry cobra, and

any hope in his life existed for his brothers. He'd do whatever it took to make sure they lived. So he stood, eyeing her. "You and *Franklin* seem to get along well."

"We do." Audrey glanced at the bed, avoiding his gaze.

Something about her posture gave him pause. Hunched shoulders, facial tic only he'd be able to discern. "What are you hiding, Aud?" he asked softly, her small feet looking so feminine and vulnerable his stomach ached.

She sighed, the darker blue band around her spectacular iris seeming to almost glow in the soft light. "So much, Nathan." She bustled over to retrieve a pair of pink panties and a couple of blouses from the floor. "Sorry about the mess. I, ah, didn't expect anybody to be in here."

"Not even Darian Hannah?" Nate asked, anger lighting through him yet again.

"No." She snagged a skirt from the bed and tossed the entire bundle into the messy closet, kicking the doors shut behind her. "Of course not."

"Really?" Nate's voice dripped with darkness as he stepped into her space to prevent her from leaving the bedroom. "Good old Franklin told you to do whatever you needed to do. Does that mean the commander is now your pimp?" The words tasted like acid on his tongue, but he couldn't prevent their slipping out.

Audrey's head jerked up. Anger flushed red across her delicate cheekbones. "You're calling me a whore?"

Not in a million years. He needed to shut up, but the hurt spiraling through him pushed him on. "Are you screwing people on command? If so, sounds like a whore to me."

The right cross to his cheekbone jerked his head back and echoed around the room. He turned his head back toward her, a smile tugging at his lips. That was his Audrey. No soft-girly slap from her. She went for the closed-fist impact.

"Feel better?" he asked.

The left cross cracked his jaw. He glanced down at her, an apology on his lips because he knew she was no whore. Which she quickly countered by aiming a punch at them.

He caught her hand in his before she made contact. Her other fist flew at his gut, and he caught that one, too. Sliding forward, he clasped her wrists together with one hand behind her back. He lifted her chin. Hurt and raw fury glittered in her eyes. "I'm sorry," he said.

Her gaze flickered, and only excellent reflexes had him shifting to the right in order to avoid the hit to the balls. Her knee bounced off his thigh.

He felt his own smile all the way to his heart. "Let me get you out of here. New identity, plenty of money. You can get that degree and work with kids like you always wanted."

For the briefest of seconds, thirst hinted in her eyes. Then the veil dropped and hid her thoughts again. "My wants and needs have changed."

"No, they haven't. You've always wanted your mother's approval, and you're working too hard, becoming somebody you're not, in order to get it." Even as he said the words, he realized he had no clue what he was saying. He didn't have a mother and would've probably done anything to get one to love him. "Please, Audrey. You don't belong in politics making deals and committing fraud."

"Yet I'm so good at it." A self-deprecating smile tilted her lips. "The girl you loved is gone, Nate."

But was she? Nate studied her guileless expression, his instincts clamoring. Or maybe he wanted to believe that girl still existed—if she ever had.

A truck engine ignited outside. The commander was leaving. Apparently he'd taken a few moments, probably to speak with the two men currently watching Audrey.

Nate leaned down and smacked a hard kiss against Audrey's lips. "I have to go. See you tomorrow."

Leaving her sputtering, he jogged through the apartment. While Nate wouldn't be able to infiltrate the commander's base on such short notice, at least he could get the lay of the land if he followed the asshole.

"Wait, Nate—" Audrey called, limping after him and into the hallway.

He turned. "Stay here." Then he had to ask. He'd wanted to hold on until he had more information to use, but he couldn't wait any longer. All hell was about to break loose, and he needed to know. "Is Jory at the base?"

Audrey frowned. "Jory? Why would he be at the base?"

Dread slammed into Nate's gut. "So he's dead?"

Audrey shook her head. "I don't know what you're talking about. I haven't seen Jory since you escaped the Tennessee facility."

Nate studied her body language and expression, listening closely to her heartbeat. She was telling the truth. Unfortunately. She didn't know anything about Jory, which meant he probably wasn't located outside of DC. Fear for his brother sizzled through his veins. "I'll catch up with you tomorrow, Aud." Turning, Nate jogged to follow the one man he wanted to kill in order to hopefully find the one he wanted to save. Where was Jory?

He had to be alive.

CHAPTER
7

Aᶠᵗᵉʳ ᴀ ꜱʟᴇᴇᴘʟᴇꜱꜱ night and a day doing nothing but putting out fires, Audrey tucked her blouse more securely into her pencil skirt and rode the elevator up to the top floor of a high-rise around the block from her office. Work had been brutal all day as they prepared for the report for the Senate. She'd asked Darian to meet her at the restaurant, mostly because she figured Nate would wait for her at home. He'd expect her to change before her date.

Since most people in her business worked well past the traditional dinner hour, Darian had easily agreed to meet her at Anchonies, the new hot restaurant in DC. She stepped into the waiting area.

The hostess nodded at her. "Miss Madison? Mr. Hannah is waiting this way." Turning on a high-heeled silver Blahnik, the six-foot blonde wove gracefully around tables to reach an alcove against the window. Audrey smiled her thanks and sat, taking a moment to appreciate the DC skyline at night. The beacon glittered from the Washington monument as if hope still lived.

Darian slid a glass of Shiraz toward her. "I ordered you a glass of wine."

"Thank you." She didn't ask how he knew what she preferred—it was fairly easy for one secretary to call another in town for details. The first sip relaxed her shoulders.

She studied the man who'd been so persistent in asking her out. Tall and broad, Darian had played college football for Notre Dame before moving on to politics. Rugged features and light mocha skin combined into a handsome configuration that reminded her of a cross between Denzel Washington and Dwayne Johnson. It was too bad Darian wanted to commit fraud with her, because he seemed like a decent guy.

He'd removed his suit jacket, and nicely filled out a green dress shirt. "Why did you finally decide to accept my invitation?"

She smiled. "I figured you wanted to talk about the subcommittee's recommendation, and since we're making it next week, we'd better talk."

Warmth glimmered in his chocolate-colored eyes. "I'd hoped my personality finally charmed you into accepting a real date."

The restaurant was set for romance. She tapped a fingernail on her wineglass stem, idly wondering when she'd last had an actual date. Nothing came to mind. "I don't have time for real dates right now, and I'm assuming you don't, either."

"I do." He leaned forward, gaze intent. "Life is too short to miss out on fun."

He had no clue. "I agree." But she'd given her heart five years ago, and she remained more sure than ever that she'd never get it back. Plus, once the commander discovered her true agenda, she'd be dead. "But now isn't a good time."

"As long as it's you and not me," Darian said.

Audrey laughed, caught off guard. Charming and funny, wasn't he? "Good one."

The waitress arrived and took their orders.

"So, talk," Audrey said, munching on a breadstick. The back of her neck tingled, and she fought to control her nerves.

Darian sipped his water. "Red Force wants badly to receive significant Senate allocations this year, and if the senator makes this happen, we'll find a way to fund his war chest in the next election."

Audrey nodded. Would she ever feel as if she wasn't being watched? The commander's men remained close. "What makes your organization a better fit than others out there to justify his recommending you?"

Darian leaned forward. "As you know, our private employees are ex-military, are well trained, and can go into areas the U.S. officially cannot. We're the best out there for covert operations needed but not sanctioned by the U.S. government."

Audrey kept an interested look on her face. Red Force's soldiers were nowhere close to the commander's forces in skill or experience. "Who do you think is your main competition?"

Darian shrugged. "There are several corporations providing covert ops, body guard services, and even wet work. Frankly, we're investigating all of our competition right now, but we're the only one that's ready to go today."

That darn tickle wouldn't leave her alone. She glanced around the restaurant...and froze. Nate sat at the next table, facing her, his eyes dark with warning. His companion reached out a slim hand and patted his on the table before glancing Audrey's way.

Audrey nodded at Lilith, who returned the smile, all teeth. A gorgeous red wrap-style dress hugged the woman's svelte figure and revealed high breasts. No matter how many hours Audrey logged at the gym, she'd never be that thin and willowy. Ever.

Darian followed her gaze. "That's Lilith Mayes from TechnoZyn."

"Yes. They're pushing hard for military funding," Audrey said, turning back toward her companion and feeling Nate's gaze remaining on her. She swallowed and reached for her wine.

"I'd heard TechnoZyn was looking for deals and making promises about their spylike computers. Who's the guy?" Darian asked.

Audrey lifted a shoulder. "Jason something. He's a lobbyist who seems to deal in land acquisitions."

"Never heard of the guy." Darian sat back as the waitress set a crab salad in front of Audrey and a steak before him. "I worked with Lilith a few years back on a deal. The woman is ruthless." Something darkened his voice.

"Ruthless? Was it personal?" Audrey asked.

Darian flushed. "We, ah, dated."

Interesting. Now Lilith seemed to be dating Nathan. Audrey dug into her salad, her appetite gone. How was she supposed to act normal when Nate persisted in looking right at her? She cut him a sideways glance to see him smiling at the blonde. Hurt sliced through Audrey, surprising in its intensity.

Why in the world did she care if Nate made a move on the other woman? It wasn't as if they had a chance to find each other again.

Darian poured her another glass of wine. "Are you all right?"

She forced a smile. "Yes. Tired of working so hard, you know?"

He grinned and held out a piece of steak on a fork. "I definitely know. Try this steak—it's amazing." His gaze was more friendly than sexy.

Audrey took the bite and chewed slowly. "Delicious." The chef knew how to cook. She glanced again at Nate, and the raw fury in his eyes nearly made her choke. He stared pointedly at Darian's now-empty fork. Recovering, she took a deep drink of her wine.

How in the world would she make it through dinner?

Somehow she managed to choke down the salad without tasting it, agree to think about Darian's business proposal without actually agreeing to anything, and fend off his increasingly obvious advances without marching over to Nate's table and punching him in the face. Again.

Finally, after Darian had paid the bill, her temper boiled with the need to let loose. She excused herself to visit the ladies' room and, while there, took several deep breaths, staring at herself in the mirror. On all that was holy. She'd been raised in a manipulative, secretive situation, and she now worked in politics. If her upbringing had taught her anything, it was how to survive the current situation.

All she had to do now was go home, get a decent night's sleep, and her mind would clear.

Her shoulders back, she exited the ladies' room—and ran right into Nate.

"Hey," she muttered, bouncing back. His hands around her biceps kept her from knocking over a potted plant. "What do you want now?"

He stood tall and ripped, a nearly animalistic tension cascading off him. His dark hair brushed his collar in an untamed way, and something wild glimmered behind his brown-colored contacts. "We're not finished with our conversation from yesterday, so I thought I'd provide fair warning," he said.

For the first time that evening, a hum fluttered through her belly. She'd spent an enjoyable evening with a handsome, smart, sexy man...and had felt nothing. Now, one second in Nate's arms, with him issuing *threats*, her body flared to life. "Let go of my arms, or I swear, you'll never walk again," she hissed.

He yanked her closer, one hand pressing against her lower back.

His erection jumped against her cleft, and she bit back a moan.

"I'll meet you back at your place. If he's there with you, I'm taking him out." Nate released her and pivoted to head back to his table.

Audrey swallowed several times, irritated beyond belief at the relief that filled her. Relief that Nate wasn't spending the night with Lilith the tigress.

Audrey unlocked her apartment door and slid inside, listening. No sounds. Nate hadn't arrived yet. Good. She'd get her bag and stay the night at a hotel before heading in to work the next day. She locked the door.

A light flipped on.

Nate sat in a leather chair, his shoes kicked off, sock-covered feet on the ottoman. "'Bout time you got home. I was about to come looking."

It had taken several moments to convince Darian she wished to go home—alone—and then the cabbie had taken the long route. "Don't you have a blonde to flirt with?" Audrey asked, her heart kicking into gear.

"Jealous?" Nate asked, looking way too comfortable in faded jeans and a ripped T-shirt. A half-full glass of red wine sat next to him on the sofa table.

Yes, actually. He wasn't hers, but at one point, he had been. He'd been everything, and the thought of him turning that all-encompassing focus on another woman hurt like a knife to the stomach. "Of course I'm not jealous. Don't be ridiculous."

The image he presented, Nate waiting for her after a hard day's work, had filled her dreams for much too long. Home. He'd always been her idea of home, and an ache pounded in her solar plexus. They'd never have that together, although sometimes, late at night when she couldn't sleep, she daydreamed. Fantasized. Wished. She cleared her throat against an impossible future. "When did you change your clothes?"

The man looked even better in the casual wear than the perfectly cut suit.

"A few minutes ago in your room. I brought an overnight bag." His feet dropped to the floor as he gestured toward the couch. "Why don't you have a seat, and we'll talk?"

An overnight bag? The breath heated in her lungs, and she shoved down interest. "You're not staying the night." Weariness weighed down her limbs. "I'm not up for another talk with you." Man, she was tired. He evoked so many emotions in her, her brain refused to think straight. "Don't you have a war to go fight?"

"Come here, Audrey." The low tone combined sexiness and command in a dangerously sensual way.

Her legs slid into motion before her mind reached a reason to refuse. She dropped onto the couch. "You have twenty minutes to ask questions, and then you're going to leave. Period."

For answer, he reached for her foot and tugged off the heel. Strong fingers began to knead the arch of her foot, and a small groan escaped her.

"Other foot," he said. Determination hardened his face while his eyes softened.

Why did he want to bring her pleasure? Was it to manipulate her, or did he remember how much they'd touched? So often and so freely.

God, she missed that.

So she lifted her other foot as if in a dream, and he plucked off the shoe. Both his hands went to work, sending pure ecstasy up her legs. Her lids closed to half-mast, and she studied him through the remaining light. "Why are you being nice to me?"

"Why wouldn't I?" he asked, his thumb pressing beneath her heel, studying her face and probing deep.

The tendons in her foot relaxed. "Because you hate me."

His head jerked. "I don't hate you, Aud." He ran his thumbs along her arches, melting her body in pleasure. "I don't understand you, and I'm not sure I ever knew you, but I could never hate you." Regret tinged his matter-of-fact tone.

"Why not?" she whispered, her body going lax.

He pushed beneath her toes, releasing pressure points as he exhaled slowly. "The only happiness I remember in that hellhole included you. Those days, even if you were acting, those were the best of my life."

Remembered pleasure soothed her nerves. Her lids opened. "You're a human lie detector."

He shrugged, powerful shoulders moving. "Yes, but you got beneath all of my defenses. If anybody could lie to me, it'd be you."

A feminine contentment overcame her. She was the

one woman in the world he'd let in. Too bad she'd taken that trust and broken his heart—even if she did so for the right reasons. "I didn't lie." If nothing else, she needed him to believe that—especially since it was way too late to turn back.

The gentleness in his touch contrasted nicely with the obvious strength in his fingers. "You knew we started as an experiment?"

"Kind of. My mother asked me to help a lost soldier who needed some kindness in his life. She wanted me to talk to you, get to know you, even become a friend. I said I'd help." Audrey's lips tickled into a rueful smile. "I had no intention of falling in love with you like I did."

"You don't leave somebody you love," Nathan said, dropping her feet, his gaze shuttering closed.

You do to protect them. But he wouldn't understand that, would he? His entire life, all he had were his brothers, and the idea of leaving them wouldn't have occurred to him. They were all or nothing, the Gray brothers. A familiar ache pounded in her chest. "I'm sorry I hurt you." She lifted her legs to sit cross-legged on the sofa.

"So why did you?"

She picked at a mar in the cushion. "We became too close, and the commander knew you wanted a life outside of the military group. He said either I ended our relationship or you were going to die as an example to the rest of his soldiers."

Nate lifted his chin. "So you trusted him over me."

Audrey started, and her breath caught. "No. I broke up with you to save you."

"I figured out why you broke up with me. But again, you trusted the commander over me. I would've figured out a way for us." Determination and anger blazed hot in his eyes. "You had no right to make that decision for both of us."

She gasped, anger biting her. "This is about your ego? You beating the commander?" Ending her relationship with him had nearly killed her, and he couldn't see that? Standing, she kicked her heels out of the way. "Forget you, Nate."

He caught her elbow and tugged her back around, his movement making no sound. "My ego? No. This is about you being too frightened to take a chance, to make a stand, and to fight for us, for what you said you wanted."

Oh, if he had any clue about her fight.

She shoved his chest. Hard.

The man didn't move an inch.

"Let go of me," she said, her chin rising.

"No." Then his mouth captured hers. The gentleness always alive in Nate had fled, leaving heated, pissed-off male.

Her knees weakened, and her breath heated. She opened her mouth to protest, to argue, but his tongue swept inside, and she was lost. Lost to the passion instantly igniting between them.

Her nipples hardened to rock, while her nails curled into his chest, no longer pushing.

He drew her into him, taking control. His tongue explored her, tasting, claiming. Taking with a desperation so hot it should've scared her. Should've provided warning that she was out of her element.

But fear remained so far in the background as to be inconsequential.

Or maybe she just wanted to feel alive. For the first time in five years, the pain of the present, the fatality of the future—disappeared.

Only here and now existed—only pleasure so sharp it cut through her with a delicious blade of ecstasy. One man on earth could provide such an overwhelming escape, and she wanted the freedom he offered. A temporary relief from the reality of her life, of who she'd become and what she must do now.

So she jumped headfirst into the storm he'd unleashed, her tongue mating with his. A low growl rumbled up from his chest like a lion about to attack.

He reached down and tugged her still-buttoned blouse over the top of her head. Cool air brushed her skin, and her nipples sang a whispering *hello*. She protested when he jerked his mouth free and then sighed when he nipped her jaw, tracing the fragile bone.

Fire lashed from his mouth, assaulting her with a need too dark to avoid. She held no illusions that this wasn't one night to scratch an itch. She'd given her heart to Nate years ago, but no future existed for them.

She had this moment, and she wanted to experience every second, no matter how quickly it ended.

Somehow her bra ended up across the room.

"Oh baby," he murmured, his gaze hot and on her breasts. "These haunt my dreams." His mouth found her, licking along her breast and engulfing a nipple.

She sighed, her hands burrowing through his thick hair and seizing tight. Both knees weakened, and only a strong arm banding around her waist held her upright.

Her wildest memories didn't come close to the hunger replacing all thought. A smart girl would stop him. She didn't want to be smart, and she didn't want careful. She wanted right now.

He switched to the other breast, laving and sucking, nipping with a hint of violence that shot liquid to coat her thighs.

Finally, he lifted up, his unique eyes a color she'd never seen. Not gray or black, but something in between. "Audrey?"

The low, guttural tone nearly propelled her right over the edge into orgasm.

She swallowed, trying to force out words. "One night, Nate. Just us. You, me, and now. No past, no future."

Regret twisted his lips, and desperation flamed across his face. He wanted to refuse, to maybe protect them both.

The time for protecting them had disappeared five years ago. She felt an apology shine in her eyes as she reached out and cupped his erection. Full and pulsing, even through the jeans, his cock overwhelmed her palm in size and heat.

A furious struggle cut grooves into his rugged face.

She squeezed.

His eyelids shut, and when they reopened, the fight was over.

CHAPTER
8

NATE BANDED HIS hands around Audrey's waist and lifted her, striding through the apartment and into her bedroom, placing her on the bed. This was a mistake. No question, no excuses, he was about to make the biggest mistake of his life.

He didn't care. God, he *really* didn't care.

Years of loneliness, years of uncertainty, all disappeared in the softness of her touch, in the gardenia scent of her skin.

He was an experiment created in a test tube, maybe without a soul, perhaps without any hope. But for a brief time, with this woman, he'd felt whole. Real. Good. Even if they just had the night, he wanted that feeling again.

Before he sacrificed everything.

He tried to gentle himself as he pulled the skirt from her body. A groan escaped him at the bright pink thong covering her mound. His Audrey had always loved bright colors.

Sliding his thumbs beneath the sides, he drew them down her curvy legs, his heart thumping at the scars. The soft scent of woman hit him, roaring heat between his ears. "I'd forgotten how perfect you are."

Denial lit her face. "Right."

He shook his head, reaching down to drag his shirt over his head. The woman had always compared herself to her cold, too-thin, unfeeling mother. She'd never understood that a guy liked curves. "I should've shot your mother."

Audrey's head jerked. "What a thing to say."

"Isobel has never treated you right."

"My mother has her failings, I agree, but she tried. She sent me to the best boarding schools in the world, and she always had a nurturing tutor or two for me when I was home."

Nate's eyebrows rose. "Probably to study how nurturing helped you to develop."

She grinned, the smile tinged with sadness. "More than likely. I know you don't like her, but she's still my mother, and I don't want to talk about her. Especially now." Audrey glanced at his bare chest and hummed softly.

Fair enough. This was about him and Audrey. So he brushed a finger along her arm. "You're beautiful."

She glanced down at her leg lying at an odd angle. "I'm damaged."

He grinned. "We're all damaged, baby. You're still the most beautiful woman I've ever seen."

Regret twisted her lip. "Don't be kind, Nate."

No problem. Kindness lived nowhere in him. "I've missed you." Damn it. No emotion.

Her eyes darkened to cobalt. "I've missed you, too."

Neither one of them mentioned that they'd never really had each other. Moments made up a life, and Nate could count his on one hand. Real moments, and most involved his brothers. Deep down, he knew this was another one that would shape him.

He couldn't stop the inevitable, so he gave himself over to it.

Her gaze traced his bare chest with a hunger that made him growl.

"The tattoo is new," she murmured, eyeing the ink above his heart.

"Yes. Means *freedom*." All four of the brothers had gotten the tat the second they'd escaped.

Audrey studied the symbol. "It isn't Japanese."

"No. It's Adrinka." The brothers all spent time on missions in Africa, and the thick symbol spoke to them. The hours they'd spent in drawing the symbol just right, and the hours they'd spent finding the best tattoo artist around had been treated like the most important mission of their lives.

When they'd all shared the same tattoo, with the same meaning, the time had been worth it.

Nate's hands shook when he unzipped his jeans and shoved them off his legs. Enough of an ego still lived in him that he smiled when Audrey's eyes widened.

He wanted to reassure her that he wouldn't hurt her, but there was no doubt they'd hurt each other. Even so, he needed to make a promise, to be who he needed to be. "I'll protect you the best I can, Aud."

She reached for him, feminine knowledge shining bright in her eyes. "I've never doubted you."

Smooth flesh tempted his palms as he skimmed them up her legs, careful of her scars, along her thighs, and over her hips to her torso, each rib a delicate bone he counted. Indulging himself, he nuzzled beneath her breasts, licking a path.

The sound she made went right to his groin.

He'd always loved her fullness. Lifting his head, he placed a gentle kiss on one nipple. Her hips moved restlessly against him, while her hands slid over his shoulder in a light caress. He flicked a nipple, enjoying how her body tightened. When he took her in his mouth, his groan mingled with hers.

Sweet. The woman tasted sweet. Skin shouldn't have a taste, and neither should nipples. But hers did. Honey and woman.

He'd wondered if his memories played with him. If he'd created his own reality. But he hadn't. This taste—he remembered it well. Keeping her surrounded by his mouth, he lashed her nipple.

Her nails bit into his shoulders.

Smiling around her, he moved to the other breast, finding it hard and needy. He knew the feeling.

Her sighs and moans rippled through him stronger than any kiss, so he continued his journey up her body. The primal being deep down, the one he often tried to tame, bellowed with hunger. With the need to take—and take hard.

So when he reached her neck, he kissed the vulnerable jugular, wrapped an arm around her waist, and flipped them around.

She yelped and chuckled, settling herself atop of him, knees on either side of his flanks. She wiggled to get her damaged leg into position and sighed in relief. The flesh from her thighs caressed him. A gentle hum whispered from her pink mouth as she leaned forward, running her hands along his chest.

Which left her pretty nipples free.

He reached out to knead, to play, to refamiliarize himself with the sounds she made. Five years ago, he'd been her first, and he'd taught her everything. How many lovers had she enjoyed since then?

His fingers tightened, and she gasped.

No. Their pasts didn't matter—neither did their futures.

Besides, he'd been taught how to use sex for intimidation and control, and he didn't want to count how many women he'd bedded. But with Audrey, he'd always been himself. He'd given, and he'd learned that taking was okay and didn't make him weak. Feeling everything strengthened him as well as the whole experience. Only with Audrey.

God, he'd missed that.

He rolled a nipple and kept control, closely gauging her reactions. Years ago, he'd been overly careful not to hurt the woman he'd put on such a high pedestal. Now, he realized, his woman liked a bite of pain with her pleasure.

Ah, the things he could teach her.

His cock lay heavy and demanding, jutting up over his abs. He lifted her, setting her cleft along his length. They both groaned at the contact, and wetness slicked along his shaft.

She paused, her back arching. "I, ah, don't think I can take you like this. You're too big."

Too much need roared through him to allow her to set the pace, anyway. Keeping her gaze, he slid his hand down her torso to reach the tight knot of her clitoris.

She gasped and gyrated against him. "I don't think I can wait."

That made two of them. But he'd dreamed of this moment for five lonely, long years, and he had to prolong it as much as possible. "You remember our first time?" he asked, brushing his thumb along the little bundle of nerves.

"Yes." She gasped, arching against his thumb, her head falling back.

"I was so afraid I'd hurt you," he murmured, pinching gently with two fingers.

She made a sound full of need and demand. Her eyes fluttered closed, the graceful line of her neck exposed. "You didn't hurt me. It was amazing."

He'd hurt her a little, which was inevitable, and even causing her that simple pain had broken his heart. "I dream about that night sometimes, and it's like I'm back in that moment. Until I wake up alone." He dreaded the heartache that followed upon waking fully each time. But now wasn't the time for emotion or regrets. There'd be plenty of moments for pain later.

Her eyelids flipped open, and her eyes softened. "Me too." Dropping forward, she scraped her nails down his chest, her sex grinding along his shaft. "Now, Nate." To emphasize her point, she pinched his nipple.

He smiled, reached up, and pinched hers.

She gasped, and her body shuddered. Sexy and feminine. Desire darkened her eyes to nearly black.

Desperate with the need to taste her, he wound a hand around her neck and drew her down. She sighed against his lips, and he took over. Holding her in place, his mouth covered hers, and he delved deep, demanding what he needed.

She was the only woman in the world who'd ever taken him outside of himself and away from his bloody life. The effort to touch her physically without allowing his emotions to reawaken strained his muscles, but he had no choice. Plus, she'd left him. Maybe this was only sex to her.

If so, he'd take the moment and keep it.

Her mouth responded to him with sweet fire. So he went even deeper, angling her head for better access.

Thunder cracked outside, and he ignored the sound. The woman destroyed him, always had, and pretending he gave a shit about the world right now would require concentration.

His was entirely centered on the little wildcat digging her nails into his shoulders and rubbing her clit along his dick. Sensations bombarded him from every direction, all smelling like gardenias and feeling like pure heaven.

She levered back, her lips hovering over his, her breath heating his mouth. "Please, Nate."

He'd never been able to deny her. Instinct and need took over, but he'd never hurt her. "Tell me if I'm too much," he ordered hoarsely. Flipping them back over, he covered her and quickly nabbed a condom from his discarded jeans and rolled it into place.

Her slim fingers curled over his shoulders, and she widened her legs, arching up against him.

It was too fast. Yet he paused at her entrance and slowly tried to enter her. Tight. Hot. Wet. So damn wet. He made it almost an inch in before she stiffened. So he kissed her, going deep, withdrawing and then working himself back in.

Her nails bit into his flesh.

"You're tight," he whispered, the roaring of his blood filling his ears. He'd forgotten her fragility or the desperate need it created in him to protect and defend. The muscles in his biceps and triceps vibrated as he held himself back, as he held himself in check.

She chuckled, need filling the sound. "It's been five years, Nate."

He paused, his head jerking up. His heart thumped. Hard. "What?"

Confusion and then alarm crossed her face. Her mouth

worked, but no sound emerged. She gave an apologetic half shrug, scraping her nipples against his chest.

He shook his head, the world silencing. She couldn't have meant…"Five years since we were together," he said, making sense of the moment.

She blinked, the thoughts smoldering across her face, in her expressive eyes.

His dick swelled, only halfway to home. "Audrey. You haven't been with anybody else?" How was that even possible?

She sighed and widened her legs, bringing her knees up. "No."

The world screeched to a full stop. What did that mean? Had she hoped they'd get back together? "I don't understand."

"You don't need to. I've been busy." Shields drew over her eyes, keeping him out.

Everything in him wanted to push for an answer—to understand. Being inside her felt real and right. The thought that the moment might mean as much to her stole his breath. But even so, he'd lose her again.

Without question.

And that hurt more than the stab wound he'd once taken to the kidney. "Audrey—"

"Enough talk." She arched against him and tightened her internal muscles.

His ears burned as she gripped his cock like a vise. The idea that he was the only man to have touched her, to have taken her, spurred the beast inside him to life. There was no holding back. Clamping her hip, his mouth covered hers, kissing her with more emotion than he'd ever be able to express.

His body took over. With a hard shove, he plunged

inside her. She cried out into his mouth, her eyes widening, her body arching.

She took a deep breath, blinked several times, and relaxed into the bed. "Wow."

Heated, internal walls clenched him fiercely, enclosing hard enough he needed to pound. Even his back muscles tensed when he held himself still. This was Audrey. "Are you all right?"

She smiled and scooted her butt even farther down. "Yes. Now move."

No further encouragement was needed. He slid out and back in, the incredible heat caressing his length. Home. He was finally fucking home.

Slowly, watching her closely, he increased his pace, fighting everything he was to be gentle.

She sighed and met his thrusts. Passion glazed her eyes in an expression of trust and vulnerability. He needed her to remember him. Even if he died in three weeks, he needed to bury himself so deeply inside her that a part of him always lived there.

Fear had no place between them, and yet it nearly choked him. She was the one person he'd truly been himself with, and she had to keep a thought of him alive. He had to matter to somebody.

The power she still held over him should have given him pause, but not right now. Not when his body covered hers, when her sighs mixed with his, when those sharp nails bit into his skin.

Now was for feeling.

Harder, faster, he began to pound, gauging her, making sure he didn't hurt her. Holding back, yet still experiencing as close to heaven as he'd ever reach. She bit her lip, need shimmering in her eyes. "Nate."

At his name, he closed his eyes and thrust even harder. How many times had he awoken the last five years to the sound of his name on her lips, only to find the bed empty? Electricity danced down his spine, sparking his balls. He needed this. Needed her.

Reaching down, he brushed her clit. He remembered exactly how she liked to be touched, rough and fast. "Now, Audrey."

She arched, screamed his name, and came with a rippling inside her that held him tight, demanding his own release. He shoved hard into her, hitting her G-spot, prolonging her orgasm until she whimpered in surrender.

Then he exploded.

CHAPTER
9

A UDREY TRIED TO roll over, her breath catching at the realization that she couldn't move. Panicked, she kicked out. Pain radiated up her bad leg.

"Whoa, darlin'," Nate murmured, his voice rough with sleep. "Hold on—we're entangled."

Oh. Oh yeah. Holy moly. She'd slept with Nate. "Okay." Taking a deep breath, she tried to calm her racing heart as he untangled the sheets from around them. Nate. Sex. Holy crap on a cracker. What had she been thinking? Nothing, that's what. Not one thought of self-preservation had entered her sex-starved head. The clock continued counting down to the most dangerous moment of her life, one she'd engineered to take down the commander's entire organization, and she'd just complicated the situation beyond belief.

Sheets untangled, Nate moved with sinewy grace to lean back against the headboard. Gentle hands lifted her to sit as he tugged her legs over his thighs. "I want to really see what happened," he said.

Realization dawned. Light streamed in from the window, fully illuminating the bedroom. The intimacy of the moment tempted her to wish for something that could never happen. Too much had occurred between them, and they both had missions to complete that would most likely get them killed. Plus, it wasn't like he'd declared love and asked to make a go of it. "No." She tried to free her legs.

"Yes." Gentle fingers tapped over the scars both above and below her knee. "How many pins in there?" he asked softly.

She swallowed. Sex was one thing, the intimacy of morning another one entirely. "Five." Well, five now. "I'll always have a limp."

He caressed her flesh, his gaze gray and strong. "I'm sorry."

She shook her head. "Not your fault. Never was."

"You don't blame me?" Incredibly long lashes rested against his skin when he closed his eyes and exhaled. "You should."

"No." She reached out and cupped his stubbled jaw, waiting until he focused on her before speaking. "None of this is your fault—it never has been. You've always done your best, and you've always sacrificed everything. I know I let you down, and I'm sorry." But she had to continue on her current path in order to make things right. If she shared with him, he'd try to stop her.

He turned his face into her palm with a soft kiss. "Let me get you out of here."

"No." She dropped her hand.

He sighed, studying her. "Tell me they made you work for them."

"They didn't." She let the truth show in her eyes.

"Then why?" His voice emerged rougher than freshly laid gravel before trucks pounded each stone into submission.

She slid her legs off his. "They agreed to treat me,

to make me better, if I worked for them. The second I regained mobility, I went to work for the senator."

"But you're better now. You can leave." Nate shoved away from the bed, dangerous and naked. Frustration cut harsh grooves along his generous mouth.

Regret and hurt ticked down her spine. She carefully stood, pausing to make sure her leg held. "I don't want to leave now." She meant every single word. For nearly five years, she'd suffered, healed, and planned. It was time to take down the commander, and only she could scream the battle cry. From day one she'd known the power of the organization and that the only way to beat it was from the inside. "I'm sorry."

"Me too." Nate ran a rough hand through his hair.

She wanted to level with him. But she and the senator had meticulously planned for three years, and Nate would complicate things. Sure, he would be a huge asset in a fight, but with his emotions in play, he'd go too far.

Audrey sucked in air. Even so, one of her main goals was to protect her mother. Whether it made sense to anybody else or not, she had to try. Nate wouldn't agree, nor should he. "What's the plan now?" Audrey asked.

He glanced at the floor. "Do you have a cat?"

"No." Had he lost his mind?

"I keep hearing a cat," he mused.

She forced a smile. "Mrs. Abernathy downstairs has a tabby named Chester. You must hear him." Man, the guy had amazing hearing. "Though Chester doesn't usually make much noise."

"I hear his heartbeat. Chester is chasing something. I'll have to block the noisy feline." Nate reached down and drew on his jeans. Sinewy muscle shifted at the graceful move.

She swallowed, heat rushing directly south. Even in

the devastation of the morning after, her body wanted him back in bed. Now. She had to focus on something else. "Tell me about Jory."

Nate turned, his jeans unbuttoned, his chest broad, devastation stamping his chiseled face to be smothered like a candlewick under a blanket. No expression remained. "We have a video of a woman shooting Jory and of him falling to the ground."

Pain slashed into Audrey's center. She wanted to move forward, but something dangerous in Nate's eyes stopped her. "When? How?" She shook her head, her mind reeling. "I've never heard a word about Jory being shot."

"Shane thinks he saw another video in which Jory moved, but Shane had a head injury, and the other video has never been found." Nate's voice remained monotone as he grasped his shirt to tug over his head. "We've looked everywhere, and the only place this could've happened is at the commander's Virginia base. Jory has to be there."

Nothing should've happened to Jory. He was a sweet, very gentle giant in a dangerous world. Tears pricked the backs of Audrey's eyes. Sure, the guy had been trained to kill, but he'd been so kind to her. Always.

While she hadn't gotten the chance to really get to know Matt, Shane, or Jory, what she'd seen, she'd liked. They acted as a solid unit, and they'd do anything for each other.

Watching the Gray brothers had made her wish beyond anything else for a sibling to have and love.

But all she had in the world was her mother.

The woman who'd tested and helped train the Gray brothers.

She and Nate would never see eye to eye on that issue. "I'm so sorry about Jory." The idea of Jory being killed would destroy Nate. How was he even standing? "Do you really think he's alive?"

"I don't know. But if he is, the commander has him, and I have to find him," Nate growled.

She shouldn't say anything. She really shouldn't. "There may be another compound somewhere." The words burst out of her like gun pellets. *Maaaan*. One night of great sex, and she started telling him things she shouldn't. Things that would get them both killed.

Nate's chin slowly lowered. "Where?"

Butterflies on cocaine winged in her abdomen. "I don't know, but I'll find out." It was the least she could do. If Jory had been shot by a woman in the commander's employ, there was a good chance Audrey's mother had held the gun. Though, maybe not. Just shooting somebody like that spoke of temper, of feeling and not thinking. That did not sound like Isobel Madison. Or maybe Audrey just couldn't bear it if her mother had killed Jory. "Tell me about the kill chips."

Anger blazed across Nate's face. "They're lodged near our spines, and if the correct code isn't entered into the correct computer with wireless communication to the chips, they explode in three weeks." Nate reached back and absently rubbed his shoulder. "I have to get the codes."

She thought she'd felt fear before, but the claws raking through her gut held poison. A chip ready to sever Nate's spine? How was this even possible? Brilliant but deadly. "Can't you take them out?"

"No. If they're touched with anything, they explode." His tone remained matter-of-fact.

Audrey poked a bruise on her wrist, her mind reeling. "How delicate are they? I mean, if you're hit just right, what happens?"

"They blow up." Nate rubbed his whiskered chin. "We've

taken nearly five years to prepare and find the commander, and we don't have anything yet. No codes, no computer program, no idea how to survive this without turning ourselves in."

"You can't." Fear bit into her. "If you turn yourselves in, he'll never let you go. Ever."

"I know." Determination made Nate's jaw look like carved stone.

Her mind reeled. "How long have you known about the chips?"

He shrugged. "They were implanted a year before we escaped."

She stilled. "So you knew about them? When we were together?"

His gaze shuttered closed. "Yes. I didn't see the need to worry you."

He'd never really opened up to her, had he? A kernel of hurt pricked her heart that he hadn't confided in her. She was tough enough to take the truth, but it was too late to worry about that now, and she still wanted to help him. "Whatever. I have doctor appointments later this week and will see what I can find out."

"No." Nate slid his hands into his front pockets. "I'm not here to put you in danger. Give me the layout of the base here, and I'll take it from there."

If he only knew. The need to confide in him tried to push words out, but she didn't want him to stop her. Darn it. Nate deserved the entire story before he took on the commander. Maybe she should bring Nate into the fold with the senator. But first she needed to get the full plan from the senator before she approached Nate, because the guy would definitely be a hard sell—and something had to happen soon. She nodded. "Okay. I'll get the layout."

He shook his head, warning twisting his lip. "Don't lie to me, Audrey. We both know I could have you contained, away from here, within seconds."

She gasped, heat spiraling into her cheeks. "And we both know I could have you contained, at the base, within seconds, don't we?"

Nate stiffened. His chin lifted at the threat while his cock hardened instantly, biting into his zipper. The threat was meant to throw him off balance, but the obvious lie inherent in the words calmed him. The challenge she threw down spurred him on. "I don't think you'll call the commander."

She lifted her chin. "Won't I?"

"No. Although, when did you start calling him by his first name?" The Audrey Nate remembered had been scared to death of the military leader.

She blew out air and leaned down to fetch a robe from under the bed. She shook the plush material out, frowning at the wrinkles. "*Asshat* didn't seem appropriate."

So she still didn't like the guy. "If you can't stand him, why are you working with him?" Nate asked.

"I explained that."

But there was more. There had to be. "Audrey?"

She sighed. "My mother and the commander are a package deal, and you know it. For whatever reason, Mother has aligned her path with his, and if I want her in my life, I have to accept him. Work is all that matters to them, so I'm part of the work."

It was the closest the woman had ever come to explaining her twisted relationship with Isobel Madison. Audrey had always reminded him of one of those abused kids who defended their abuser to the last breath. "Neither one of them are good for you," Nate said quietly.

Audrey lifted a shoulder. "They're all I have."

He wanted to argue that point, but how? They weren't together, and even if they were, there was a good chance his spine would explode in a few weeks. She'd be alone again. "You don't owe them anything."

Audrey's eyes flashed fire. "I owe my mother everything. Life is the only thing that matters, as you know, and she gave me that."

Nate shook his head. Dr. Madison had preached "life" and experimentation from the beginning. Maybe she'd manipulated Audrey with the thought from early childhood. "If you think that way, then I owe her, too." Dr. Madison had created him in a test tube. That was life, right?

Confusion clouded Audrey's eyes. "It's different," she said slowly.

A surprising hurt wound through his chest. "So being created in a tube isn't life?"

"That's not what I meant." The words burst out of Audrey. "I mean that she raised me and paid for schooling, tutors, and doctors like a parent does."

"What was she to me?" Nate asked, truly wanting an answer. He'd always wanted an answer to that question.

"I don't know." Sorrow and regret echoed in Audrey's tone.

Nate studied her, wondering how their very different childhoods had somehow brought them to the same place once again. "Why haven't you slept with anybody but me?" he asked, surprising himself.

Her head jerked up. Vulnerability paled her delicate face to be quickly hidden as she slid her arms into the robe and belted it around her tiny waist. "I haven't had a lot of time, with being blown up, operated on, and trying to commit fraud on the U.S. government on behalf of your sworn enemy." Sarcastic humor lifted her top lip, but the lightness failed to reach her eyes or display that devastating dimple. "Sometimes a girl has to prioritize."

He'd loved her younger sense of humor. This one? Not so much. Sarcasm and fatalism didn't fit with the person deep inside Audrey, the one she'd shoved down to survive. "I understand why you stayed to receive medical attention." The commander's medical team and facilities beat any other in the world, without question. If anybody could have saved her leg, it was them. "But now it's time to go." As much as the thought cut through him like a blade, he didn't trust her enough to send her to his brothers in Montana. But he could find her safety. "Let me help you."

"I don't want your help." Her stance widened slightly as if they faced off under high noon.

Worse yet, absolute truth lived in every word. The woman really didn't want his help. A surprising hurt compressed his lungs. "Why are you still working with him?" he breathed out. Could her mother's approval mean that much to her? After everything?

Audrey lifted her chin. "They saved my life and gave me a second chance. It's the only life I've truly known, and I'm doing some good with the senator."

"Find another life," Nate ground out.

"No." Regret filled her sigh. "You're the one who told me that our childhood shapes us. I'm doing what I can right now."

He shook his head. Why did he get the feeling she hid too many secrets? Enough truth breathed in her statement that he couldn't find the lie, but one lurked deep. He was sure of it. "I'm going to kill him, Aud. Then I'm going to blow up every facility he owns and make sure they never function again. You don't want to be here for this."

Awareness pursed her lips as she studied him. Her

breath hitched as her chest lifted. Those amazing eyes widened. "Suicide mission?"

"Probably." Which was yet another reason the previous night had been a one-shot deal. Chances were slim he'd survive the attack he planned after saving his brothers.

She nodded, regret twisting her lip. "Hasn't that always been your plan?"

"Yes." Except for the brief time she'd been his. Then his plans had changed dramatically to a future with possible kids and even a fucking picket fence. He'd known better, without a doubt. A bullshit everyday life had never been for him. He'd been created to kill, and through a lucky turn of fate had been given brothers to love—to protect and ultimately save. They were happy, and once the chips were deactivated, they wouldn't require his skill set any longer.

He wouldn't be needed, and he needed them so very much. Too much.

"Hmmm." Pain lived in her eyes, but no give existed in her jaw. "I just realized...I can't save you."

"No." He frowned. What was she talking about? "I don't expect you to save me."

"I know." She tightened the belt, her eyes glimmering with tears. "I'll get you the codes and any info on Jory, but you need to decide to save yourself. When this is all over, if you and your brothers survive, you need to save yourself. Decide to keep going."

That was the rub, now, wasn't it? The life he'd been created for, the one he'd excelled at, was over. Where exactly was he supposed to go?

CHAPTER
10

AUDREY LEFT NATE at the apartment, arriving at work a few minutes late for the first time since taking the job. As usual, she paused at the entrance to search her vicinity. A man stood across the street and saluted her with two fingers.

She turned to face him, and he grinned.

So the commander's men weren't hiding any longer. What did that mean? The guy stood tall and muscled in jeans and a dark T-shirt. Glancing at the traffic, he stepped into the street.

Panic strangled her, and she turned, shoving open the door.

She hustled through security and jumped into an elevator, smashing into a man wearing a gray suit.

"Sorry," she muttered, turning and straightening her skirt. Finally, she burst onto her floor and hustled through thick oak doors into a waiting room decorated in navy blue and white. Seated behind a hand-carved reception desk, the receptionist, a diminutive redhead who looked like a teenager, handed her a couple of messages with a murmured, "Everything all right?"

"Yes, thanks," Audrey answered. "I'll be in my office."

"The senator is waiting in his office," Red said.

What was her name? Audrey mentally listed the choices. "Thanks, Julie."

"No prob." Julie reached to answer the phone.

Good, she'd gotten the name right. The regular receptionist was on maternity leave after giving birth to twin boys. Audrey had given her a baby shower at the office, trying to enjoy the woman's bliss while still feeling empty inside. When would she get over the loss?

With a shrug, Audrey stretched out of her trench coat and tossed the heavy Chanel into her office as she hustled by. Her leg hitched, even with her feet encased in the solid boots she'd donned under a gray pantsuit. Knocking quietly, she pushed into the senator's office and stopped short.

"Hi, Audrey," Darian Hannah said, standing from one of two leather guest chairs.

"Darian." Audrey shut the door and strode forward, concentrating on diminishing her limp. What in the heck was he doing there? When she sat, Darian followed suit.

"How's the leg?" the senator asked, leaning forward from behind an antique walnut desk.

"Great." The man might be a sweetheart, but he had no clue about boundaries. Audrey shook her head. It was all she could do to get him to agree to wearing ties on the Senate floor for debate. Requiring him to hide his concern in front of visitors was out of the question. "Thank you for asking."

The senator tapped long fingers on his desk. "Audrey was in a car accident."

Darian frowned. "I'm sorry to hear that."

Audrey forced a smile. "My leg has healed, although I still have nightmares about the accident."

The senator blew out air. "My wife died in a similar car accident, and I miss her daily. She was all I had in this too-short life. You're fortunate to be alive."

"Definitely." Audrey smiled gently, well used to the senator talking about his deceased wife. He spoke fondly and with a certain sadness that the woman had passed. Audrey had made up the lie years ago about her damaged leg, and people usually believed her. Of course, she'd told the senator the truth, but in front of other people, they stuck to her old story. He was getting better at subterfuge, wasn't he?

She glanced at Darian, her mind still reeling. "Did I miss a schedule for this meeting?"

"No. I dropped in unexpectedly," Darian said, adjusting his purple tie, which contrasted nicely with his black shirt and suit. Sleek and stylish, the lobbyist showed a flirtatious side to his charming personality.

"Okay." Audrey lifted an eyebrow and concentrated on the senator.

A smile lifted the corners of the senator's eyes. "Darian came to me with information today, and I realized we're on the same side."

The breath left Audrey's lungs. *Okay. Relax.* She forced a smile. "What kind of information?"

"I know about the commander and his organization," Darian said.

She blinked. Irritation grated along her spine. "So our date last night was a fishing expedition for you?"

Darian's eyes glittered with genuine amusement. "Of course not. Our date was me using business to try to get you to see me socially."

The senator chuckled. "That was probably your only chance."

Darian grinned. "I know. The woman is all about business."

"How was the date?" the senator asked, his chair creaking as he shifted in his seat.

"Boundaries, Senator," Audrey murmured as heat climbed into her face. She'd been used as a pawn before, and the thought that Darian just wanted to see her socially warmed something inside her.

"That good, huh?" The senator guffawed. "Ah, to be young again."

Audrey shook her head. She needed to regain control of the situation. "You were saying about an organization?"

Darian sighed. "After we left the restaurant, I went back to work. My computer hackers told me everything about our main competition for funding. An organization run by some commander." Darian's smile revealed strong white teeth in a handsome dark face.

Audrey held perfectly still. No way did Darian know *an inch* of everything. "Who's the commander?"

Darian sighed as if disappointed at her secretiveness. "The Red Force has amazing computer hackers. Believe it or not, some of my soldiers are excellent. We've been following the senator, who had a meeting with the commander, so we began investigating him."

Three meetings, actually. Audrey crossed her legs, her pulse increasing. "Do tell."

Darian picked a piece of lint off his pant leg. "We started investigating and discovered this commander guy is our main competition for funding. Digging deeper, we realized some of the missions that have been going on for decades."

Audrey tilted her head. "Digging deeper?"

Darian lifted a football-player-sized shoulder. "Digging,

hacking, you know, the stuff we're not supposed to do but all do anyway."

Hacking? Darian's guys managed to hack into the commander's computers? Audrey's lids half lowered. "What's the commander's first name?"

"Don't know. Do you?" Darian asked, challenge lifting his chin.

Audrey's gaze slashed to the senator.

He lifted gnarled hands. "It's okay, Audrey. We can trust Darian—he wants the commander shut down as much as we do. I told him about your mother working there and that you know about the organization."

Audrey shot to her feet. "Are you kidding me? You *told* him?" This was bad. This was beyond bad. "I trusted you." The man shouldn't be a politician—he didn't have it in him.

Which was why she liked him.

He pushed back and stood, looking every one of his sixty years. "You have to trust somebody sometime. I made you the guarantee that your mother would be safe when we took down the commander, and I've expressed that to Darian." The senator pressed his palms against the desk and leaned forward. "Darian has more information than we do, and if we work together, we'll be successful."

Nausea swirled in Audrey's stomach, and she frantically gulped in air to keep from diving for the garbage can. Her entire reason for going along with the senator's plan was to protect her mother—right or wrong. She had no guarantee Darian would follow the plan, no matter what he said. "You're crazy."

Darian stood and gently grasped her arm. "I have the means to find out where the commander's other facility is located."

Audrey's mind spun. Darian even knew about the commander's secondary facility?

The senator nodded. "As soon as we discover the location, we're going public with the information about him and the inhumane missions he has created and endorsed. Plus, we can't forget the men who have had to work for him. They must want freedom. I give you my word your mother will be protected in any governmental sweep."

Audrey had made the deal on day one. While her mother didn't deserve leniency, the woman was still Audrey's mother. What child wouldn't try to protect their one parent? But what about Nathan? What about all of the supersoldiers who'd escaped five years ago? Audrey couldn't ask the question, because it was possible neither the senator nor Darian knew there were any freed soldiers. But if files were found, if records were deciphered, their secret would be out.

The door opened, and Ernie Rastus poked his head in. "Sorry I'm late. Long meeting." He glanced from Audrey to the senator and back. "Um, what's going on?"

Audrey whirled. "Senator Nash told Darian about our hidden agenda, because apparently we're on the same side."

Ernie hurried inside and shut the door. "We are?"

"Yes." The senator sighed. "Darian wants the commander out of commission as badly as we do. We're on the same team, and he even has discovered the experiments to create human soldiers from birth."

Ernie swallowed and gave Audrey a look. "We need to use caution here, Senator."

A hard gleam entered the senator's eyes. "The time for caution is over. We have to take them out. On all that is holy, the atrocities must end."

Wow. Audrey frowned and focused on Darian, still

trying to keep her coffee down. "What did you find out about experiments?"

"Not enough. Just that the commander has been creating soldiers to fight. Supersoldiers...and training them as killers." A veil dropped over Darian's eyes.

Audrey nodded. "I see." Either Darian didn't know about the intense training, or he was damn good at hiding the truth. Either way, nobody knew about Nate and his brothers' extra abilities—the hyper-hearing, the reading of body language, the impossible strength...those had never been documented, even by the commander. "Where are these soldiers now?"

"A disaster happened in Tennessee five years ago." Darian shook his head. "We think the commander might've killed his creations, or maybe the explosion was an accident and they all died."

Audrey exhaled. "I see." So Darian didn't know about Nate or any of the other soldiers being alive and free in the world.

"Or, perhaps, the creations escaped and blew the place up." Darian's gaze narrowed. "What do you think?"

"I think you're crazy." Audrey swallowed. "The commander is a bad guy who trains soldiers to work outside of the United States. He's so good at his job, there's no way any soldiers could've escaped him. Whatever happened in Tennessee was executed by the commander, I'm sure."

The senator shook his head. "What if some of the commander's soldiers actually did escape? What if we have created killers out there with no hope of living among society?"

Anger and panic threatened to bubble up, so Audrey forced a chuckle. "You both are getting way into a conspiracy theory here. Who else have either of you told about the commander or his organization?"

The senator shook his head. "Only you."

Darian nodded. "I have two men, hackers, who have discovered the information for me. Only we three from Red Force are privy to the truth. Right now, anyway."

Audrey wished she could trust Darian. Unfortunately, a woman who kept secrets didn't trust anybody, a lesson she'd learned at her mother's knee. Trust was a luxury she couldn't afford—especially right now.

If she told the truth to Nate, the smartest thing for him to do would be to take out both Darian and the senator— maybe even Ernie. He'd do it, too. To protect his brothers, he'd do anything.

What a complete mess. "Our recommendation is due next week, and the Senate vote is a day later, so we only have a few days for one of you to discover the commander's alternate base, if there even is one." Oh, there definitely was one—she knew it. "Then we either have to give the money to the commander, or we have to shut them down. Quietly."

"Publicly," Darian said.

The senator glanced from one to the other. "Now that I think about it, Audrey is correct. If possible, we should do it privately. While the group hasn't been sanctioned by our government, well, it has done a lot of governmental work...with taxpayer funding. We can't go public with all of the information. We want to shut them down for good with the smallest of fanfare."

Audrey turned toward Darian. She needed to at least look like she was playing ball. "If you guarantee privacy and you won't go public, we'll guarantee your organization will receive the recommendation for the funding this year."

"The next five years," Darian countered, his eyes darkening to black.

"Deal," Audrey whispered, caring little that it was the senator's place to make the promise. At this point, he'd screwed up enough. She was two seconds from puking on his shoes to make her point. They'd rocked her world, and she needed a moment to figure things out. How could she protect her mother and Nate? Right or wrong, she needed to protect both.

Nate had been her one love, and she refused to let him be taken into captivity again. He'd die first, and while they'd never be together, she needed him out in the world living. Hopefully finding happiness, or at the very least, some peace.

And Audrey had been a disappointment to her mother for years, a fact she deeply regretted. Logically she knew the fault lay with Isobel, but in her heart, a young girl still lived who wanted to do better. Who only wanted her mother to be proud of her. Audrey wouldn't fail her mother at this juncture—she refused to do so.

What if to save her mother, she had to hurt Nate? Or vice versa?

She coughed and glanced at her watch. "I have a meeting with Senator Wilcox's chief of staff about the arms appropriation vote. Don't do *anything* about the commander's group without talking to me first." That quickly, that smoothly, power shifted, and she became the ringleader of the hodgepodge group dealing with the commander.

A position she wanted less than she wanted to be shot in the head.

She hustled back to her office, her gut swirling. What in the world was she supposed to do now? Calling her mother would be a mistake and would alert the commander to the senator's duplicity.

With everything she was, she wished she trusted her mother.

What about Nate? She glanced at her phone but didn't trust her phone enough to call Nate with. Not even her cell phone was secure enough. She sat and grimaced. Even if she wanted to call him, not only did she have nothing good to say...but she also didn't have his phone number. A slightly hysterical laugh bubbled up from her chest. She'd slept with a guy, the only guy she'd ever loved, and she didn't even have a way to get a hold of him.

Life was truly fucked.

CHAPTER
11

NATHAN HELD OUT a chair for Lilith at the coffee shop located conveniently across from where Audrey worked. He made sure to seat himself with his back to a post and an unfettered view through the window. While he didn't expect Audrey to be leaving work any time soon, he felt better watching the exit.

As well as the soldier pretending to read a newspaper on a bench near the entrance. So the commander was still having Audrey followed. Why?

Lilith pushed her blond hair off her face, her eyes glimmering under a smoky shadow.

Audrey's natural look appealed far more to Nate. He'd spent his life with people changing reality, and while a bunch of eye shadow didn't qualify as subterfuge, he liked the natural look. Or maybe he just liked Audrey.

Yeah, that was probably it.

Good thing he was so self-aware, wasn't it?

The waitress deposited their coffees in front of them, and Nate reached for his steaming cup.

"Why are you scowling?" Lilith straightened her posture, revealing breasts lifted by a bra working hard. She pressed her arms in, pushing the mounds higher, just in case he hadn't noticed.

"I'm not." He forced a smile, keeping his gaze above her neck.

"Oh." She pouted out full lips. "I thought we might relax over coffee. Didn't you have a good time at dinner last night?"

His mind counted back. Dinner? Sure. Watching Audrey on a date with another man had been incredibly fun. "We were spying on Darian Hannah and Audrey Madison, remember? Our goal was to investigate Audrey Madison before making the senator our next offer to create more manufacturing plants in his state."

Lilith's eyes narrowed. "Was that it? For some reason, it seemed like your interest in Audrey went beyond politics."

His interest in Audrey went straight to the bedroom. Screw politics. Nate rolled his eyes. "Don't be silly. I was merely doing my job."

Lilith sipped her drink. "If you say so. Though I invited you in that night, and you kindly refused. I don't get turned down very often, Jason. Is there somebody else?"

"No. I had more work to do. You know from my résumé that I'm a workaholic." His fake résumé and falsified background, that was. Heaven save him from forward women. He didn't have the energy to deal with Lilith.

"Maybe. What about another night?"

The woman wasn't going to give up. "I'd love to make it another night—when are you thinking?" Hopefully he will have skipped town by then.

"I'm thinking right now, if you'd like to get out of here." Lilith licked coffee off her lip, making a slow swipe of doing so.

He tried to pretend interest, but the image of Audrey's stunning face, eyes glazed with passion, kept filling his head. What in the hell had he been thinking? One touch, one night with her, and now he was staking out her place of work. Just to make sure she remained safe.

Forcing himself back into the mission, he smiled at Lilith. "Work first, play later. Right now, I'd like to know more about lobbyists in the area. What is Darian Hannah's bio?"

Lilith tapped red nails on the table. "Lately he's been lobbying for a security firm that hires ex-soldiers and mainly provides bodyguard services. He goes where the money is."

"Don't we all?" Nate sat back, pleased that Sins Security, the company he and his brothers had created, would never even remotely seek funding from any government. Way too sticky, that. "Who did Darian work for before?"

"I think a teacher's union, and before that, the beef industry. As a lobbyist, he is one of the best." Lilith gave up all subtlety and ran her bare foot up Nate's pant leg. Her toes were long and without stockings, and the big one dug into his sock and tugged down.

Thank goodness she'd ditched the three-inch high heel first. All Nate needed was a cut along his leg to explain later. He shifted to the left, and she dropped her foot with a large pout.

"I thought you liked me," she murmured.

"I do." He lied his ass off. The woman could probably eat him for breakfast and then go hunting again. "I like to be the one to make a move." Which, frankly, was rather true.

"Oh." She sipped her drink, looking thoughtful. "I see. You have to be in control."

The woman had no idea. "I like to hold the reins." It was the most truthful he'd been with her. Maybe now she'd back off.

"Why?" She ran her tongue along the rim of her cup.

He shook his head. "I don't think we have that much time right now, but doesn't everything go back to childhood?"

"I guess." She studied him. "Did you have a good childhood?"

"Yes. I have two older sisters living in Alabama, where my parents still live and run a small restaurant." He recited his cover story.

Lilith smiled. "Two older sisters? No wonder you want to be in control. I bet they dressed you up to play."

What did that mean? His playtime with his brothers had included blade fighting and target shooting. He laughed. "Funny."

"Thanks. So why haven't you taken the reins with me?" Her voice lowered to husky.

Because he'd rather mate a grizzly? "I like to know a woman before I make a move. All I know about you is that you took a job with the PR department of Techno-Zyn years ago. Before that?" He listened with half an ear, keeping his focus on the myriad of people exiting the building across the street.

"Before that? I went to college, and George Fairbanks gave me a good offer to work for the tech firm upon graduation. PR is my game." Something clicked under the table. She must've slipped her foot into the shoe that more than likely served as a weapon for fresh kill. "Now you know all about me."

Somehow, he doubted that. "All right."

She took another sip, nearly humming. "Do you believe in destiny?"

"No."

"I don't, either." She set down her drink. "But I'm drawn to you. Do you know why?"

He lifted an eyebrow. "I have no idea." Which was true. Everything he'd garnered about the woman told him she went for the king of fish, the head dog, the big cheese. In his current cover, he played a lobbyist. One who answered to her, actually.

She sighed. "I don't know why, either." The scent of expensive perfume clouded his nose when she leaned forward. "But I have excellent instincts, which means there's more to you than you've let on."

He tuned in completely to her from heart rate to respiration rate. No stress, but definitely some arousal. "What do you mean?"

"Why are you a lobbyist?" she asked, her lids dropping to half-mast.

He hardened his gaze. "I like money, and I make a lot of it as a lobbyist. Much more than you make."

"So you care about money." Respect filled her eyes.

Only for the freedom it provided and the weapons it allowed him to buy. "Of course."

"I think we have a lot in common," she said.

Somehow, he doubted that. "How so?"

"You're determined and dedicated, and I think you'll end up much wealthier than you are right now." Her focus dropped to his lips. "More importantly, I can help you become a powerhouse in DC. Power is so much more important than money, and I can tell you want it."

Wow, had she pegged him wrong. Power meant nothing to him unless it kept his family safe, just like money. He'd like nothing better than to go live a quiet life in Montana away from power, people, and prestige. "You read people so well."

The outside door opened, and Fairbanks strode inside. He made his way to their table.

Lilith scooted over to make room. "I told George we'd be here, and he thought we should meet."

The last thing Nate needed was actual work from his current cover. "Great."

"We need to finish wrapping up the agreement with Senator Nash before he changes his mind." Fairbanks signaled the waitress and ordered a vanilla latte.

"Trouble?" Nate asked, finishing his drink.

"Yes. The senator is a crusader who needs funding for his state. If he finds a more above-board method to accomplish his goals, he'll drop any deals with us." A thread of desperation wound through Fairbanks's words.

Nate concentrated on the man's heartbeat. Too fast. "Why do you really want to build in Wyoming? Besides providing a type of kickback to the senator?"

"We need the tax breaks and the subsidies," Fairbanks said bluntly. "The economy hit us harder than most, and we're going under if we don't get a home base that works."

Odd that he said a home base. Nate nodded, wondering if he should dig deeper into his temporary boss's finances. Something was up, but since it didn't deal with Nate or his family, did he really care? "Why Wyoming?"

Fairbanks shrugged. "The senator is a good guy, and Wyoming is a long way from DC. We can work autonomously out there, and we can pursue the scientific world we've earned."

"Huh?" Nate asked.

Lilith laughed. "These days, George here likens modern technology to divination from God, and he doesn't like the safeguards put into place by the government."

Fairbanks leaned forward after glancing around. "I'm working on nanobite technology that will revolutionize medicine and disease treatments. It's beyond anything natural, and it'll make us billions."

Computers as weapons. Who knew. Nate's shoulders slowly relaxed. Nanobite technology was theoretical, or was it? Either way, it was normal science. Except... "I'm assuming your problem with governmental oversight is the prohibition against human testing?"

"Exactly." Fairbanks nodded, pleasure lighting his face at finding an ally. "If someone consents in exchange for payment, why shouldn't we experiment? It's for the greater good."

That one phrase made Nate see red, and his hand curled into a fist with the desire to punch Fairbanks in the face. Yeah, obsession ruled the man, and it was an obsession that had nothing to do with Nate or his mission. Even so, he'd like to knock good ole Georgie out. "I'd sure like to see your research." Not.

"You got it. But we need the perks from the senator and his home state to really get the project off the ground. Do you have an in there?" Fairbanks asked.

"Not really." Not unless one counted the woman Nate had made orgasm three times the previous night. "Do you?"

"Maybe." Lilith tapped her fingers along the back of Nate's hand as if she couldn't help but touch him. "Nash's chief of staff and I go way back. I have a dinner meeting with him tonight to talk about it. Don't worry, I'll do what I need to do."

For the first time, Nate really wanted out of DC. Away from politics, away from murder, away from people. He needed to get Audrey to safety as soon as possible. Not only for her safety, but also for his damn sanity.

He was finally losing it.

CHAPTER
12

AFTER AN EXHAUSTING day, Audrey stepped outside the building into a pounding deluge. Of course, she'd left her umbrella in her office. This day sucked.

She turned toward the parking garage, and a strong hand banded around her arm. "What the—"

"Shhh." Darian towed her through the rain and toward a yellow taxi parked at the curb, his hold relentless. "We need to talk. Things are so much worse than you think." He opened the door.

She yanked back, surprise and fear making her knees shake. A man sitting on a bench jumped up and began to jog toward them. One of the commander's soldiers? Why had she forgotten her umbrella? It'd make a good weapon. Where should she go to get away from the soldier and from Darian? Back into the building. She turned to run. "I'm not getting in the cab."

"Yes." In one smooth motion, Darian turned and all but shoved her into the cab. Her leg buckled, and she cried out, her arms flailing.

He slid in beside her. "Go," he said to the driver.

The taxi drove out into the busy street. The soldier

jumped into traffic, running for the cab. He soon disappeared from sight.

Audrey regained her equilibrium and shoved Darian. "What is wrong with you?"

He closed his eyes and sighed. "We're going to Milly's Bar in Georgetown. We can talk there." He opened his eyes, the darkness full of a plea. "Please. Trust me. This is important."

Audrey scrambled for the other door handle. "This is crazy. I don't know what your problem is, but you need to take it up with the senator—"

"Shhh." Darian wrung her back around, desperation paling his face. He nodded his head toward the taxi driver. "It's okay. One drink, and I'll explain everything. It's so much worse than we feared. Please."

Audrey glanced up to see the taxi driver's curious gaze in the rearview mirror.

"You okay, miss?" he asked with a thick Bostonian accent.

Audrey looked over at Darian, who seemed to be holding his breath in an impressive chest. Fear cascaded off the big guy. "Um, yes." She settled back into the seat and slid her bad leg into a more comfortable position. If necessary, she could dart out into traffic and take her chances. But something in Darian's expression kept her in place. He'd been investigating the commander. Had he found out about the Gray brothers? Or was it something even worse? "We're fine."

The driver nodded and instantly honked at a Mercedes trying to cut him off. Darian exhaled in a burst of air and ran a hand over his wet, curling hair. "I should've never traded sports for politics," he muttered.

Amen, buddy. Audrey pressed her lips together to keep

from asking any questions until they exited the cab. What had Darian discovered? Her mind reeled. She had to get to Nate in case his cover had been blown. "Take a deep breath," she whispered. If Darian kept panting like that, he would pass out.

He nodded and sucked in air, his gaze darting outside the cab. He turned to frantically stare out the back window, his hands shaking in his lap.

Audrey turned to see regular DC traffic behind them, cars darting in and out, cabbies honking, and mud puddles splashing up. Nothing like a good rainstorm during rush hour. She studied the cars behind them, seeing no pattern to discern a tail. The commander's men wouldn't leave a trail. Nausea and adrenaline slammed simultaneously into her stomach.

Calm and cool would save the day. Winding her fingers around Darian's beefy ones, she tugged. "How was your day?"

He swung a wild gaze toward her. "What?"

She flexed her fingers. "Your day. How was it?" Lowering her chin, she kept his gaze. Would he understand? Appearances would save them—probably.

He blinked. "Oh. Ah, I had a good day. You?" As he turned to look out the back window again, she jerked his hand toward her and waited until his gaze followed suit.

"Mine was great." She forced a smile. He had to stop looking so suspicious. If somebody was following them, there wasn't a thing they could do about it. But acting suspicious would get them killed.

His gaze narrowed on her, and he tilted his head. Finally, intelligence rather than terror filled his eyes. "We should do dinner again. Soon."

Yeah, she'd played her hand. The man now probably

realized she had training beyond a lobbyist for a senator. "I did enjoy the steak."

"You are full of surprises." Now he clamped her fingers with a strength far beyond hers.

He had no clue. Silence wrapped around them, broken only by the smattering of rain on the roof. Darian's spicy wood cologne filled the cab. *Clive Christian?* Probably. The lobbyist had money, that was for sure. Working for a top private military organization in the United States came with a fat paycheck. Audrey scooted forward and eyed the front seat. Dark sunglasses and a wide rain hat perched atop a wet newspaper.

She smiled. "How much for the glasses and hat?"

The driver frowned, turning over his shoulder. "Seriously?"

"Yep." She gestured toward Darian. "The guy has a freaky ex who scares me. I'd like a little protection in case she's waiting at his favorite bar."

Cool calculation narrowed the cabbie's gaze in the rearview mirror. "Benjamin is my middle name."

Audrey reached for the wallet in her trench coat and counted out twenties. "Five Andrews." She reached over the seat and swung the hat onto her head, stuffing her thick hair up in the roominess. The dark glasses finished the look.

Darian frowned. "You look like a 1950s movie star trying to remain not-so-anonymous."

Audrey shrugged and tugged the brim of the hat down farther. So long as she remained difficult to identify, she didn't give a fig how she looked.

Darian whistled, glancing out his window. "You've obviously done this before."

No. But she had a brain, and she'd keep her gaze down to avoid any cameras from businesses or ATM machines they passed. Too bad she didn't have any real training. In boarding school, she'd studied English, and in college, she'd studied education, hoping to teach at preschool or the kindergarten level. Somewhere with young kids. Then she'd fallen in love with Nate, had been blown up, and now worked in politics.

Life didn't make any sense.

Finally, the cab rolled to a stop outside a bar in Georgetown. Audrey released Darian and stepped into the rain, her boots splashing the wet sidewalk. Milly's Bar sat proudly in the center of a long block of businesses ranging from a scarf store to a specialty pet store. Without glancing at the street, Audrey steeled her shoulders and strode toward the bar doorway, careful not to limp.

Darian's voice echoed as he told the cabbie to keep the tip, and his hand slipped along her elbow. "We'll go toward the back where we can watch the door," Darian whispered, opening the door and escorting her between tables and along a bar lined with bright red stools.

The guy had seen too many James Bond movies.

Even so, adrenaline flooded Audrey's system, making it hard to breathe. Danger had dropped into her world and taken hold. Heck. She'd sent the invitation, now, hadn't she?

"Hey, Darian," a fiftysomething woman with long pink hair called cheerfully from behind the bar.

"Hi, Milly. Heading to the back—meeting," Darian yelled back, waving at several folks throughout.

They ended up at a round table set against a wall decorated with football paraphernalia. A picture of Darian in his college uniform proudly held center stage. Darian scooted a chair around so both he and Audrey faced the door.

Milly sauntered up, a wide grin on her face. "Good to see you again. Whatcha all want?"

Darian's gaze remained on the closed door. "The usual for me, and a—"

"Gin and tonic." Audrey cut him off before he ordered her a Shiraz. Her disguise wouldn't mean much if she gave herself away through habit. "My favorite." For good measure, she added a slight French accent to her tone. Might as well try to match the hat and glasses.

Darian's gaze swung to her, and his mouth dropped open.

"No prob." Milly turned around on a sparkly pink boot and glided back toward the bar.

"Who are you?" Darian hooked Audrey's elbow and leaned close.

Audrey pushed the glasses higher up on her nose. "You're the one acting so weird. I'm trying to survive here." Without any training or experience. The French accent was probably stupid.

"You're no ordinary operations director." Darian frowned, wiping rain off his forehead. "How much are you involved in this group?"

"Which group?" These days, so many groups surrounded her, it was amazing she didn't get them confused.

"I don't know who to trust." Darian shuddered.

With a hop in her step, Milly returned and deposited a glass of gin and tonic in front of Audrey and what looked like a Greyhound in front of Darian. "Here you go, kids." She smiled, pressing a beefy hand on an ample hip. "It's so nice to see you out on a date, Darian."

Darian nodded weakly. "Thanks, Milly. Genevieve here is a sweetheart."

Audrey bit back a smile. He'd even gone for a French

name. "I like your bar," she said, trying to lower her voice and add the accent.

"Thanks. You're not from around here, huh?" Curiosity quirked Milly's lips.

"How did you know?" Audrey asked. The accent didn't even sound authentic to her.

"Oh, I meet a lot of people. You a model?" Milly asked.

"Um, no." Not unless she lost twenty pounds and learned how to sashay without a limp. "But you're very kind."

Milly scratched her nose. "Okey dokey. You kids give a holler if you need anything else." She hurried over to help a boisterous group of men all wearing Armani.

Audrey kept her fingers off the glass. "Genevieve?"

"I don't know. Sounded French." Darian took a large gulp of his drink. Then another.

Audrey leaned toward him. "Now talk." How much danger had Darian discovered?

"Okay." He swallowed and set down his drink, his hand visibly trembling. "I stayed for a meeting with the senator after you left and—" He coughed and paled as the outside door opened. "Oh no. They found us."

Audrey swirled her head around. Three men, all in black, all staring intently at her. Her brain fuzzed, and the world narrowed in pinpoint sharpness. She scooted her chair and stood. "The back way. Let's go."

Darian stood and instantly cried out, hitting the wall. Blood spurted from his shoulder.

Audrey turned to see a silver gun held low in the first man's hand. They were moving fast.

A woman at the bar screamed, and everyone in the place seemed to drop to the floor at once.

She grabbed Darian. "Let's go."

"No." He shoved her toward the back, reaching for the table with one hand. "Run. Run now."

"Come with me." She tried to tug him.

"No time." He shoved her harder, and she slammed into the far wall. Her leg bellowed.

Milly screamed and disappeared behind the wide bar. Everyone turned toward the three men, glasses and drinks flying.

Crap. Audrey's heart kicked into a fast gear, and she gasped for air.

"Run!" Darian yelled, charging the table into the oncoming men.

Left with no choice, Audrey turned.

And ran.

CHAPTER
13

AUDREY HURTLED THROUGH the doorway into an empty storage area, pushed through another door, and ran as fast as her cramping leg allowed for a back door. Rain slashed into her as she stumbled outside to a narrow alley. The stench of wet garbage assailed her, and she sucked in air. The smattering of more gunfire pattered behind her. Bile rose in her throat, and she shoved the acidic taste down.

Two long brick buildings extended for almost a block on either side of the alley.

She'd never be able to outrun those men.

Glancing frantically for a weapon, she grappled for a rusty tire iron near the steps. The metal scraped her palm, but the heaviness felt good. She could brain somebody with it if necessary.

Limping down the chipped stairs, she started to run. Or rather, jog with a hitch.

She reached the next doorway and tried to open it. Locked.

Her fists ached as she pounded, but nobody came to her rescue.

Two doorways down, a teenager with bright purple hair hefted a garbage bag out of a door. Audrey called out and ran toward the girl. The girl stepped back, her fingers wrapping around the doorway.

"Men with guns," Audrey yelled, reaching the girl and pushing her back inside.

A shout echoed from the back door of the bar. The men were outside.

Audrey pulled the door shut and turned toward the terrified girl. "Lock it." Turning, Audrey ran through a series of scarves and into a store as a pounding echoed on the doorway. She had barely enough time to get outside and find a hiding place before these men could run the entire alley and end up out front.

Her leg hitched, and she went flying, hitting the smooth wood floor with enough force to decompress her lungs.

A shopper with three scarves in his hands gasped and tossed the silk patterns onto a table. He leaned down to help her up. "Are you all right?" Quickly releasing her, he backed away from her sopping wet clothes.

"Yes," Audrey gasped, wiping rain off her face, regaining her breath. Her ribs protested with a sharp pain. "Thanks." She turned and hustled toward the outside door, running into the now pelting rain. A quick survey of the street showed no taxis.

The men in black hadn't made it around the block yet. They'd expect her to run and hide in another business. So she shot into the street, dodging cars and ignoring angry honks. Reaching the other side, she ran into a coffee shop, turning frantically to view the street. The men in black had seen her come in. They stopped traffic as they chased her.

Crying out, she dodged through tables and behind the counter.

"Hey, lady—" a kid with a goatee yelled out.

She ignored him and shoved herself into the kitchen, knocking down a busboy. Coffee grounds sprayed, covering her front. "Sorry," she yelled, trying to run toward the back door. A table edge caught her hip, and she stumbled. She hurt, but she refused to stop. Opening the door with one hand, she bulldozed outside, scanning yet another alley. A shout echoed from the closest side. This row of buildings wasn't nearly as long as the one she'd just fled from.

The door locked behind her.

Pounding footsteps echoed through the rain.

Clutching the tire iron, she limped to the other side of the alley and ducked down behind a wide garbage receptacle. No more running. Her leg ached, and even her ankle trembled. Time to fight.

She held no illusions she could take all three men. But if she managed to knock one out, his gun would be free. From the age of ten, she'd learned how to shoot. Unfortunately, working in a Senate building and having to go through security daily meant she couldn't carry regularly. She'd give anything for her Lady Smith & Wesson right now. Anything.

"Where the fuck did she go?" a deep voice hissed as boot steps came closer.

"Dunno. Who is she?" a voice with a thick Russian accent muttered.

Good. They didn't know who she was. What did that mean? The wet brick cut into her back while she huddled, her leg crying, her fingers tightening around the crowbar.

"Who cares?" the first voice shot back. "If Hannah had time to tell her anything, she has to go, too."

Too? Had they killed Darian? Fear stuttered up

her spine, shaking her shoulders. She braced herself to attack.

Movement sounded, and one of the men rounded the garbage can. "There you are," he murmured, a smile flashing a gold front tooth.

She leapt up onto her good leg and swung, hitting him squarely in the gut. He doubled over with a muffled *oof*, and she swung for his head. The iron impacted with a sickening thud. The guy flew sideways.

The next man whirled around and kicked the weapon out of her hands.

She backed up until reaching the building again.

He smiled. "You're a feisty one. Sorry about this." Almost in slow motion, he lifted a gun to point between her eyes. Even through the pouring rain, the silver barrel glinted.

Audrey gathered her strength to duck and attack.

A body dropped from above, landing on the gunman. They hit the concrete, sending shards flying. The gun spun around and around, landing under the huge garbage receptacle.

Nate!

He'd dropped from a fire escape three floors up. Without missing a beat, he rolled over and snapped the gunman's neck with one smooth motion before backflipping to his feet and kicking a black gun out of the third guy's hand.

Audrey gasped and dropped to her knees. She hadn't even seen that guy. Reaching down, she patted the ground under the receptacle, trying to reach the gun. Rocks and glass sliced into her hand, but she kept searching, biting back a wince at the pain. Her fingers touched something smooth, and she tugged it out. Crack pipe. Bending lower, her cheek almost to the ground, she kept searching as she watched the fight.

Male grunts filled the alley as the men threw punches and kicks. The guy in black was well trained, but he didn't have a chance with Nate. Nate punched him in the gut and followed up with a high front kick that jerked the man's head back with an audible snap. The guy died before he hit the ground.

Nate turned and stalked over to the man half crawling away. The man Audrey had hit. Nate wrestled him up, and the guy pivoted on one knee, slashing out with a wicked-looking knife. The blade sliced across Nate's upper chest, spraying blood.

"Damn it." Nate twisted and slammed his closed fists together on the other guy's wrist. The knife dropped.

Nate punched him in the jaw. Once, twice, a third time.

Swinging around, Nate finished the fight with a choke hold. "Why are you after her?"

"She was with Hannah," the guy gasped, his legs kicking out.

"Who wanted Hannah dead, and why?" Nate hissed, his mouth at the other guy's ear.

"Don't know. I was hired by Frankie." The guy pointed toward one of the dead men. Then he glanced down at the blade still resting on his chest.

Audrey cried out a warning.

The man grasped the blade and stabbed up toward Nate's face. Nate leaned to the left, the knife whizzing by his head. He encircled the guy's wrist, lowered his arm, and plunged the blade into his neck. The guy's eyes opened wide in shock and pain. Then they closed.

Shoving him aside, Nate stood and strode to Audrey, grasping her arm to help her up. "Keep the hat and glasses on." He quickly dragged her to the other end of the alley, glancing up and around. "I don't see any cameras from businesses recording us. We're safe."

Audrey's knees wobbled. The pounding rain failed to cover the stench of instant death. She'd forgotten. During the explosion that had injured her leg, she'd nearly suffocated from that scent. Not flesh, not fear, but something else. Death had its own smell...its own existence. The world fuzzed, and she started to go down.

Nate pressed her against a building, his head dropping toward hers. No emotion showed on his face, but those eyes teemed with hell fire. Fury. "Not now, Audrey." He shook her. "Dig deep, darlin'. Suck it up and move."

She nodded, blinking against the wetness. Tears or rain? She wasn't sure. But she moved into a fast walk, her mind spinning. Nate had killed—so easily and without a second thought. Yes, he'd been protecting her. But taking a life had to mean something, didn't it? Her stomach lurched, and she forced herself not to throw up. Not now, anyway.

Never in her life had she seen somebody kill. Sure, she'd known that Nate was trained to kill, but knowing and seeing were different. The smell of blood and death sent her senses into panic. Somehow, she kept going.

How well had she known the man she'd loved? The idea of his being dangerous had seemed romantic to her. The reality of seeing him kill opened her eyes in a way nothing else could have. Dangerous meant deadly. Cold, purposeful, and intense.

Her ears burned at her foolishness in romanticizing his training. "I'm sorry, Nate," she whispered while trying to keep up.

He stiffened but didn't turn back.

They reached the end of the alley, and Nate shoved her into the back of an older Chevy Cavalier. "Get down and stay down," he ordered, shutting the door and running to slide into the driver's seat. A second later, he'd ignited the engine and ripped into traffic.

Audrey stayed down, hidden behind the passenger seat. "Are you all right? You were cut."

"I'm fine. Stay down." The car swerved.

"Where did you get the car?" Her lips quivered as she began to shiver.

"Stole it. I followed you from work, to the bar, to the alley." He hit the steering wheel. "Damn it, Audrey. What were you thinking?"

She sniffed and wiped tears from her eyes. "I trusted Darian. He had something to tell me."

"Did he? Please tell me he told you whatever got him killed." Sarcasm filled Nate's voice.

"Screw you." Audrey began to sit up.

"Get down." Nate leaned over and pressed her head down. For the first time, raw emotion darkened his voice. "There are cameras watching sidewalks everywhere. Just hold on."

She sniffed again and wiped her nose. "What's the plan?"

"Hold tight for a while—we have a bit of a drive. I'm going to drop you off at a store entrance to the mall. You go inside, find a bathroom, and ditch the hat, glasses, and coat. Buy yourself a new coat with a scarf to cover your head. Take a different exit, find a taxi, and get home." He paused. "Use cash only."

She gulped. How had her life become a suspense movie?

Nate handed over a bunch of twenty-dollar bills. "Here's money—don't use anything bigger than a twenty."

She took the cash and shoved it into her wallet. "When can I sit up?"

"Be patient." He glanced back. "Are you all right?"

"Fine." Her bad leg felt like somebody had beat it with a bat. "What are you doing after you drop me off?"

He turned back toward the road and switched lanes. "I'll ditch the car and meet you back at your place. Leave your bedroom window unlocked because I'll need to time my entry when the commander's men aren't looking."

"One guy started running toward me when Darian shoved me into a taxi."

"One of the guys in black?" Nate asked.

"No." She coughed, once again wanting to throw up. "Do you think those were the commander's men?" Maybe Darian's hackers had discovered something bad about the commander. If so, who was the guy running in the street?

Nate remained quiet for a moment. "I have no clue."

Great. Could things get any worse?

Nate waited until the man guarding the back alley to Audrey's apartment rotated position before climbing up the fire escape to her downstairs neighbor's apartment. What was her name?

Mrs. Abernathy. Yeah, that was it. He swung inside and quickly found what he needed, all but running into the shower to get rid of blood and dirt. He'd donned his boots and a pair of faded jeans from his bag in case he needed to move quickly.

Finally, he sat at Mrs. Abernathy's cheery kitchen table, stitching up the wound across his chest with thread from the woman's sewing basket. A quick glance at the ultra-large calendar stuck to the fridge showed that the elderly lady had bridge at "Ellie's house" that night. Hopefully she wouldn't be home for a while yet.

Chester rubbed his big orange butt against Nate's legs. "I don't like cats, buddy." Nate tied off the end of thread and reached down to scratch the cat's ears. "I've been listening to your heartbeat all week—good to know you're not having an attack." As usual, Nate had to filter out a million sounds to concentrate on the ones that mattered, so he shoved Chester's heartbeat into the abyss and focused on the men outside and the woman upstairs.

The commander had three men watching the building. Two out front and one to the side—they rotated on seemingly random sequences. Nothing was random. Nate had about sixteen minutes and seven seconds until he could scale the fire escape to Audrey's bedroom.

Her heart beat steadily, punctuated every so often with a glitch. Probably from pain. Her leg had to be killing her.

Nate might never be the same. When he'd seen those three men find her in the alley, it was all he could to remember training and go high to drop. He'd wanted to rush to her aid, forgetting the consequences.

When she'd nailed the bastard with the tire iron, pride had filled Nate until he wanted to clap. What a woman. She might not be his, but damn, he wished she were. That they could ride off into the sunset like one of those corny movies his sister-in-law Josie loved.

But they'd never see eye to eye about her mother. The psychotic bitch had made his childhood hell, which he might be able to overcome. But she'd also hurt his brothers, and she may have had something to do with Jory's death. So Nate wanted her to pay.

Audrey wanted to protect her.

Nate had never had a mother, so he didn't fault Audrey. But he couldn't be someone other than who they'd created. His job was to take out the threat, and that bitch would always be a threat.

Steeling his shoulders, he forced himself to focus and get back to work. Freeing his secured phone from his pocket, he dialed his brothers.

Shane answered with a barked, "Status."

"Secured." Nate sat up. "What's going on?"

"We've been monitoring the DC police force as well as the news. Darian Hannah, a man who'd been on a date with Audrey Madison, was gunned down in a Virginia bar earlier today. What is going on, Nate?"

"Well, it wasn't me," Nate said dryly.

"I know it fucking wasn't you," Shane exploded.

"Give me the phone," a deeper voice ordered. There seemed to be a bit of a struggle, and Matt came on the line. "Nate?" Matt asked.

Nate exhaled. Good. Matt was always calmer than Shane. "I'm here."

"What the blazes is going on?" Matt bellowed.

Okay. Not so calm. "Geez. Remember before you were both tied down by women? You used to be calm and collected—unflappable, really."

"Unflappable?" Matt asked, his voice dropping dangerously low.

"I'm fine, Mattie."

Quiet seconds ticked across the line. "Stay where you are. I'm catching a flight out of here in the morning. Don't. Fucking. Move." Matt rarely used that voice any longer.

"I'm going, too," Shane echoed in the background.

Nate's gut clenched. How did they not get it? "Stay there. Keep Josie and Laney safe. I'm fine."

Matt exhaled in an old trick to control his temper. "You're as important as they are, Nate. Deal with it."

He blinked. That wasn't how things happened. "I'm fine. Stay safe." Did they not understand his role in the family? His head spun.

"You're *alone*, Nate," Shane bellowed.

Nate blinked.

Matt cleared his throat. "Shane's right. You're so fucking alone right now, you're not thinking. Never alone, Nate. *Ever.*"

Pins pricked the backs of his eyes. If God existed, He'd done Nate a solid by giving him brothers. *These men* as brothers. But he had to take care of the situation before both of his brothers ended up in the commander's cross-hairs. They had families now, and they needed to stay safe. It was his job to protect them. "No. Everything is secure here, and I don't need help."

"You do need help." Matt sighed. "The reports show that a woman was with Hannah when he died. Was Audrey present at the bar?"

Nate thought about lying, he really did. But he'd never, *ever* lied to his brothers. "Yes. She ran, the men followed her, and I took them out."

Matt inhaled sharply. "We can be there in hours."

"I know. The second I need help, I promise I'll call." Not a chance. He'd handle the commander and anybody else who came along. "I'm getting closer to the codes and to finding out what happened to Jory. Trust me, Mattie." He waited a moment and then sweetened the pot. "There's a good chance the commander has another base some-where, and it might be closer to you. If Jory is there..." The Dean brothers would fill in the rest.

"Fine. When are you going to infiltrate the commander's Virginia base?" Matt asked, his words clipped.

"Soon. I'll keep in touch." Nate disconnected the call before his brother argued more. Time was running out—Nate needed to destroy the commander soon, and hopefully he'd come up with a plan. For now, he had five minutes until he could see how badly Audrey had been injured.

Five minutes seemed like forever.

CHAPTER
14

AUDREY SAT ON the bed, pretending to read a magazine. Warmth cascaded from the heating pad on her leg but failed to provide any relief. She hadn't healed to the point of engaging in hand-to-hand combat. In fact, since she'd returned home, she'd thrown up twice.

Now, after having taken a hot shower, brushed her teeth, and eaten some leftover banana bread, she could finally breathe.

Her phone rang, and she glanced at the caller ID. "Hello, Mother."

"Hello, Audrey. Was that you on the news?" Isobel Madison asked in cultured tones.

Audrey sat up on the bed and reached for the remote control to turn on the television. "I don't know what you're talking about."

From a flat-screen across the room, the news droned on about Darian Hannah's death. His biography and life were listed, as were his affiliations with technology firms and DC powerhouses. A witness from the shooting confirmed that a woman had been with Darian when the shooters arrived. Another witness concurred, saying the woman had been a blonde with dark glasses.

Good. Score one for the hat and glasses. Witness recollections were notoriously off base.

"That wasn't me, Mother."

Isobel sniffed. "It better not have been. Franklin is quite worried."

Which made Isobel worried. Hurt spiraled through Audrey's chest, and she bit back a sharp retort. What kind of a life might she have had if the commander hadn't manipulated Isobel so? "While I appreciate his concern, there's no need." Would Isobel finally admit the commander was having Audrey followed? "Why would you think that was me?" Audrey asked.

Isobel cleared her throat. "Franklin has had bodyguards on you for weeks, and one of them saw Darian Hannah throw you into a cab. Care to explain?"

Audrey stiffened, her mind reeling. "Why would I need bodyguards?"

"Answer the question, please." Isobel's tone snapped a warning.

"It wasn't me." If all else fails, lie. "I don't know who is following me, but they suck. I wasn't with Darian, and the bodyguard must've gotten confused."

Silence reigned for a moment. "Very well. I'll speak to Franklin."

Audrey shoved down impatience. "Why am I being followed?"

"You'll have to ask him." Isobel hung up.

Isobel had to care somewhat, right? Audrey punched a pillow into a better shape for her back and increased the volume on the television.

The reporter recapped the news while standing in front

of the U.S. Capitol Building. When the senator's name came up, Audrey groaned. The reporter, a stacked redhead with voracious eyes, nearly hummed while reporting that Darian had met with Senator Nash earlier that day. Unfortunately, according to the reporter, the senator was unavailable for comment.

Audrey's phone rang again as if on cue. "Hello?"

"Audrey. Have you seen the news?" the senator asked.

"Yes. I can't believe it. Poor Darian." Audrey sat up straighter on the bed.

A voice cleared. "A woman was with him. Was it you?" Ernie Rastus asked quietly. Resigned intelligence echoed in his weary tone. The guy had been in politics for too long.

Oh. A conference call. "Of course not." Audrey picked at a thread on her bedspread, forcing her voice into calmness. "I have no idea who would've been with Darian, but I didn't know him very well. The news is reporting his meeting with you, Senator. Do we have a statement ready to go?"

"We're working on it," Ernie said. "We're having a five a.m. meeting tomorrow beforehand. Can you make it?"

"Of course." She'd have plenty of time for the meeting before her doctor's appointment out at the facility, which took hours to reach via car. "We need to make the point that whatever got Darian killed had nothing to do with the senator, and the senator needs to send condolences to Darian's family."

"Already done," the senator said. "I'm glad you weren't the woman in danger today, Audrey."

"Me too." The man showed far more concern for Audrey than her own mother had. Why couldn't she have had a parent like the senator? Heck, she didn't even know who'd fathered her. Audrey finished the conversation and hung up the phone as Nathan slipped inside the bedroom, closing the window and blinds.

The scent of male permeated the space. Cleanly washed male.

Her breath caught, and nerves flared to life along her entire body. He'd saved her life. And he'd killed so brutally without thinking twice. But for her. He'd *protected* her.

Her heart thumped into overdrive. She pushed the heating pad off her leg and eyed the stitching across his bare chest. "Where did you shower?"

His duffel bag dropped with a muffled thump. "Mrs. Abernathy kindly let me use her shower."

"She's at her weekly bridge game." Audrey winced as she tried to slide her leg free.

Nate instantly slid onto the bed, large hands enclosing her aching flesh. "Let me."

She shouldn't. The second he touched her, she short-circuited. But as soon as he began to massage her aching leg, she fell back onto the pillows in bliss. Pure, deep bliss. He had magic fingers. Or maybe her muscles responded only to him with pleasure. Simple release and pleasure. "How bad is your chest?" she murmured, her eyelids fluttering closed.

"Shallow cut." He continued to kneed, wringing a blissful groan from her.

His hands tightened.

Rain splattered against the window, the storm increasing with a mournful wind. Audrey shivered, her eyelids opening, the intimacy of the moment wandering through her like a fine wine. "Did you lock the window?"

"Yes." Nate reached and removed a gun from the back

of his waist. The weapon thumped softly on the night table when he released it. "Where's your gun?"

Audrey pointed to the drawer.

He opened the drawer and removed the silver gun, checking it carefully. "Cocked with one in the chamber." Approval lit his gray eyes. "Good girl."

Warmth spread around her heart. Darn it. She shouldn't give a fig if he was proud of her or not. Yet she wanted to bask in his approval anyway. "I'm surprised your brothers aren't already here after seeing the news report." Without a doubt, those men knew everything about her, and that she'd been with Darian. Nate would've told them.

"They have other things to worry about." Nate's tone didn't invite discussion.

Audrey frowned. The television report caught her attention as a reporter noted that three men had been killed in an alley very close to the bar where Darian Hannah had been gunned down by three men. It was too early to report, but a source in the police department had identified the dead men as the ones who had killed Hannah.

"Shit," Nate said mildly.

"It took them longer than I would've thought to make the announcement," Audrey mused.

Nate nodded and turned toward her. "I agree. Who do you think they were?"

Audrey had been running it around her brain. "I don't know, but my best guess is that the commander sent them." But something didn't feel right about that analysis, so maybe the soldier running in the street had been the commander's. Maybe they all belonged to the commander, and the guys in black were a kill squad for her and not for Darian. Or they were after Darian because of something his hackers had discovered. Life was way too confusing.

Nate rubbed his stubbly jaw. "The men in black weren't that good. I mean, the commander would've sent better skilled soldiers. Although you lost the one he had on you when Darian shoved you into that taxi."

"So much for training." Audrey smoothed down her threadbare T-shirt. She should've put on a bra, but she'd been too tired. "For the sake of argument, let's say that the commander didn't send those men. Now he'll be wondering who the woman is and who took out those guys." The commander would have to at least consider the idea that Nate or one of the Gray brothers had done the damage.

"The bigger question is who wanted Darian dead, and why." Nate reached for her injured leg again. "Unless you were the target."

Her ears rang and heated. "The men didn't know who I was, so they weren't initially after me." Warmth of a different type slid down Audrey's abdomen as she moved her legs away. The tiny shorts she wore to bed didn't hide much skin. She should've thought harder when getting dressed, but her mind had all but shut down. In fact, life remained hazy. However, her body was springing to life with all sorts of interesting tingles brought on by the half-dressed man sitting on her bed. On. Her. Bed.

His gaze wandered along her bare legs, eyes flaring ten kinds of fire. Gray and dark at once. Glittering. Hungry.

No, this wasn't going to happen. Not again. If she didn't protect her heart, she'd lose it completely this time. Getting over him had almost been too painful for her to bear. She couldn't do it again.

"Audrey—"

"No."

"I know." Yet he reached out and slid a knuckle along her bare thigh.

Fire licked along her skin, and her lids dropped to half-mast. The earlier fight, the crazy adrenaline, the inevitable release... all made her thankful to be alive. Alive and feminine.

He'd always done this to her. There was something so basically *male* about Nathan that being near him made her feel feminine and powerful. A heady combination. One she'd missed so very much.

Keeping her gaze, he reached over and switched off the television set. In the same graceful movement, he pressed PLAY on the iPod docked next to her bed. The mellow sounds of "Colder Weather" by Zac Brown Band crooned out.

She breathed out. Fitting. If anybody was a rambling man, it was Nathan.

His fingers skimmed up her good leg, feathering against her thigh. "Audrey?"

"It's a bad idea." Her body didn't care—and deep down, neither did her heart. Some temptations were too strong to deny, and sometimes the pleasure was worth the ensuing pain. Only with Nate.

"Definitely a bad idea." His hand flattened over her leg. Red spiraled across his cheekbones as he glanced down at his hold. "We were never a good idea."

No. But she'd never trade the few moments of true happiness she had found with him—not for anything. She studied him, and desire hit her hard. Man, he was beautiful. Smooth, tight skin over his muscled chest tempted her far too much. Ruthless angles and hard ridges made up his entire body, even to the point of creating interesting hollows in his rugged face. He made her forget the fear of death and the pain of the past, however briefly. "Nate?"

"Just one more time, Audrey," he whispered, his voice so husky it slid straight to her heart.

One more night, to celebrate their living through the day, if nothing else. She blinked. "I've missed you," she whispered, finally letting her shields drop. This wasn't a guy a girl could shield herself from, so why waste the energy? Plus, he deserved to know he'd meant something to her. If that kill chip detonated, then somebody would miss him. That mattered, right?

"I've missed you more." He stood and unzipped his jeans. Then he toed off his boots, dropping the jeans with them. Leaving him nude, his impressive cock jutting out.

She swallowed. Truly amazing, and for the moment, all hers. But she needed more than his body. "Tell me you forgive me. For buckling to the commander's threats and breaking up with you." Yeah, it was unfair to ask him that while he was hard and ready, but the words slipped out before she could stop them. She needed to hear them before one or both of them ended up dead—which probably wasn't far away.

He paused, one knee on the bed. His eyes darkened. Then he moved up her to place a soft kiss against her lips. Lifting her chin with one knuckle, he looked her directly in the eyes. "I forgive you."

Tears sprang to her eyes. Something inside her released, a ball of pain she hadn't realized still lived deep within her. "I'm so sorry."

He shook his head, dropping his mouth to lick along hers. "It's in the past." Then he kissed her, going deep, keeping his weight off her but still lighting her on fire.

The bittersweet moment stole her breath while the sexy

male filled her heart. *They* were in the past, and there was no going back. But she had this moment, and she had this night. Maybe as a remembrance, perhaps as a way to say good-bye the right way—if that's what was needed. She held no illusions about their lives or of any longevity. Reaching out, she ran her palms along the hard ridges in his arms. So much strength.

Which made his gentleness all the more breathtaking as he drew her T-shirt over her head, humming with appreciation as her breasts sprang free. Tucking his thumbs in her shorts, he slowly drew them down her legs, tossing them atop the dresser. Settling in, he kissed along her calves, over her knees, spending precious time on her scars. As if he knew exactly the placement of each pin, he kissed the areas, warming them.

Need roared through her, more powerful than any shot of whiskey. "Nate—" she groaned, reaching for him.

"No." He licked his way up her thighs, nipping softly but with enough bite to still her.

Yearning beyond reality filled her, and she dug her nails into his shoulders, finally within reach.

"Careful, baby. I scratch back." The next bite to her inner thigh held an erotic warning.

Her abdomen spasmed.

He chuckled and licked her slit. "We didn't have enough time together, Aud." He inserted one finger in her and twisted.

Electricity rippled up her spine, and she arched her back. It was as if he felt inside her skin and knew exactly how to touch her. He kissed her gently, the stubble from his strong jaw burning a path across her thighs. Tempting her. Marking her.

She looked down her body as he lifted his head, his

expression free for once. Hungry. A wicked smile quirked his full lips, and he dropped back down, his shoulders settling in, spreading her thighs wider.

As if fully in tune with her, his hand moved up and repositioned her left leg so it didn't cramp.

Her heart opened completely. She couldn't help it.

With pinpoint accuracy, his tongue lashed her clit.

She hissed and arched against him, an electrical zap circuiting from his tongue to her nipples. They ached, so full and ready. He licked her clit again and slipped another finger inside her. Playing. Seeking. Twisting.

His fingers and his tongue set up a rhythm that had her swelling, aching, unwinding. Her body moved of its own volition, moving against him. The tension wound so tightly inside her she tried to still herself. "No." She gasped. "Not yet."

He chuckled around her clit.

The vibrations wound everything even tighter. So incredibly tight. Her eyes rolled back as she fought the energy coiling inside her. "Not. Yet," she hissed through clenched teeth. It all felt too good... She had to hold on to the good.

He rubbed his whiskers against her thighs, the slight bite nearly pushing her over the edge. "Ah, baby," he rumbled against her clit, "you'll come when I say." One slow swipe of his tongue stopped time. "I say... *now*." He sucked her entire clit into his mouth, crisscrossing his fingers along her G-spot.

Everything in her, the wicked and the good, the soft and the hard, the past and the present, all exploded into a blazing-white hotness that poured through her in heat and fire. She arched into his mouth, crying out his name, her entire being undulating. Her mind went blank as her body detonated. Lost in a world of sensation, she finally whimpered her final bit of tension.

He released her, one hand flattening across her abdomen as little aftershocks took her. He kissed her abdomen. "Beautiful." Moving up, his body covered hers, his mouth sliding against hers. "You're okay, Aud."

She'd never be the same. Sliding her arms around his broad back, she opened her legs wider to accommodate him. "Please, Nate. Just, please." She had no defenses and didn't feel the need to find some. This was Nate, and it had to be everything between them.

He nodded, gentle understanding filling his eyes. Quick movements had him rolling on a condom.

One thumb rubbed against her cheekbone in such a tender touch she barely felt it. As if he understood fully, he pressed his forehead against hers and slowly penetrated her. Inch by swollen inch, he moved with complete control as her body accepted his. He was so big he filled all of her and then some. Even after the incredible orgasm, only now did she feel filled. Complete. The words from her heart hovered on her tongue, but she bit them back.

His broad shoulders vibrated as he held himself in check. "Is your leg all right?"

That quickly, with the simple question, he ripped out what was left of her heart. He'd always owned it, but she'd fooled herself into believing she'd kept a small part for herself. "Yes. I'm perfect." Tilting her hips, she brought him even deeper inside her. If possible, she'd keep him there forever.

Unfortunately they didn't have forever.

But as he slid out and back in, her dreams took over. So she did the only thing in her power and opened herself completely to him. He began to thrust harder, faster, his body taking hers. She skimmed her fingers down his flanks, caressing a truly fine ass. He groaned and pounded, staying careful of her bad leg.

"Faster," she murmured.

Unbelievably, everything inside her began to coil again. To spiral into a coil of need that tightened so hard it hurt. Her nails bit into his flesh, and she met him thrust for thrust. How was this possible?

He thrust hard, angling over her clit, and she detonated. Flew through the air, fire consuming her, waves pummeling her as she held on to him with everything she had. With one hard push, he stayed inside her, his body convulsing as he came. Slowly, they both stopped moving.

Lifting up, his eyes darkened with emotion. He leaned down and kissed her so gently tears sprang to her eyes.

What now?

CHAPTER
15

NATE SETTLED AUDREY more securely against him, keeping his weapon in sight. Peace threatened to dull his senses. In the aftermath of the passionate storm, with Audrey sleeping in complete trust against him, he allowed himself to relax.

She murmured and cuddled closer, her hand curling on top of his chest. Her warmth and soft skin offered comfort he wasn't strong enough to turn away from. The defenselessness of her position made him want to tuck her close forever, but he couldn't do that, even if she'd allow it. In three weeks, he'd probably be dead, and she'd have to pick up the pieces again. Why do that to her?

The constant tension always riding his body finally calmed. She was the only person in the world who'd ever been able to bring him peace. For that alone he'd love her forever.

Add in her courage, incredible intelligence, and the inherent kindness she'd had to bury, and Audrey Madison was a miracle.

Just not his. The truth of that carved a hole in his chest more painful than any injury he'd ever sustained.

He needed to stop pretending and living in the moment or they were both going to die even before the chips exploded. How loud had they been? The music had played, and surely the commander's men didn't have Nate's hearing. Even so. For a precious few moments, Nate had forgotten about the threat outside. That couldn't happen again.

Checking in outside, he listened for the heartbeats of the three men, scrubbing out all other sounds. They were still out there but not moving. Good.

Nate could afford to sleep for a brief time. He allowed himself to drop off, somehow not surprised in the least to have the one dream he had more often than any other— the day he'd met Audrey.

The sun was strong, the smell of dirt stronger, and he'd had no clue his world was about to change. The first time he met her, he had blood on his face. The training exercise had been brutal that morning; he'd been brutal. He was tired of training, tired of killing. Most of all, he was tired of being controlled by the people who had made him. But he knew the rules. If one of them failed to return from a mission, they all died. He had three brothers, and he'd die for every single one of them. He killed for them now. But a change was coming, and he held on to that hope.

"Hi," she said as she stood in the sun next to the dark doorway, the red highlights in her black hair absurdly out of place on the outskirts of the dismal training field.

He took the towel she offered and tried to wipe off the blood. She looked to be about nineteen, younger than him, and innocence shone bright in her eyes. That wasn't a place for innocence.

One look, and he could tell she was far different from the women who had shaped them in the last ten years; they were hard, cynical, and had taught them more than anyone should know about inter- rogation, sexual and otherwise. He had learned a long time ago that softness was an illusion.

"Are you Nathan?" she asked.

"Yes." He growled it, uneasy as hell with her.

"I'm Audrey." She held out a small hand for him to shake.

He shook her hand, feeling the fragile bones tremble slightly in his. She was afraid of him, but her gaze remained calm and direct. Admiration welled through him.

"You're supposed to train me," she said.

"In what?" The thoughts of some of the ways he might train her ran unwelcomed through his head. Beautiful and delicate, the woman drew him to her. Big blue eyes set in an oval face with ivory skin tempted him, while she barely reached his shoulder in height.

"Basic hand-to-hand"—she gave a self-deprecating shrug—"just in case."

"In case of what?" He could break her in two with minimal effort, and there wasn't enough time in the universe to protect her from somebody with his kind of training. Besides, why would anybody want to hurt such a sweet little thing?

"I don't really know."

"Who would bring you here?" The question surprised him even as he asked it. Whoever had brought her into hell should be shot. Twice.

She sighed. Her gaze darted to the ground, away from him, while her shoulders hunched forward in defense. "I guess you're going to find out anyway."

"Find out what?" He reached out and placed a knuckle under her chin to lift her gaze back to his. Her pretty eyes held more warmth than he'd ever seen, and he wasn't ready to relinquish the heat.

He was surprised by the sheen of tears in their blue depths as well as the shamed flush that stole across her pale skin. He suddenly wanted to defend her against whoever had brought that look onto her face.

"My mother brought me here," she said.

He didn't understand.

Audrey sighed again and tried to tug her face away from his hold. Although he knew better, he kept her in place.

She stopped struggling and met his eyes directly. "My mother is Dr. Madison."

He dropped his hand, and his shoulders went back. Shock and anger tightened his muscles.

"I know." Pain and regret filled Audrey's voice. "I have some understanding of the experiments she's conducted on you because of the commander, and I'm sorry. So sorry that they hurt you."

He stared at the top of her head, shining so brightly in the sun. Confusion made him blink. He hated the sociopathic psychologist with every fiber in his being and had since she'd forced him into the training field with the three older Brown boys. Nate had held his own, but he'd still ended up with several broken ribs, a broken femur, and a cracked wrist.

He hadn't healed by the time Matt had returned, and Matt had gone berserk, ending up in the brig for two weeks after going after the Brown brothers. Christmas had rocked, though. It was the best memory the brothers had, and neither Nate nor Matt regretted it.

Years later, Nate wanted Dr. Madison dead nearly as much as he wanted to see the commander bleeding out over the packed earth of the training field.

"I'm sorry." Audrey's voice remained muffled as she scuffed one small shoe in the ground.

Nate brushed aside anger and opened his senses, studying her closely. His odd gift of being able to discern a falsehood assured him she told the truth. The poor girl really was sorry and actually felt shame.

Now she needed his assistance.

His heart warmed as the wish to help her roared through him. They shared an enemy, now, didn't they?

He snaked out a hand, tangling his fingers in her silky tresses. Desire unfurled through his gut. They needed to understand each other, so a quick twist of his wrist jerked her head back to meet his gaze. "If you're playing me, you'll regret it."

"I know." Her easy acceptance bothered him more than it should have. Then she smiled, and he forgot how to breathe.

Years, scars, and pain later, Nathan awoke to a slight drumming of rain on the window and a sleeping woman curled into his side.

Slipping out of the bed, he secured his gun to go check on the threat. He turned back to study the only woman he'd ever loved, the one he'd have to let go in order to save his brothers. For the first time in five years, he wondered if he could do it.

After scouting outside the building for almost an hour, Nate stepped back into the apartment, smiling at the scent of cooking eggs. "Morning," he said as he stalked into the kitchen.

Audrey jumped and flipped around, a spatula in her hand. "Where did you go?"

"I wanted to check on the men watching you. They're not bad." Not that great, either. No wonder the commander wanted the Gray brothers back so badly. "Why are you up so early?"

She expertly tossed the eggs. "I have an early press conference."

About that. "I'd like you to call in sick and maybe take a vacation." If he got her to safety, he could better concentrate on killing the commander and decimating the entire organization.

"No." Audrey slid eggs onto two plates and added a toasted bagel to each. She handed them to him. "Table."

He followed the order, slid the plates on place mats, and turned to face her. "Why not?"

She moved back to the stove. "Because I have work to do."

He rubbed his chin, his instincts humming. "Turn around, Audrey."

Her heart rate increased, so he tuned in to her breathing. Slow, calm, purposeful breaths. What in the world was she hiding? "Now."

She turned, her face placid. "What?"

Slowly, flexing his biceps, he crossed his arms and studied her.

She tilted her head to the side, sliding on a curious expression. "Nate?"

Oh, she was good. But he was better. So he remained silent, keeping his expression closed and his eyes hard.

She blinked but kept his gaze.

He purposefully didn't move. An inch.

A pretty pink flared at her chest and wound up her neck to cover her face. The blush had to burn, but she didn't turn away.

Admiration melded with irritation. He'd been trained by the best, and he'd spent too many moments interrogating people and figuring how to break them. He wouldn't break Audrey, but he'd get her to talk.

She rolled her eyes. "Is this really necessary?"

He knew she'd talk first. So he stayed silent.

Her fine eyebrows drew down. "Fine," she huffed, slamming the spatula onto the stove and beginning a lovely storm from the room.

He took a step sideways to block the exit.

She halted, her breath catching. Then she lifted her head, sparks glinting from stunning eyes. "Get out of my way, or I swear, I'll shove your balls through the roof of your mouth."

Yeah. He loved her spunk. Slowly, he lifted one eyebrow.

Fire burst across her face. "What the heck do you want?"

"The truth."

She backed away, her gaze darting away. "About what?"

He waited until she focused back on him. "On why you can't leave. What's really going on?" His mind spun different scenarios, and nothing made sense. Except—"Why are you really working for the commander?" She could find another way to be close to her mother without working for evil. Audrey would never work for evil.

She swallowed. "I told you why."

"You lied."

She took another step back. "How dare you." Her voice lacked any conviction.

What was going on? "You're not leaving the kitchen until you tell me the truth."

Defiance lifted her chin. "You want the truth? Fine. I'm working with the senator to close down the commander's organization and put the bastard in prison."

Everything in Nate stilled. "Excuse me?"

Audrey hissed out air. "He needs to be held accountable, and you can't do it. Sorry, but I'm in the position to do it, and you need to get out of the way."

Oh, hell no. "The senator knows?"

"Yes." She put both hands on her hips. "I'm sorry I didn't say anything, but I wasn't sure how to say it, and I knew you wouldn't want my help. And I couldn't tell you about the senator, because you'd be pissed, and I couldn't tell him about you, because I wouldn't do that to you."

The long string of words made his head ache, and a tension began to coil in his gut. This wasn't going to be good. "What are you talking about?"

"The senator and I have ulterior motives in working with the commander. We're going to find out all about the current organization, and then we're going to expose him." She belted her robe tight, determination tightening her jaw.

Nate's mouth went dry. "Expose him? You can't expose him." Letting the world know about the experiments, about Nate's brothers, would be a disaster. "He has to be killed."

"No. The man deserves prison—forever. Trust me, we'll bury any information about you or any other soldiers. Darn it. I have to get ready." Audrey limped toward the bedroom.

He stood and manacled a hand around her arm. "Ah, darlin', you're not going anywhere."

She blinked, her gaze sparking to his. "Excuse me?"

He walked her backward to sit, every muscle he had turning to rock. "Start at the beginning." Sheer determination kept his voice gentle when all he wanted to do was bellow. But as he eyed her, sitting so small and defenseless next to her scrambled eggs, her midnight-hair a mess from his hands, her lips a well-kissed red, something in him awakened. Something dark and dangerous, something undeniably *male* raging with the urge to protect and defend. Whether he liked it or not.

She rubbed the bridge of her nose. "I knew I shouldn't tell you." Creamy flesh beckoned when the neck of her robe opened.

His gaze dropped, and he mentally shoved down interest. "Too late. Spill it."

The plan she detailed made his blood slow down and go cold. It was crazy. They planned to trick the commander into giving up all intel, and then they planned to have him arrested and incarcerated.

The naiveté nearly made him dizzy.

"Audrey, there is no way the commander is going to give the senator information that would hurt him. There's also no way that monster is going to jail." The commander probably had more escape plans than Nate did, if that were possible. "You're going to get both yourself and the senator killed."

Audrey shook her head, her body visibly vibrating with temper. "You're wrong. We can do this the right way."

To have such trust. "What about your mother?" Would Audrey be able to testify against her mother, if there actually was a court case?

"The senator promised she'll be protected." Audrey glanced down and picked at a loose thread on her robe. "I know she doesn't deserve it."

Everything in Nate loosened. After how Isobel Madison had been to Audrey, after she'd used her, sweet Audrey still wanted to protect her. Sweet and terribly sad all at once. And wrong. No way would the commander or Madison go easily. They'd fight until the last second.

"Your plan won't work, and it's not going to happen." Nate stood, his mind reeling. Where should he send Audrey? "We need to get you out of town."

She stood again and poked him in the chest. "No. I have a job to do, and I'm going to do it. Besides, you need me to find out about the commander's other facility. The senator will be able to get the information, and you know it."

Temper tickled the base of Nate's neck. "Don't think for a second of manipulating me like that. It's not going to happen."

The stubborn tilt of her jaw seemed to harden. "Too bad, because I'm taking that bastard down."

"Why?" Nate asked. "Why do you hate him so much?" It wasn't as if the guy had trained her to kill or ever beat her when she'd failed. Nate had a scar on his back that'd never fade because of the commander's cruelty.

Vulnerability and fury commingled in her eyes. "Everything is his fault. He hurt you, he hurt my mother, and—"

Oh. Nate exhaled slowly. "Your mother made her own choices. Right or wrong."

"Wrong." Audrey raked a hand through her tousled

hair. "She loves him, and she's followed him her entire life. My mother is a brilliant scientist, sought after by many institutions. We could've had a good life."

Ah. Realization finally cleared Nate's thinking. Audrey couldn't blame her mother, because, what kid could? But it was easy blaming the cruel military leader. And who knew? If Isobel Madison hadn't aligned herself with the bastard, maybe she would've been a different person. "I'm sorry, Audrey," he whispered.

Tears glimmered in her eyes. "There's nothing to be sorry about. But I do have to get to the press conference, and whether you like it or not, the senator is the only person who can find out where the other military base is—the one where Jory might be."

Nate hated that she was probably right, and the second he found the other location, he would take her from DC whether she liked it or not. "Fine. But we do things my way, or I'll take your butt out of town right now."

She sighed, her shoulders dropping. "Of course."

CHAPTER
16

B LACK AND FORMFITTING, Audrey's slim pencil skirt hugged her legs and ass while her bright yellow shirt yelled hello. She'd curled her hair to land sexy and wild on her shoulders and had taken extra care with her makeup, adding bright red lipstick. A completely different look than the muted gray pantsuit worn by the woman with Darian Hannah the other day.

Flat black boots shined but allowed her free movement if necessary during the press conference. She leaned against a wall over to the side, watching as the senator used his country accent to pacify the crowd.

A push woman from DCNT shoved her way to the front. "Senator, an anonymous tip came into the news station earlier today that one of your aides was with Darian Hannah prior to his death. Can you answer that?"

The senator beamed a genuine smile. "None of my aides were with Darian, so I think you should be careful of anonymous tips."

The reporter elbowed a guy from the *Times* out of the way. "Our sources confirm the woman was Audrey Madison, your operation's director."

Audrey's heart dropped to her toes. How did they get her name? Ernie gave her a sympathetic smile and shoved his glasses back up his nose.

The senator gestured her forward, and she stepped briskly up to the podium of microphones. Plastering on her most rueful smile, she shrugged a shoulder. "I'm deeply saddened by Darian's death because he was a good man, and we worked well together. But I promise you, I wasn't with him at the time of his death."

The reporter pushed forward. "You were identified by the cabdriver who dropped Darian off at Milly's Bar. He said you paid him for a disguise of a hat and glasses."

Audrey shook her head again, keeping her smile in place. "That's impossible, because I wasn't there."

The senator leaned toward the microphones. "As I understand it, the woman with Darian ran from three killers, who ultimately died in the next alley. Unfortunately, with Ms. Madison's crippled leg, there's no way she could run from anybody."

Audrey bit back an angry expletive, fighting every urge in her body to keep her smile in place. Enough information about her to reporters. "I have five pins in my left leg, that's true."

"Why?" The reporter's green eyes gleamed like a cat's spotting a rushing mouse. "What happened to your leg?"

"Old hunting accident," Audrey snapped out. Then she sighed. "My personal life is exactly that—personal. But since I know you're going to dig until you find the information, I was injured in a car accident years ago that resulted in my leg breaking in several places. After many surgeries and way too much physical therapy, I can walk with barely a limp. What I can't do is outrun killers or fight anybody with any strength." The commander had created false medical records for her years ago, and she had no doubt they'd stand up to scrutiny.

"So who do you think killed the men who murdered Darian Hannah?" the reporter asked.

"I don't know any more than you do, and I'm sure the police department will find the killers and bring them to justice." Carefully turning on her heel, Audrey made her way back to the wall, this time allowing her limp to show.

Things were turning south, and fast. The press and now the world knew too much about her—it'd be time to flee soon. As soon as she discovered the location of the commander's other facility, she was out of there. Maybe to somewhere warm this time—somewhere she could lounge on a beach and not worry about killers or war. Or Nate.

Even the thought of his name sent her body into overdrive.

The night before had been . . . monumental. Darn it.

The senator stepped up to the podium to speak about Darian and his work and how important the type of businesses he represented meant to the American people.

As one, a ripple went through the gathered reporters. Several read smartphones, and one tapped some sort of ear communicator. Bluetooth?

Audrey fought unease as all eyes turned toward her and then back to the senator.

The pushy woman from before put a hand on her overly curvy hip. "Senator, it appears that the cabdriver who'd driven Darian and a woman"—she gestured toward Audrey—"has been found dead this morning in his cab over on B Street. Care to comment?"

Audrey coughed, her head blanking.

The senator stilled. "Ah, well, no. I mean, our sympathies go out to the cabdriver's family, but I don't have any knowledge of his death. Neither does anybody on my staff."

"Don't you think it odd that the driver who positively identified your employee as the last person to see Darian Hannah alive is now dead by having his throat slit?" the woman persisted.

Audrey kept her calm façade in place while her mind full-on sprinted. Had Nate killed the cabbie? He wouldn't have done so, would he? To protect her? Maybe. She hoped not. It was one thing to kill in a fight, but to murder an innocent guy just doing his job? She wanted to pray Nate hadn't turned that cold in the last five years.

What if he had? If he killed that easily, the man wouldn't hesitate to kill the commander or Audrey's mother. As a child, Audrey had feared her mother's death because of all the guns and soldiers around, because then she'd truly be alone. As a kid—alone.

Even now, as an adult, that fear never quite abated. And if Audrey's lover killed Isobel?

Her heart would shatter with guilt and regret.

How could she have such all-encompassing, confusing feelings for a man who ended life so easily? Sure, he'd been trained from birth to fight and kill, but he'd had five years to find another way.

What if there wasn't another way for Nate?

The senator concluded the press conference and followed her through the building and into their offices.

Where two uniformed police officers waited to take her downtown for questioning.

Nate sat on the couch in his remote cabin, his head pounding as he concentrated on the television. His heart actually kicked against his ribs when Audrey stood in front of the cameras lying her ass off. She looked sexier than sin.

Of course, she'd donned the outfit to contrast with what everyone thought the woman with the dead Darian had been wearing, but something bright gleamed in her eyes. A look Nate had brought to her last night.

What had happened last night? He'd meant to reassure them both, to calm them, and instead he'd planted himself so deeply inside her he'd never be free. Ever.

Flipping open his laptop, he dialed up his brothers.

Matt and Shane instantly filled the screen. "What in the world?" Shane asked.

Matt rolled his eyes. "We're making plans to head your way."

"Not yet." Nate hit a button to widen his lens so he didn't see every pissed-off pore in his brother's face. "Your huge heads take up a lot of room."

Shane flipped him off. "Get ready, Sally, because we're coming to dinner."

Nate shook his head. "We may need you there and able to move to the commander's alternate location on a dime. If I find the place, we might not have a lot of time, and you know it." The idea of saving Jory was the only leverage Nate had, and he was more than ready to use it. "Trust me. The second I need you, I'll call." Never going to happen.

Shane glanced at Matt. "I'll go to DC, and you wait here for instructions on Jory."

"No." Matt kept his level gaze on Nate's through the secured computers. "I'm going to DC."

Warmth spread through Nate. They didn't get it. He needed to protect them. His entire life had been dedicated to them, and he couldn't stop now. Without his brothers, he was a cold killing machine, and he needed them alive and finding peace. Jory was the one who mattered and had a hell of a lot more than Nate to offer the world. "I'm close to finding out the truth, Mattie. Trust me." Yeah, he used the one lever that always worked with Matt. Trust.

Shane turned to the side and punched in a bunch of keys on another computer. The guy had the finesse of a drunken elephant, and it was lucky the keyboard didn't break. "Damn it," he muttered.

"What?" Nate asked.

"I hacked into the police file on the dead cabbie. He was found in his cab—with a picture of Audrey Madison next to him. Covered in blood." Shane eyed Matt. "We're in trouble."

"We're always in trouble," Matt muttered, scrubbing his hands over the dark circles under his eyes. "Obviously somebody is trying to set Audrey up, but who and why?"

Nate's mind calculated every possible scenario in a matter of seconds. "I have no clue." The commander wouldn't bring attention to her, and neither would the senator. Darian's group wouldn't know how, so who did that leave? "Describe the picture," Nate said, anger and helplessness boiling through him.

Shane clicked a couple of buttons, and the picture came up on Nate's screen. "This is her ID photo for the Senate building." He rubbed his chin. "Easy enough for a reporter to get a hold of. Maybe the picture is from a reporter trying to ID Audrey." That was the easiest and the best-ass explanation they could hope for.

"Maybe." Matt's frown deepened.

Nate peered closer. "When the hell is the last time you slept?" *Haggard* didn't come close to describing his older brother.

Matt shrugged. "I won't sleep until we deactivate the chips."

Nate nodded. More than ever, his brothers had too much to lose. "Where are Josie and Laney, anyway?"

Shane rubbed his rough whiskers, appearing almost as exhausted as Matt. "Josie is working on the books for our security company, and Laney is making breakfast because she's now convinced protein will save us all." A genuine smile lifted his lips.

An odd and shameful jealousy rippled through Nate, and he shoved it down. He wanted his brothers happy, and that made him happy. Love and forever had never been in his future, no matter how badly he wanted it.

When he'd been old enough to pick a path in life, he'd chosen his role with his brothers. Without it and without them, he was the darkest side of what the commander had wanted to create. It was too late for a different path now.

He purposefully shoved down all memories of the previous night with Audrey into a dark hole. "Do we have the resources for a full-out attack if necessary?" he asked quietly.

Shane nodded. They'd created Sins Security after escaping the commander, which was a company that employed ex-soldiers to carry out services the U.S. government couldn't or wouldn't. Their employees had no clue who they worked for, but they were paid well. And the Dean brothers had invested their profits wisely. "We have money, weapons, and soldiers if we need more. We're ready to go, Nate. Just say the word."

"You got it." Relief tickled down Nate's spine, but he kept his expression bland. Once again, he'd convinced his brothers to hold tight where it was safe—and where they could keep their women safe. "The time is coming soon."

Unless he found Jory first, and then he'd go in and get his brother. Dead or alive.

Something dinged offscreen, and Shane turned toward the sound. "Interesting," he said as he typed in more commands.

"What?" Nate asked.

A series of photographs came up on his screen. Autopsy pictures of Darian Hannah. The man had been built and in excellent shape—apparently having continued to work out after his college football days.

"Take a look at this one," Shane said, swiping something.

Nate peered closer. The picture focused in on Darian's upper right shoulder, where a wound festered. "What the fuck?"

"Branding." Shane fiddled with something, and the picture cleared. "I think it's a sword with letters down the blade. PROTECT."

What in the world? "That looks new." Who would've branded Darian?

"The coroner's report said it was fresh—very fresh. Probably occurred hours before death," Shane said.

"For sure? It happened before and not after death?" Nate took a screen shot of the picture and e-mailed it to his smartphone.

"Yes. Definitely before death based on the swelling and burn marks." Shane scowled. "What in the world is going on in DC?"

"Don't know, but I will find out." Nate glanced at his watch. "Audrey has a doctor's appointment at the commander's compound, and I'm going to follow her to survey the security in place for known arrivals." While the press conference had been fairly safe because of the sheer number of reporters around, nobody would be recording her visit to the military facility. He hated the thought of allowing her to go into the commander's den with every square inch of his being. But it had to be done.

"Fair enough. Just so you know, we're making plans to head your way, like it or not." Matt's hard jaw set in a way that guaranteed a fight.

"Fair enough." Nate would get the intel before his brothers could make it to DC. "I'll call if I need help. Bye." He shut the laptop, determination coursing through his veins. Time to make something happen.

CHAPTER
17

AUDREY'S MORNING HAD sucked the big one, without question. The senator had defended her and insisted the police interview her in his office, with him present. They did so, and Audrey had basically lied yet again. But they were local cops, not federal, so hey, she hadn't broken any laws. Well, not really.

The drive to the commander's facility had taken forever, and she'd had the oddest feeling of being followed, but she couldn't spot a tail. Considering she was ensconced in the commander's limo, it wasn't his men. It had to be Nate. She just knew it.

Pain dragged Audrey back to the present as Dr. Washington finished twisting her bad leg. She winced while sitting on a plush leather examination table in a medical room painted a soothing peach color. Top-of-the-line machinery surrounded her on pure marble countertops with Brazilian maple cabinets. A medical facility for only the very special . . . or those with amazing connections.

The doctor straightened, his dark eyes warm. "Well, I know it still hurts, but it's amazing you can walk now." He spoke without ego or self-congratulations, and more like an overall gratefulness for the status of modern medical achievements.

"Thanks to you." This doctor was one of many who'd worked on her leg, but he'd done a good job, and he'd always treated her like a patient and not a science experiment. Audrey glanced down at the scars on her leg and grimaced as the Band-Aid on her elbow tightened. The nurse had taken blood the second Audrey had arrived.

The doctor smiled. "I think it was more your own stubbornness in the recovery process. For years I've performed surgery on some of the best trained, toughest soldiers in the world, and you beat all of them in heart and determination, hands down." He slipped the sheet back over her bare legs.

"Thanks." The months and months of physical therapy had almost broken her, but she'd kept going with one thought in mind: revenge. For her childhood and for the brainwashing Isobel had endured for years.

The doctor typed onto a tablet, taking notes. "Are you seeing Dr. Zycor today?"

"Yes." Audrey settled more comfortably onto the examination table. "My last internal surgery was over three months ago, and this is a follow-up to check for scar tissue."

Dr. Washington nodded and rubbed the back of his neck with a large-boned hand. "Excellent." He swiped something on the tablet and patted her shoulder. "Let me know if you have any further discomfort, and please consider returning to physical therapy."

"I will." Not. Physical therapy had brought her as far as it could, and she would do the remaining exercises at home. "Have a good one."

"You too." The doctor turned and quietly exited the room.

Audrey took a deep breath, swinging her legs under the sheet. The A/C flipped on, and she shivered.

The door opened, and she began to smile, only to stop halfway when a woman entered. She swallowed. "Hello, Mother."

Isobel Madison lifted her chin, her dark blue eyes appraising. "Audrey, how are you feeling?"

"Better. My leg is hanging in there." For the past five years, since Audrey had worked with the commander, she and her mother had reached a mutual agreement. Maybe, for once, her mother was actually proud of her. Audrey didn't want maternal approval, or rather, she didn't want to need maternal approval. But she sat straighter and with a lighter heart. "I'm waiting for the next doctor."

Isobel nodded. "You could've done something with your hair."

Irritation chilled Audrey's chest along with an odd hurt. "I could always go for the bun look, but it's patently yours."

Her mother sniffed and flipped over the metal chart in her fine-boned hands. "Sarcasm is beneath you."

Audrey tried to shrug but ended up patting her hair instead. How could she and her mother be so different? She'd inherited her mother's blue eyes and black hair, but Audrey was much taller and curvier than the genius scientist. Even now, as Isobel perused her daughter's medical chart, scientific curiosity lit her eyes. "Why are you here?" Audrey asked wearily, searching for concern in her mother's expression. There had to be some.

A familiar hurt assailed her. She knew her mother felt love because that sentiment had motivated the woman for decades with the commander. So surely her mother loved her, too. She just didn't show it well.

Isobel closed the chart and smoothed down her perfectly pressed lab coat. "I'm here to review your current medical progress, of course. Some of the surgeries we performed on you were experimental and will change the medical community forever."

Science and exploration ruled and motivated Isobel Madison like nothing else. "Of course," Audrey muttered.

"Have you been taking the concoction of natural vitamins and muscle-healing tissues we created for you?" Isobel asked.

"Yes." Audrey warmed a little. Isobel had been pushing those vitamins that really did help Audrey to feel better, and plus, she trusted the science and the doctors. Her pathetic gratefulness at thinking her mother cared tasted like sour lemons on her tongue. They'd never really had a heart-to-heart, and it was time. Since the commander would surely kill Audrey if he found out her deal with the senator, she might not have long to get the answers she needed. "Why did you have me?" Audrey asked quietly.

Isobel tilted her head. "You've never asked me that."

Frankly, Audrey had never wanted to hear the answer. "I'm asking now."

Isobel sighed and pushed a strand of hair away from her timeless face. "I found myself pregnant and wondered at the experience. Plus, it seemed a shame to waste my intelligence and not pass it on." She tapped long nails on the metal clipboard. "These last couple of years since you've been working with us, I've truly seen your potential."

It was as close as Isobel had ever come to expressing pride in her daughter. Audrey's throat clogged. "Thank you."

"You're welcome. I take satisfaction in seeing my child succeed."

Audrey swallowed, wondering if she could finally gain answers. "Who was my father?" She'd asked the question many a time, never receiving an answer.

"No clue." Isobel glanced at the gold watch around her narrow wrist. "Could've been any number of soldiers— it's not like I've ever denied myself."

No, the woman had slept with dozens of soldiers through the years. Maybe more. But...to say her IQ went beyond genius was accurate. Wait a minute. Audrey thought about the myriad of emotions that struck her because of Nate. She'd never want to have somebody else's child if she was around him every day. Her mother couldn't be that different from her. "You wouldn't have let yourself get knocked up." Fire washed through Audrey's torso. "You would've chosen carefully." Why had she never figured that out? "Somebody with good genes and high intelligence."

Isobel chuckled and shook her head. "Not exactly."

Oh no. Audrey gasped and clutched her stomach. "You didn't—"

Her mother frowned and then laughed. "The commander isn't your father. While he's tough and sexy, his intelligence isn't quite what I would've hoped."

Wait a minute. While Isobel lied to herself, Audrey knew full well the woman loved the cruel commander. She would've wanted his baby—intelligence or not. "I don't believe you."

Isobel started. "Excuse me?"

"You would've wanted Franklin's offspring." Audrey narrowed her gaze as her mind clicked facts into place. "He said no."

A glimmer of hurt lightened Isobel's eyes to be quickly dispelled. "Fine. Franklin said that since we worked together every day that a child between us would complicate things."

Audrey bit back a gasp. How could such an intelligent woman like Isobel let a man treat her so poorly? In the name of love? "Why do you love him, Mother? He's terrible to you."

Isobel scoffed. "Love? Don't be ridiculous. This is about the pursuit of perfection."

"At what cost?" Audrey murmured. Was she like her mother? Falling in love with the wrong man—a man who could kill so easily? One who'd put his mission before her?

"Any cost is worth it if we create the perfect soldier." Isobel shrugged, her eyes veiled.

Audrey shook her head. "You wouldn't have picked somebody to knock you up." She'd been wrong and hadn't figured in Isobel's inexplicable feelings for the commander.

"I've told you for years that I have no idea who fathered you." Isobel's expression didn't change. "There was a time when I experimented a bit with hallucinogens, trying to expand my mind, and it often led to recreational activities I can't quite remember."

Audrey's head jerked back. "So my father might not even be a soldier?"

Isobel glanced down at the chart in her hands. "It's possible, but usually I took a cadet or two home with me."

Audrey shook her head and dropped her head into her hands. "So it's possible I was conceived in an orgy after you'd popped shrooms. Really?" She lifted her head, finally, and with a bone-deep sadness, accepted the possibility that she'd never know her father. Maybe he would've liked her.

"Again, I have no clue who fathered you, not that it matters," Isobel said.

Audrey gathered the sheet more protectively around her legs. "So why have me?"

Isobel shrugged. "Why not? There was a chance you'd inherit my brilliance."

"Apparently not," Audrey said, her mind calculating scenarios. She needed answers. "Does it even bother you that you set me up with Nathan? It nearly broke me when our relationship ended."

"Oh for goodness' sake. Nathan was just a man—get over it."

"Just a man? I loved him!" Everything inside Audrey exploded at once. Just like Isobel loved the commander. Life was so screwed up, and the one person who was supposed to have protected Audrey had actually thrown her under the bus. "You used me. You used us both—as an experiment. As a way to motivate a soldier."

Isobel sighed. "Well, get over it because he's never going to want you back. You broke his heart, and there's no forgiveness in that man."

Nate would agree with her, and they were both wrong. The man had more capacity for love and loyalty than anyone Audrey had ever met, and forgiveness was a part of that.

Audrey knew him, and it was time to seize the opportunity to delve deep and manipulate Isobel into giving her information about the kill chips. No matter how screwed up Audrey's feelings were for Nate, she wanted to save him. She had to save him. "You don't know Nathan."

"I know everything about that boy—I've studied him since birth. You took away the only thing he ever truly loved besides his brothers—you. Nothing in him will ever be able to forgive you for that. It's how I made him." Isobel frowned and eyed her watch again. "What in the world is taking so long?"

"You're wrong. Nate will be back for me someday." Audrey tipped her hand in order to gain information, her fingers tapping nervously on the leather table. "Don't you think?"

Shrewd blue eyes narrowed on her. "No. Why—do you?"

Audrey sat up straighter. "I wouldn't, except the commander has had men following me for the last three weeks. Why would they be watching me, if there wasn't a credible reason?"

"Interesting." Isobel pursed bright-red lips. "Soldiers, hmmm?"

"I can spot a tail, Mother." Good Lord, she'd been partially raised in a military environment. "Why. Am. I. Being. Followed?"

Isobel rolled her eyes. "I assume it has something to do with the subcommittee for military funding. Franklin is hedging his bets."

"Why haven't you been able to find the Gray brothers? The commander is the best at tracking and, yet, nothing." How could she get Isobel to admit the truth about the kill chips?

"I'm not the soldier here, and I have no idea." Isobel tapped a high heel on the floor.

No way would her mother let the truth slip. Well, one action left. Audrey launched off the table and shoved her mother against a cabinet, forearm against the older woman's throat. She cared little that she stood in a T-shirt and underwear. "Tell me the truth, now. I have no trouble killing you."

Surprise widened Isobel's eyes, and she burst out laughing. "You forget—I made you, too." Genuine amusement and no anger crossed her face. She shoved Audrey's hips, pushing her back a couple of inches. "You always have

amused me. Like you'd ever really kill your own mother.
Sit down before the doctor gets here."

Audrey waited several heartbeats and then slowly
backed up, reclaiming the sheet to sit on the table. Yeah,
the woman did know her. She'd never kill Isobel. But
she would and could catch her off guard. Her mother's
security card cut into her palm, and she discreetly tucked
it under the pillow. The older woman may have made
Audrey, but she didn't know her as well as she thought.
The security card would get Audrey access into any area
of the entire facility. "I apologize. I'm not quite myself
today," she said quietly.

"I understand." An indefinable gleam filled Isobel's eyes.

Audrey swallowed as unease straightened her spine.
What was going on?

A discreet knock sounded on the door, and Dr. Zycor
slipped inside. Small of stature, the Asian doctor was the
smartest person Audrey had ever met—and that was saying something. Audrey instantly smiled. While several
doctors had operated or rehabbed her leg, only Dr. Zycor
had fixed her insides. He remained a calm and gentle man
in a dangerous facility, and he'd been on her side.

He silently handed a sheet of paper to Isobel, who
breathed out while reading. A pink flush rose from her
neck across her face.

Audrey's heartbeat kicked into a full-out gallop. "What
is that?"

Isobel giggled. "Good news. Very good news."

Dr. Zycor pushed an ultrasound machine toward the
table. "You're completely healed, Audrey. It's almost a
miracle."

Oh. So her crazy mother wanted grandchildren someday, was that it? Audrey lay down and shook her head.

"There's no way I'm procreating, Mother." Yet, the thought of being healed, of actually having a child, created a burning need inside her. The feeling had been there since she'd first met Nate, actually.

The doctor squirted gel on Audrey's stomach and pressed the receptor against her abdomen. Audrey settled back, relaxing. She'd had hundreds of ultrasounds through the years.

A rhythmic *thump, thump, thump* echoed throughout the room.

Audrey frowned and turned toward the screen. "What is that?" Her gaze landed on the outline of a baby with something fluttering in the center. The heart. Shock nearly stopped her breathing. "What—"

Isobel clapped her hands. "It worked. I can't believe it worked."

Audrey's chest constricted and her breath caught. She began to pant, and a ringing filled her ears.

"Hold on." Dr. Zycor pressed a dry hand against her head. "Panic attack. Hold your breath for a moment."

Audrey held her breath, allowing the carbon dioxide to dissipate. She'd fought panic attacks for a while after the explosion, but she'd learned to manage them and hadn't endured one in over a year. She sucked in air. "I'm pregnant?"

"Yes." Isobel peered closer to the baby moving on the monitor. "About fourteen weeks. Your last surgery wasn't really a surgery. We sedated you and inserted sperm into you—after you'd been ingesting a series of hormones, of course." She frowned. "I'd hoped for a multiple birth, but apparently there's only one little genius soldier in there."

Audrey shook her head, the room hazing. Pregnant? "How—who?"

Isobel's eyes glittered with satisfaction. "Nathan's, of course."

"No." Audrey shoved the ultrasound receptor away and sat up. The thumping stopped. "All of their specimens were destroyed in the blast." She'd double-checked.

Disappointment filled Isobel's face when the screen fuzzed, and she turned toward Audrey with a resigned sigh. "We had one vial for each Gray brother stored at a safe location, because as you know, we always wanted to create offspring from them. They're the most talented and gifted soldiers we've ever created, so who knows how gifted the next generation might be? How much they might help the commander's cause? We used all of the samples over the last five years—unsuccessfully—saving Nathan's for you in case we healed you. You were the only woman ever to be impregnated by a Gray brother, so we had to take the chance that it wasn't a fluke."

Audrey swayed. "Wh-why Nathan and not one of his brothers?"

"Because Nathan had managed to impregnate you before, even though that was natural and not via test tube. Sometimes there are chemicals and hormones at play we can't pinpoint." Isobel beamed, a maniacal glint in her eyes. "Since you and Nate had created life once before, we hoped against hope the result might happen again."

Audrey shook her head, her mind swirling. Fear and a dangerous hope burst through her. She was pregnant. Again. With Nate's baby.

The room went dark as she fainted completely.

CHAPTER
18

W HEN AUDREY CAME to, her mother was gone. Audrey sat up on the examination table, her head pounding. She put a hand to her forehead and murmured a soft "ow."

Dr. Zycor, sitting on a rolling stool, finished typing onto a tablet and glanced up, his eyes soft behind the wire-rimmed glasses. "Are you feeling all right?"

Fury consumed her so quickly she nearly hissed. "You bastard. You fucking bastard." She'd trusted him. Hurt and disbelief nearly propelled her from the table, but her legs shook, and she didn't trust them to hold her up.

From day one, when he told her he'd be able to heal her internally, that he'd be able to save at least one of her ovaries, she'd thought they were on the same page. In the same corner. She'd thought she wasn't so alone in the sterile medical environment. "I'm going to kill you."

He nodded. "I can fully understand your anger."

"Can you, now?" Disbelief flooded her. "My mother was aware of the plan from the very beginning?" she whispered, already knowing the answer.

"Of course." Sympathy glittered in his dark eyes. "It was her idea, actually."

Betrayal melded with outrage until focus escaped Audrey. Her mother had allowed the commander to impregnate her against her will and without her knowledge. How could she have done that?

Rage overtook the hurt.

Audrey reached under the pillow to draw out the card and jumped off to snatch her skirt off the chair. Why hide her body? The man had seen her both inside and out. "I trusted you." She kicked one leg into the silk, discreetly sliding the card into a pocket.

"I know." He stood and whipped off the glasses. "I apologize for deceiving you, but you knew I worked for the commander from the beginning. And the medical advances here—"

"Shut up." If one more person talked about her body and the incredible medical advances, she'd break their nose in one punch. "Where's Dr. Evil?" She hadn't called her mother by the sarcastic nickname in way too long.

Zycor glanced at the closed door. "I assume she went to update the commander on the news."

The news. Audrey's hands trembled as she zipped up her skirt. A baby. Her baby. And Nate's baby.

They'd used condoms when they'd had sex. Yet here Audrey had become pregnant with Nate's baby via in vitro when he'd been nowhere around and she'd been sedated. The irony nearly choked her.

Danger instantly threatened the barely formed human for the mere fact of its parentage. Nathan's child. The commander and Audrey's mother would never let the child live a normal life—never let him or her see freedom. Unless Audrey stopped them.

Maternal rage surrounded her heart. This was her baby, and she'd protect it. No matter what. Its father was

one of the most deadly men in the world, and he needed to
live in order to help. So she had a job to do. Now.

Air swished as she shot an uppercut to Zycor's throat,
sending him sprawling against a cabinet. He cried out,
arms wide, and medicinal cotton balls rained down.
Twirling him, she forced him into a choke hold, fighting hard as he struggled like a caught carp. But she held
fast, taller and with better leverage, until he dropped
into unconsciousness. "Sorry, Doc," she muttered while
removing his lab coat and taking his security clearance
card just in case.

Her shoulder ached when she shrugged into the lab
coat, which smelled like bleach. Then she reached for a
rubber band in a drawer and put her hair in a bun. The
final accessory was the doctor's eyeglasses.

She was well known in the facility, and she might be
able to fool people into thinking she now worked with
her mother. Maybe. Time ticked down. Her mother would
return soon.

Audrey hurried through hallways toward the secured
areas, fear and adrenaline flooding her system. Was that
bad for the baby? She pressed a palm against her still-flat
abdomen, trying to force herself to be calm. Her knowledge about pregnancy and forming fetuses could fit on
a note card. Last time, she hadn't been pregnant long
enough to figure out how to do it right.

Maybe she should hit the bookstore on the way home.
For now, she needed to center herself and relax as she
committed treason, trespassing, and disloyalty. The third
element was the one that would send the commander over
the edge.

Her mother's card swiped easily in a reader, and
Audrey stepped through a new doorway into an area she'd

never visited. A narrow hallway led to another locked door, and her boots swished on bleach-clean tiles as she made her way through the next security point and into a small vestibule leading in several different directions. She headed to the right and peered through a window in a door where a myriad of scientists worked at different stations in a lab. A series of doors led to other areas—probably more labs.

Too many people.

So she hustled back and took a different hallway, this one leading to several armories and conference rooms littered with battle plans. An office at the end smelled like the commander and was decorated with pictures of war. His computer beckoned her, but she probably had a better chance with her mother's.

A hand on her elbow stopped her. She gasped and glanced up at a man in a black soldier's uniform. Dark brown eyes focused on her. "Miss Madison? Where's your escort?" he asked.

She slipped her arm free, almost surprised when he released her. "Dr. Zycor let me in and told me to go to my mother's office for some assignment. I wanted to pop by and say hello to Franklin."

Suspicion tightened the soldier's solid jaw. Standing almost as big as Nate, the guy lacked any kindness in those eyes. "I was not informed you'd be in the secured area today."

"Need to know, buddy. I'm now working with my mother." She turned on her heel and tried to keep her shoulders back as her stomach objected. "Get back to work."

He escorted her down the hallway, past several offices to a large one at the end. The scent of rose water smacked

Audrey, and her gut revolted. Now she got morning sickness? Swallowing, she loped inside and dropped into a chintzy guest chair. Her mother's desk was glass, and pictures of the brain covered the walls. No pictures of Audrey. "I'll wait here."

The soldier reached for a phone and talked into a speaker. "I need confirmation that Miss Madison is now allowed in the secured areas without an escort."

Shit. Shit. Shit. Audrey eyed him, looking for an opening. How was she going to take him down? What if she put the baby at risk?

A crackle echoed across the speaker, and a voice hissed through. "I'll alert the commander and track down Dr. Madison. She mentioned she had a meeting later today. For now, your orders are to get on the plane for China, Daniel," a voice ordered. "We're under the gun here."

Daniel eyed Audrey. "Stay here and don't touch anything." Turning on his heel, he disappeared.

"No problem," she whispered, hurrying around the desk to the computer. She punched in a couple of keys and waited until the sign-in screen came up. What would her mother's password be? She had no clue. Taking a chance, she tried several variations for "brain" and Franklin and war. Frustration welled up. It couldn't be. So she typed in AUDREY.

Denied.

Why would she have even thought her mother would've used her kid's name as a password like a normal mother? Why did that hurt? She shoved down any pain because now wasn't the time to deal with childhood issues. If ever.

Oh well. Audrey rolled up her sleeves and went to work. Having a superior IQ that was shaped by the best in the world came in handy. If anybody could hack her mother's computer, it'd be Audrey. Unfortunately, she didn't have much time. The algorithm she ran had been created by a genius ten years ago, and she'd made it even better. Faster. Trickier.

The computer dinged exactly five minutes and twenty-three seconds later, giving up the code made up of a random set of letters and numbers. Figured. Audrey sat forward and searched for "kill chips." The computer offered no results. What would her mother call the chips? Audrey sat back, her mind reeling, and typed in "C4 neutralizing measure." C4 came up on several documents, and Audrey began clicking through them.

She needed to vomit halfway through reading, and it wasn't from pregnancy. How could her mother be so evil? The chips had been inserted and would certainly detonate. The only man she'd ever loved and the father of her baby.

Baby.

This baby would have a father, damn it. If Audrey didn't find a way to deactivate Nate's chip, he'd die. She would not allow her child to be abandoned by its father, even by death. Pressure threatened to choke her.

An outside door slammed. Air filled her lungs as she sucked it in, trying not to puke. One more page. She clicked on it and finally hit pay dirt. All the details about the computer program that controlled the chips.

Quickly printing the page, she folded the paper to cram in her back pocket. She erased her search, and instituted the password page right before her mother's high heels clicked into the room.

Isobel sighed and clipped around the desk to see the now blank page. "Impressive move taking my security card." She held out a hand.

Audrey slapped the card into her mother's palm with a bit more force than was necessary. "How could you do this to me?"

Isobel sighed. "For goodness' sake. You were so sad when you lost the baby before, I figured you'd be pleased."

"Pleased?" Audrey leaped to her feet. "You did this without my consent and without Nate's consent. You had no right."

"Sometimes sacrifices are made in the pursuit of excellence." No emotion showed on Isobel's face.

Fine. There was no getting through to her mother, and Audrey would never receive an apology or even an understanding of how badly she'd been violated. Her shoulders slumped. "I need to know more about this pregnancy." Hopefully her mother wouldn't search too hard into the computer, even though Audrey had erased her trail. Nothing was ever really erased.

"Why didn't you ask me?" Isobel asked.

"Because I trust you as far as I can throw your skinny, neurotic, narcissistic ass," Audrey said. "I even tried to use my name as your password."

Isobel's dark eyebrows both arched high. "Why in the world would I use your name as my password?"

That pretty much said it all, didn't it? "What now, Mother?" Audrey asked.

"Well, now we go back to the lab where you're supposed to be"—Isobel pointed toward the doorway—"and we go meet with Dr. Zycor to come up with your treatment plan . . . after you apologize to him, of course. You'll need to take vitamins and have a weekly check-in here."

"No." Audrey shook her head as she lurched into the hallway.

"Listen, Audrey." Isobel grasped her arm and twirled

her around. "We don't have time for theatrics. Either you agree to our terms or you stay here."

Audrey towered over her mother, stepping into the older woman's space. "I work for a United States senator. If I disappear, I guarantee he'll call out the National Guard to find me. Plus, I'm a person of interest in an ongoing investigation."

"The National Guard would never find you if Franklin decides to hide you, and you know it. Besides, he has taken care of the investigation." Isobel lifted a shoulder.

Audrey coughed. "Who did he set up as Darian and the cabbie's killer?"

"Who cares?" Isobel gestured toward the doorway. "Regardless, the police will make an arrest later today, and you'll be in the clear."

The commander cared little for Audrey and had put her in the clear for his own benefit. Audrey tried to concentrate, when all she wanted to do was run for safety. "I'll check in about the pregnancy, but only if you take the tail off me. The men following me are making me nervous, and the second I see them again, I'm done cooperating."

Isobel pursed her lips. "I can speak with Franklin, but I'm sure he's concerned you'll run."

Audrey forced a grim chuckle. "Run where? There's nowhere to go."

Isobel nodded. "Well, I suppose that's true. All right. I'll speak with Franklin, because we are willing to let you continue in your work and in living on your own, so long as you report in once a week."

Aha. They needed Audrey to continue with the senator in gaining funding. The second funding was obtained, no doubt the commander would "secure" Audrey in a place far away from DC—where he and Isobel would control the baby's life. They had no interest in her living her own life. "Fine. Give me the prenatals, and I'm out of here." She turned toward the secured doorway.

"I will—after the amniocentesis. We need to make sure there are no fetal defects, and you want to find out the sex of the baby, don't you?" Isobel asked, swiping her card through the door.

Audrey stumbled. The sex of the baby?

Nate kept his position in Audrey's living room, his gaze focused through a slat in the blinds. One man had been watching her apartment all day, while two had accompanied her to work and then to the commander's local compound. Everything inside Nate had rebelled at allowing Audrey to go into the area secured by Nate's greatest enemy. But his focus had to remain on saving his brothers.

Wishing for something different wasted time and energy.

Yet the muscles along his spine relaxed when she unlocked her door and stepped inside. The scent of gardenias wafted along his nose, tempting his taste buds. His groin warmed while his heart thumped. "How was your appointment?" he asked.

"Fine." Her gaze darted around the room, and she dropped her briefcase onto a chair. "I, ah, really want to change out of this skirt, and then we can talk. We, ah, need to talk."

"Okay. I picked up sandwiches earlier." He didn't know if she still liked veggie, so he'd bought veggie, ham, roast beef, and turkey. Whatever she didn't want, he'd probably eat.

"Great. I'm starving." She turned and headed into the bedroom, her gait stilted.

Whatever tests they'd conducted had left her sore. Maybe he should force her somewhere safe now instead of later.

Nate strode into the kitchen to fetch the sandwiches from the refrigerator. The cat downstairs suddenly came alive, its heartbeat hammering. There must be a mouse or something down there, because Nate hadn't heard the little bugger all day. Weird.

He set the food out and waited for her. Should he say something about the previous night? If so, what?

She stepped into the room wearing cropped yoga pants, a blue tank top that showed full breasts, and bright-purple fuzzy socks. A band secured her thick hair in a sexy mass, and no makeup remained on her face.

The woman was fucking perfect.

She eyed the food and then him. "I think you need to sit down."

Pale. All color had fled her face, leaving her skin nearly see-through.

Nothing could've kept him from reaching for her arm. "Sit down, Aud. Are you okay?"

Panic lightened her eyes. "No. I mean, yes. We can't talk about this in the kitchen." Slight hysteria lifted her voice. Slender fingers tangled through his as she led him into the living room and all but pushed him onto the sofa. "Yeah. This is better."

What in the hell was going on?

He reached for her, and she waved him off.

"No. I need to be standing." She turned toward the window and rubbed a hand over her eyes. Then she took a deep breath, her chest moving. "Okay. You need to keep calm."

Instantly he became anything but calm. "What happened?" He shot to his feet, already planning an attack on the compound. "What did they do to you? How hurt are you?" He studied her from head to toe, calculating the weapons he'd need.

"I'm not hurt." She gently pushed him back down on the couch. "Take a deep breath."

Was she talking to him or to herself? He frowned. *Oh God.* "Did you find out about Jory?" He braced himself for the pain. Jory was dead.

"Jory?" She shook her head, her hair band letting go. The dark mass fell around her shoulders. "No, sorry. I didn't find out anything about Jory."

Oh. Nate shook his head, trying to regain his bearings. Okay. Well, good. He forced himself into a calm place and smiled. "What's going on, Audrey?" He kept his voice low and soothing, like he'd been trained.

He frowned. That cat downstairs was distracting him again.

Audrey drew in air. "My last surgery wasn't needed. At all."

He tilted his head to the side. "Okay..."

"No." She shook her head, her hands trembling as she clasped them together. "I'm doing this wrong."

"Just tell me. It's okay." He'd help her—he'd have to.

"I'mpregnant," she said in a rush. Then she took a deep breath. "Oh, good. Okay. I said it."

He blinked. Once. Twice. "You're what?"

She stepped forward and dropped next to him on the sofa. "Pregnant—about fourteen weeks."

Oh. Holy fucking shit. Pregnant? In a fight years ago, he'd taken a sledgehammer to the gut...and that was a tickle compared to this. He pulled away from her to stand, facing her. She'd lied to him? So much for not being with anybody else. The thrumming of the cat's heartbeat became louder in his ears, and his gaze dropped to her abdomen. Oh. Not a *cat*. "Congratulations."

"Thanks." She rubbed her eyes, her body relaxing. "I've been freaking out about telling you all afternoon."

Yeah, considering she'd lied. Something hurt deep in his chest, and he fought the urge to rub it. His brain suddenly slowed, each neuron in pain. "Who's the father?"

She stilled, her chin lifting, her brows drawing down. "Huh?"

"The father." That was *not* a tough question.

She shook her head. "Oh. I didn't explain. Um, you're the father."

He coughed, his breath heating. Damn her. "I'm sure my sperm is super and all of that, but we only just had sex. Plus, I used protection both times. So I'm going to ask you again—who's the father?"

She rolled her eyes. "You. Are." With a sigh, she drew her legs up to sit cross-legged, wincing as she set the left one in place. "My surgery three months ago wasn't a surgery. They inseminated me with the last vial of your sperm that had been kept at a different place than the one you blew up."

His vision grayed.

She nodded. "Yep."

His mind shut down while his chest expanded until he couldn't breathe. Panic? He staggered over to drop next to her on the couch.

"I told you to sit down." She reached out and patted his knee. "By the way . . . it's a boy."

CHAPTER
19

AUDREY SAT ON the couch, munching on a turkey sandwich. She'd wanted the veggie but figured a baby needed protein. Right? Man, she needed to get ahold of a few pregnancy books. Last time she hadn't been pregnant long enough to really study the situation or get a feel for it, so right now, confusion ruled her mind. Although, the turkey tasted delicious. She extended her legs onto the coffee table and watched Nate pace the room.

He scrubbed both hands down his face. "A boy?"

"Yep." Audrey took another bite. She wasn't sure about the tomatoes—they tasted too soft.

"A boy? Oh no." Nate paced faster, pure panic on his face.

"I know." Maybe she'd have texture problems while pregnant, because she definitely didn't want the tomatoes.

"I mean, I'd love a boy. Or a girl. But in this case, a boy—"

"I know." Yep. Audrey took out the remaining tomato and tossed it on the paper wrapping on the table. The commander would want to study and train a girl, but to have a boy with the size and strength of the Gray brothers? Yeah. He'd never let that kid go.

"Wait a minute." Nate shook his head. "Why do you trust them? You could be pregnant with anybody's kid." His eyes widened. "I didn't mean that the way it sounded."

Yeah, he did. But it was a good question, and she'd already thought it through. "I think the baby is yours because you'd impregnated me before, the first and only time a Gray had impregnated anybody. It makes sense they'd try again. You know how many times they'd tried to impregnate surrogates with the Gray brothers' specimens. The commander is desperate to have a next generation of Gray boys."

"Why?" Nate asked, his voice hoarse.

"Because you're the most successful experiment they'd ever conducted." Audrey lowered her voice in sympathy. Now wasn't the time to sugarcoat the truth, even though she wanted to ease his pain. Now was about the baby and not either one of them. Man, she loved turkey all of a sudden.

"I'm not an experiment." Fire lit his eyes.

"I agree, and neither is this baby." She tried to clear her cloudy mind. "But that's not how they see you or junior here, and we can't forget that."

Nate whirled toward her, his eyes a wild stormy gray, dark grooves lining the sides of his mouth. "How are you so calm?"

She shrugged, finishing off the sandwich. "I had the long car ride back to freak out, and well, I think I may still be in shock." The satisfying numbness surrounding her brain felt good, and she didn't want to let it go. The second that calmness disappeared, she'd freak out like never before. Her feet hit the floor. "I have to stay calm for the baby."

Nate dropped to his haunches, his hands warming her knees. "You're right. Calm. That's good."

Poor guy couldn't even talk in complete sentences. She reached out and cupped his whiskered jaw. "Take a breath, Nate. We'll protect this baby with everything we have." Nobody was going to hurt the little guy.

"I know." Determination and something else lit his dark eyes.

What was that? Oh. Fear. She'd never seen Nate afraid of anything. Ever. Drawing on a store of strength she hadn't realized she owned, she fastened her hands over his shoulders. Hard. "Trust me. *Nothing* is going to happen to this baby. Period."

He nodded, the fear vanishing and leaving a deadly light. She shivered.

"We need to plan." He strode out of the room and returned with a glass of milk. "I think you're supposed to drink this."

She hated milk unless it was on cereal. "Sure." Taking the glass, she set it down on the coffee table. He wouldn't notice in his current state. "Oh, hey." She reached for her briefcase and drew out a picture of the ultrasound Dr. Zycor had made for her. "Here's a picture of the little Gray guy."

Nate took the picture, his hand visibly shaking. "He's real. I mean, I can hear his heartbeat, but... he's real."

"You can hear his heartbeat?"

"Yes. Thought it was the cat's."

"Yeah." She took another piece of paper from the bag. "Here are the results of the amnio that show he's a boy and that he's yours." She'd insisted on the report in case her mother and the commander were lying in order to trap Nate. "It's conclusive." Of course, they could've easily doctored the test.

"I know." Nate scanned the paper. "I'm not sure how I know, but now that I can focus on him in there, I can tell he's mine. Don't ask me how." He shrugged. "Or maybe I just want him to be mine. I don't know."

Audrey nodded. The Gray brothers harbored gifts nobody could explain, so why question it? Besides, deep in her heart, she knew the baby was his. Sometimes you just knew, and the explanation from Isobel had made sense. "Besides that, I accessed the secured headquarters and found some interesting information." She tugged out the printout from her mother's office.

Nate stilled, every muscle along his chest clenching visibly beneath his T-shirt. "You what?"

Audrey sat up straighter. "Um, I broke into my mother's computer."

Nate's gaze lasered in on her, making her feel like a specimen squirming on a slide. "How did you gain access to her office?"

"I, ah, stole her key card." Audrey swallowed, but once she started confessing, she couldn't stop. "I knocked out the doctor and stole his, too. After that, I just went through secured doors until a soldier found me and escorted me to my mother's office."

Nate paled. He went from bronze to ghostlike in less than a second. "You knocked out a doctor." Lurching over to the overstuffed chair, Nate fell like an anchor. "Then you snuck into a secured area." He dropped his head into his hands. "That's where a soldier found you."

"Um, yeah." The roast beef sandwich in the other room seemed to be calling her name. Hopefully there weren't any tomatoes on it.

"Are. You. Crazy?" Nate kept his head down and his voice low, but a tenor of raw fire whipped through the words.

"Maybe a little." Audrey wiped her hand over her head. Based on her parentage alone, there was a fair to middle chance she had some insanity in her. "Don't panic here, Nate. The good news is that I'm fine, and I found information about the computer program that will deactivate your codes."

Man, she was way too calm. Must still be the shock. Plus, even after eating that entire sandwich, she was still hungry. "Relax."

"Relax?" He leaped to his feet, steam all but shooting from his ears. "You're incredibly lucky you're pregnant right now, because I'd like nothing better than to flip you over my knee and paddle your butt. You'd be so sore you couldn't sit until Christmas."

"You're mad?" What in the world was wrong with him? She'd found valuable information, and he hadn't even glanced at it. Anger whirled through her like a tornado, so she stood. "Listen, buddy. I did what I had to do, and you'd better get on board. We're in this fight together, and you're gonna need me to get you access. Deal with it."

"Deal with it?" Red spread across his rugged cheekbones. Yeah, he was bewildered and pissed.

"Yes." Audrey blew out air.

"Oh, baby. You're on your way to a safe house the second we pack you a bag." His voice lowered to a softness with no give.

"Think, Nate." She drew in air, trying to keep from punching him in the face. Could the baby hear yet? If so, she didn't want him hearing her become violent. "I'm your way in to save your brothers. That's your goal."

He shook his head in slow motion, his gaze tapping hers, raw determination stamping an already hard face. "You and the baby are my *only* goal. If you don't understand that one simple fact, then you never really understood me."

She stepped back. Yes, she'd expected him to go caveman protective, but she had underestimated the primal being at the core of Nathan. "What about your brothers?"

"The second I get you safe, I'll figure out a way to get the codes. But *nothing* happens until you're secured."

"Nate." She drew on every ounce of patience she'd cultivated through the years. "We're in this together. I need you alive as much as I need this baby to live. Do you honestly think I can protect him myself while on the run from the commander?" Yeah, she was smart, and she had contingency plans. But the commander had an army, and someday, he'd find her. "I need you alive. I need the Gray brothers alive." She needed all the help she could get.

"Dean brothers." Nate still hadn't moved, but she knew he could launch at any second.

"Huh?" She frowned.

"Dean brothers. We took a last name years ago—only family gets to know it. That kid in there? He's a Dean." Nate eyed her stomach with a fierce possessiveness.

"Good name." Great name, in fact. Much better than hers, considering she shared it with a sociopath.

"Glad you like it. You'll be wearing it soon." Nate finally glanced down at the paper in his hands.

She coughed and fought the urge to fall to the sofa. "Excuse me?"

Nate answered without stopping reading. "I, ah, think we should get married."

Well, if that wasn't the most romantic proposal on record. "Why? What does a piece of paper have to do with anything, Nate Dean?" Yeah, it felt good to slap a last name on that one.

He stilled, vulnerability digging hollows under his cheekbones. "Nothing, really. But, I mean, I would've wanted my parents to be married, if I'd had parents. I mean, right?"

This side of him tore her apart. All of a sudden she could see the lost little boy who just wanted a family and didn't want to learn how to kill. "I guess. How about we think about it?" She shrugged, her mind whirling.

"There's a good chance I won't make it past the next few weeks." His voice lowered with pain. "I'd like for the kid to know I wanted him and gave him a name. That he mattered."

Audrey lifted her head as comprehension dawned. Nate had always wanted to matter, which is probably why he'd taken such good care of his brothers. "This kid will know he matters. I promise."

"Okay. Good." He glanced down at the paper again. "This is excellent. It describes the computer program that sends out the wireless code to deactivate the chips."

"Yeah, but I didn't find the actual code." Yet.

"This is a good start, and Shane will be able to duplicate the program." Nathan tossed the paper onto the chair. He scrubbed both hands down his face. "We have to deactivate these chips. We just have to."

Well past midnight, from behind the rainy window, Nathan scouted the area outside the apartment, the cold metal from his gun offering comfort in his hand. He wanted to go outside and start taking out the men watching his family, but for now, he needed to stay close and not tip his hand. Soon, he'd wreak havoc. In the other room, two heartbeats thrummed. One slower as Audrey slept, and one faster. The baby. His baby.

He'd already searched on the Internet the correct speed of a baby's heartbeat, and his was doing fine. A baby. Talk about changing the game midway through the second half.

The love he felt for the forming body held enough weight to crush him, so intense was the need to protect.

The intense craving to live, to have a future to see the miracle he'd been given was new and not what he ever would've expected based on his past.

When he'd arrived in town, he'd been crushed the baby from five years ago hadn't survived. But now? Now he had another chance. With Audrey. With a kid he could love and protect—and teach football, not fighting.

His spine hurt in an unconscious reminder of the device set to kill him.

He couldn't die. He had to live. For Audrey and the baby.

Hope was a terrible thing, because it was crushed so easily. Yet he couldn't protect himself from hoping a little.

How odd that he'd used a condom with Audrey, and she'd ended up pregnant with his kid anyway. But the betrayal from her mother and the doctors infuriated him. How dare they use her like that?

He scrubbed both hands down his face. What did Audrey really feel about the baby? She had to be angry and hurt that she'd been taken advantage of, and she had to be scared. Did it matter to her that the babe was created in a lab instead of naturally? He hadn't been created or conceived naturally, and look how he'd turned out.

A killing machine.

But his kid would be different.

Intensity lived within him and always had. But he'd tempered his natural fire in order to calm Matt and protect Shane and Jory. Now, with his own child being threatened, nothing on earth would temper him. Ever again.

His feelings for his child's mother were even more confusing. He'd loved Audrey Madison from the first second she'd flashed those innocent baby blues at him, and he wasn't a guy who loved twice. He'd always known that fact with a certainty that had helped him take risks in the field since he figured he'd never have a chance with Audrey again.

Talk about a new chance. Now she carried his child, which made his hands shake and his ears heat. If anything happened to either Audrey or the baby, more than his body would die. He'd never figured on having a soul, but for the first time, as he sensed the existence of his child with a preternatural surety, he wondered. If he did have a soul, it was encased in Audrey and that baby. Losing them would be worse than any death the commander might devise.

The cabin he'd commandeered wouldn't be a safe enough place to hide Audrey. She'd made some good arguments earlier, but the idea of her returning to the facility shot cold sweat down his back.

But he had to survive, and he did need her help to do it. How could he risk her in such a manner? How could he not?

His life had always been such a straight line, and he'd never questioned his place on the path—until now.

Audrey had been correct. Smart and tough, the woman would give the commander a good chase, but ultimately, he'd find her. Nate had always intended on taking out the man, but now, more than ever, he needed to end the organization. Cripple it, kill it, so nobody could threaten his child or Audrey.

He'd do his damnedest to survive, but odds still weren't good. His only chance was to clear the path for Audrey.

So he sat down, opened his laptop, and made the one call he *never* thought he'd make.

His older brother took shape on the screen, concern gleaming in his familiar gray eyes. "Nate?" Matt asked.

"I need help, Mattie."

CHAPTER
20

ACROSS THE COUNTRY from Washington, DC, on a rural ranch outside of Rebel, Montana, Mathew Dean drummed his fingers on the kitchen table, waiting until the shocked silence ended. His brother, Shane, sat to his right, and the woman who held his heart, Laney Jacobs, sat to his left. Josie Dean, Shane's wife, sat next to her husband.

"Pregnant?" Josie whispered, her pixie-cut blond hair swishing when she shook her head. "Really pregnant? Are we sure it's Nate's baby?" So much hope lived in Josie's tone that Matt's heart thumped.

"Yes." Matt reached out and grounded himself by slipping his fingers through Laney's. "Nate has the amnio results, and he also has a sense of the baby and can hear a heartbeat. Chances are good it's Nate's kid, considering the scientific exploration and past history."

"Wow." Shane leaned back in his chair and drew in a deep breath. He smiled, showing dimples that might be charming in any other face. In Shane, they appeared dangerous. "We can have kids."

Matt nodded, surprised by the emotion welling inside him. Through him. They could have kids.

Laney tightened her grip on his hand, as if she felt his turmoil. "This is wonderful news." Her voice, cultured and sweet, served to calm him as nothing else on earth. "After all the failed tests from Dr. Madison, it turns out the Dean brothers can have kids—with the right woman." She snorted and shook her head. "Who knew?"

Matt chuckled. Her sense of humor always eased his stress. However, he seriously doubted his sperm could tell the difference between eggs, but what the hell. Maybe God did give a shit and was actually looking out for them.

Shane rested muscled forearms on the heavy oak table. "Nate honestly asked for help?"

Yeah. For the first time in, well, ever. "Yes." Matt eyed Laney. "He needs us to prepare for Audrey to come here." Three days ago, Matt would've said no way. Now? Things were different.

"Of course," Laney said, as always waiting patiently. "What else?"

"Shane and I are going to DC in an hour."

Shane narrowed his eyes. "No way did Nate ask that."

"No." Matt shook his head.

"I can be ready in ten minutes." Shane pushed back from the table.

Laney nodded, intelligence shining in her brown eyes. "Good plan. I'll get my bag in case you need help—we can leave Josie in charge of the ranch."

"No freakin' way." Josie's eyes shot sparks. "If Nate needs help, we're all going."

Matt had expected the fight, and he appreciated everyone's desire to help. While Nate had told him to stay in Montana, no way would he leave his brother alone right now, and the women would be safe in Montana.

The ranch was secured with fences, electricity, land

mines, and a cache of weapons. In addition, Nate had created several escape routes if necessary. The safest place for Laney and Josie remained in Montana, and he couldn't do what he needed to do in DC and worry about them. "You're both staying here, because our trip to DC will be short."

"How so?" Shane asked.

Matt flattened his free hand on the table. "We get in, get info, and get out. With Nate and Audrey." And the baby.

How messed up was Nate's head right now? Matt cleared his throat. Nate had never gotten over Audrey, and now she carried his baby. There was no way his younger brother remained clearheaded right now, and confusion got soldiers killed. An urgency to get to DC propelled Matt from the table.

Shane rubbed his neck, no doubt feeling the same pressure. "We need to hurry."

Matt nodded and said a quick prayer to a God he wasn't sure existed to protect Nate. The guy would go off half-cocked to challenge the commander in order to protect Audrey, and that wasn't the way to go. For the first time in his life, Matt worried about what Nate would do.

Matt turned toward Laney, a former surgeon. "Start researching pregnancies and births, and get me a list of what we need here. An ultrasound machine, a crib, all those other baby things people need. I'll buy them under the radar and get them here."

"Put them somewhere secured," Shane said quietly.

Matt started and focused on his brother. "Right."

"Why?" Josie asked.

Matt took a deep breath. "Audrey lost the baby last time, and I'd rather Nate didn't see all the baby stuff here in case something goes wrong." Frankly, medical experiments had never gone quite right for the Dean brothers, and hoping for a different result might end in further heartbreak.

Shane sighed. "We need to be prepared in case the baby makes it, and we need to be prepared otherwise. For Nate."

Nate wouldn't survive if he lost another baby. Matt hadn't known Audrey very well, but his gut whispered that she couldn't take the loss, either.

For years, Matt had relied on Nate to keep him sane, and now it was Matt's turn to protect the brother who'd never wanted protection. "Let's go get him," Matt muttered as he went to pack a bag.

Laney followed him quietly, and in the other room, Josie argued vehemently with Shane about going to DC. It was an argument she'd lose, but Josie gave everything her all, which was one of the many things Matt adored about his sister-in-law.

Matt threw supplies into a bag and turned to eye Laney. "You going to argue with me?"

Tall and curvy, the brilliant woman nevertheless barely reached his chin. Delicate and strong, she held his heart in her hands every day. Soft, doelike eyes studied him. "I'm not going to argue." Stepping forward, she slipped her arms around his waist and rested her head against his chest. "I understand you have to go. It's Nate."

Matt closed his eyes at her open acceptance of who he was and what he had to do. "Thank you."

She squeezed harder, her breasts pressed against his ribs and awakening his groin. "You're welcome. But don't think for a second I'm staying here if you're in danger. Get your job done, and get back here before I sign on with Josie and we head south."

Matt smiled over her head. His woman didn't bluff—a fact he'd learned early and the hard way. "We'll be careful, and I'll check in." Reaching down, he lifted her chin and slid his lips against hers. "You're my everything, Laney."

She returned his kiss, leaning back to stare into his eyes. "Right back at you. Be careful, and bring Nathan home."

"I will." As a vow, it was absolute. Matt only hoped his brother would be in one piece when he brought him home. He'd already lost Jory; he couldn't take losing Nate, too. As Laney relinquished her hold to go find him some fresh laundry, he allowed all semblance of humanity to release him.

It was time the commander came face-to-face with the killers he'd created.

Audrey snuggled into the sheets as the storm raged outside. Hopefully the men watching her apartment got nice and wet... and ended up with pneumonia. Unlikely, though. *Tough* was the kindest word to describe anybody trained by the commander.

Her stomach growled again. Interesting. All the nausea lately... all the exhaustion—turned out it wasn't stress. Neither was the five pounds she'd put on.

A part of her, the rebel deep inside, wanted to strike out at being violated in such a way. Her doctor, the one she'd trusted, had impregnated her against her will. Without her consent.

Fury threatened to choke her. They'd taken control of her body to impregnate her, and they could've chosen anybody's sperm. She could be pregnant with a complete stranger's kid right now—even one of the commander's psychopathic soldiers who enjoyed the killing. Who lived for it.

The only reason they'd chosen Nate's specimen was

because he'd impregnated her before, so they had at least a little success to draw on and try to copy. Thank goodness it was Nate's kid.

A baby. A real baby, inside her. Even more so—Nate's baby.

The miracle of that curbed Audrey's anger while also filling her with a determination only a mother trying to protect her child would understand. Sharp and fierce, the feeling grounded her like never before.

For now, she needed rest. Nathan Dean patrolled the apartment like a Doberman looking for dinner, and at least for the night, she felt safe. He wouldn't let anything or anybody come near her.

She'd offered him half of the bed, but one look at the war raging in his eyes had sent her to bed alone. There was no way that man would be sleeping any time soon.

But she had the baby to think of, and babies needed sleep. Probably. She should get ahold of some of those baby books. At that thought, she slid into a sleep punctuated by moments from the past.

Her dream was more of a memory of when she'd sat on an examination table in the main lab, her mind calculating the different ways of navigating the compound to get to Nathan. She'd been exiled from the facility since the breakup, and only the current medical issue had forced Audrey's mother to bring her to the facility.

She was bleeding.

Fear for the baby welled up in Audrey as she waited for the results of the internal ultrasound.

She had to find Nathan and had been trying to reach him from the second she'd discovered the pregnancy. He deserved to know, and he'd figure out what to do. Once she made sure everything was all right.

Pregnant women spotted. She'd read it in a book, so this was okay. Everything was going to be okay.

Isobel Madison's high heels clicked into the room, her gaze on a series of printouts. "We lost the fetus. Fetal development ended a week ago." She pursed her lips, her thoughtful gaze now on Audrey. "We'll need to do a D and C so we can examine the tissue."

Audrey swayed, catching herself on the wrinkly paper. "Wh-what?" That couldn't be right. Her mother was wrong.

Isobel frowned. "Get ahold of yourself. The pregnancy was unheard of, so we can't be too shocked. Start thinking like a scientist, would you?" She turned for the phone, ordering a medical team to perform the D and C.

So much pain welled up in Audrey that her eyes stung. Her entire body ached. She watched, almost in a daze, as the woman who was supposed to love and protect her calmly proceeded to make plans.

This was wrong. So damn wrong.

Audrey shoved off the table and drew her dress over her head. She'd get to Nathan. He'd figure everything out. They could save the baby.

Deep in her heart, she knew it was too late. The tests didn't lie.

But she needed to find Nate anyway.

With a rough shove, she pushed past her mother and ran into the narrow hallway.

"Audrey—" her mother called out, pure exasperation in her tone.

Audrey didn't look back—just kept going. Then running. Running toward the exit to find the barracks.

A crack of thunder ripped through the day. Then another.

The ground shifted. Tiles slammed up into the air. Audrey cried out, hands protecting her face.

What was happening?

A wall collapsed in front of her.

She fell, tiles cutting into her knees.

Fire.

Booming, angry, licking…fire suddenly surrounded her. A beam fell, and agony ripped up her leg. She cried out, her vision graying.

Another beam fell, hitting her shoulder. Smoke filled her lungs. As she fell back, hurt and helpless, she screamed one more time, "Nathan!"

A hand shook her shoulder, and there he was.

"Nate." She launched into his arms, her heart beating enough to hurt. "Blood. I'm bleeding."

He quickly carried her through the bedroom and deposited her in the bathroom. "Bleeding?"

"Yes." She gulped down air, trying to differentiate from the past and the present. Panic and fear fuzzed her vision. "Give me a second." She gestured him out and shut the door. Her stomach hurt. She'd been through this before.

Not again.

How could this happen again?

Sitting down, she used the toilet and then looked. The breath swooshed from her lungs. No blood. None.

Oh. She dropped her head into her hands. It was just a dream. This was different, and this baby would live.

"Everything is fine," she whispered in case she'd scared the baby.

The door flew open. "I can't wait outside," Nate said.

Audrey slowly lifted her head and shut her knees. She was on the toilet, for goodness' sake. Her face heated. "I'm fine."

Nate dropped to the ground and leaned against the counter. His normally tanned face had gone white. "You're not bleeding?"

"No." She wanted to reach out and reassure him, but right now, her body remained in a curled-up position. "I had a bad dream. About last time."

Nate scrubbed shaking hands down his face. "You screamed out my name."

"Um, yeah." She sat up and nonchalantly pulled up her panties without standing. Her knees trembled. Sitting seemed like a good idea for a few moments.

He lifted his chin, gaze piercing. "Did you yell my name that day? When the world blew up?"

Her mouth opened, but no sound emerged. Sometimes the truth should remain in the past. But there were some people on earth you couldn't lie to, and the father of her child, even without his amazing gifts at finding the truth, deserved honesty. "Yes."

His deadly eyes closed.

Seconds passed. Nate didn't move, and Audrey slowly hugged herself. No aches—no pains. Good. She shivered in the cool morning air.

Nate's head jerked up. In a smooth motion, he stood and lifted her right off the toilet to place back into the bed. Without a word, he stalked from the room and reappeared a few seconds later with a glass of milk. "Drink."

Audrey sat up, eyeing the thick white liquid. "Ugh."

"Calcium."

Okay. One of them had to speak in a complete sentence. "I'm not sure cow's milk is so good for you anymore. Last week at the coffee shop, the barista and a customer got in a huge discussion about cow's milk versus almond or soy milk, and the barista said that we're the only species on earth that drinks another species's milk, and now there's a bunch of added hormones in it." Besides, she really didn't like the taste of milk. Never had.

Nate scratched his head. "Almond milk?"

Audrey lifted a shoulder. "We should get some books."

"Yeah." He reached for the e-reader on her small desk. "I'll start downloading."

Audrey yawned. "What time is it?"

"Almost dawn." Nate pressed several buttons and nodded to himself. "You should get more sleep."

She blinked, her heart rate finally slowing down. Nausea swirled around her stomach. "Nah. I'll get up and maybe stretch a little bit."

Nate set down the tablet and tugged his gun from his waist to place next to it. A deadly weapon near the tablet downloading information about babies. The paradox wasn't lost on Audrey.

"These will take time to download." His gaze remaining on her, he tugged his shirt over his head and kicked off his jeans. "Scoot over."

Her heart fluttered. "Um, I'm not sure—"

One muscled knee pressed down on the mattress before he nudged her to the other side. He lay down, turned, and pressed her back against his front. "Just to sleep."

Instant warmth, safe and male, surrounded her. She wiggled a little to get comfortable, her butt caressing his erection. She froze.

"Relax," he whispered, heated breath warming her ear.

Desire uncoiled throughout her neck to her sex. "I am," she breathed. "Maybe we could—"

"No. Not until we read the books and know it's okay." Nate flattened his palm across her abdomen.

The gentle touch contrasted so completely with the hard-muscled body cradling her that emotion sparked alive in her. He filled her so completely just by being near. The idea that he might be taken away in a second by the deadly chip plagued her until she could barely breathe.

Fear had a weight, and she needed to fight that. So she cleared her throat. "We should come up with a plan we can all three live with." How odd to say "three" like they were a real family.

"I know." Nate kissed her gently on the ear. "Now sleep."

CHAPTER
21

NATE AWOKE QUICKLY, immediately reaching for his gun and sliding from the bed. Somebody was in the apartment.

Somebody good enough to get inside without alerting him.

He left Audrey sleeping and crossed the room, gun low and ready to fire.

At the doorway he paused, listened, and stepped into the hallway to shut her door. They'd have to go through him to get to her.

Two guns cocked simultaneously, one at his left ear, and one at his right.

He froze and his shoulders relaxed. "Damn it," he muttered.

Ignoring the weapons, he moved forward and into the living room, pivoting around to glare. "What the holy fuck are you two doing here?"

Matt grinned and slipped his gun into his waist. "I love such a heartwarming welcome, don't you, Shane?"

Shane rolled his eyes, eyeing the antique rug covering some of the wood floor. "I think my boots were dirty. Sorry."

Nate shook his head, his carefully laid plans dissolving on the dirty rug. "I told you to stay in Montana, and I'd bring Audrey to you." What the hell were his brothers thinking? They couldn't be this close to the commander—not all three of them at once. It was too risky.

Matt shook out his wet black hair. "Oh. Is that what you meant by telling us to stay the fuck out of DC?"

"Yes." Exasperation filled Nate's head with static.

"Humph." Shane gingerly stepped back onto the rug. "We must've got that wrong. We thought you were in trouble and needed help." His lip lifted in a smart-ass grin. "Oops."

Nate stilled and tried to remain cold. He studied his brothers. Both stood well over six feet and had taken natural, muscular builds and honed them to deadly efficiency. Matt's black hair curled over his collar, while Shane's shaggy brown hair almost reached his shoulders. A *fuck you* to their military upbringing.

Both men returned his stare with identical gray gazes—full of understanding.

"You shouldn't be here," he said, close to breaking, as rain slashed against the windows.

"*Never alone*," Matt whispered.

The mantra they'd coined as scared children—a promise to each other. A vow.

Nate shook his head, his heart pumping hard. "You have more important things to think about than me." Josie and Laney for a start.

"No." Shane stood even taller. "We don't."

"Shane—"

"No." Shane lowered his chin. "Do you think we don't know you? Know what you've done to protect me and Jory? How you sacrificed yourself to give us a childhood?"

"Or fought to keep me from going insane?" Matt asked. "Why would you expect us to be any different than you? If you're in trouble, we're here. Period."

Nate swallowed. Those were *not* tears pricking the backs of his eyes. He didn't cry.

Two of the deadliest men in the world stood across from him, offering help. Offering themselves. His *brothers*. He blinked and nodded, both humbled and taken aback. "Thank you."

"Sure." Shane shrugged and strode toward the kitchen. "I'm starving. Any good food here?"

"Leftover sandwiches," Nate said, his gaze remaining on Mattie. "The ranch is secured?"

"Yes."

"You engaged the outside tracking field?"

"Of course." Matt sat on the couch. "Is your head on straight?"

Nate sat on a chair, curling his bare toes into the rug. "I don't know."

"Well, why don't we start there?" Matt leaned his massive forearms on his knees. "A baby. You're having a baby."

Warmth that might be joy welled up through Nathan. Followed by terror. The bittersweet moment caught him hard in the chest. He wanted to be ecstatic, but the kill chip in his spine counted down the end of his days too quickly. "Yes. I'm going to be a father." Putting aside the fear that he didn't know how to be a father seemed appropriate since he needed to find a way to stay alive first. One challenge at a time.

"Congrats, bro." Mattie smiled, delight in those deadly eyes. Hardness and determination filtered through. "So. I guess we'd better start planning how to survive."

• • •

Audrey shook sleep from her eyes and wandered through the apartment to the living room, where she stopped short.

"Hi, Audrey," Matt said gently.

Shane waved, his mouth full of food.

Nate smiled.

She gulped. The Gray brothers. In her living room—three of them. And here she stood in tiny shorts and a see-through shirt. Slowly, she slid a foot backward. "I, ah, need to get dressed."

Matt surveyed her. "You're supposed to wear loose clothing during the second trimester. It helps with circulation and nausea."

Shane swallowed and nodded. "And nonslip socks. You could easily fall on that wood floor."

Nate leaned forward. "You read up on pregnancies?"

"Yep," the other two Gray—make that Dean—brothers said in unison.

"What did you read about cow's milk?" Nate asked, reaching for a pen and notepad.

Twilight Zone. Crazy Town. Alternate universe. There was no way Audrey stood, half dressed in her own living room where the Dean brothers currently discussed cow's milk, magnesium, and something called a breast pump. No freakin' way.

She turned. "I need a shower."

"Make it under a hundred degrees," Matt called after her.

Where had reality escaped to?

She nodded and kept walking, her mind fuzzing. *Under a hundred degrees?* Mathew Dean, the deadly soldier who'd furiously and sometimes cruelly trained his brothers to kill, *to survive*, under impossible odds, was giving her pregnancy advice? In a cheerful voice?

No, no, no. She shook her head, trudging into the bathroom to drop her clothing as she made her way to the shower to turn the knob to warm. This had to be another dream. No way were three Dean brothers, the commander's *most wanted* on earth, hanging out researching pregnancy in her living room. Impossible. It was more likely she'd been transported to an alternate universe. One where up was down and grass was pink. Or purple.

Warm spray cascaded over her as she stepped inside the roomy shower, allowing the heat to soothe her tight shoulders.

One tiny groan escaped her when she pressed a palm against the dark tile to lean into the water, inviting warmth to wash down her back. Heaven—and possibly a bit more than a hundred degrees.

Apparently she'd need to get caught up on pregnancy before Nate knew more than she did. The man would be a steamroller at that point—making sure she followed all the rules.

She took her time shampooing her hair, breathing in steam and calming her lungs. Finally, the water began to cool as she finished shaving her legs. She lifted her head...and the world spun.

Crazy, wild, and hazy, the tiles spun around her. She pushed out of the shower and cried out, going down. A thick rug cushioned her fall.

Boot steps echoed, and the door flew wide open.

"Aud?" Nate skidded to his knees in front of her.

"Is she breathing?" Matt asked, grunting as he was pushed aside.

"Make sure she's breathing," Shane said urgently, dropping to his haunches.

Audrey blinked, trying to clear her head. She was buck-ass naked. "G-get out," she croaked.

Matt knelt down, his eyes dark with concern. "What did she say?"

Nate ran a hand down her arms, obviously looking for broken bones. He quickly moved on to her legs. Her very bare legs.

Audrey sucked in air. "Get the fuck out—now!"

Shane chuckled. "Honey, it's not like we haven't seen—" He lurched back, alarm on his face, as she lunged at him.

She could kill them all. Scrambling on the carpet, she sprung, only to have Nate catch her and take her back down.

"Towel," he ordered, holding out a hand.

A towel suddenly appeared, and he covered her from neck to knees. "Hold still, Audrey," he said, his face giving no quarter as he felt for the pulse under her neck. Counting, he waited, his gaze staying on hers. "What happened?"

Her mind fuzzed again. Good thing she was lying on her back. "I got a little dizzy."

Matt leaned around Nate. "You have to take it easy."

Shane nodded, peering around Nate's other side. "You should've sat down."

Fire raged through Audrey, and she stretched to jab his nose.

"Whoa." Nate captured her hand and pressed it on the carpet. "Guys? Do you mind giving us a second?"

Matt ducked his head to get a better look at her face. "You sure she's okay? We should take her to a doctor."

"I'm fine," Audrey said through gritted teeth. "Except there's way too much testosterone in my bathroom all of a sudden with three of you here."

"Four. The baby makes four guys." Shane grinned quick dimples and stood back. "She's okay." He disappeared, whistling down the hallway. The tune was horribly off-key but sounded familiar. *Mission: Impossible*?

Matt patted Nate on the shoulder. "Call me if you need me." The door closed quietly behind him.

Audrey struggled to get up, only to have Nate press both her shoulders to the ground.

"Stay still for a moment." He remained on his knees, caressing her shoulder as if he couldn't quite stop touching her. "I want you to take inventory from head to toe, right now. Slowly."

"Nate—"

"Now."

She rolled her eyes. "Fine." Taking stock, she mentally checked on every bone, every muscle, and all her skin. "I'm okay."

"So what happened?" His huge hand smoothed back her hair as if she were something infinitely fragile and breakable.

For some reason, his kindness pissed her off. "Don't worry, your baby is fine." No way would he be so nice if she wasn't carrying his child. At the thought, her eyes filled. All her life she'd been an experiment, cared for because of something having nothing to do with who she was or wanted to be. Her mother had wanted a daughter to carry on her own brilliance, and the commander had wanted to use her as a pawn. Even the senator needed her for intel.

And now Nate wanted her because she happened to be pregnant with his child.

Part of her knew she was being unreasonable, but the emotions wouldn't stop bombarding her. Darn hormones.

"Okay," he said slowly, his brow furrowing. "How are you?"

"You don't care." She sniffed, trying to turn away.

He bit his lip. "Is this hormones?"

"Yes." She sniffed again. "I'm suddenly having a lot of them."

"That's normal, Audrey."

"Oh, shut up, Nate." She pushed him away to sit. What did he know about normal? "You're only being nice to me because I'm knocked up with your kid."

He cupped her jaw, his smile sweet. "Do you really believe that?"

"No." She sat with her back against the wall and picked at a nub on the towel still covering her. "I feel weird."

Nate sat back. "Weird how?"

She shrugged. "All of a sudden, things are popping out of my mouth I don't mean. And I really, *really* wanted to punch your brother in the nose a few seconds ago."

"Sweetheart, don't worry about words—you can say whatever you want. As for Shane, we all want to punch him on a regular basis. That's normal."

Audrey huffed out a laugh. "Your brothers saw me naked."

"I'll kill them if you want." He managed to keep his lips tight as he offered.

"Funny." Embarrassment hunched her shoulders.

Nate leaned forward and glanced down the front of the towel. "First of all, they were worried about you and didn't have time to appreciate your marvelous assets." His lips wandered along her collarbone. "Unlike me."

A quiver wandered down her back.

He tugged the towel down to kiss along the tops of her breasts. "My brothers should be the least of your worries."

Warmth flooded her veins. "What should I be worried

about?" she murmured, leaning back and allowing the towel to slip.

"I just read that having sex during the second trimester is fine," he murmured, licking along her skin.

She blinked while desire awakened inside her. He was trying to calm her, to distract her, and it was working. Wait a minute. She threaded her fingers through his hair and clenched. The scowl across his features made her smile as she held him off of her. "Your brothers both can hear as well as you do."

"So?" Nate's frown deepened.

"So?" She pushed him away and shoved herself to her feet. "No way, buddy." She couldn't be quiet, no way, and she wasn't giving the Dean brothers a free show. Or listen. Or whatever.

Nate smoothly stood. "You're kidding."

"Nope." She gestured him toward the door. "Now, if you don't mind, I'd like some privacy."

He stepped into her space. "Last time I gave you privacy, you ended up on the floor."

She lifted her chin to meet his gaze. "If you don't get out of the bathroom, I'm going to make sure you end up on the floor."

He held up his hands in surrender and opened the door. "More hormones," he muttered as he disappeared from sight.

She sighed. "Nate, you know I'm going to work today, right?" she called out.

"The hell you are," came the swift response.

Yep. She might as well get dressed before the battle of the day began. Now she'd have to take on all three of the stubborn Dean brothers, but not until she'd had breakfast.

• • •

She felt more human when she'd gotten dressed and fixed her hair, going minimal with the makeup. Her stomach rumbled, so she reluctantly exited her room to head to the kitchen.

"Nice boots," Mathew said, his back to her as he finished scrambling eggs on the stovetop.

Audrey paused and glanced behind her to the empty living room.

"Shane went to scout the area and take notes on the men watching you, and I sent Nate for a run," Mathew said, not turning around. "Sit down, Audrey. We need to talk."

She hovered, her nerves firing. Matt Dean had always seemed larger than life—dangerous and hard as steel. Until she'd gotten to know him through Nate's eyes, she'd feared him as much as she feared the commander.

Steeling her shoulders, she crossed to sit at the table, where two places had been set with milk, orange juice, fruit, and plates. How mad was Mathew at her for hurting Nate? Would he want her to disappear, even though she was pregnant?

He turned, a massive man—wearing a bright yellow apron at his waist.

Humor bubbled up and she coughed into her hand.

"What?" Mathew frowned down at the apron and shrugged. "Seemed appropriate." Stalking forward with the grace of a hunting wolf, he slid eggs covered with cheese onto her plate.

Slipping the empty pan into the sink, he took a seat. "The eggs and cheese are good protein, and the fruit has all sorts of vitamins."

She couldn't do this. "Mathew—"

"Matt." He unfolded his napkin, his movements graceful

and deadly all at once. "Family calls me either Matt or Mattie."

She swallowed. "We're not family."

Matt pinned her with those odd gray eyes. "You're carrying my nephew. That makes you family."

She frowned and reached for a fork. "But Nate and I—"

"Need to figure things out." Matt nodded for her to eat her eggs. "Whatever you two decide works for me. But that doesn't mean you're not family now, whether you like it or not."

Being part of Matt's family didn't seem like an easy road, but it might be the safest one available to her. "I'll do anything to protect this baby," she said, not sure if it was a threat or a statement.

Matt wrinkled his nose. "I wonder what that feels like." He eyed her, cocking his head to the side.

"What?" Being pregnant?

"Having a real mom—one who cares." Matt shrugged. "Through the years, we've all wondered what that would be like." He pointed to her abdomen. "The little Dean in there is a lucky guy."

Surprise and warmth flushed through her. "Um, thanks." She took a bite of eggs and nearly groaned at the wonderful flavor. "I guess I don't really know what that feels like, either." Her mother truly didn't give a fig about her and never had. Not really.

"Yeah." Worry creased Matt's forehead. "Talk about a bunch of lost people trying to raise a baby. None of us know what a normal family is like."

She chuckled, finally relaxing. "No, but at least you know what family feels like. That'll help."

"Yeah." Matt dug into his fruit and grimaced.

"What?" Audrey asked.

"I hate grapefruit." He took another bite. "But I figured if I was going to talk you into eating it, I should try it, too."

What a sweetheart. The guy would make an excellent uncle. "I thought you'd hate me for hurting Nate." Crap. She hadn't meant to bring that up during their peaceful breakfast.

Matt pushed the fruit cup away. "I've never hated you. For the brief time you were together, you made Nate happier than he'd ever been."

"But I hurt him."

"You did, but none of us ever thought it was because you'd stopped caring. We knew the commander forced your hand. You just made the wrong decision." Matt happily scooped eggs onto his fork.

"The wrong decision?" She dropped her fork. "Are you crazy? You all sacrifice yourselves on a daily basis for each other, and I made the wrong decision to keep Nate alive?"

"Yep." Matt eyed her downed fork pointedly and didn't continue speaking until she'd regained it to eat more eggs. "Call it old-fashioned, but you don't get to sacrifice for Nate. You know him better than that."

The eggs were good. It was hard to hold on to temper with good eggs warming her tummy. Yet she gave it a good shot. "That's Neanderthal-like and ridiculous."

"Yep."

Audrey tried to think of a rejoinder, but the lug was agreeing with her. She studied him, suddenly curious. "Did you ever find somebody, Matt?"

He stilled, sitting back to study her.

For some reason, she held her breath.

Finally he nodded, his entire face changing into something more approachable. "Yes. Her name is Laney, and she's a pistol. Sweet, tough, and brilliant." The love in his words held a determined strength.

Relief and the oddest gratitude filled Audrey. Matt trusted her. Really had made the decision to trust her. "Laney sounds amazing."

"She is." Matt grinned, looking almost boyish. "I have to admit, learning that Nate could have kids has given all of us hope. We'd love kids..." Something dark swirled in his eyes as his grin slid away. "If we live."

"I know." Audrey finished off her eggs, her stomach aching. Survival seemed nearly impossible sometimes, and she had to dig deep for hope. She eyed the orange juice. Nope. No acid for her today.

Matt leaned forward and rubbed his chin, his smile appearing forced. "Shane is married to a woman named Josie who gives him fits on a daily basis. It's hilarious." More sadness than humor colored Matt's tone.

Apparently Matt was as worried as she was about the kill chips. Audrey's head jerked up. "Shane is married?"

"Yes." Matt nodded. "You'll meet both Laney and Josie soon, when we send you to headquarters."

Ah. Okay. Audrey took a deep breath. If she could get Matt on her side, Nate would be easier to deal with. Either way, she needed to stay in DC until she discovered the commander's alternate training facility. "About that. I'm staying here." She sat back to convince one of the most stubborn men alive to help her convince *the* most stubborn one. Either way, she was staying—with or without their agreement.

CHAPTER
22

HOURS LATER, AUDREY congratulated herself on a feat beyond most human beings: defying three Dean brothers at once. Even though she'd almost convinced Matt by the time Nate returned, Nate made some good arguments. They'd objected, but she'd persevered, saying she had work to do and wouldn't leave the building—and she promised to head out of town the second they discovered the commander's alternate training area.

She'd driven herself to work and hadn't spotted or sensed the commander's men tailing her, so maybe her mother had convinced them to back off.

However, now the Dean brothers had staked out the three entrances, so there was no way for her to leave without being seen. With the brothers so close, their enhanced hearing allowed them to listen in on her conversations. Was it enough for them? No. They had to give her a minute earpiece so they could communicate with her, too.

Her hair covered the device, and the volume refused to be turned off.

"What are you doing now?" Nate's voice echoed in her ear, sending delicious tingles just under her skin.

She shifted her legs under her desk. "Trying to work on a budget for the senator's Christmas party next year. Now stop bugging me."

"Funny."

She frowned. Oh. Bugging. Yeah, that was funny.

The senator limped inside to drop into a chair. "Mornin'."

Audrey released her pen and leaned forward. "Are you all right?"

"I tripped while running last night." The senator wiggled gray eyebrows. "Not as swift as I used to be, I guess. How was your medical appointment at the facility?"

Audrey coughed. "Fine. My leg is as good as it's going to get." She wasn't quite ready to share her pregnancy news with the senator.

Nash sighed. "I do worry about so much medical knowledge and power being in one place without oversight. While I'm thankful the doctors were able to save your leg, I do fear what havoc they might wreak."

"I agree." The experiments conducted by the commander's scientists needed to be revealed and studied. Who knew what laws had been broken and what victims had been used? She'd even been impregnated without her knowledge or consent. Who else had they used for experiments?

The senator leaned forward. "There are some laws of nature that can't be broken. You don't think they've tried to clone human beings, do you?"

Audrey shrugged. "I've read it's medically impossible to clone humans, but who knows? I've never heard of it."

"That's an abomination against God." The senator rarely let his religious roots show, but when he did, it was absolute. "You can't create a soul from another human."

Audrey kept silent, not wanting a debate so early in the

morning. She figured if somebody was alive, they had a soul. But since the science of cloning had only reached sheep, cows, and possibly organs, she didn't find the point relevant.

She also didn't want Nate hearing such silly nonsense. The guy had always wondered if he had a soul, and she knew with every inch of her being that he did have one. "I'm sure everyone has a soul, Senator." She shuffled papers. "Any news on Darian's death?"

"My contacts confirm that the police have zeroed in on a suspect. Some crazy stalker from Darian's football days." The senator sighed. "He was such a good man. I can't believe somebody would kill him."

Audrey nodded. The commander had found a scapegoat to get her out of the limelight, now, hadn't he? Even though the commander hadn't been involved, he'd still set up some poor sap to get Audrey free and clear to continue working on his behalf. Somehow, when the truth came to light, she'd expose that lie, too. "Why did the guy kill the cabbie?"

"I don't know. Something about wanting to kill anybody that had been in Darian's vicinity." The senator shrugged. "Crazy, crazy stuff. The guy is in custody, so you're safe."

"Good." She'd always been safe from the setup crazy guy.

The senator sighed. "To be honest, I wondered if the commander had Darian killed."

Audrey shook her head. "Doesn't make sense. While Darian worked as a lobbyist for a rival military firm, his death doesn't really change anything when it comes to funding or your recommendation. The firm is still strong and wants funding."

"I know, but I thought maybe it was a warning to me?" The senator rubbed his wrinkled forehead. "You and I have both been working with Darian."

"No." Audrey's mind reeled as she tried to make sense of chaos. "The entire situation is too obvious. The commander would never have sent three men into a public bar to kill. He would've sent men late at night, and there wouldn't have been witnesses." Plus, no way would Audrey have been able to escape three of the commander's men.

The senator leaned forward. "Who do you think the woman was? The one with Darian?"

Audrey smoothed her face into curious lines. "I have no clue. More importantly, why hasn't she come forward?"

"Good question." The senator stood, and his briefcase slipped open. Manila files, pictures, and a bunch of papers spilled out all over the floor.

Audrey chuckled and hurried around the desk to help. It was amazing the senator rode horses—the guy was such a klutz. Her knowing that fact made her feel like an insider, like they were close. Although she hadn't met the senator until adulthood, the affection she felt for him seemed daughter-like. They'd both been alone in the world, so why not bond? He was the only man she trusted besides Nate. "Let me." She scooted everything into a pile and stilled, taking up a piece of paper.

"What's this?" she asked.

The senator peered over her shoulder. "That's a drawing of the brand found on Darian's shoulder. I copied it from the FBI interviewer."

Great drawing with wonderful detail. Smooth ink lines showed a deadly, sharp dagger with the word "PROTECT" on the glinting blade. The menacing nature of the form sent shivers down Audrey's back. "Did you draw this?"

"Yes." The senator puffed out his chest. "You should see the charcoal drawings I've done of my ranch at home. When I retire, I may paint."

She nodded and slowly stood to hand him the bundle of papers, wincing as her leg protested. "What do you make of the brand?"

"I've been researching it on the Internet." The senator glanced around as if to make sure nobody listened. He lowered his voice. "I haven't found anything yet."

Audrey bit her lip. The last thing she needed was a U.S. senator acting like Sherlock Holmes and getting himself shot. "I suggest you leave the investigation to the FBI. Whoever sent those men to kill Darian meant business."

The senator shoved the mass back into his briefcase. "I know, but I'm so curious. The FBI agent said Darian had recently been branded, so it had to have something to do with his death, right?"

"Maybe." Audrey discreetly backed up to her desk to place the drawing behind her. "But we have work to do, Senator."

"Right." The senator shook himself and angled his body toward the doorway. "I have a meeting with the commander tomorrow morning, and I hope to get the information from him. Would you like to attend?"

"Yes," she said, just as a resounding, "Absolutely not," echoed in her ear.

She swallowed. "I would love to attend."

Nate growled over the transmitter stuck in her ear. "You are not attending any meeting with the commander."

"What time and where?" Audrey asked the senator.

"He's having a car pick us up at eight, and we're having breakfast at the facility," the senator said.

An instant flurry of threats and expletives poured out of the device in Audrey's ear. She blinked several times and tapped the device, clearing her throat. "That sounds lovely, Senator."

"No fucking way," Nate said.

The senator glanced down at his white dress shirt. "Should I wear a tie tomorrow?"

"Yes." Audrey smiled as her ear finally went silent. "Maybe the blue and white striped one? It's in your top desk drawer."

"Ah, good." The senator grinned, suddenly looking years younger. "You're the best."

"Thanks."

The senator reached the doorway and turned back around. "I'm quite curious to meet your mother. Are you sure you don't mind tagging along?"

"Not at all." Audrey leaned back against her desk. "My mother is quite charming, if she wants to be. I imagine you'll see her good side tomorrow." Not the real woman, without question.

The senator's faded blue eyes filled with sympathy. "Don't worry, Audrey. We're gonna take them down."

Nate quit swearing and rolled out a blueprint he'd created of the commander's local facility. The rickety chair squeaked loudly around the cabin when he moved. "The weak points are here and here," he said, pointing to the south and east of the area. "Though, it's obvious those are the weak areas."

Matt nodded and tapped an entrance to the west. "This one looks well manned, but I think we could get through there the easiest. The other two are traps."

"Yeah." He reached back and rubbed the rock-hard muscles in his neck as Audrey hummed show tunes in his ear. The woman probably didn't even know she was singing. "Aud? I'm going to tune out for a few minutes. Don't leave your office," he said.

"Bite me," she answered cheerfully.

He removed the earpiece to toss on the table. "I'd forgotten how crazy she makes me." Romance and rosy glasses shaped his memories of Audrey. Now, having her in his world again, reality arrived with a bite. The woman drove him insane sometimes.

Matt nodded, his gaze serious. "I have Shane out acquiring materials to wire Audrey tomorrow when she goes into the facility. You need to decide right now if we're taking this route or not."

Nate's temples began to pound. "If I say no?"

"We find another plan." Matt's voice stayed level. "I can't make this decision for you, and I won't. If you decide we force her to Montana, then that's what we do."

"But the intel she could gather tomorrow might be invaluable." Nate wanted nothing more than to force Audrey to safety—and not only because of the baby. The idea of anything happening to the blue-eyed smart-ass shot spikes of terror through his brain.

"Definitely." Matt leaned back, stretching. "If Audrey didn't want to go, it'd be a done deal, and we would come up with plan B. But Audrey wants to go. So the ball is in your court. Does she go or not?"

"I don't think she'd appreciate our deciding for her—or even our thinking we had a right to decide." Nate wondered again why he couldn't have fallen for a nice, compliant woman.

"Definitely not." Matt snorted. "When she went after Shane this morning, even after almost fainting, I almost laughed my ass off. I always knew she was tough, but the woman has no clue how delicate she is. I really like that."

"I like that, too." Nate shook his head, trying to uncover the fine line between protecting someone and making them want to kill you. "While Audrey was raised by Dr. Madison and knows the commander, she truly doesn't realize who he is. She spent so much time in boarding school and then college abroad that she doesn't realize what he's capable of."

"I know." Matt's gaze shared remembered horrors of being trained by the monster. "So your point is that Audrey can't really make an educated decision based on her knowledge of the situation?"

Man, that sounded good. Too bad Audrey wouldn't fall for it. "While that's true, I don't think Audrey will care."

Matt leaned forward. "She's trying to save you and now this baby. You can't blame her for taking risks."

"I don't." But that didn't mean he had to allow her to take the risk. While she'd probably hate him, he did have the strength and the determination to get her out of town against her will. But something in him, something deep, wanted her to work with him instead of against him. "What would you do?" Nate asked Matt.

Matt exhaled and rubbed his eyes. "Fuck, I don't know."

Yeah, that about summed up the shit-storm going on.

The door burst open, and Shane lurched inside. "You guys watching the news?"

Nate sat straighter. "No. Why?"

Shane hurried over to flip on a flat screen he'd bought the day before. The scene filled with reporters outside of Audrey's apartment building.

"What now?" Nate stretched to his feet.

"Dead body." Shane turned toward Nate, his eyes wide. "Found inside Audrey's apartment. Some guy named George Fairbanks."

CHAPTER
23

AUDREY SAT AT the senator's conference table with him protectively flanking her right. Two FBI agents sat across from her, one gently asking questions and the other staring at her as if measuring her for a prison jumpsuit. Obvious interrogation tactic.

"As I was saying," Agent Clacker said, elbows resting on the table. A kind smile lifted his lips, making him appear about thirty years old and earnest. Very earnest. "We agreed to this interview at the senator's office because of our respect for him and his office."

Audrey nodded, noting that any respect for her wasn't mentioned.

"Tell me about your relationship with George Fairbanks," Clacker said.

Audrey shrugged. "The senator and I have had several meetings with George Fairbanks regarding TechnoZyn and its possible building of manufacturing plants in Wyoming, which as you know, is the senator's home state."

"Have you met George Fairbanks alone?" Clacker asked.

"No."

"Unlike your relationship with Darian Hannah." Clacker slipped a picture of Darian across the table. A dead Darian on an autopsy table.

Audrey swallowed, nausea rising up. "Not true. I had a business relationship with both men."

"Both men?" the up-to-now silent Agent Farland asked. He frowned down a hawklike nose, his gray hair curling over his collar. Definitely the more seasoned of the pair.

Temper flared at the base of Audrey's neck. "We weren't having a devil's three-way, Agent. I knew both men in a professional capacity, as did the senator."

Senator Nash leaned her way. "What's a devil's three-way?" he whispered.

On all that was holy. She kept her face bland and turned toward him. "Kind of like an orgy with one woman and two men. It's the rage in erotic romances right now."

A bright red crawled up the senator's weathered face. "For goodness' sake, Audrey." He cleared his throat and faced the agents. "I can vouch for Audrey, here. She wasn't romantically involved with either Darian Hannah or George Fairbanks, and I believe I attended every meeting she had with them."

"Except Audrey and Darian's date two nights ago at Anchonies," Clacker said, a gleam in his dark eyes.

"Wasn't a date," Audrey returned.

The door opened, and a man in a poorly cut beige suit stomped inside.

"Excuse me, but we're in the middle of an interview," Clacker said, rising to his feet.

"I know," the man said, waddling around the table toward Audrey. "I'm Miss Madison's attorney."

Audrey frowned and looked closer. *Nate?* Couldn't be.

The man making his way laboriously toward her weighed three hundred pounds—very soft pounds. He wore blond hair to his shoulders, with the mustache and beard covering his face a slightly darker blond. Brownish eyes squinted out from behind large spectacles.

"Um, I didn't call for an attorney," she said, watching him closely.

"Yet here I am." He reached into his pocket and took out cards. "Bubba Jenkins, at your service."

Holy crap, it was Nate. Even though his voice was higher and carried a Southern twang, she'd know his voice anywhere. He'd chosen the name Bubba? Her make-believe name for a dom who spanked him. Very funny. What in the heck was he doing?

She nodded slowly, searching his ruddy face. How had he turned his complexion so sallow? "I barely recognized you."

He beamed a wide smile, showing several silver caps on back teeth. "Thank you for noticing. I just lost seventy pounds." Grunting, he tugged back a chair to wedge his bulk in between the armrests. "So, what are we talking about?"

Her mind reeling, Audrey turned back toward the agents. "We were discussing the dead body found in my apartment."

"How did he die?" Nate asked, twirling the picture of Darian's body around and around with one finger.

"Somebody slit his throat," Agent Clacker said.

"At her apartment?" Nate asked.

"No. The lack of blood spatter in Miss Madison's kitchen indicates George Fairbanks died elsewhere before being dumped at her apartment."

Her kitchen. Her bright, cheery, undecorated kitchen

where she'd eaten breakfast with Matt that morning. She eyed Nate. Would Matt have killed George Fairbanks? She crossed her legs, trying to get comfortable. "How was George Fairbanks found?" she asked.

"Anonymous call," Clacker said.

That was odd. Audrey eyed Nate. "Obviously somebody is trying to draw attention to me. Why?"

"Or maybe they're trying to scare you," the senator mused. "With Darian dying and now George Fairbanks being found in your apartment, it seems like this is directed at you. Why?"

She shrugged. "I work for a U.S. senator and am easier to get to than you are. Maybe this is about you, Senator." Though something in her gut warned her the murders were all about her. She sat up straighter. "What if—"

"No conjecture," Nate cut in smoothly.

Her head jerked. He was right. Her thoughts had instantly gone to the commander and the myriad of soldiers who'd escaped five years ago. Maybe one of the freed soldiers was going after the commander and Audrey's mother, and she was the best course to do so. The Dean brothers weren't the only men out there who hated the commander.

Audrey had almost said too much.

Agent Clacker leaned forward. "What were you going to say?"

"Nothing." She clasped her hands together on the polished table. "I was wondering what Darian and George Fairbanks have in common besides both meeting with the senator this week." Darian worked as a lobbyist for a military organization, and George Fairbanks was a top executive for a technology firm also vying for military funding. "Do you have a connection?"

"Not yet, but we're working on it. So far, you're the only connection. Well, you and the senator." Agent Clacker's tone made it all too clear he considered her the key.

Nathan hitched his created bulk around in the chair as if unable to get comfortable. "George Fairbanks died earlier today when Miss Madison was meeting with the senator. Her alibi is solid."

"We agree Miss Madison didn't kill George Fairbanks, but she may have knowledge about the crime." Agent Clacker's expression softened as he turned his attention toward her. "Lying to federal agents is a crime, and I want to assure you, we're here to help. Don't be afraid."

Audrey bit back a laugh. Lying to federal agents? If the guy only had a clue. "Thank you for your concern, but I've told you everything I know."

Agent Clacker sighed. "There's one more thing the men had in common." He slid another picture across the table. "George Fairbanks had the same brand on his back—a much older brand—as Darian Hannah. What does the brand mean?"

Audrey's mind spun as she glanced at the PROTECT brand down George's back, the edges blurry and gray with age. "I have no idea."

Farland's phone rang, and he lifted it to his ear. "Yes." He listened for several moments and then clicked it shut. "Miss Madison, we'd like you to view your apartment to see if anything is out of order or missing. The body has been removed."

Her hands shook, so she slid them off the table to her lap. "Um, okay."

Nate pushed back from the table, his chair protesting. "I'll drive Miss Madison, and we will meet you there."

Audrey stood, the world morphing. Oh no. She gulped.

Her mind spun. Nausea slammed into her. Covering her mouth, she pushed by Nate to bolt from the room, barely making it to the bathroom before she threw up her entire breakfast.

Heaving, tears in her eyes, she flushed the toilet and limped to the sink to wash out her mouth. She spit and held her stomach, taking several deep breaths. She could handle this. Time to buck up.

Patting down her hair, she turned to head out of the bathroom so she could view a crime scene in her own apartment.

Nate kept one hand on the steering wheel and one on her thigh. "Are you sure you're all right?" he asked again, weaving her car in and out of traffic as they entered Virginia.

"Yes. Morning sickness is normal." Well, she'd probably thrown up because of the picture of a dead body, but why admit that? She tugged on the seat belt to give her belly a break. "How did you get rid of the FBI agents?" When she'd finally exited the restroom, only Nate had been waiting.

Nate grinned beneath the thick beard. "I told them they'd upset you and that I'd bring you to the crime scene when you were good and ready. Then the senator pretty much kicked them out of the office. I like that guy."

"Me too." Audrey glanced at her watch. "He better have gone to the budget meeting."

Nate turned a corner and glanced in the rearview mirror of her compact. With his disguise, he barely fit behind the wheel. "The senator said you'd be worried about the meeting and to let you know he left for it."

"Good." Audrey glanced at the storefronts outside the window. "This isn't the fastest way to my apartment."

"I know." Nate released her leg to press a button on his cell phone. "Matt?"

Something crackled over the speakerphone. "I see him," Matt said. "Gray SUV, no plates. Two cars behind you. I'm behind them in a white Escalade."

Audrey gasped and started to turn around.

"No," Nate said, bite in his tone. "Look forward and act normal. Matt? Can you tell how many men are in the SUV?"

"Negative. The windows are tinted." Matt swore, and a horn honked in the distance. "Freakin' cabbies can't drive. Take the next left onto Wilson, and I'll cut these guys off."

Nate reached down and unbuttoned his jacket. "I'm not armed, Mattie. Just left the Senate building."

"I know," Matt returned.

Audrey glanced at Nate and opened the glove box, taking out a Glock 23. "I'm armed." She released the clip, tapped it against the side of the car, and slammed it home.

Nate's left eyebrow lifted. "That's my girl." He eyed the console between them. "Any chance you have a knife in there?"

"Um, no." She tugged open the middle console. "Two pens, leather gloves, and a notepad."

"Great." Nate held out one arm. "Pull, will you?"

She nodded and yanked on the arm of the cheap suit. Between the two of them, they managed to get the roomy jacket tossed into the backseat. Audrey peered closer at the rubbery suit covering Nate's chest. "What in the world?"

"Pretend fat." He cranked the wheel to the left. "I'm leading them away from the public—we can't afford witnesses," he muttered.

"Affirmative," Matt responded through the phone. "Take a right on Jones and a left on Mayberry. I'll ram them into the fifth empty lot I see, and you head out."

"We don't know how many men are there," Nate snarled.

"Doesn't matter. Get Audrey to safety. I can handle anybody in the SUV."

Audrey's eyes widened as she watched the unmoving phone. "He sounds different when he's giving orders."

"I know." Nate glanced in the rearview mirror, obviously torn between loyalties.

Audrey grasped the gun. "I say we help Matt. Don't worry, I'll shoot if necessary."

Nate eyed her and turned back to the road. "No."

She gulped, her gaze searching outside at crumbling buildings and empty, littered lots. "I've never been to this part of town. Where's Shane, anyway?"

"Acquiring materials." Nate jerked the wheel to the right and hit the accelerator. "Matt, we just passed a lot that slopes down. If you hit them right, they'll go spinning down and maybe out of sight. Keep going, and we'll rendezvous at Audrey's apartment."

"I'd rather chat with them and see what they want," Matt said tersely.

Nate exhaled, his nostrils flaring. "Me too. But not without backup—one of *your* rules, Mattie."

Matt muttered what sounded like expletives in German. Or maybe Russian.

Nate reached over and tugged on Audrey's seat belt. "Face forward, relax your body, and get ready for speed. I'm going to take a hard right, and then we're going fast."

Adrenaline flooded her bloodstream. She nodded and dug her nails into the armrest. "I'm ready—"

A rush of movement burst from an alley to the left, silver glittered, and a car smashed into them. The screech of metal cutting into metal filled the air, and Audrey screamed. Momentum threw her head sideways into the window, shattering glass. Pain radiated down her face and through her head. The world fuzzed. Her seat belt tightened, holding firm and bruising her chest.

Nate swore and tried to control the car. The vehicle spun around, twirling.

Twin airbags exploded, sending dust flying. Audrey's hit hers mid-center, shoving her back into the seat. The gun flew out of her hand. One of their tires exploded as the car tipped up and over a curb.

"We've been hit," Nate yelled to the phone, which had spun onto the floor. "Three men in a silver SUV."

Panic cleared Audrey's vision, and her hands went instinctively to her abdomen. The baby.

The car finally stopped spinning, dropping onto flat tires with a hiss. Nate glanced down at the floor and picked up the gun and the phone. Less than a second later, he'd kicked open his mangled door with above-human strength. His unnatural bulk caught on the dented steering wheel and he shoved himself out, already firing.

Calm. Determined. Cold.

No emotion, no wasted movements, no humanity.

Audrey gulped and smashed the now deflated airbag off her legs. Dust whirled around. She coughed, her hands shaking as she tried to unbuckle her belt.

Nate would certainly put his body between her and bullets. She had to get out of the car. Now.

Return fire impacted the hood of the car. Fear rushed her movements. Crying, trying to see, she finally unbuckled her belt. Hard and unyielding, her door hampered her efforts to get out. She had to get out. Finally, her slapping hands found the knob, and she pushed open the door, instantly hitting the rocky ground. Glass cut into her knee, but she stayed down and shut the door, crawling to the rear of the vehicle.

A black SUV jumped the curb, propelled by an even bigger Escalade. Two men jumped out of the SUV, while Matt Dean barreled out of the Escalade, gun out and blazing.

She back-crawled down the side of her car toward the front.

Gunfire echoed all around her.

In the span of three more heartbeats, the world silenced.

CHAPTER
24

NATHAN DROPPED THE empty gun and surveyed the scene. A kill shot between the eyes had taken out the first guy, and a bullet to the heart had stopped the second. The third guy, the one yelling directions at the other two as he had hidden behind an open car door, had taken a bullet to the knee. He finally moved away from the SUV, his eyes a wild black and filled with desperation. Not exactly someone trained in combat. Good.

No emotion, no frantic thoughts zipped through Nate's brain. Immediate calculations clicked through his thoughts. One target, holding a Smith & Wesson Black Ops Spring Assist Knife. Two dead from his hands, no threat there. Over to the left, Matt fought hand to hand with one man, while another bled out on a pile of old newspapers.

Audrey's heart beat rapidly from the other side of the car, and the baby's kept pace.

With measured steps, Nate kept advancing on the wounded man. "I have one alive here," he said loud enough for Matt to hear. "Finish yours."

A neck snapped with the finality of a quick death,

and Nate didn't bother looking. His brother wasn't even breathing heavily.

Only one survivor. That's all Nate needed.

His heart rate remained calm and steady, and no emotion clouded his movements. Just as he'd been trained. Quick as a snake, he kicked the knife out of the guy's hand.

Blood slid down the guy's face from a head wound probably sustained in the crash. Fury lit his black eyes, and more blood matted his stringy blond hair to his head. "You're dead," he growled.

Nate struck for the gut, doubling the guy over. A kick to the injured knee, and the man went down near the blade embedded in a discarded A&W Root Beer cup. Almost casually, Nate lifted the phone to his ear and speed-dialed Shane.

"What?" Shane asked, chewing on something.

"How soon can you get a tow truck to the middle of Jackson Street outside of Arlington to the west?" he asked, pressing his boot against the downed man's jugular. The guy started to flop like a snake worshipper about to sing in tongues.

"Fifteen." Shane stopped chewing and started moving. "I'll have to steal it."

"Hurry." Nate clicked off.

"You have any tape?" Matt called.

Nate pressed harder with the heel of his boot. "No." He slid his foot free, leaving an imprint of his boot swelling on the guy's neck. Dropping to his haunches, Nate claimed the knife still stuck in the soda cup. He stood and stabbed himself in the chest.

The guy screamed.

Nate smiled and drew the knife down through the fat

suit. He couldn't stand the heat any longer, finally shuck-
ing the stupid thing. Cool air brushed his bare chest, and
he nearly sighed in relief. "That's better."

With now-smooth movements, he dropped to his
haunches, hand on the knife. He struck with a clean swipe
to the chin. Red spurted instantly. "Hello," he said casually.

The guy's dark eyes darted around frantically. His
hands curled into fists on the dirty rocks.

"There's nobody left but you." Nate wiped the knife off
on the man's dark shirt. "Know why?"

The guy swallowed, his eyes filling. "No. Why?"

"You're the guy in charge, right?" Nate ignored the
sound of Matt opening and shutting SUV doors as he
searched for tape. "I heard you calling the shots."

"Yes." The guy looked over at his dead buddies, his
face contorting in pain and fear.

Nate tapped the knife against the guy's chest, regaining his attention. "What's your name?"

"Jon." He swallowed several times. "I have money.
Anything you want. Don't kill me."

"How much money, Jon?" Nate opened his senses to
the empty lots and abandoned buildings all around them.
No heartbeats, no cameras. A report of shots may have
been called in, but the police wouldn't arrive to this area
any time soon.

"Anything you want." Jon eyed the knife. "Just don't
kill me."

"Found duct tape," Matt called out. "Not ideal, but
it'll do."

Relief loosened the rigid muscles in Jon's face. "You're
taking me hostage?"

"No." Nate maneuvered the blade under Jon's chin.
"The tape isn't for you."

Fear scented the air. "What do you want?" Jon asked.

"I want to know why." Nate didn't see a need to expand.

"The woman." Jon glanced at Audrey's demolished car. "I'm supposed to get the woman."

For the first time, anger pricked between Nate's stoicism. "Why?"

Tears filled Jon's eyes. "I can't tell you."

"Then I don't need you alive." Nate lifted a shoulder in a shrug and started to dig in with the knife.

"Wait!" Snot slid from Jon's nose. "They'll kill me if I say anything."

"You have a more immediate threat to your life." Nate saw no reason to lie. "I have no problem ending you right now."

Jon sniffed. "Okay. We were told to get the woman. She was with Darian Hannah when he died, and she has information we want."

Nate leaned down. "Information about what?"

"Beyond my pay grade, buddy." Jon sighed, his body relaxing. "The people I'm with, they don't share everything. She knows something."

Nate scraped the blade over Jon's Adam's apple. "Does her knowledge come from Darian or somewhere else? Something from the senator?" Or the commander?

"I don't know." While Jon's heart beat rapidly, the rate didn't change a wit. "I truly don't."

"I believe you." Nate stood and turned toward Matt, who'd finished taping the fingers of the two men he'd taken down. "Get prints?"

"We'll see." Matt headed over toward the two Nate had killed.

Nate looked back down. "How many of the men here are with your group?"

"Just me. The rest I hired. They sucked." Jon's lip twisted.

"Who's your group?" Nate asked.

Jon shook his head. "We don't have a name—we exist to make things right. To protect the sanctity of life."

The asshole sounded crazed. "What does that mean?" he asked.

A maniacal light entered Jon's eyes. "It means life is pure, and we have to fight for it. We will win."

What in the world?

"Who else is in your group?" Nate asked.

"I'm new. Darian and I were inducted at the same time." Jon started coughing, his body convulsing.

Nate nodded and turned to see Audrey standing on the other side of the demolished car. Her skin nearly glowed she was so pale. Blood flowed from a cut along her face, and pure terror darkened her eyes to cobalt. Several rips marred her shirt, and one hand pressed protectively against her abdomen.

"The baby is fine," Nate said quietly. "I can hear his heartbeat." Actually, that didn't mean the baby was fine, but Nate needed her calm. The baby needed her calm. He began to stride toward her with the intent of sitting her down.

Her eyes widened. "Nate—"

Faster than a thought, he pivoted and threw the knife to land squarely in Jon's neck. The man dropped the gun he'd tried to draw from his boot, blood gurgling out of his mouth.

Nate turned and kept walking toward Audrey.

She blinked, sucking in air. "You didn't check him for another gun?"

Nate shook his head. He hadn't needed to check Jon— he'd seen the outline in Jon's boot. As Nate reached

Audrey, more emotion tried to break through his training. He shoved it back and reached for her chin. "How bad is the cut?"

"I don't know."

A vehicle rumbled in the distance, and a beat-up tow truck came into view. Shane reached the scene and jumped out. "What happened?"

Nate lifted Audrey and strode to deposit her gently in the passenger seat. "Get her car."

Shane nodded and leaped back into the driver's seat to maneuver the truck into place.

Nate turned toward Matt as he finished taping Jon's fingerprints. Nate reached down and ripped open the man's shirt. Bruises and cuts marred his skin, but no tattoo. Using one hand, Nate flipped him over.

"Shit," Matt said.

"Yeah." Nate eyed the fresh brand of a sharp blade with the word "PROTECT" down the middle. "Looks fresh. Maybe as fresh as Darian's was."

Who were these people, and what did they want with Audrey?

Nate snapped a picture of the brand with his phone. "We need some answers. Let's go."

Audrey swallowed and tried to look innocent from the dented examination table. Cool air brushed her bare tummy since she'd tucked her shirt under her bra. Talk about different than the commander's medical facility.

The doctor slipped on rubber gloves, her red hair wild around her shoulders. Laugh lines fanned out from her green eyes, while dark circles marred her pale skin. "You folks just caught me. We close at seven. Bad accident, huh?"

"Yes, but I'm not spotting or anything. No cramps, either." Audrey nodded, her heart thundering. The accident had been a bad one. She couldn't lose another baby. Fear tasted like metal in the back of her throat. "My purse is still in the car," she whispered.

Nate clasped her hand, dropping to his haunches next to her. His face remained calm, but a quick glance at his hands showed that one trembled. "I have cash, Doctor."

"This is a free clinic, folks." The doctor squirted gel onto Audrey's stomach. "Pay what you can, but don't worry about it. I'll give you the best medical care I can." She pressed the wand on Audrey's abdomen.

The baby chose that moment to flip over.

Nate straightened. "Did you see that?"

Audrey gasped. The baby was moving, so that meant he was alive. Relief clouded her eyes with tears. Her throat clogged. "The kid is an acrobat," she breathed out. *Please, let him be okay.*

The doctor hummed to herself, pressing the device along Audrey's stomach, staring intently at the screen. Finally, she turned off the buttons. "The baby is developing well, and I see all the major organs are functioning," the doctor said, turning off the machine. "He's pretty well insulated in there." Reaching for a towel, she gently wiped off Audrey's stomach before lifting her shirt. "Your uterus and the amnio sac both look healthy. I'd be more worried about this bruise from the seat belt."

Relief burst through Audrey, and she shut her eyes for a moment before opening them. The baby was all right. She was so afraid for the little guy, but she had to calm herself.

Nate frowned and stood, leaning over for a better look. "How worried?"

The doctor shook her head. "Not that worried." She

smiled at Audrey. "But definitely take it easy for the next couple of days."

"Bed rest?" Nate asked.

The doctor laughed. "No. You can do all normal activities, but no running marathons or digging ditches for a few days."

"Sex?" Audrey asked, fascinated by the red flush suddenly crossing Nate's face. She had never seen him blush.

"Sex is fine." The doctor helped Audrey pull down her shirt. "Just don't try to hang from the ceiling for a few days."

"Well, there went that idea." Audrey winked at Nate.

Nate lifted his head as the shower in the other room turned off. Audrey had been in there for nearly thirty minutes, and he'd started to worry. The shower wasn't that luxurious in his cabin, and he hadn't figured there would've been enough hot water for such a long shower.

"Relax," Matt said softly, finishing his Internet search. "We made her lie down for an hour, and both of us listened to the little guy's heartbeat. He's fine."

Nathan nodded. "I know." The baby seemed fine, and Audrey hadn't bled or cramped or anything. Besides a shallow cut above her eyebrow and a bruise across her chest from the seat belt, she'd left the crash relatively unscathed. Physically, anyway.

Matt shut down the computer. "I sent an anonymous donation to that clinic for a million dollars. Good enough?"

"Perfect. Thanks." Nate needed to relax.

Matt leaned back. "I hacked into several databases, and the men who attacked us all have records. Robbery, drug possession, intent to distribute, one kidnapping, and two manslaughters. Hired muscle."

"And Jon?" Nate asked.

"No criminal record. He's ex-military, honorably discharged. IRS records show he worked as a bouncer at J&D's bar in DC." Matt stood and stretched his neck. "We have to find out what Darian knew—what everyone is afraid he told Audrey before he was killed."

"If that's the information they're seeking." Nate bit down a growl.

Matt nodded. "Good point."

"Did you do a search on the brand? The PROTECT knife?" Nate asked.

"Yes. There isn't anything on the Internet that I can find." Matt maneuvered around the couch to reach the door. "I need to go get supplies for tomorrow, and you need some time with Audrey. He drew on a jacket. "Shane will be back by morning. I told him to take her car several states away and burn it. The thing won't be found for quite some time."

Nate nodded. "Thanks, Mattie."

"No problem." Matt paused at the door, his gaze serious. "How pissed was the FBI that you didn't take Audrey to the crime scene?"

"Pissed." Which was all Nate needed. "But as her attorney, I explained that they'd upset her too much, and she'd be by tomorrow to look at the scene."

"Will she?" Matt asked quietly, the question loaded.

"I don't know." Everything in Nate bellowed for him to get her to a secured location before something happened to her. "She's pretty determined to go with the senator tomorrow and act like a spy." Plus, although she wouldn't admit it, he knew she wanted access to the facility's medical advancements to make sure the baby was all right. He couldn't blame her, even though she'd just seen a doctor.

The commander had the best doctors in the world under his thumb.

"Let me know." Matt shut the door behind him.

Nate sighed and scrubbed both hands down his face. A fire crackled in the corner and rain pattered softly on the windows. Now that he could finally relax, emotion slammed into him with the force of a dropping anvil. Not soft, not sweet, he burned with energy. With the need to hit something. Hard. So he stood and stretched his neck, drawing in several deep breaths to calm himself.

He refused to let Audrey see him out of control.

Shit. He didn't get out of control. Ever.

But at the memory of that SUV slamming into them, of the airbags deploying, of gunfire splattering the car where Audrey had sat...rage rolled through him. Too strong, and too hard to fight. He should've had Matt stay so he could go for a run. Maybe burn off the lava burning his blood. Yet he smoothed his face into calm lines as the door opened and Audrey walked out, wearing only his T-shirt.

He swallowed. Anger swiftly morphed into something else. Something dark and with an edge. "Are you all right?" he asked, his voice lowering to a huskiness he couldn't hide.

She nodded, smoothing the bottom of the shirt down. The boxiness of the shirt emphasized her femininity. Naked. She was naked under there. "Yes." Her bare feet made little sound as she pattered across the room to reach him.

The scent of woman and gardenias nearly dropped him to his knees. If anything happened to Audrey or the baby, the kill chip would be welcomed to do its job. Her intelligence intrigued him, while her spirit challenged him. But the woman deep down, the one full of kindness and generosity...that one owned him. "Are you sure you're fine?" he asked, tuning in to her vitals.

"Yes." She took a deep breath. "I'm fine, although I could use some clothes." Her nipples poked out from under his shirt, and her taut thighs led down to toned calves. Even the scars along her left leg appeared graceful somehow. The symmetry of the pins seemed perfect. "How are you?" she asked.

Having totally inappropriate thoughts, considering what they'd been through. The fact that she stood so close, happy to be bearing his child, humbled him. Protecting her was all that mattered. "Good." He had to get away from her before he grabbed her. "I'll make dinner."

Her hand on his arm stopped him. "I don't want dinner."

He started, glancing down at her eyes. They'd turned the color of the ocean depths...dark and barely blue— sensual in a powerfully feminine way. Hunger simmered there along with emotion. A turmoil no doubt brought about from their close brush with death and the gratefulness at being alive. Maybe by something more...him? He didn't deserve love from somebody like her, but if offered, he'd take it with hunger and never give it back. "You should eat," he managed to grind out.

He sensed her fear and tasted the tears she'd shed earlier. Deep down, he understood her need to get lost in the present.

But his present was full of danger, and he shouldn't relax.

"Where are your brothers?" She kept her gaze on his.

"Out for the night." The words barely made it out of his mouth. The entire night. With Audrey, alone. What had he been thinking? As gently as he could, he unraveled her fingers from his wrist. "I need a moment, Audrey." It was as close to admitting a weakness as he'd ever come with her.

"Too bad." She pivoted to put her body between his and escape.

"Audrey—"

"Shut up, Nate." She stepped into him, her body flush with his.

He shut his eyes, pummeling down instant lust. Way down. The events of the day, his woman so close, the rage against the time counting down on his life—it was all too much. No way would he hurt her, so he needed time and space to rein himself back in. "Please move," he whispered.

"No," she whispered back, her hands sliding under his shirt to press against his abs. "I'm perfectly fine, and you're perfectly fine. A couple of bruises for either of us is no big deal."

The gentle touch from her shot his body into overdrive. "I'm not in control." He opened his eyes. Everything in him hated admitting that to her.

Her smile held power. "So?" Stretching up on her toes, she kissed the pulse suddenly pounding at his neck. "We're alive. At least for a very short time, we're here and together."

Unable to help himself, he cinched her arms. Too hard and too tight. "You'll be here for a long time, I promise. No matter what happens to me, you'll be okay. You and the baby." He'd clear a safe path for her if it was the last thing on earth he accomplished. His back muscles vibrated as he held himself back. "Now step away."

"No." As graceful as any dancer, she slid down him, her palms along his legs, to land on her knees. "I don't think so."

His cock hardened and pressed against his zipper, fighting to get out of his jeans. Nate held perfectly still.

Don't move. Her mouth was way too close to his dick. Way too close. The beast inside him, the one he secretly doubted held only human DNA, roared with the need to pounce. To take Audrey all the way down and make sure she knew exactly who she belonged to. *His woman*. Now and forever. "What are you doing?" he asked.

She chuckled, the sound all female and challenging. Staying on her knees, she skimmed her palms up the inside of his legs and his thighs. "I'm perfectly fine, and so are you."

He groaned, fighting against self-imposed chains. But his feet wouldn't move. He could easily jump over her and leave the cabin. Yet his feet remained in place, his thighs tightening, all the blood in his body rushing to one place.

The sound of her releasing his zipper echoed much louder than he'd expected in the small cabin. Not even the rain gathering strength outside masked the sound. When he'd changed after the fight, he'd just donned jeans. No shirt, no boxers. With a happy hum, Audrey took him in her hand.

His knees nearly buckled. "Don't—"

Her tongue flicked out and licked him.

At that one contact, in that one second, the beast in him took over.

CHAPTER
25

AUDREY LICKED NATE again, electricity dancing through her veins. Kneeling in front of the deadly soldier gave her the most satisfying sense of empowerment. She trailed his jeans down his legs. A vibration settled through his thighs, and yet he kept still. So painfully still.

But he wanted to move, didn't he? The poor guy wanted to get away from her—to keep her safe.

The real Nate Dean, the kind, gentle man deep down... she saw him. The sexy soldier and hard-bodied charmer had intrigued her right from the start, but the man inside had stolen her soul.

She'd never gotten it back.

It was a freakin' miracle they were both healthy and fine... and she wanted to celebrate that fact. Plus, she'd spent most of her shower time thinking and remembering the attack and how easily Nate had shifted into soldier mode. The cold, deliberate killer who'd run toward spraying bullets in order to protect her had scared her a little bit. In their time together years ago, she'd never truly seen that side of him. The side created by her mother and the commander. The aspect in him that made him such a good soldier—deadly and strong.

She needed the *man*. His courage, his strength, his gentleness with her. Only her. Even more so, while he might not realize it, he needed her.

They were lost souls, without a doubt. Maybe they'd found each other for this brief time. For so long, she'd been alone. Had her own space and plenty of room to plan her life. Once she succeeded in taking down the commander, she'd planned to disappear. To find a small house in a small town and become part of a community.

Not now. Now she had Nate to save and a baby to protect. Suddenly, her life was full. Because of Nate.

So she licked along his shaft to the base, smiling when he groaned again.

Intense passion lived in Nathan Dean, and she'd caught glimpses of his true nature. The loyal brother who loved so completely, who sacrificed so easily, had taken on that role with his brothers on purpose. Even after Audrey had hurt him so badly, he'd been kind to her. Before finding out she was pregnant, he'd been protective.

The coldness in him was necessary for surviving his childhood and for working through his adulthood as a soldier. But his perfect control didn't belong between them, and it was time she showed him he could trust her. Trust her with everything.

So she tipped her head back and took him deep.

"Holy shit," he muttered, his hands threading through her hair.

He tasted like male and spice—all Nathan. Drawing him out, she caressed her tongue along his base.

"Audrey," he murmured.

"What?" She sat back and looked up at him, pleasure

rippling along her nerves. As she focused, her breath caught.

The expression on his face was new. Raw need, male demand. Heavy-lidded, his eyes glowed a darkened gray. Strong and cut hard, his jaw clenched, crimson spiraling across his rugged cheekbones. His hands tethered and then released her hair, sliding down to her biceps to lift her. Easily. Very easily.

Once she reached her feet, he kept lifting until her thighs tightened against his hips.

Strong fingers latched on to her butt, and he kicked his jeans away. He strode through the room, avoiding furniture while keeping his gaze completely focused on hers. No hint of gentleness, no inkling of concern glimmered in those unreal eyes. Just hunger.

When her ass hit the table, she gasped. Cold and rough, the wood scratched her skin. Fire exploded inside her, dampening her thighs. She'd assumed he would take her to the bedroom, and the idea that he wanted her too much to wait melted her from the inside out. Made her wet and soft.

The thin T-shirt covering her flew across the room, baring her. His eyes flared with a predatory light.

Delicious and wicked, a shiver tingled down her spine. Keeping his gaze, she slowly widened her legs on either side of his thighs. Daring him.

His jagged chuckle nearly threw her into an orgasm. Rough and thick, the pad of his index finger drifted along her bottom lip. Smiling, she opened her mouth and sucked it in. His nostrils flared. He tugged, and she released his finger with a soft *plop*.

With a primal gaze, he watched his finger as the pad brushed down her chin, her neck, and wandered between her breasts.

She breathed out, heat flaring along the path of his wet finger. A hollowness set up deep inside her, an ache only he could fill. Yet his finger trailed traitorously slow, over her naval, down her shifting abdominal muscles, right to her clit.

He pressed.

Sparks torpedoed inside her. Her mouth opened on a gasp, and she tilted toward his hand.

His upper lip quirked in male satisfaction. In an emotional connection.

Keeping his finger right on her, he leaned in, his lips grazing hers. Not enough. Nowhere near enough. So she reached up and snagged his arms, yanking until he bent down and she could seize his hair. Digging her fingers in tight, she pulled him to her mouth. Taking.

Her tongue swept inside as he remained still. As if he could remain in control. So she softened her assault, teasing and tempting. Layer by layer, she felt his control shred. His breathing sped up first. Then he slowly, easily kissed her back, taking over so smoothly she didn't realize it until she couldn't get enough oxygen into her lungs.

Her body flared alive, tingling. Finally, he released her mouth and kissed a path down to her breasts, where he nipped hard enough to make her catch her breath in her throat. Smiling, he laved the small wound. She moaned, trying to move against his too-still finger. Desire flared so hot it burned, and she couldn't get enough.

The thought whispered through her that he'd taken control again as he gentled his movements, as his kisses softened.

So she tightened her hold on his thick hair with one hand and anchored his cock with the other. No hesitancy, no subtlety, she gripped him hard. From shaft to tip, she caressed him, her fingers not reaching all the way around but staying firm.

His mouth on her skin, he sucked in air, the muscles in his arms visibly fighting.

"Give it up, Nate," she murmured, leaning even farther down and grasping his balls.

He levered back, the snapping of his control confirmed in every line of his body. Catching her hips, he flipped her around, a firm hand pressing her down to the table. Her breasts scraped against the wood. She turned her head to the side in order to breathe, yet her lungs wouldn't cooperate as her heart rammed a staccato beat against her ribs.

Unyielding hands manacled her hips and slapped her back into a rock-hard erection. With one strong push, he thrust into her completely, not stopping until his balls hit her thighs.

Oh God.

She closed her eyes and tried to breathe out, tried to anchor herself in a wild storm she'd created as he pinned her to the table. He somehow shoved even deeper inside her, leaning over her, his chest against her back, his breath at her ear. "If your leg hurts, tell me."

Her leg? What leg? She may have whimpered a response.

He stretched her, filling her until he was all that existed. His skin against hers, the hair on his thighs tickling hers, his scent covering her. He rocked inside her, withdrawing and driving forward with a force that would've sent her across the table if he hadn't been holding on. Tight.

Hard and fast, the rhythm he set up coiled need tighter and tighter inside her. She gasped and tried to dig her hands into the table, shoving back. Close, she was so close.

Only Nate could do this to her. Make her forget everything but him. Any future she had included him—he couldn't die.

She tried to fight falling over, to hold on to the delicious ecstasy riding her, but he wouldn't let her. The powerful, steady pace increased, and he angled her slightly to the left. As her clit slid along the side of the table, the coils inside her detonated. She screamed his name, riding the waves, her mouth closing suddenly as the room sheeted white. The sensation shut down her system, so perfect and so intense. Finally, she came down from the heights, her body going lax.

The second she softened, his hold tightened, and he began to pound harder. She closed her eyes, lost in the bliss. Finally, he ground against her, his body convulsing. After what seemed like eons, he fell over her, his mouth at her ear. "No way in hell am I letting you go this time," he whispered.

Dawn broke with an angry storm matching the one building inside Nate. After he'd taken Audrey against the table like they hadn't just been in a car accident, he'd tucked her into bed, watching her sleep. The woman had slept like she hadn't slept in years.

He couldn't find it in himself to regret the previous night. She'd enjoyed him, and he'd enjoyed being himself with her and letting go. But now, more than ever, he couldn't lose her. Or the baby.

Awakening her had been one of the hardest things he'd had to do lately, but they had to get a move on.

"Stop frowning," Audrey said as she stood in her bra and pencil skirt.

"I'm not frowning," Nate said, frowning harder. Shane

had broken into Audrey's apartment to get her a full cache of clothes after ditching her car the previous night, so she had something to wear.

Matt glanced up from where he was taping a wire along Audrey's lower back. "Do you want to do this?"

"No. You're better at placing wires." Nate crossed his arms. "I don't give a crap if you see Audrey's pretty bra, Matt. Jesus. I trust you and my woman." It was the plan of the day that pissed him off. Completely.

Shane turned around from the computer on the table and gave him a look.

He looked right back. Yeah, he'd called her *his woman.* So what? Shane rolled his eyes and went back to the computer.

Nate smirked. If Shane had any idea what had happened on the table the previous night, he wouldn't be so comfortable sitting there.

"That's better, Nathan." Audrey smiled at him, lifting her arms for Matt to tape the wire closer to the back of her bra.

He smiled back, his mind reeling. "We need a different plan."

Matt sighed, his shoulders bunching. "We've been over this. If we need another plan, that's fine. But enough already."

Audrey put both hands on her hips. "The plan is for me to go in and videotape the facility so you have a better understanding of the layout. That's where we'll find information about Jory, which is our next step before we expose the commander. I understand your concerns, but I promise I'll take good care of the baby. Nothing will happen to him today."

"Damn it, Audrey." A rush of pure anger flooded

Nate's veins. "I'm as worried about you as I am about the baby. This is a bad idea."

She shrugged, glancing over her shoulder at the wires. "This is the only idea we have. The senator has invited me to the facility, and the commander is fine with me there, so I'm the right person to go. Plus, I wouldn't mind another ultrasound to check in on the baby, and Dr. Zycor has technology way beyond the hospitals in the area." She kept her voice level and her head down while she spoke.

Anxiety felt like needles in the brain. "Is something wrong?" Nate asked quietly.

She looked up and smiled. "No. I want to double-check, and Matt placed the wires along my back, so nobody will see them." Her cute hips wiggled when she reached behind her and tugged out a security card. "I still have Dr. Zycor's card, so maybe I can get into the secured areas, even if the commander doesn't invite the senator back there."

"They would've changed his card upon discovering you had it," Matt said, standing up.

"Maybe." Audrey reached for a shirt hanging on a table chair, donned it, and then buttoned up.

The ticking clock in the kill chips hung over their heads like an invisible mantel of sheer stone.

Tension oozed through the room, but nobody acknowledged it.

Matt handed her a pair of earrings that looked like man-made sapphires. "You'll need to keep your hair up so you don't block the camera. It'll be in your right ear."

Audrey slipped the earrings into place. "I understand." She walked in stylish flats over to the window and glanced out. "I can't believe you stole a car that looks exactly like mine."

Matt shrugged. "Red Toyotas are easy to find. We hammered out your license plates to put into place, and nobody should notice the VINs don't match. By the time anybody figures anything out, we'll be long gone from here." He gathered up extra wires and put them away in a metal case. "We're all set to go here. Nate?"

Nate studied Audrey. She was smart and quick. The commander wouldn't hurt her, especially since she now carried Nate's child. "If you think you're in any danger, you give us the code term. We'll launch everything we have to get you out."

She moved toward him and patted his arm. "Stop worrying. I've got this. We'll head to my place to appease the FBI, and then I'll go scope out the commander's base for you. Everything will go perfectly."

Nate swallowed. Never in his life had anything gone perfectly. By the looks on his brothers' faces, they had the same thought. He scrubbed a hand over his face. "Let's go over today's plan one more time."

CHAPTER
26

A FTER HOURS OF traveling, Audrey smoothed down her skirt while sitting in the back of a plush limousine. The urge to let her hair down hit her again, and she fought it.

The senator tipped back his head to drink a bottled water. The good kind. "It was nice of the commander to send a car for us," he said pleasantly.

Audrey smiled and tried not to laugh. The senator hated limos and anything with pomp or luxuriousness. "The partition is up, Senator Nash. The driver can't hear you." Although it had been fun to listen to the senator be polite for the long drive.

He rolled his eyes and leaned toward her to whisper, "I bet the place is bugged."

Audrey coughed into her hand. The place *was* bugged—by her. Maybe it wasn't ridiculous to wonder if the commander had bugged the limo, too. "Good point."

"How bad was your apartment this morning?" the senator asked.

She swallowed down bile. "Actually, the only thing out of place was a big pool of blood on the floor. I didn't find anything out of the ordinary." Nate had thrown on another fat suit and accompanied her to the apartment before she'd gone in to work. "My lawyer called a cleanup crew, and it should be good as new tonight." Of course, the smell of death might take a while to leave.

"I'm glad to hear it." The senator plucked on his tie, only stopping when Audrey lifted an eyebrow. "Why would somebody plant George's body in your apartment? Any new theories?"

"No, and I don't understand the connection to Darian and his death. I mean, with both men having that odd brand on their bodies." Audrey studied the senator, wondering how the commander was going to fix this one, considering he'd already framed somebody for Darian's murder. "Any thoughts?"

"No." The senator rubbed gray whiskers. "I forgot to shave, darn it. Oh well. Let's see if we can figure it out. Darian was a top lobbyist who wanted funds for his military group, and George was a brilliant scientist who considered building manufacturing plants in Wyoming. They both wanted something from me—money."

Audrey eyed his whiskers. He should've shaved. "That's not a motive for murder."

"I know." The senator tensed as they approached the first guarded gate. "Plus, they found Darian's murderer. So what's up with the weird tattoo? Here come the guns."

Audrey nodded and scooted closer to her window, making sure to point her ear toward the soldiers manning the gate. "They do have a lot of firepower," she murmured. The enforced gate connected to a small hut where one man stood in a standard black uniform, his hands and weapons out of sight. Two men flanked the gate outside the hut, each armed with automatic weapons, sidearms, and knives. After looking inside the limo, a guard opened the gate.

Two gates later, the car finally pulled up in front of the main building of the compound.

The commander waited, dressed in the standard black uniform, his hair cut like a steel brush even in the rain. The downpour didn't dare muss his hair. At the odd thought, Audrey accepted his hand in exiting the limo.

He glanced down at her, black eyes fathomless. "How are you feeling?"

"Fine." She brushed by him, not wanting to discuss the pregnancy.

He shook hands with the senator and led them both inside to a common conference room. The senator protested without sitting down. "I'd like to tour the entire facility, if you don't mind."

"I don't mind." The commander executed a perfect pivot, his hands clasped at his back, his boots polished until they reflected the light. "This way." He led them through the main facility and right into the private areas.

Audrey's heart galloped, and she made sure to look around so the camera could catch everything. While she could've drawn the layout for the Deans, there was nothing like a live recording. They went through the armory, the offices, and finally the labs, where people in white lab coats worked with vials, microscopes, and buzzing machinery.

At the last lab, the senator glanced through a closed door with a hazard warning on the window. "What type of experiments do you do here, anyway?"

The commander glanced at Audrey, and she nodded. While she certainly hadn't told the senator about the creation of soldiers in laboratories, he'd gotten the information from his sources.

"We use the labs for medical research in order to assist soldiers in healing quicker and better." The commander stood straight and tall. "We did have a failed experiment when we tried to raise soldiers from birth, but that program is long shut down."

Baloney. Audrey smiled and nodded. "That makes sense." She slowly walked around the lab, her camera catching everything.

A clicking of heels on tiles announced her mother's arrival. Audrey turned. "Hello, Mother."

Isobel slipped an arm around Audrey's shoulders and gave a somewhat maternal hug. "Audrey. How good to see you." All manners, the brilliant doctor held out a hand for the senator. "This handsome man must be Senator Nash. We haven't formally met."

The senator took her hand, standing tall and tugging on his tie. A dark flush covered his weathered face. "It's my pleasure, ma'am."

Good Lord. Audrey stifled a grin.

Isobel twittered. "My daughter didn't mention how handsome you were."

The senator snorted. "That's kind of you. I was asking about the experiments here."

Isobel patted his arm. "We try to make things better for soldiers. That's good, right?"

"Maybe." The senator glanced around at the expansive equipment. "But you don't clone people, do you? I mean, you don't use science that would be better left to God?"

Isobel's eyebrows lifted to her hairline. "Of course not. God has His place, now, doesn't He?"

"Yes." Relief crossed the senator's face.

"But weren't you offering good deals to George Fairbanks and his crew if they built in your state?" Isobel asked sweetly.

"They work on technology that speeds up computer processing," the senator said softly, as if speaking to a lady of years ago.

If the man had any clue how tough her mother really was... Audrey glanced down at the small-boned beauty who'd held the lives of thousands in her hands at one point or another.

Isobel nodded at the senator. "Yes, George's former group does work on computers, but they also have a grant for nanotechnology that might be used to change human biology if it works out. How do you feel about such matters?"

The senator's eyes widened. "I do not agree with changing biology at all, and I had no idea Fairbanks was into such experimentation."

Audrey coughed. Wow. Talk about a bad turn of events for Fairbanks. First he gets murdered, and then he loses an in with a senator.

Isobel turned back to her daughter. "If you gentlemen don't mind, I'd love to steal my sweet daughter for a moment."

Warmth flushed through Audrey, even though she knew her mother was playing it nice for the senator. So she forced a smile. "Is it all right, Senator?"

"By all means," the senator said, his smile wide.

"Good. Plus, Audrey should take a break. Pregnant women need rest, you know." Isobel beamed.

The senator's gray eyebrows rose to his forehead. "Pregnant?"

Isobel clapped a hand over her mouth. "Oh my. I let the cat out of the bag."

Heat rose through Audrey's face. "That's all right. Um, I'm pregnant." She felt like she'd been caught making out in the barn.

"That's wonderful." The senator beamed, reaching out to pat her arm. His chest puffed out. "I'm so happy for you."

Audrey shuffled her feet. "Thank you."

He studied her, obviously trying to think of a way to ask the obvious question.

She forced a smile. "Um, I briefly dated a college professor for a while. We kept our relationship very quiet."

"I understand." Delight filled the senator's eyes. "A baby. Oh, I can't wait to go shopping. Do you have a crib?"

She faltered. "Um, not yet."

"Excellent." He rubbed his hands together. "Ernie has been teaching me woodworking, as you know. I'll make one for you." Pure, unabashed delight filled his face. He smiled again at Isobel. "Ernie is my chief of staff."

Audrey's heart thumped. Chances were she'd be long gone when the baby was born. She was going to miss the senator. "That would be very nice."

He nodded. "Well, you go rest. The commander and I are going to look at the outbuildings where weapons are stored and the barracks where the soldiers bunk down." He gave a short bow and turned to follow the commander.

Audrey glanced down at her mother. "I'd like another ultrasound."

"Why?" Isobel's brow furrowed.

"Just to make sure everything is all right." Audrey shrugged. "Maternal worry."

"Very well." Isobel slipped her arm through Audrey's as they walked back toward the main medical facility. "I remember being pregnant with you. Morning sickness for the entire nine months." She smiled and revealed perfect teeth.

Audrey stumbled. Were they having a moment? Actually bonding? "I haven't been too sick." She glanced behind them. "Mother, the senator believes there's another compound somewhere, and he isn't going to recommend funding for you until he knows where it is." Maybe she could get her mother to reveal the information.

Isobel hissed out a breath. "Why does he think that?"

"I don't know, but he's certain." Audrey smoothed her face into concerned lines, actually feeling a little bad to be manipulating her mother in such a way. "He won't give the money."

"You'll have to convince him." Isobel led her into the examination room.

"I tried," Audrey lied again. "Why not tell him the truth?"

Isobel shook her head. "We can't. You know the kind of experiments we do—and you heard what he said about science. He can never know."

Audrey's stomach lurched. "You're still creating soldiers?"

"Of course." Isobel tsked and gestured toward the examination table. "I thought you were on board with us."

"I am. It's just a surprise after the fiasco five years ago. I'd assume you'd be afraid those soldiers would be coming back for you." Audrey unzipped her skirt and lay back on the table. Fear trembled down her spine. Nate was listening in, and he'd just discovered Isobel was experimenting again.

He might kill her this time. Dread dropped like a lead weight into Audrey's stomach.

"Oh, the soldiers from years ago will probably seek us

out at some point." Isobel smiled, her canines seeming a bit too long.

"Why?" Audrey asked, holding her breath.

Isobel squinted behind the glasses. "No reason. This is where they belong."

Baloney. But there was no way Isobel would confess about the kill chips.

"Where's the other compound?" Audrey asked idly, as if they discussed the weather, her heart battering against her ribs.

Isobel's gaze narrowed. "I don't think you need to know that."

"Okay." Audrey shrugged, letting go for the moment. Isobel was still creating soldiers, and the commander was training them to kill. But at least Audrey had gotten her mother to admit to there being another facility. That was enough for now. "Let's check out this baby." She sat back to watch the monitor.

Nate turned his rented BMW onto the newly asphalted road and glanced at his watch, his muscles relaxing for the first time that day. Audrey's ultrasound had proven the baby was fine, and now Audrey sat safely in her office returning e-mails and phone calls as the day wound down. She'd done an excellent job recording every section of the commander's facility.

Pride filled Nathan at her resourcefulness.

Now he had a meeting at TechnoZyn, and it was time to quit. Since he no longer needed the cover, he was happy to move on, and after quitting, he'd drop by and escort Audrey home. But first he wanted to ask some questions. The connection between the deaths of Darian Hannah and George Fairbanks remained unclear, and he had to find out who wanted to point the finger at Audrey.

The three-story building sprawled in an industrial area of Virginia, complete with its own parking lot. Nate had liked the strong lines and square concrete shapes forming the outside walls on sight. The place looked like a successful technology firm should. Not for the first time, he wondered what career he would've chosen if he hadn't been created to kill.

Probably not one in computers, although his skills reached well above normal. But Jory was the computer genius in the family. Maybe Nate might've done something with his hands, like building boats or fixing cars. Or even racing cars. He'd always loved speed.

Thunder cracked overhead as he parked near the exit and dodged out of the car. He'd donned slacks, a white shirt, and a dark gray jacket, nixing the tie. No need for a tie since he'd be tendering his resignation. Even so, he tugged at his collar while striding inside. Give him worn jeans and a ripped T-shirt any day of the week instead of a monkey suit.

He showed his security card to the yawning guard in the vestibule and rode the elevator to the third floor. Long paces brought him to Lilith's corner office.

She glanced up from reading a printout, her blond hair mussed, a drink at her hand. "Rotten day."

"I agree." He settled his bulk into a guest chair, facing her over a mountain of papers on her glass desk. A sophisticated set of cabinets made up one wall, while an original oil painting of a mountain range took up the other. Windows spread out behind her. "Sorry about George."

"Me too." Lilith made a production of standing and stretching her pencil skirt over her toned butt. Moving with sinewy grace, she crossed to open two doors in the cabinets. A myriad of crystal and bottles filled the space. "Join me in having a drink?" she asked, pouring him a glass without waiting for a response. Leaning a bit, she dropped ice into the glass with sharp *tink*s. Gliding toward him, she handed him a drink and sat in the other guest chair, her shapely legs crossed.

Nate accepted the drink and held out the glass. He needed to get a move on to meet Audrey after work. "To George."

"To George," Lilith repeated, clinking glasses. She took a deep swallow and sighed. "The poor lost soul."

Nate took a drink of the Scotch and hummed with appreciation. "Good Scotch."

Lilith smiled, her gaze remaining sad. "Yes." She lifted her glass. "Where have you been all day, anyway?"

"I told you when you brought me over from Neoland that I didn't sit in the office very often." Taking a moment, he punched a button on his phone and pretended to read notes. "Mangatech is going public next year, the CEO of Talcon is resigning due to scandal, and RT Technologies just lost its biggest benefactor when Frank Filsome married some model who talked him into donating to monkeys instead of technology."

"Monkeys?" Lilith sat back. "You found all of that out today?"

"Meetings and gossip," he said. Actually, Shane had hacked into computers and e-mail accounts all morning for the information, but close enough.

Lilith leaned forward, her blazing pink blouse gaping open. "What's the scandal at Talcon?"

"CEO and underage nanny." Nate forced a shrug, hoping the guy got the book thrown at him. Hard. "How was your day?"

She sighed, rubbing under her eyes. "Exhausting. I've been trying to make sense of George's files and not having much success. He did so much around here."

"I know." Nathan leaned forward and slid charm over his face. "Have the funeral arrangements been made?"

"Yes. The funeral is next Saturday." Lilith sat up and stretched her arms over her head. "No news on who killed him, though."

Sadness filled the woman's eyes, and Nate nodded with sympathy. "You've known George for a long time?"

"Ten years." She smiled, making her look years younger. "He recruited me right out of college, and we've worked together ever since. For so long, we shared the same vision. Faster computers and government assistance."

Nate extended his legs and leaned back. "Have you heard about the brand on his back? The same one as Darian Hannah recently got?"

"Yes." Lilith lifted a small shoulder. "Though I have no clue what it means." She relaxed in her chair. "If you ask me, the police should take a gander at Audrey Madison's ass. I bet she has the same brand."

Nate knew for a fact that Audrey's butt remained unmarred by any brand. "Why do you say that?"

Lilith scoffed. "Everybody knows the woman who was with Darian when he died had to be Audrey. Then George is found in her apartment? There has to be a connection, and I bet a trip to Vegas it's all about that brand."

"I wonder what it means?" Nate scratched his neck. He took another drink, his mind calculating facts. "Why was George a lost soul?"

Lilith uncrossed and recrossed her legs. "He went from computers to science and tried to mess with biology. Tried to do unnatural, unclean things."

The facts slowed in Nate's brain. His feet suddenly became too heavy to move. "Unclean?"

"Yes." She claimed his glass before it fell to the floor. "Do you know that when we acquired Neoland, we didn't have time to properly vet all of the employees and independent contractors before getting to work?"

"Is that a fact?" His head lolled forward. He struggled to stay awake, and realization smacked him in his fuzzy brain. "Wh-what did you give me?"

"A drug stronger than morphine—much stronger, actually." She leaned into him and brushed his jaw with her lips. "I did so like you, but you're going to tell me everything. I promise."

"Don't know what you're talking about." He fumbled for his phone, and it fell to the floor.

"Sure you do. I have connections that would shock you." She bit his chin. "But I don't like secrets. You're keeping secrets from me, and Audrey Madison is keeping secrets about Darian. My sweet Darian."

Nate shook his head, and the room whirled around him in slow motion. "I'm not connected to Audrey."

"Sure you are. I saw you at the restaurant, and you two are definitely connected."

He thought he'd been discreet. "You and Darian?"

"Yes. I trusted him, and not only with my body." Lilith's hand slipped down Nate's neck. "We believe the same things—and he joined us. But he turned against us."

"Leave Senator Nash and Audrey Madison alone," Nate ground out, his eyelids fluttering shut.

"Not a chance. Nash believes as I do and is valuable to me. Audrey, though, according to Darian, is connected to people who create evil, and she's going to tell me all about it. Tonight."

"Darian told you?" Nate gasped out.

"Yes. Darian told me all about Audrey, the senator, and somebody named the commander who's doing all sorts of terrible things," Lilith said.

Nate reached for Lilith's neck, and she slipped easily out of his way. What had she given him? How had this happened? His last thought as he fell forward was that he had to protect Audrey...and that he was a complete dumbass for making such a rookie mistake.

CHAPTER
27

AUDREY FOLLOWED MATT'S directions and untangled herself from the wires along her back, putting those and the earrings into her briefcase. Relief washed through her as she kicked back in her office and sipped herbal tea. She'd successfully captured the entire facility on camera while acting normal—maybe she had more of her mother in her than she'd thought.

Her mother. Dr. Isobel Madison, a woman soon to be a grandmother.

Audrey blew on the tea and sipped some more. She and her mother had gotten to know each other better during the last five years, but it had all been in pursuit of the commander's goals.

Her mother had done terrible things—unforgivable, really—and Audrey probably didn't know the half of it.

Yet the young girl trapped deep inside Audrey still craved the approval of her only parent. Intellectually, she knew better. But sometimes emotions and thoughts didn't connect. At some point, Audrey would have to let go. The idea of giving up hope with her only blood relative hurt worse than the beam dropping on her leg five years ago.

Ernie walked by the office door and backed up, poking his head in. "Why are you still here?"

She shrugged. "I'm having some tea before heading out."

Ernie nodded. "The senator said the trip to the facility went well and that you saw all of the labs, but the commander wouldn't admit he has another compound somewhere. Do you think the senator is wrong?"

"I don't know," Audrey lied. "The commander seemed quite open today, and he showed us everything."

Ernie shook his head. "If the commander is experimenting on people, we have to stop him. Especially if his victims are unwilling."

"I agree."

"Go home, Audrey. I'll see you after my vacation."

She'd forgotten. "Oh yeah. Italy with the wife and kids. Should be fun."

He smiled and rolled his eyes. "You haven't traveled with teenagers before. It will be memorable. Now go home and relax." Whistling a roaring-twenties tune, Ernie sauntered back down the hallway.

Good advice. Audrey slid her cup onto her desk and drew on her coat. Man, she was exhausted. Acting like a spy and forming another human being took up a lot of energy.

She hummed softly to herself while riding the elevator down and walking to her car. Nate had said he'd try to pop by and escort her home, otherwise they would meet at his cabin. If she arrived first, she'd love to cook him dinner this time.

Sliding into her car, she headed out of the parking area and into the street. Minutes later, DC traffic slowed. Ugh. She wondered if Nate had already arrived at the cabin.

The previous night had been amazing. At the thought, her thighs softened. Nate Dean was sex personified, and that was fine with her. She was ready to see him again. To figure things out. Every block she drove took her closer to the warmth that would be waiting for her at the end of this long day. She exhaled to keep calm as the traffic slowed to a crawl.

Finally the gridlock released and she ended up heading into Virginia. She stopped at a light, humming along with the radio.

Suddenly her door burst open, a knife flashed to cut her seat belt, and unrelenting arms forced her from her car. Fear accosted her until breathing became impossible. She screamed, hitting and kicking, and found herself tossed into the back of a van. A hood slammed over her head, and something scratchy wound around her wrists, binding her. The door slammed shut, tires screeched, and they started to move.

She huddled against the metal side, her mind whirling, her body shuddering. They'd taken her so quickly.

But who?

After reaching a parking garage and walking down several stairs, Audrey's hood had been removed, and she'd been shoved into a passageway far underground. Her hands shook and her throat clogged. What in the world?

Rough and uneven stones hindered her movements through the underground passageway reminiscent of a catacomb in a movie. But this wasn't a movie. She stepped around a jagged edge, careful of her damaged leg.

She had to be ready to run. Her knees trembled so much her teeth chattered. Calm. She needed to calm herself.

Two men guided the way with flashlights, while a third

prodded her in the back every once in a while with the barrel of a Ruger 358. The deadly thing would cause quite a hole in her center if it went off.

He stood close enough for her to try for the weapon, but the two guys ahead of her also held weapons. Plus, any fight would risk the baby. Fear buzzed confusion into her brain, and she gulped several times to regain control.

The drip of water on stone echoed around them, and the scent of mildew tickled her nose. She coughed and sneezed into her elbow.

"Bless you," said the guy from behind her.

"Thank you," she automatically replied before her brain kicked in. *Bless you?*

A rock caught her toe, and she stumbled, reaching for the mossy wall for balance. Wet slime covered her hand, and she grimaced before wiping it off on her skirt. Ewww.

Twists and turns through the pathway kept her head spinning until she wasn't sure how to find the way back out. Finally, they reached a large metal door set into the rock. How had they gotten such a heavy door down so far under the building?

The first man rapped several times on the door, and it slowly and rather majestically opened. Then the two men flanked the door, while the third pushed her between the shoulder blades and then shut it, remaining on the outside.

Bracing herself, she walked into a circular room cut smoothly into rock. A massive table sat in the middle, surrounded by hand-carved wooden chairs. Old and magnificent. At least twenty people could comfortably sit around and plot whatever it was they plotted there so deeply hidden.

Right now Lilith Mayes sat at the head of the table wearing a white robe with a blade insignia over her left breast. Senator Nash sat to her right with two men wearing black robes sitting next to him. Two other men, also robed in black, sat to Lilith's left after one empty seat.

Shock filled Audrey at recognizing both Lilith and the senator. Hurt came next. Her hands shook and her knees wobbled.

Heat of betrayal attacked her, followed by an icy knife of reality. She'd trusted him—genuinely liked him. He was the closest she'd ever had to a father figure who cared. He'd wanted to carve her a crib.

Her throat clogged. Why did she keep choosing the wrong people to trust? Her breath caught and she searched for an escape.

Lights, probably powered from a generator, lined the walls in intricate sconces. Silver and glinting, a sword hung from the ceiling a little way from the table. At least seven feet long, the sharp blade held the insignia PROTECT down its graceful edge.

Beautiful and deadly.

Audrey cleared her throat. "Where's the sacrificial altar?" Her gaze landed on the senator.

Lilith laughed, the sound tinkling oddly through the room. "No altar. Sorry." She gestured toward a seat next to her. "You're going to want to sit down."

A barrel between Audrey's shoulder blades propelled her toward the seat, where she couldn't help sending the senator a hurt look. He'd gone pale, his expressive eyes full of sorrow. His hands shook as he rested them on the table. "Why is Audrey here?"

Lilith smoothed a curl off her forehead. "She's here because we need access to the commander's data, and she's our way in. We have to purify what that man and his people have done."

Audrey blinked. "Purify? What does that mean?"

Lilith gestured behind her to the iconic sword. "Life and humans need to be pure. For decades, our group has shut down all experiments to change DNA of humans. No cloning, no testing, no aberrations."

Audrey gulped down bile. She really needed to throw up. "I don't understand. You worked with George Fairbanks for almost a decade, and he wore the sword brand."

Lilith sighed. "Yes, George and I were the best of friends, and he was the one who initially inducted me into this marvelous society. But he let his scientific curiosity get the better of him. For years, we worked on computer technology together that assisted us in our fight, but then George discovered nanobytes, and he changed."

Audrey straightened her shoulders. "So you killed him."

"Of course," Lilith said.

"Why leave him in my apartment?" Audrey asked.

"Why not?" Lilith lifted a shoulder. "Since we also killed Darian, and you easily connected the two, why not use you to deflect the attention a little bit?"

Audrey's head spun, while her instincts hummed. "Bullshit. There's more."

Lilith's upper lip curled. "This is business."

"No. This is personal." Audrey leaned forward, her hands fisting. "You and Darian had a thing, right? Did he dump you?"

Lilith's nostrils flared. "I'm going to kill you."

"Maybe." Maybe not. "Why did you kill Darian?"

Lilith sighed. "I just went through all of this. Darian was on our side, and he was inducted, but when he discovered our plan to take you, he turned rogue and tried to warn you. So he had to die." She brushed lint off her robe. "Plus, the bastard did dump me."

"Yet you went out with, uh, Jason." Crap. Audrey had almost forgotten Nate's undercover name. "I saw you making a move."

Lilith's eyes glittered. "Jason watched you all night, even on a date with me. *With me.* I don't know what your draw is, but I'm going to end it. You have been such a complete pain to me. Torturing you will be a pleasure, so please don't give me all the info I need up front."

What a nutjob.

Audrey swallowed. "I don't know anything."

"Exactly." The senator leaned forward. "Let her go, and I'll do whatever you want."

Audrey frowned. It was a little late for him to help, wasn't it? "You have no idea who I am or the connections I have. Let me go, or I promise you'll die and fast."

"I can't wait to cut into you." Lilith drew out an intimidating knife—the exact replica of the one suspended from the ceiling.

"You can't cut her—she's pregnant," the senator said, his eyes widening.

Oh God. Oh no. Audrey shot him a black look.

Lilith frowned, studying Audrey. "Really? Well, you started dating Darian, and he's dead. I know you spend a lot of time with the commander, and I know all about the madman from my sweet Darian." A wild gleam entered her eyes. "Are you part of the commander's experiments?"

"No. One-night stand," Audrey said, trying to sound calm.

Delight lifted Lilith's eyebrows. "You're lying. Wonderful. Just wonderful. You have an aberration inside you."

Terror nearly lifted Audrey from the chair. "You're

crazy." She donned a bored expression and focused back on the senator. "I know you have strong religious beliefs, but I can't believe you aligned with this crazed bitch."

In a surprisingly smooth movement, the senator lunged for the knife, snatching it from Lilith's hand. He stood, jerking her back to his chest, the blade at her throat. "I haven't aligned with this lunatic," he said.

All four men flanking the table shoved away and stood, two of them drawing Glocks, the other two pointing Sigs.

Audrey pushed back from the table. "Um—"

Faded blue eyes shot sparks over Lilith's head. "You thought I had something to do with this?" Long and lean, the senator loomed over the deadly blonde.

"Um, no?" Audrey stood, her gaze on the man she'd trusted. "Okay. I'm confused."

The senator nodded. "I get that. This witch drugged me, and I ended up here in this bizarre chamber. Kidnapping a United States senator is a federal crime, you know."

Relief almost dropped Audrey back down. The senator was one of the good guys. Thank goodness.

Lilith rolled her eyes. "Senator, I've been trying to make you understand. You believe in life, and not in experimentation. We're on the same side."

"The hell we are," the senator boomed. "You're crazy."

Audrey shook her head. She was right to have trusted him. "I'm sorry," she whispered to him.

He grinned. "That's okay. I feel like James Bond."

An explosion ripped by Audrey's ear. Red bloomed across the senator's upper right chest, and his jaw dropped open in shock. He released Lilith and backed away, falling to his knees.

The guy to Audrey's right chuckled, his gun steaming. "The robes aren't for show, asshole."

Audrey cried out and ran around the table, sliding onto her knees. Pain radiated up her bad leg, but she didn't care. "Senator?" she asked, lifting his head to her knees.

His eyes widened with shock, and he coughed. Fear and pain crossed his face.

Audrey shrugged out of her coat and balled it up to press against the wound. Her gaze darted around for help and landed on Lilith. "He needs medical attention."

Lilith pursed red lips, regret twisting them. "I'm afraid not." She shook her head. "I do wish you would've joined us in our quest, Senator."

Blood seeped between Audrey's fingers and helplessness flooded her. "Please let me get him to a doctor."

Lilith sighed and focused on the shooter. "Finish him off, and dispose of his body. We can't be linked to this." Reaching down, she clung to Audrey's arm. "We need to get to a medical facility to see what exactly is growing inside our new member here."

Audrey ripped her arm free. "Screw you."

"Classy." Lilith nodded at the two men closest to Audrey. "Please remove her so we can finish off our business here." Thoughtful contemplation filled the woman's expression.

She didn't care one wit about life.

Audrey pressed harder against the senator's wound, and he groaned. "How can you so easily kill if your mission is to protect life?" She directed her question to the silent men in black and not to their leader. Lilith had killed too many people to care.

The shooter grinned. "We care about pure life, not all life. Some people are collateral damage in our war."

"You have no idea about war," the senator hissed, pain filling his face. "No idea at all."

"It's okay," Audrey murmured. The senator had fought in Korea and had the medals to prove it. He was tough, and she could figure out a way to save him. But the warm blood rushing along her fingers promised she didn't have much time. "Stay still so you don't bleed as much."

Lilith glared down at Audrey. "Get away from him, or I'll make you regret it in ways you can't even imagine."

"Think so?" Audrey eyed her immediate area for any type of weapon. Only smooth, stone floor met her gaze.

"Yes." Lilith nodded at a man covering the far door. "Let me show you what we do with our enemies. Now, Freddie."

The man who'd shot the senator opened the door and reached inside to remove a man wearing a black hood. He fell to his knees, his arms bound behind his back. With flourish, Freddie snagged off the hood.

Nate. Audrey blinked, time grinding to a complete halt. Bruised and battered, his clothing ripped and filthy, Nate Dean kneeled on the stone floor, pure fury in his gray eyes.

CHAPTER
28

NATE EYED AUDREY, tuning in to her heartbeat as well as the baby's. Steady and strong, both. Audrey's thumped much too quickly, however. He smiled, ignoring the crack in his bottom lip. "Hello, Miss Madison."

Audrey's face paled to the color of white chalk. "I don't understand."

Lilith giggled and clapped her hands together. "Life is weird, right? Jason has been investigating me, and it turns out, his past is a little hazy. I thought Freddie could get answers from him, but so far, Jason has been tougher than I'd expected."

Realization flickered in Audrey's eyes.

Nate gave a short nod. Lilith had no clue about their real connection, nor about his true identity.

Audrey frowned, surprise twisting her lip. "So you, ah, captured Jason?"

If there was a *what-the-fuck* expression, Audrey wore it right now. Embarrassment flooded through Nate. "It wasn't as easy as she's making it sound." Why was he defending himself? He'd been knocked out by some good drugs, for Pete's sake. Yeah, it was a rookie move. He sighed.

Lilith sauntered over and ran long fingernails through Nate's hair.

A small growl emerged from Audrey's chest, and Nate cut her a hard look to knock it off. If Lilith discovered their connection, she'd turn on Audrey.

Right now, Nate had enough problems. The senator was bleeding out, Audrey was unarmed and pregnant, Lilith was crazy, and several men with guns seemed ready to happily kill him. But he'd spent the last hour trying to get his hands free, and he was almost there.

The first one he'd take out would be Freddie. The guy had enjoyed kicking Nate in the face for information, but Nate hadn't given him anything interesting. He'd been tortured by the best during some of his missions, and this guy hadn't come close.

Lilith tugged his head back, nails scraping his scalp, as he finally worked the ropes free around his wrists.

Yep. His chance. He leaped to his feet and secured her in a headlock while kicking Freddie in the back of the knee. Freddie went down, and Nate stole the gun from his holster.

Four guns instantly pointed his way. He pressed the barrel to Lilith's throat, ducking down to keep her as cover. "How loyal is your little band of morons here, Lilith?" he asked, making sure to press hard enough that she winced. "If anyone even flinches, I'll blow your head off."

She held perfectly still. "I didn't think you had it in you, Jason."

He eyed a twitchy guy to the left of the table. "Getting drugged and kicked around for a few hours can change a guy. Just so we're clear, I have no problem killing you."

"I believe you." Her gasp echoed around the chamber. "Why do I have the feeling you're not quite what you've let on?"

"I don't know." Nate leaned closer to her ear. "Tell them to drop their guns, or I swear, I'll shoot."

She chuckled. "No, you won't. If you shoot me, they'll have no reason not to kill you."

"We both know I don't have a chance of getting out of here in one piece," he said quietly. The woman had planned to kill him, without question. "So if I'm going to die, you are, too."

She kept silent for several moments, obviously thinking.

"Okay," Nate said, bracing himself against her back, "I guess we all die."

"No," she gasped. "Fine. Do what he says—put down your guns."

Nate kept Audrey in his peripheral vision. Her eyes widened, and she slipped her hands under the senator's armpits.

The smartest thing to do would be to run and call for help to retrieve the senator. But one look at Audrey's determined face promised she wouldn't leave him. Nate sighed.

The men in black hesitated.

"Now!" he barked.

Finally, one by one, they dropped their guns.

"Kick them under the table," Nate said calmly. His face ached, his chest throbbed, and his temper threatened to take over. So he shoved all emotion into the netherworld and fell back on training.

The sound of metal spinning across stone filled the chamber.

"Good. Now everyone in black back up to the far wall and slide down to your bellies." Nate kept bite in his words. Freddie didn't move quickly enough, so Nate shot a sidekick to the guy's jaw. Freddie's head snapped, and he dropped, unconscious.

Asshole.

The men in black began to move.

The one closest to Audrey ducked down and lifted her by the neck, his muscled arm against her windpipe.

Nate's attention focused completely and absolutely on him. "Let her go, or I'll kill this bitch."

The guy slid a knife against Audrey's carotid. "Let's work on a win-win situation here." Backing up, he dragged Audrey toward the main exit. "I won't kill the brunette, if you don't kill the blonde."

Nate kept his gaze off Audrey's vulnerable neck. Blood covered her hands, and fear lit her eyes. So he focused on the determined ones of the man holding her. "I don't know the brunette. You need the blonde."

"Somehow, I don't think you'll let me kill the pregnant chick." The guy shrugged, lifting Audrey up onto her toes. Her eyes widened, full of panic. "If I'm wrong, then I'm wrong." He reached the door and shoved it open.

This guy had better training than the rest. "I'm holding your leader. Let the pregnant chick go, and I won't kill Lilith." Nate ensnared Lilith's hair and wrenched back her head, exposing her neck and the bruise the barrel was creating next to her jugular.

The guy smiled again. "She's not my leader." Carrying Audrey through the doorway, he kicked it shut.

Terror ripped through Nate until he saw black. They had Audrey.

His hands shook, and his knees weakened.

He had to save her.

Drawing on every ounce of training that had been beaten into him, he dug deep and shoved all emotion into a box. Cold and merciless, he surveyed the situation.

Smoothly, he slipped an arm under Lilith's neck and

squeezed, pointing the gun at the remaining men in black. "Get down on your stomachs. Now."

They followed suit, a couple of them eyeing the guns under the table. "Hands behind your heads," Nate ordered.

The senator groaned and rolled over to crawl under the table, his hand pressing Audrey's coat to his wound. Mumbling to himself, he gathered the weapons and crab-walked backward to use the wall to stand.

Nate nodded at the former soldier. "How badly are you hurt?"

"Flesh wound," the senator lied, blood dripping from his lips. "Go after Audrey."

Nate applied more pressure, and Lilith struggled against him, trying to get air. Finally, she passed out. He let her drop to the floor, the white robe fluttering around her. "I should kill you," he muttered. But he'd never kill a helpless woman, no matter how dangerous she might be.

He hustled toward the door, swearing at finding it locked. He glanced back at the senator. "You have a phone?"

"No." The senator's lips were turning blue. Not a good sign.

Nate reached down and frisked the guys on the ground. "How is it none of you have phones?"

The closest guy turned his head and grinned. "No service down here, asshole."

Nate punched him in the jaw, somewhat appeased when his eyes fluttered shut and his nose landed on the concrete. Blood slid around a stone.

Fury and fear commingled in Nate for the briefest of seconds. So he grabbed the next guy by the hair and lifted his head. "If Lilith isn't your boss, who is?" In other words, where was the kidnapper taking Audrey?

The guy shook his head. "Way above my knowledge. I've only been in five years, and Lilith gives the orders. If she's answering to somebody, I don't know who it is."

The guy told the truth. Nate had to find Audrey. He reached into the guy's boot and drew out a nicely sharpened knife. Time to pick the lock.

Audrey sat in the back of the SUV as it wound through DC and into Virginia, her hands tied before her. The guy who'd kidnapped her drove, while one of his buddies sat next to her, a Glock perched casually on his knee.

The swish of the windshield wipers competed with the pelting rain, fogging the windows.

She tried to rub her tethered hands together to get rid of the sticky, dried blood. Her stomach grumbled and hurt. When was the last time she'd eaten?

A quick glance at the bored guy next to her had her mind reeling. She sighed and looked out her window. She could do this. Taking a deep breath, she lunged for the gun. The guy easily shifted the weapon to his other hand, his huge paw smashing the side of her face.

"Nice try." He still sounded bored.

Pain cascaded through her cheekbone to her neck. "Jerk. Why don't you sit up front?" she muttered, stretching her aching jaw.

"It's safer in the back." He turned to look out the window again.

Audrey cleared her throat. "Where are we going?"

"Here." The driver wound the SUV through an intricate gate. Trees lined the luxurious driveway, perfectly tended, until they reached a two-story Tudor, fit for one of DC's finest.

Audrey peered out of the window. "Nice house."

"Very." The driver hopped out and crossed to open her door. A strong hand banded around her arm. "Watch out for puddles."

Yeah, because wet feet were the worst of her concerns. She trudged along the brick walkway to the double blue doors. "We're going in the front?" she asked.

The guy knocked, and the door opened.

Audrey gasped and stepped back. "Ernie?"

Ernie Rastus stood aside and gestured them in. "Is Lilith dead?" he asked quietly, looking stately in a maroon sweater vest over khaki pants.

"Probably not," the soldier said. "But this chick is pregnant. Seemed to matter to Lilith."

Ernie's eyes gleamed. "Good job, Buck," he said, shutting the door.

"What have you done, Ernie?" Audrey asked, her mind calculating facts into a scenario that made sense. "Oh." Ernie had been the one to educate the senator about cloning and scientific research. He'd also been the one to get George and Lilith into the same room with the senator. "You're the leader of the PROTECT group."

"These days, anyway." Ernie smiled sparkling dentures. "You've put a serious dent in our numbers, but I can rebuild. Come into my study, would you?" He turned and led the way through expertly decorated rooms to a study fit for a high-level policy maker.

After Audrey had been deposited in a seat, he extended the handset to a phone toward her.

She swallowed. "What in all that is holy does PROTECT mean?"

He sighed. "For generations, a select few have worked within the DC political structure to protect the sanctity of human life. We've lost some battles, but we've won some, too. Stem-cell research has been put back years through legal means, and other labs have been blown up... accidentally. We do what we have to do."

"You're a cult." Audrey swallowed, wondering how in the world they'd gotten away with it for so long.

Ernie shrugged. "We're a legitimate group of concerned citizens who do what needs to be done. I'm a legacy, because my great-grandfather created our society."

Her breath sped up, and she tried to fill her lungs. "Why Senator Nash?"

Ernie smiled. "The subcommittee, of course. We had intel that a couple of military groups seeking funding were conducting inhumane experiments. I was in place to stop that—and we had no clue how bad things were until the senator started working with the commander and his godforsaken creations."

"You have no idea what you're talking about." What a jackass. Audrey wiped rain off her cheeks.

Ernie nodded. "There's no need to discuss it. Please call your people. It's time to negotiate."

"My people?" She shook out her wet hair. "What people?"

Ernie chuckled and reached for a half-full glass of whiskey on his executive desk. "The commander. It's time we got to know him better. Tell him he'd better cooperate, or you're dead."

Audrey bit back temper. How had she missed the darkness in Ernie? The senator had really liked him, so she'd really liked him. Talk about being blind to someone's faults. Intelligence didn't equal honor, unfortunately. How had she forgotten that one simple fact? "Why do you think the commander will help me?" she asked.

Ernie leaned down, his gaze serious and deadly. "I

know who you are, and I know who your mother is. In addition, I know you're pregnant, and I'm fairly certain I know how that happened."

Fire lanced through Audrey, bordered by fear. "There is a book about a stork I'll buy for you if you don't really understand how babies are made."

The backhand to her face took her by surprise. He'd hit the exact spot the soldier had in the car. Hurt pounded through her cheekbone, and her temple began to thrum. "Ass."

He nodded. "We understand each other." Taking her bound hands, he shoved the phone into them. "Make the call."

Audrey took a deep breath, her stomach churning. "You really don't want me to call him like this. Trust me." The guy had no clue who he was dealing with.

"Do it. Now," Ernie said.

Audrey shrugged and slowly dialed, calling the one person she'd never believed she'd call on purpose.

"Yes?" a deep male voice answered.

She cleared her throat. "Commander? It's Audrey Madison. We have a problem."

CHAPTER
29

AUDREY'S ARMS HAD grown nearly numb after two hours of being tied up in Ernie's study. For the first hour, she'd struggled against the bindings attaching her arms to the heavy sofa with no success. For the second hour, she'd sat quietly and watched the clock on the mantel count down. How could she get free?

The door swished open, and Ernie entered with a large vest in his hands. His soldier entered behind him and crossed the room while tugging out a sharp knife.

Audrey gasped and pressed back against the cushions, her heart racing.

"Hold still," the soldier said, leaning over her to saw through the rope.

Raw feeling returned to her hands, and sharp needles dug into her wrists. She rubbed them, trying not to cry.

With a swoop of movement, the soldier forced her up and against his chest, securing her arms being her back. She kicked out, struggling. "Stop—" she said, tears streaming down her face, terror raising her voice to shrill as she took in the explosives attached to the vest.

Ernie restrained her arm and shoved it through the

vest. "You know I can't expect the commander to come alone or even to listen to me. This will ensure he has to."

It was a real bomb. Audrey shoved back against the soldier, kicking out as Ernie pushed her other arm through and fastened the front with a lock.

"There we go. Try to disengage the lock, and . . . *boom*." Ernie nodded for the soldier to release her and withdrew some sort of detonator from his back pocket.

Audrey stilled and glanced down at the explosives now strapped to her chest. The bite of fear weakened her knees. How could she get away from the bomb and get the baby safe? She eyed the remote resting in Ernie's hand.

"Don't even think about it." He reached over and increased the volume on the television across the room. "I suggest you sit."

Her legs wobbling, Audrey maneuvered over to sit on the sofa. Would the bomb explode if she moved too much? How stable were the explosives? "Please let me go, Ernie."

"No. Now watch the news—it's full of all sorts of interesting stuff." He threw back his head and laughed, the sound maniacal.

The commander would strike hard and fast at the house. What about the bomb? It might explode before the commander even realized it existed. "The commander might shoot you before you can speak with him," she said.

"Shhh." Ernie focused on the television reporter, who confirmed that Senator Nash had been kidnapped earlier and that several people, including Lilith Mayes, had been taken into custody, but nobody knew where the senator had been taken.

Trembles wound down Audrey's spine. Had the senator really survived, and had Nate been taken into custody?

No way. The reporter, a vivacious blonde, told the audience that the FBI was searching furiously for the senator.

Audrey glanced at the bruises around her wrists. At least they'd unbound her. She eyed the lock atop her chest and the wires extending from a black box to some cream-colored putty stuff. "Don't you have to be at the hospital, considering you're Nash's chief of staff?" she asked.

"I'm on vacation—out of the country with my family," Ernie said, frowning at the television. "But I did just call and say I'm on a flight headed back home and will be in tomorrow. Of course, by then, I'll be long gone from here."

Audrey shook her head. No wonder the house was so quiet—Ernie's family wasn't home. "The senator trusted you. Completely."

Ernie rubbed his graying beard. "I know, and I'd hoped to bring him on board. He has such lovely thoughts about science and the sanctity of human life. I'm afraid Lilith will have to kill him once she's out of custody. So much for life."

Audrey gasped. "You can't have a U.S. senator killed."

Ernie shrugged. "Sure I can. You don't really understand the scope of our society, do you?"

"I guess not. How big are you?" Who were these people?

He took a deep swallow of whiskey. "Considering the amount of people we've lost lately, or had taken into custody, we're not very big. But like I said, I can rebuild."

That's what he thought. Audrey fought the urge to rub her pounding cheek. "What's your plan, anyway? You got the commander to agree to come alone and talk, but what then?"

Ernie rubbed his chin. "I kill him."

Audrey's shoulders straightened. "Excuse me?" How was that a plan?

"Cut off the head of the snake, and the body will fall." Ernie reached for the bottle behind him to refill his glass. "After the commander is dead, we'll dismantle his organization piece by piece. Your mother is next, but my scientist wants to have a nice long talk with her first. I assume she'll cooperate."

Audrey glanced at the clock on the wall. She swallowed the acidic taste of fear, and her stomach lurched. Nate had to be going out of his mind, but there had been no opportunity to reach him. She jerked her head. "Wait a minute. If you kill the commander, am I next?"

"You should be." Ernie glanced with derision at her stomach. "I know what an abnormal creation you have in there. But our scientists want to study you and this aberration briefly, before we rid the world of the anomaly."

The world narrowed to pinpoint focus. She'd take out Ernie long before he had the chance to study her child. "You think you've thought all of this out." She shook her head. "Boy, are you a moron."

"Think so?" Ernie's eyebrows rose.

An explosion sounded right outside the door.

"Yes," Audrey whispered, instinctively edging toward the floor, curling over to protect the baby. She tried to sidle closer to the detonator.

Gunfire pattered outside, and then inside the mansion. Ernie jumped up and drew a gun from the bookcase, his eyes a wild hue. "What's going on?"

The soldier at the door backed away, two guns pointed at the entry. "I'd say we're under attack."

Cries of pain littered through the night, and smoke wound under the door. Terror flooded Audrey, and she glanced frantically around for an escape. The vest lay heavy around her middle. Taking stock, she crept toward the desk while the two men in the room focused on the door. Saying a quick prayer, she slid down in front of the stable mahogany.

On the other side of the desk, glass shattered with a resounding crack. Sparkles rained through the air— deadly pieces of the window.

Both Ernie and the soldier pivoted and fired over her head toward the window. Return fire dropped the soldier. In the distance, one more explosion sounded.

Her hands shaking, her head pounding, Audrey waited for silence. Ernie hauled her in front of him, the detonator in his other hand. She gulped and faced the window, her entire body shuddering.

The commander stood with a wide stance, a Glock in his hand, the rain splattering down to cover his black uniform. A landscape light focused up on him, making him seem like an antihero from an action flick. Hard, dangerous, and emotionless.

He beckoned her with one finger. "The house will blow in two minutes," he said, his voice easily carrying through the storm.

Ernie laughed. "She blows in thirty seconds."

Tears streamed from Audrey's eyes, and she blinked them out. The commander would let her explode before he allowed himself to be taken hostage. The baby was her responsibility, and she wouldn't let him down.

Terror threatened to consume her, but she had no choice. Taking a deep breath, she shot an elbow into Ernie's gut. With a muffled "oof," he bent over. She pivoted and snatched the detonator from his hand, whirling away from him.

The commander calmly plugged him three times in the chest.

Blood splattered toward the window. Ernie's mouth opened wide as he went down.

Dead.

The commander stepped over the broken windowsill, already unfolding a Swiss Army knife. He leaned down and studied the lock on the vest.

Audrey held her breath. *Get it off, get it off, get it off.* She didn't twitch.

The commander inserted a small knife and twisted. The lock popped.

Audrey's heart dropped to her feet.

Silence. Nothing blew up.

The commander unzipped the vest, and the sound magnified in the death-filled room. He expertly removed the explosives and took the detonator from her hands. Placing both on the desk, he jumped through the window and held out a hand.

She paused. The building was going to explode, and yet, she had to gather her strength to accept his outstretched hand. "Thank you," she said, her mind fuzzing.

"Of course." He kept her hand in his while leading the way to a Hummer idling in the long driveway. "Keep your head down and hurry."

She ran and jumped into the front seat of the Hummer. The commander followed suit, driving away from the palatial home. "You can't blow up the home of a U.S. senator's chief of staff," she said, her gaze on the side-view mirror.

The commander pressed down on the accelerator with more force. "Why not?"

Indeed. In his world, there was nothing wrong with

blowing up the home and killing people still in it. Audrey shook her head. "I guess this will be one more mystery to go along with the senator disappearing."

The commander glanced down at her. "Maybe. Don't really care. Are we going to get his recommendation for funding or not?"

"I don't know." Probably not.

The world lit up bright yellow and orange behind her, and she leaned away from the side mirror, even as her gaze remained glued to the image of fire and wood roaring through the night. Glass shattered in every direction, and smoke billowed up.

She'd been so close to exploding. So far, her baby had been in more danger in the past few days than most people saw their entire lives. Sorrow and fear threatened to swamp her. Where was Nate? More than ever, she needed him.

The commander steered onto another street and the image disappeared.

Sirens sounded in the distance.

"Explain about this group," the commander said, his gaze on the dark street in front of them.

Audrey put on her seat belt and told the commander everything she knew as they drove through Virginia. Finally, she wound down. "That's all I know."

He nodded. "I surmised most of that explanation." A quick glance at his watch had him focusing out the front window again. "Lilith Mayes and three of her men were released from custody an hour ago, and their car should've gone off a cliff by now. No need to worry about them any longer."

Audrey's ears rang. "You had them killed."

"Of course." He increased the speed of the windshield wipers.

Her vision blurred. "I don't suppose you're taking me to my apartment?"

"No. It's time you came in-house," he said. "The senator isn't likely to give us funding, and your time under-cover is over."

"What about funding?"

"I have other sources. Always have a contingency plan." He rubbed a large hand over his wet spiky hair.

She cleared her throat, her mind reeling. Yeah, she'd known the commander would try to sequester her some-where else at some point, but she hadn't known it would be so soon. It would've been easier escaping from outside the organization. "I don't want to go in-house."

No expression crossed his hard face. "How else am I going to get Nathan to come home?"

Audrey's breath caught. "Nate? Why would he come home?"

The commander glanced at her, the skin twitching at the corner of his eye—the closest he'd ever come to roll-ing his eyes. "Please. We know Nate is here, and we know you've had contact. He'll come home in order to save his baby."

They'd been so careful, but the commander had known them all since birth. "What if he doesn't?" Audrey asked, focusing outside the front window.

"He will. Plus, I assume you know about the kill chips?"

Audrey thought about lying, but why bother? The com-mander knew all. "Yes. How could you do that?"

"Plan B." The commander turned the Hummer onto the interstate.

"Where's your other facility?" Audrey asked. Since she'd been truthful, maybe he would be, too.

"You'll see the other facility soon enough."

There had been very few times in her life that she'd been alone with the commander. She'd been raised by nannies, attended boarding school, and then went to college abroad. But she'd known him her entire life. Kind of. "I used to wonder if you'd marry my mother," she said quietly.

He started. "Your mother and I have a good relationship."

They'd been together, nonexclusively, for Audrey's entire life. "Why haven't you married each other?"

"Why would we?" he asked.

"Love?" She breathed out the word, knowing it was a mistake.

"Don't be silly. Love is a chemical reaction. You know better." Disapproval firmed his lips. "My Gray boys know better."

Audrey kept silent. Even after raising them, training them, studying them, the commander didn't know Nathan or his brothers. Love had kept them together and had helped them to survive. Then it had nearly destroyed them.

She loved Nate. Completely and truly...and she'd fight for him. For both of them. Maybe they had a chance, and maybe not. But she'd go down fighting.

Since the commander was taking her in, maybe he would finally level with her. "Is Jory still alive?" she asked, holding her breath.

The commander twisted a knob and sped up the windshield wipers. "Are Shane and Mathew with Nathan?"

Audrey pressed her lips together. "No. He's alone."

"Pity. Well, he'll bring them back to me."

"Why?" Audrey turned to face the commander. "Why do you want them back so badly? They don't want to work for you."

He leveled a surprised look at her before focusing on the road. "I created and trained them to be the best. They are the best. Right now, more than ever, with the competition out there, I need them back."

"What competition?"

He sighed. "We're not the only group vying for funding, and we've actually been attacked. I need the Gray brothers to defend us as well as take out the competition. They owe me."

"They don't owe you anything." Audrey sighed and settled back into her seat. She could try and jump from the vehicle, but taking such a risk with the baby would be a mistake. Plus, her face hurt, her head ached, and her leg pounded. She needed to regroup before fighting again.

The commander switched on the radio, and classical music filled the vehicle. "How badly are you injured?"

"I'm not."

"Did your abdomen take any impact?" he asked.

"No." Of course he was only worried about the baby. Audrey swallowed, allowing her mind to drift a little bit. When she'd called him, she'd known he'd come, even though his motivations weren't what she'd like. She sighed again. "Thank you for coming to get me." To save her.

"Of course." He glanced her way, a massive man with ramrod posture. "I own you."

Nate stared at his cell phone while the storm raged outside the small cabin. Over at the table, Shane kept track of all news reports regarding the senator and the explosion at Ernie Rastus's place. The commander's fingerprints dusted all over that one.

Matt organized and cataloged weapons on the sofa, checking clips and muttering to himself.

The cell phone remained silent. "Why hasn't he called?" Nate asked no one in particular.

Nobody answered him.

The commander hadn't called because he wanted Nate to sweat it out. To be so desperate when the call finally came that he'd agree to almost anything.

Senator Nash suddenly appeared in the bedroom doorway, a sling around his arm. "What's going on?"

Nate frowned. "We took a bullet out of your shoulder. You need rest."

Nash shrugged and then winced. "I want to help find Audrey."

"I've got this." All Nate needed was one more person trying to get shot in his stead. "You, ah, need to worry about your future."

Matt nodded. "Senator Nash disappeared and will never be found."

The senator shook his head. "I don't understand. Why did I disappear?"

"Chances are the commander has figured out you're double-crossing him, but even if not, he'd kill you because you know too much about his organization," Nate said slowly, his vision graying. "After this whole fiasco, he'll take Audrey and run before tying up any loose ends." Where was Audrey?

The senator reached out to clutch the door frame with one gnarled hand. "You're telling me the commander would actually kill a U.S. senator and that I'm a loose end?"

"Without a hiccup," Nate said. "I'm not sure about that PROTECT group, either. They might want you dead."

Shane typed more keys on the laptop. "I can create an identity for you, Senator. We can also make sure a body is found that is identified as you, but you'll have to stick with it."

The senator ran a gnarled hand through his gray hair. "Okay. I'm staying with you guys. With Audrey. I mean, a kid needs a grandparent, right?"

Nate stilled. He wasn't adding to family here. "Um, one of the most powerful organizations in the world wants us captured or they want us dead. Sticking with us is a bad idea."

The senator smiled. "I'm glad we're in agreement." He swayed. "I guess I'll go take a nap." He shut the door behind himself.

Nate shared an amused look with Matt.

"Let's worry about him later." Shane unrolled a map Nate had created of the compound. "We need to go over this again. The plan sucks."

"The plan really sucks," Matt agreed without turning around.

Nate stalked over to study the map once again. "The plan is my only chance." The clock was counting down, and he had no good options. This was do or die, and the odds stank. Something in his chest hurt.

"I hate statistics, but the odds of you surviving this are not good," Shane said, his gaze down, his shoulders rigid. "We have to find a better way."

"What would you do?" Nate asked softly, heat filling his head. "If the commander had Josie right now, what would you do to get her back?"

"Anything." Shane smoothed out the paper, a muscle in his jaw visibly tightening. "But that doesn't mean I like this. We should all go in at once."

"No." Giving the commander exactly what he wanted would be suicide for all of them. "I know I can't control either one of you, but this is the way it has to go down right now. You have Josie and Laney to worry about." Nate left fear in the dust and allowed the soldier inside him to take over. "And Jory. We have to find out about Jory."

A strangled groan rumbled up from Shane's chest. "We will find him, and we'll do the job without sacrificing you."

Nate fastened his brother's arm and turned him. "My woman is in there, and so is my baby. I have to go." His entire life was being held hostage by the commander. He waited until Matt turned to face him. "If I don't make it, promise me—"

"You'll fucking make it," Matt growled, fury hardening his jaw. "That's an order."

Nate nodded, his throat closing. There were so many words he needed to say, so many in such a short time. "Thank you both." The multitude of words wouldn't come, so he did his best. "For being my brothers."

Shane's eyes darkened, and he yanked Nate close for a hug. "Shut up," he muttered.

Nate hugged back, his heart aching. "You shut up."

"Both of you shut up." Matt clicked a clip into place. "We're going with the plan, but we all survive it. I trained you until my head nearly blew off my neck, and you'll fucking remember every single session we had. Remember who you are, what you can do, and who needs you."

Nate swallowed, his shoulders going back. "I'll remember."

Matt threw him a weapon. "Take this."

Nate tucked the Glock into the back of his waistband. "If you say so."

"I do." All soldier, Matt stalked forward to view the map. "I think you should go in this way." He pointed to an area heavily patrolled to the north. "They won't expect it."

Nate sighed. "Mattie, we have the plan they won't expect, and that's what we're going with." He understood Matt's need to protect him, but there wasn't time for another debate. "You know what I can do, and you know what you would do if Laney was in there." Hell, Matt would lay siege to the place to get her out. "Trust me. I know what I'm doing."

Matt eyed him for a moment and then grabbed him for a quick hug. "Okay." He let go and turned to study the map again. "I guess we go with your plan."

Good. Nate nodded. He needed his brothers on board. "We're good to go."

On the table, his phone rang the tune assigned to unknown numbers.

Nate swallowed and answered the call on speaker. "Yes."

"Nathan! So good to find you, boy." The commander's voice had gotten even deeper in the last five years, if that was possible. "It's time to come home. Your woman and baby are here."

CHAPTER
30

A UDREY SAT IN the conference room and twirled the new box of prenatal vitamins across the table. Her stomach hurt and her eyes burned from lack of sleep. She'd spent the night at the facility in a rather plush room complete with attached bath, but sleep had eluded her. She needed to save Nate. Somehow. "Mother, I've never asked you for anything."

Isobel glanced up from a stack of papers, her brow wrinkling. "Why would you? I gave you life."

"Thanks for that." Audrey reached over and clasped her mother's chilly hand. "I'm asking you for help now. Please help me save Nathan—help me get out of here." The genuine plea came from her heart and asked for more than just help. She wanted to add a request for Isobel to care.

Isobel tilted her head to the side. "I'd think you'd want Nathan to come be with you. This is the best course for everybody."

"No." Audrey tightened her hold. "The best course is for me to leave with Nathan and give this baby a chance for a normal life. He's your grandson. Don't you want that for him?" So much need roared through her that Audrey's hands trembled. Even if Isobel didn't care enough about Audrey to give her freedom, maybe she'd care enough about a grandson. Sometimes bad parents made good grandparents, right?

Isobel frowned. "But the boy will be special. We need to study him, to make sure he trains in the correct manner. Just think how powerful he'll be and what an asset he'll become to Franklin."

Ah, Franklin. So Isobel cared about the baby because of what he might do for the organization, and not as a grandson. In that second, Audrey let go of any childhood dream she'd harbored of her and her mother finding a common ground. A relationship. Resignation and a sad wisdom filled her. "You love the wrong man, Mother."

"I most certainly do not." Red slid over Isobel's porcelain skin. "How ridiculous."

"You do." Audrey gentled her voice. "Mother, the commander is a sociopath. He's incapable of loving anyone or feeling anything. You know that."

Isobel freed her arm. "I do know that he's unencumbered by emotion or weakness. He's invincible."

"Nobody is invincible." Sorrow and sympathy softened Audrey's tone. "You've said all these years that you experimented in the name of science." Which was somewhat true, definitely. But Isobel's motivation was stronger than just the quest for answers. "I've known that your love for that man has colored everything you've done." Including sacrificing her own daughter's happiness and health.

"My entire life is dedicated to science." Isobel patted Audrey's hand as a commotion set up outside the compound. "Let's go see what's happening." Holding her tablet to her chest, she led the way from the room.

Audrey's shoulders slumped, and she pushed up from the chair. She followed her mother, her heart hurting, her leg hitching as she tried to keep up. She walked outside into the drizzly rain and gasped. Armed soldiers lined the area, guns all pointed at a van pulling up. One of the commander's vans.

The door opened, and Nathan Dean stepped to the ground.

Guns cocked all around them.

His hands held harmlessly at his sides, he stalked forward, wearing only faded jeans and a ripped T-shirt.

A soldier jumped out of the van behind Nate. "He's not armed, and we searched him for visual or audio devices. There are none."

The commander took strong, measured steps from the building to stand before Nate. "You came in the front door," he said, frowning.

Nate cocked an eyebrow. "You invited me."

Audrey measured the two men. The commander had always seemed too large to be real, but now, in the murky rain, she realized Nate stood at least two inches taller. Maybe three. His chest stretched wider, and his muscles cut a sharper image. "My boyfriend can beat up yours," she whispered to her mother.

"What?" Isobel asked, her gaze wide on the action.

"Nothing." Audrey fought down instant panic at the sheer number of guns pointed at Nate.

Nathan's body didn't move, but his head tilted just enough that he could meet her gaze. "What the hell happened to your face?" he asked quietly. Too quietly.

She gingerly touched her still-aching cheekbone. "Rough night. Before I arrived here."

The commander glanced at her over his shoulder

before turning back to Nathan. "I wouldn't hit a woman, as you know. Anybody who harmed her is now dead, I assure you."

"That's nice to hear." Nathan glanced at the myriad of guns pointed at him. "This is overkill, don't you think?"

"Maybe." The commander's stance widened. "When is the surprise attack coming from your brothers?"

Nate smiled, challenge filling his eyes. "They're not coming."

"Bullshit." The commander stepped toward Nate in an intimidating move. "They wouldn't let you come in here by yourself. That much I know."

Nate didn't look intimidated in the slightest. He looked...triumphant. "That's true. If they'd known I was coming here, they would've either tried to stop me or they would've joined me. But. I. Didn't. Tell. Them." He kept the commander's gaze, sardonic humor twisting his lip.

"The kill chips will end them," the commander said.

Nate's smile widened, and he shook his head. "We have the computer program and can hack the codes."

"You do not," the commander scoffed.

Nate held out his hands and then gingerly reached into his back pocket.

Soldiers tensed on either side of him.

He sighed and extracted a piece of paper to hand to the commander. "The program."

A deep red flushed across the commander's cheekbones. "Where did you get this?"

"Who cares? We have it." Nate's lids half lowered, and his smile disappeared. "You lose."

The commander took a deep breath and crumpled up the paper. "Do I?" He smiled. "I have you, and I have your progeny. That's a win, as far as I'm concerned."

Nate shrugged. "I have mere weeks to live."

"I can fix that." The commander turned and nodded at Isobel. "Please post on all crucial Internet sites that we have Nate Dean, and his brothers have one day to show up and save him or I'll cut him up to study for years."

Isobel nodded, already moving for the door. "Standard encryption and multiple codes?"

"Yes. We don't want anybody but the brothers to know we have Nate." The commander clasped his hands behind his back as Isobel disappeared into the building. "Do you think they'll discover the message before I torture you enough to find their location?"

Nate shrugged. "Why don't we find out?"

Audrey's knees weakened. Torture?

The commander gestured for Nate to turn around.

Nate lifted his chin, amusement lighting his eyes before he complied, hands behind his back. "Afraid of me, Commander?"

"No, but I trained you and know what you're capable of." The commander nodded to a soldier hovering by the building to come forward.

"You have no clue what I'm capable of," Nate said softly.

The soldier held restraints and approached gingerly, looking ready to sprint away at any second. After he'd wound Nate's wrists tight with chained-together cuffs, he bent and followed suit with Nate's ankles. Then he slowly backed away.

When Nate pivoted back around, he looked... bored.

This was all so wrong. Audrey took in the soldiers, trying to make sense of how everybody could be so wrong. They looked... scared. Very alert. She shook her head. Why would they be frightened of Nate? "Nathan's the good guy." Her voice sounded shrill, even to her ears.

Nobody looked her way. They all kept their focus on Nate.

Why wasn't the world exploding? Where were Shane and Matt? Audrey swallowed. They had to be coming, right? But only the sound of rain falling on concrete filled the air.

The commander smiled. "Let's get started, shall we?"

Exactly seven hours after arriving at the commander's Virginia facility, Nate sat, battered and bleeding, on an examination table in a lab. Thick cuffs secured his wrists to a post behind his ass, which wasn't helping his broken ribs in the slightest. He'd spent his first hour having blood drawn and medical tests conducted—all while being bound. Every doctor and scientist had approached him cautiously, and he'd held still for each, amusement keeping him from going insane.

Then he'd fought for six hours straight.

In a training field much like the ones he'd grown up on, he'd fought highly trained soldiers. With knives, with poles, even with guns, they'd come at him—often two or three at a time.

The commander had watched while several others had filmed him and taken copious notes. After the fights, they'd brought him here. He glanced down at his bare chest and already purpling ribs. Blood and mud covered his ripped jeans and combat boots. He smelled like blood, death, and dirt.

Some doctor had taken more blood and made notations of Nate's breathing, heart rate, and blood pressure before disappearing.

High heels clicked outside the door, and every muscle in Nate's body stiffened.

Dr. Madison entered the room, her dark hair up in a bun, a tablet in her hands.

Great. Nate lifted an eyebrow. "Seems like old times." Except for the tablet—she used to scribble in notebooks. Score one for technology. The woman had tended to his wounds many times through the years, although she wasn't a medical doctor. Not once had she offered sympathy or kindness. Just Band-Aids and medical jargon.

She smiled and eyed his bare chest, interest gleaming. "You've filled out even more in the last five years."

He swallowed down nausea. "I've made it all day without puking. Let's keep it that way."

She giggled.

The sound assaulted every muscle in his gut. For years, he'd heard that giggle—unnatural and weird from such a brilliant scientist. "I've always thought you might be crazy," he said conversationally.

She shrugged and moved forward to tap her fingers along his ribs. "You've broken a couple."

No shit, lady. "They'll heal." He tested the ties at his wrist—solid.

"Yes, they will." She hummed to herself. "Do you still heal quickly?"

Faster than ever, actually. "Not as fast as Jory. Where is he?"

Madison giggled again. "I'm asking the questions today. You fought well—kept up the training, have you?"

"Did you think I'd get fat and slow after I escaped you?" he asked lazily.

"No." Madison shook her head, reaching for disinfectant and a cotton ball. "I figured you'd prepare to come back and try to take the commander out."

Nate gave a short nod. The woman had studied him since

birth, and she was an expert in psychology and all of that crap. "I considered it. Planned it, in fact. But things change."

"I've noticed. Where are your brothers, anyway? They should be mounting a rescue by now." She dabbed the cotton along a cut above his right pec.

Pain bit into him, and he kept his expression bored and his body relaxed. "Like I said, things change."

She leaned into him, wiping blood off his shoulder. "Don't be silly. There's no way you and your brothers have had a falling out bad enough that they wouldn't save your sweet ass."

He swallowed and turned his head so they were eye to eye. "We're as solid as ever, but now they have something else to protect."

Madison breathed out, her gaze dropping to his mouth.

He levered back.

She sighed and stepped away. "You don't mean those silly women, do you? I met Josie once, and I've read all about Laney. Those twits wouldn't come between you."

Nate chuckled and shook his head, ignoring the strained muscles in his neck. For once, he could give her the truth. "My sisters-in-law haven't come between us. But they've given my brothers a reason to keep living, and nothing, not even me, will keep my brothers from protecting them." Nate tugged on the restraints. "You don't know either one of them if you think they're sacrificing those women for me, and you don't know me if you think I'd let them."

Madison clucked her tongue. "I taught you all better than that." She studied a cut above his right eye that was still bleeding. "When you're fighting, when such pain is inflicted on you, I figured you'd be thinking about your brothers. Or escape. Or some beach in Cabo. Is that true?"

"No."

"Then, what?" she asked, reaching for the tablet, fingers poised to type.

"Fuck you." The woman would never understand. When he fought, when pain tried to trap him, he thought of *nothing*. It was a trick Mattie had taught him early on, and it had saved his life more times than he could count. Think nothing, feel nothing, and just fight back.

His childhood had shaped him into a survivor, into a predator, and those lessons had taken hold and dug deep.

Madison reached over and jabbed a bruise along his jaw. "Not nice, Nathan. Considering we're going to share a little boy, you might want to be nicer to me."

Rage ripped through Nate, and only a tight rein on his control kept him from showing it. "Audrey and I are going to share a little boy. He won't need nutty granny, you bitch."

Madison barked out laughter. "Did I hit a nerve? Sweet boy."

Nate shook his head. "I really don't get it. How can you not care a whit about the baby? Or Audrey? She's your daughter."

Madison gave him a blank look. "I do. Audrey is safe, and we're going to train that boy to be even better than you."

No way was his kid going to be a cold-blooded killer. No fucking way. "How could you impregnate her like that? Without even asking her?"

Madison smiled. "Why ask her? The girl has loved you since day one. She would've said yes. And the baby is yours, Nathan. I promise."

She was telling the truth, but he'd already known the kid was his. Regardless of the sperm donor. "Don't make me kill you, Madison." His voice became hoarse.

She blinked and then scoffed. "You couldn't kill me, Nathan. Not only did I raise you, but I'm also Audrey's mother. She might not understand me, but like any child, she wants to love me. She does. No matter how much you might dislike me, she'd never forgive you for killing me." Dr. Madison patted him on the top of the head. "You sweet boy. Think."

Nate jerked his head away. As much as he hated it, the woman was right. Audrey wouldn't be able to deal with him killing her mother. Plus, he wasn't quite sure he could handle killing the woman, as horrible as she'd been to him through the years. Unless—"Did you shoot Jory?" he asked.

Madison stepped back. "How did you know Jory had been shot?"

"I saw a video." Nate watched her closely.

Her eyebrows rose. "Interesting." She reached out and brushed a finger over his tattoo. "Freedom."

"Yes." He kept his face stoic, wanting nothing more than to kick her away from him.

"I don't understand you." Dr. Madison frowned. "We could give you the world. A freedom you can't even imagine."

"That's not freedom. That's fear." Nate shook his head. "No matter how smart you are, you'll never understand." The way the commander and Madison had controlled them, with threatening harm to their brothers, guaranteed no other outcome but escape. "We will never want what you have to offer."

She scratched her chin, frowning as if trying to solve an impossible puzzle. "You and everybody you love are going to die in slightly more than two weeks if you don't come back."

He lifted his chin. "I'll take freedom and death over the life you're offering."

"For your brothers, too?" she asked, her painted lips coy.

"Yes." He kept her gaze, allowing no expression to cross his face. The thought of his brothers dying hurt deep inside him, but the thought of them being subjected to the commander's whims again sliced deep beyond the here and now.

Her head jerked up, and her frown deepened.

The door opened, and Audrey rushed inside and toward him. "Nate!" Her eyes widened when she eyed the damage marring his chest. She touched a bruise under his eye. "Are you all right?"

"I'm fine." He glanced at Dr. Madison as she turned to furiously type on her tablet. "Taking notes, are you?"

"Yes." Madison didn't lift her head. "The emotion in your relationship intrigues me. It'll be interesting to see how it changes when the baby arrives."

Audrey went pale.

"Audrey," Nate said softly. "Look at me."

Her tear-filled eyes lifted to meet his.

He forced a smile through battered lips. "We're going to be fine. I need you to stay calm."

"What should I do?" Her brow furrowed as she leaned around to look at his restraints.

"Nothing." He wished he could hold her. "Trust me. Please."

Dr. Madison leaned against the counter. "I'm sure he has an escape plan. Don't worry." The scientist didn't seem too concerned with the possibility.

Nate gave a short nod that hopefully only Audrey caught.

The door opened again, and two soldiers stomped inside. "The commander is ready for him," the taller one said.

Dr. Madison nodded and slid her tablet onto the granite counter. "Very well."

One of the soldiers reached behind Nate and released him from the table. Unfortunately, his wrists remained bound. He jumped off, smiling when both men tensed.

Audrey backed toward her mother. "Where is he going now?"

Dr. Madison rubbed her neck. "The tests have just begun. Next we're going to see how well Nate handles pain. A lot of it. Plus, we do need to show other soldiers what happens when the commander is betrayed. Nate will make a good example."

"No." Audrey darted toward him, and one of the soldiers snatched her away.

Nate growled low.

Audrey furiously struggled, tears sliding down her pale face.

"Audrey." Nate put enough bite into his voice to halt her movements before she got hurt. "Stop it. Now."

She paused, confusion clouding her eyes.

He kept her gaze. "Stay calm and take care of the baby. I'll be fine."

"But—"

"Now." This time his voice cut hard.

Audrey blinked and stilled.

"It'll be okay," he murmured as the soldiers shoved him out of the room to head toward pain.

CHAPTER
31

Whips and electricity hurt less than simple needles pumping drugs into his veins. Nathan spit out blood, aiming for the commander's boots. Chains held his arms high above his head while cold concrete bit into his bare feet. Blood and other fluids slid across the floor and into a drain in the despondent cell.

The commander threw an electric prod across the room to smash against a table holding all sorts of interesting devices. "How's the head?"

Cloudy as fog. "Fine." Nathan concentrated on the concrete beneath his toes. Cold. Hard. Real.

"I doubt it. There's enough sodium barbital in your veins to make a priest confess." The commander eyed a grate in a far corner of the ceiling. Through the night, rain had poured down the grate, and a couple of trucks had passed over it, sending down leaves and water. "Dawn is breaking."

So dawn had broken before he did. Nathan eyed the locks on the one door and smiled with cracked lips.

The commander nodded, an odd pride glowing in his black eyes. "I made you tough."

"No, you didn't." Nate tried to roll his bellowing shoulder to snap it back into place. "Matt made me tough." Nate tried to bite back his comment, but the words flowed freely. Stupid drugs.

"Yes, he did." The commander twisted his wrist, frowning at a growing bruise from one of Nate's early kicks. "Mathew's obsession with training, with learning, with becoming so deadly—I was impressed. Not once did I see his true motivation."

"Which was?" Nate fought to keep his head from lolling forward.

"Escaping me." Injured ego and bewilderment glimmered in the man's eyes for the briefest of seconds. "Training you. Training Shane and Jory to survive. To someday leave."

"Yes. Leaving was always our plan." Nate couldn't stop the truth.

The commander's gaze hardened. "But your duty, your role, differed from your older brother's, didn't it?"

"What role?" Nate's words slurred on the end.

"Oh, don't think I don't know you, Nathan." The commander chuckled, low and deep. "Matt taught Shane and Jory to avoid death. You taught them to embrace life."

Nate shook his head. He'd never embraced shit. "You're crazy."

"Am I?" The commander scraped blood and tissue off one boot with the heel of the other. "You tried to give them a childhood. A sense of normalcy, of being wanted and protected in this environment."

Nate spit out another clot of blood. "You've been reading too many of Madison's psychology journals."

"You gave them the one thing you wanted more than anything else in the world. To belong. To have a *family.*" The commander smirked.

A slow smile lifted Nate's bruised lips, the feeling malicious. "I succeeded, you prick."

"Think so?" Anger burst red across the commander's face. "You will never have normalcy. You're abnormal. We created you like a science project."

Nate started to laugh. "So?"

"So? Freaks can't have family."

Nate laughed harder and rattled a broken rib. "You tried so hard. So damn hard to make us cold killers. I'd never realized how badly you'd failed."

The commander shot a punch into Nate's gut.

Nate folded over with a harsh *oof*. He spit blood. And laughed harder. "No wonder you're pissed."

"I'm not pissed." The commander straightened his bloody uniform. "I won. You are a killer."

"Maybe, but I ain't cold." The current environment notwithstanding. "Neither are my brothers. You tried so fucking hard, but you couldn't break us. Not one of us." The muscles in Nate's back vibrated from the pressure of keeping him from dropping and injuring his wrists. "Matt survived the pressure you put on him. Even more so, he survived the pressure he put on himself to save us. He fucking survived and found love."

The commander punched Nate in the face, sending spittle flying from his mouth.

Nate's head rocked and his vision fuzzed. Pain radiated through his ear. So he smiled. "Shane is happily married. Fucking married, Commander."

"And Jory?" the commander said softly. "You didn't save him."

"Maybe not." Nate lowered his chin to look evil in the eye. "But I gave him the best childhood possible here, and he thrived. When we escaped, he became truly happy.

Almost twenty, a trained killer, he went to Disneyland and rode the rides like a kid on holiday." The memory would always warm Nate.

The commander reared back. "Disneyland."

"Yep." Nate finally let the past go. "If he's dead, he's in a better place."

"You think you creations go to a better place?" the commander spat.

"Yes." Nate exhaled in release. "I actually do."

"You're still in this place." The commander manacled Nate's hair and jerked back his head. "What if I forced you to choose?"

"Chocolate chip. Forget the vanilla." Nate forced his eyes to remain open. "You meant ice cream, right?"

"No." The commander smiled, malice carving grooves next to his mouth. "How about a choice between Audrey and your brothers?"

Nate tried to chuckle, but more blood slipped out of his mouth. "My brothers are free, and Audrey will be soon."

"I'll kill her. Cut her into little pieces while you watch, unless you get your brothers here." The commander reached into his boot and drew out a fresh blade he hadn't used yet on Nate.

This time Nate did chuckle. "Right. Killing Audrey while she's pregnant with my baby. Not a chance would you do that."

"I can wait six more months." Sharper than the blade he played with, the commander's smile promised pain. "Let's be honest. While she's done a good job with the senator, Audrey lacks commitment to my organization. Once the baby is born, Audrey will be a hindrance." The commander lifted a muscled shoulder. "I will have to kill her."

"You fucking touch her, and I'll rip you apart tendon

by tendon." Rage sped up the drugs in Nate's blood, making him even more light-headed. Even so, he held the son of a bitch's gaze. "Trust me. I. Will. End. You."

Dark amusement echoed on the commander's chuckle. He peered closer at Nate. "Listen to you tell the truth. Your pupils are three times normal size."

Not a big surprise considering the drugs infecting his blood. "What'all did you give me?" Nate's long-hidden Southern accent broke free.

"Truth serum, drugs to increase pain, and some others we're not quite sure about." The commander tightened his hold. "Now that you're in a talkative mood, let's talk."

"Fuck you."

"Good start." The commander smiled. "Where is your new headquarters?"

"San Diego." Nate let the truth slip out, not sure if he could stop it. Sins Security was based in San Diego and counted as headquarters. Of course, it wasn't where the family had dug in, but the commander hadn't asked that question. "Why did you let somebody shoot Jory?"

The commander sighed. "I needed Jory to bring you all back in."

Needed? For the first time, real pain sliced into Nate's chest. "So he's dead?"

"I didn't say that." The commander leaned closer, his minty breath brushing Nate's skin. "How's the heart? I had to restart it twice."

So he'd died twice during the night. Interesting. "Still pumping. Where's Jory?"

"I can stop your heart again if I wish. When are Matt and Shane coming to get you?"

Nate smiled and fresh blood washed down his chin, cooling aching bruises. "They're not coming here. Period."

The commander blinked.

Triumph, almost sadistic in its intensity, flew through Nate. He'd made the bastard blink. "You know I'm not lying." He couldn't at this point.

"Hmmm." The commander rubbed his chin. "Yet they know you're here."

"Yes."

The clinch on Nate's head loosened, and the commander stepped back to study him. "Why aren't they coming?"

"I told them not to. It's more important that they figure out the codes to the chips... and find Jory." Nate spit out more blood. "We have the computer program but not the codes. Yet." He should probably worry about the internal bleeding going on right now.

"No." The commander shook his head. "They wouldn't have listened."

"They did." Nathan's voice sounded oddly strangled and hoarse. How long had he screamed during the night? The whole thing was a blur. "I thanked them for being my brothers and hugged them."

"And they?"

"Shane told me to shut up, and Matt told us both to shut up. That was the end." Nathan rose up on his toes as his leg cramped.

"Interesting." The commander drew out a cell phone to type in a text. "So they figure I won't kill you... might even reprogram your chip. You're here to get information."

"I would like information." Nate's vision blurred. "Why do you want Matt and Shane here, anyway? We won't work for you."

The commander's jaw hardened. "You will work for me. There's important missions to be accomplished, and after I filet Matt in front of all of you, you'll do what I want."

"Filet?" Nate's brain fired.

"Yes. He took my training and betrayed me. He tried to take my place with you and your brothers." The commander nabbed the back of Nate's head and jerked. "You follow *me*," he spat.

It had always been personal between the commander and Matt. "So you want him dead?"

"Yes, and I want his brothers to follow my command." Spittle flew from the man's mouth. "Forever."

The commander truly hated Matt.

Nate spit out blood and spoke directly from his heart. "You will never beat Matt. Ever. He's twice the soldier and man that you'll ever be. And. You. Know. It."

The commander yanked hard, and Nate's vision blurred. Then the leader released him. "I'll kill Matt slowly."

Nate grimaced. "Where's Jory?"

The door opened, and a soldier wheeled in a laptop. "I received your text."

"Thank you. Leave." The commander pressed a couple of keys on the keyboard, and the soldier scrambled out of the room.

Nate tried to raise an eyebrow. "We're going to watch a movie? I haven't seen the new Disney one. I love monsters that talk."

The commander glanced over his shoulder. "You're under the influence of potent truth-inducing drugs. You really do love Disney movies."

Nate tried to shrug. Disney movies rocked.

The commander chuckled and rolled the screen closer to Nate. "This is a different movie."

Nate tried to focus and keep his gaze stoic as Jory came into focus. His baby brother, the one who'd grown huge, the one who never exploded in temper, sat bound on a chair, bloody and furious. A woman's high heels came into view as she shot three rounds into Jory's chest. Jory fell to the floor, and the screen went blank.

Nate's heart thundered fast enough to hurt his broken ribs. "I've already seen that movie." Hundreds of times, actually. He'd studied it frame by frame, trying to find any clue.

"Yes, I figured." The commander leaned over and punched in a new code. "But you haven't seen this one."

Everything in Nate stilled. The drugs disappeared, the cold room faded into the background. The screen showed Jory's massive body on a surgical table, surgeons scrambling to save his life. They lost him once, but he came back.

Nate lifted his chin. "He survived being shot?"

"Not exactly." The commander pushed a button, and the video fast-forwarded through the surgery to Jory lying unconscious in a hospital bed, tubes hooked up to him everywhere. "Coma. Brain dead."

Please, no. Nathan turned a cold look on the commander. "This won't break me, either." But he'd watch. If these were his younger brother's last moments, he'd watch and experience them with Jory. He'd be there for his brother, even if it was too late.

"I think it might." The commander smiled without humor. "I've always known that physically, you can't be broken. Emotionally, you're the easiest target in the Gray family."

"Isss that a fact?" Nate slurred.

"Yes. You need them so much more than they need you. Without them, you'd free that beast I know lives in you. You'd be the cold-blooded killing machine I fucking created. It's in your DNA." The commander's smile turned triumphant.

The truth of the words slithered deep into Nate's gut, taking root. "Maybe you're right. Maybe not." He levered up to get better balance, even as his wrists bellowed in pain. "But I do have brothers, and Matt made sure I stayed human. Jory and Shane kept me good instead of bad."

The commander shook his head. "But that need in you? The need to be other than who you are? That's what makes you weak."

Did it? Or did it give him strength? Nate blinked blood out of his eyes. "You'll never understand me."

"Oh, I get you. Let's see, shall we?" The commander turned back toward the video and fast-forwarded through scenes, each day documented with a date. Day by day, Jory didn't move. He became paler and his muscles lost definition... but he didn't move. For nearly two years, he didn't even twitch.

Nate allowed no emotion to show on his face, but inside, knives sliced through everything he was. Everything he'd hoped for, and everything he'd wanted to be. He'd failed his little brother, the one he'd promised to protect. Jory, so good and powerful, had wasted away in a hospital bed. *Alone*.

The commander pushed PAUSE at a date six months ago. "I actually hadn't planned on showing you this, but you've left me no choice."

"Finish it," Nate ground out.

"Fair enough." The commander pressed PLAY and stepped away.

The date blinked on the bottom of the screen, and the beeping of medical machinery filtered through the speakers. A monitor to the side of Jory's bed blipped with his heartbeat.

Nate watched three months pass, waiting for the final moment when the beeping ended. Something inside of him started to crack.

Jory opened his eyes.

CHAPTER
32

THIS WAS DEFINITELY a bad idea. A horribly bad idea. Audrey crept through the hangar storing three helicopters. Only three? Yeah. The commander had another base somewhere, without question. The smell of gasoline and motor oil assaulted her.

She'd seen the commander have Nate brought to the building late last night, and it had taken this long for her to gain access. She'd only had to knock out one doctor to reach the secured part of the main building. Exiting that building had taken several more hours, after she'd acquired a gun off a soldier she'd injected with morphine. Then she'd threatened two scientists, stolen several ID cards, and tied people up.

For nearly another hour, as dawn broke, she'd hidden behind a fuel tank until the guards around the hangar rotated. Finally, she'd managed to slip inside using one of the secured cards.

The people she'd tied up would be discovered soon.

She didn't have much time.

Unnatural quiet surrounded the silent beasts. She maneuvered around them, her damaged leg hurting deep inside. Her activities of the night had strained her beyond her capabilities, and everything ached. Even her stomach.

But she had to save Nate.

Finally reaching a doorway in the far metal wall, she swiped a card, and the door opened. Thank goodness. A quick glance inside showed a rough cement stairway leading down. She swallowed. Nothing good happened down there.

Steeling her shoulders, she took the first step and closed the door quietly. She listened.

Silence.

She'd worn yoga pants, a sweatshirt, and tennis shoes for her night of creating havoc. The soft-soled shoes made no sound as she carefully took each step, her back to the wall, and the gun pointed down. The landing faced a wall, and she had to turn right. Taking a deep breath, she turned, her gun pointed directly at the soldier manning the door.

He opened his mouth to shout a warning.

She fired.

The bullet hit him in the chest, sending him down.

Oh God, oh God, oh God. She scrambled for the door and swiped the card through the reader. Nothing happened. Her fingers shook. Her heart pounded. She swiped again, and the door clicked.

Please, don't let it be too late. She ran inside a small cell and stopped cold.

Nathan hung suspended from the ceiling, his hands holding chains, his knees twisting the commander's neck. "Where the hell is Jory?" Nate yelled, veins popping along his jaw.

The commander fought back, punching up, turning and biting Nate's thigh.

Nate bellowed in pain and struggled against the chains. "Why did you show me that video?"

The commander gurgled for air, reaching for his back pocket. "Because I'm not deactivating your chip or Jory's chip, and I'm keeping you separated. Matt and Shane will have to separate to rescue you both, and that's when I'll reclaim all four of you." He slowly drew a jagged-edged blade from his back pocket.

Audrey didn't stop to think, didn't stop to reason. She pointed the gun at the commander's back . . . and fired.

The bullet hit him in the shoulder and knocked him across the room. He crashed into a metal table. Instruments of torture clattered to the concrete floor. His arms flailed, and blood sprayed from his chest. Must've been a through and through. His eyes closed and he hit the ground.

Nate swung his body toward her. Cuts, stabs, and burn marks violated his chest, legs, and neck. Bruises mottled a frightening purple across his strong face. "Get something sharp."

She scrambled toward the bloody instruments on the floor and clasped a knife glinting red and silver. She turned, her breath heaving, and studied him. Reaching for the damaged table, she rolled it toward him. "I've got this." Gingerly easing her good knee on the table, she leveraged herself and slowly stood up. The knife sliced easily into the leather cuffs around Nate's wrists, although she had to saw for precious moments to free him.

He dropped with a groan, scrambling for the table and still going down.

Panic flooded her, and she leaned to balance on the table and hop down. "Nate?" She knelt next to him and held his shoulders. "How bad?"

He shook his head, and blood arced across the room.

"Couple of broken bones, internal bleeding, and vision hazing." Curling bloody fingers over the table, he hauled himself to his feet and hitched over to a laptop opened on a narrow table.

"Nate, let's go." She stood and reached for his arm. "Bring the laptop." Was his brain even functioning?

As he brought up a Pinterest site for some artist from Alaska, she shook him. His brain had been fried. "We have to go."

"Hold on." His fingers fumbled on the keys. "I can't function. Audrey, pin a picture of high-heeled shoes on this site, would you?"

She coughed. "You're going to be okay. Trust me. Let's go." She tried to drag him toward the door.

"Now." He tugged her back. "Pin."

On all that was holy. She couldn't move him. "Fine." Leaning around him, she searched and pinned a sparkling pair of Louboutins onto the page. "Happy now?"

Satisfaction quirked his lips. "Oh, yeah." He closed the laptop and shoved it into her hands. "Do not lose this." He turned back toward the commander, who remained motionless on the floor. "This will only take a minute."

"We have to go." Audrey glanced at the downed man. "Right now. More men will be coming."

A bellow sounded from up above, and boots clamored on the stairway. Nate growled, frustration flushing his face red as he tore himself away from the commander's prone body. Nate claimed a knife from the floor and ran out in front of her, slicing one man across the face and the next across the neck.

He lurched on the stairs, and Audrey jumped forward to help him up. Grabbing her elbow, he stumbled for the door. "We have five minutes."

He tripped several times on the stairway up, and she tried to stabilize him, even with her leg buckling. She tucked the gun in the back of her yoga pants. They reached the top stair, and Nate shoved open the door. She followed him into the hangar.

Strong arms hooked her and threw her across the room.

She cried out, landing hard and bouncing. The baby! Her ears rang. She slowly sat up to see Nate and a soldier grappling at the doorway. Nate jabbed an elbow into the soldier's neck, and the soldier punched Nate in his already damaged face.

Nate fell back, crashing against the metal wall.

Audrey shook her head, trying to focus. The gun. She set the laptop on the concrete and took the gun from her waist. Rising, she started to aim and then stopped. Nate had the soldier in a headlock, and the guy's neck snapped with a quick twist.

She gulped down bile.

Nate turned toward her, a bloody mess, pure fury in his gray eyes. "Are you all right?"

No. Not even close. "Yes. What's the plan?"

He grinned bloody teeth. "Sparkly shoes mean we're heading out via air."

"Huh?" Her brain had slowed to a crawl.

"Get in that helicopter while I sabotage the other two." He staggered toward a helicopter.

Oh. The Deans used a fake Pinterest site to relay messages? Audrey tried to ignore the immense pain attacking her body. What had she injured when she'd hit the ground?

No time for that. She reclaimed the laptop and limped over to crawl into the front seat of a Black Hawk. She kept the door open and her legs out just in case. A sharp pain stabbed along her ribs, and she bent over. "Ow."

Nate whirled toward her. "What's wrong?"

"I don't know." Another pain hit. Not again. "Please, Nate. Let's go."

Nate finished whatever he was doing with the other two vehicles and hitched over to her. "Get secure. This is going to be bumpy." He frowned. "Hasn't it been five minutes?"

Audrey wiped dirt off her chin. "Why?"

The outside door opened, and almost in slow motion, Isobel Madison clicked into the room. Her gaze on the tablet before her, she stilled, her head jerking up.

Isobel reached for her cell phone.

Audrey jumped from the helicopter, gun out and pointing. Her ribs ached. Bad. "Drop the phone, Mother."

Nate stood next to the helicopter, his gaze going from one woman to the other. "Nobody has to get hurt here," he said through swelling tissue.

Audrey swallowed and set her stance. "I will shoot you. Drop the phone."

"You will not." Isobel sighed and glanced at Nate. "Where's the commander?"

"I shot him." Audrey's knees began to tremble. She'd shot two people. Her breath caught, and she tried to remain standing.

Isobel's eyes widened. "Where?"

"Down there. Go check on him but drop the phone first." Audrey's knee buckled, and she kept upright only through pure stubbornness.

Isobel's gaze darted to the far doorway and back to her daughter. She glanced at her phone. "You won't shoot me."

"I will." Audrey's hands trembled, and she tightened her hold on the gun. Another pang rolled through her abdomen, and she swayed. "I don't want to shoot you, but to protect this baby, to protect Nate, I will. I swear,

Mother. I. Will. Shoot. You." She meant every word, but she hoped she didn't have to shoot.

"Audrey, don't," Nate said softly.

She kept her aim steady and turned slightly to look at his battered face. "I love you. I love this baby, and nobody is going to hurt either one of you. Get in the helicopter, Nate." If a choice had to be made, she'd choose her baby and Nate. "I'm sorry, Mother. But I'm taking a stand."

Her mother's eyes blazed a light blue. "I can't believe you're mine."

Audrey sighed and allowed sorrow one brief moment. "I'm not." She turned toward Nate, wincing at her aching stomach. "Let's go."

He eyed her and nodded before hitching his bulk around the front of the bird. Audrey turned back to her mother. "Drop the phone. Now."

Isobel's eyes flared. "I will never understand you." She threw the phone onto the ground.

"I know." Sadness filled Audrey as she turned and lifted herself back into the bird. "Go check on Franklin. He may be dead."

With a soft cry, Isobel ran for the back door.

The world exploded outside. Even protected by metal, Audrey felt heat. Oh, no. What was happening? Even though she had emotionally let her mother go, she was pathetically grateful Isobel had headed downstairs in the metal shop and hadn't been caught in an explosion. Maybe Audrey hadn't let go completely, but who could?

She hurried to shut the door and turned toward Nate.

He frowned. "That was more than five minutes. I had my brothers set the explosives and get back to safety where they could remote detonate." He leaned over and pressed a hard kiss against her mouth. "I love you, too."

She gulped as he flicked a bunch of levers. "Your brothers?"

"Bombs and other explosives set around the entire perimeter. The commander's forces won't know where to concentrate." Nate pressed a button, and the ceiling folded in two. "We'll go pick my brothers up now."

"Okay." Audrey buckled in, her mind reeling, her abdomen undulating. Something bad was happening, but they had to get free. "Um, can you see to fly?"

"Sort of." He ignited the engine, and a second later, they lifted into the air.

Audrey's stomach cramped, and she squeezed her abdomen. "Oof."

"What?" Nate kept his gaze outside.

She tried to take several deep breaths, her gaze outside at the fires billowing up from all around. Soldiers scurried to and fro, shooting, but not at anybody. "I'm not sure." Trying to remain calm, she pressed a hand to her inner thigh. "I'm bleeding. The baby."

CHAPTER
33

NATE FLEW THE copter through the storm, his heart thundering. Visibility sucked. "Lean back and take several deep breaths." He had to get Audrey to a doctor. Now.

She nodded and leaned her head back, closing her eyes. Even so, a tear leaked out to wind down her face. "This is my fault."

"No, it isn't." He needed both hands on the stick, or he'd reach for her. His hearing was off, and he couldn't get his bearings. "You'll be okay. I promise."

A light glimmered up from below, and he followed it, setting down right outside his cabin.

Shane and Matt ran out through the swirling wind and angry rain, both loaded down with gear. The senator jogged out afterward, his arm in a sling.

Matt opened the back hatch.

Nate ensnared Audrey and gently lifted her, stepped into the storm, and into the hatch. "I can't see to fly," he muttered. The senator scooted in next to him.

Matt nodded, shut the door, and jumped into the pilot's seat. Shane stretched into the passenger seat, and they rose back into the rumbling clouds.

Nate gathered Audrey close, his breath heating. She felt so small and defenseless in his arms, and for the first time, he didn't know what to do. She huddled into him, her head on his chest, her knees gathered to her stomach.

"Audrey?" He leaned close to her ear.

She sniffed. "I hurt. Something's wrong. Cramps."

No.

Matt reached a low flying altitude and glanced over his shoulder. "We'll reach the SUV we have hidden in five minutes. Be prepared to run for it."

"No." Nate swallowed, his ears buzzing. "We need a hospital, Mattie. Now."

Matt stilled, his gaze lashing to Audrey. "The copter is probably tracked, Nate. We have to ditch it. Now." The helicopter rocked to the side as the storm battered it. Lightning blazed outside.

Nate rubbed a hand down his face. "Drop us off and keep going. It's the baby. Please."

Matt cut Shane a look. "They're tracking us right now. If we make a stop, they'll know it. They'll come after you." He grimaced and turned back to the stick.

Audrey groaned, her body shaking.

Nate tucked her closer. "There's no choice. Drop us off and get to safety." He'd figure something out after seeing a doctor. Even if he had to call the real cops, he'd do it to protect her. As if they could.

The senator patted Audrey's shoulder. "I'll come with you."

"No." Nate shook his head. "You've disappeared, and you have to stay that way." He leaned to better view Matt's face. "Audrey shot the commander. He's slowed down."

"Dead," Audrey moaned.

"No." It wasn't a kill shot. "You didn't kill anybody,

baby." Even the soldier outside the room had been wearing a vest. "I promise."

Her body relaxed against him as if she'd been carrying a weight. "Okay."

Nate bit back a growl. He'd been so close to ending the commander, but he hadn't had time with the soldiers descending on them.

Shane looked back at Audrey, concern cutting grooves near his mouth. "Inova in Falls Church has one of the best neonatal programs in the world. They have a heliport." At Nate's raised eyebrow, Shane shrugged. "I memorized hospitals from here to home just in case."

Thank God for his brothers. Nate nodded, emotion tearing into him. "Drop us off and go hide the copter. We'll meet you at home."

Matt fought the storm while Nate fought the fire inside him. He'd been so cocky. So sure he'd be able to get Audrey out safely. Shane strapped on a headset, his deep voice making arrangements with the hospital.

Nate tuned him out, listening for the baby's heartbeat. His vision sucked, and his hearing remained static. The drugs still thumping through his bloodstream messed with his entire system. The second they landed, he was going to hand Audrey to Shane to see if Shane could hear anything.

The city flashed by below them.

Matt glanced back. "Put on some clothes."

Oh, yeah. Nate reached for a duffel with one hand and tugged on a dark shirt. He moved Audrey as gently as possible to the side, pressing a soft kiss to her forehead. The senator tucked her into his good side and murmured calming words.

Nate exchanged his jeans for clean ones and also threw on socks and boots. Reaching into another bag, he took out some antibacterial wipes and removed most of the blood and grime from his face and hands before slapping a Yankees cap on his head.

As smooth as silk, Matt landed the helicopter. Orderlies rushed toward them, and Nate lifted Audrey out before depositing her on a gurney.

Shane jumped to the ground and slid a gun in the back of Nate's waistband.

Nate nodded, his throat clogging. "I'll be in touch. Watch the videos on the laptop. Jory's alive."

Shane blinked and took a step back. His eyes blazed dark and gray. "Are you sure?"

"I'm sure." Nate gripped his arm and leaned toward his brother. "I'm positive."

Shane swallowed.

Nate turned to run after the gurney and his family.

Seconds later, the helicopter rose slowly into the sky.

Nate followed Audrey until a nurse made him stop and fill out a bunch of forms. He used one of his many identifications, citing a car accident that would explain both of their bruises. Then he had to wait. He sat in the waiting room on an orange chair, one eye on the hall for a nurse, the other on the door for the commander.

The outside door opened, and he tensed.

Matt and Shane jogged inside, their hair wet, jackets covering what had to be a cache of weapons.

"What are you doing here?" Nate whispered, leaping to his feet.

Shane frowned. "Where else would we be?"

Matt clapped Nate on the shoulder. "We deposited the helicopter in the middle of a grocery store parking lot, secured transportation, and high-tailed it back here."

Nate shook his head. "Where's the senator?"

"Waiting with the engine running," Shane said, his gaze encompassing the entire room.

Nate had to get them out of the hospital. "The commander will know we stopped here."

"No shit." Matt frowned and brushed water from his hair. "But we didn't want to block the heliport with his piece of crap. We moved it." He reached under his jacket and drew out the laptop. "Any news on Audrey?"

"No." Nate swallowed, too much emotion swamping him at once. "You need to go."

Matt's eyes darkened. "*Never alone*, Nate. Period."

The back of Nate's eyes stung.

Matt glanced down at the dented silver computer. "This shows Jory is alive?" Matt's voice broke on the end.

"Yes." Nate patted his older brother's arm. "Watch it. You'll see."

A nurse hurried down the hallway toward him. "Mr. Jones?"

"Yes." He moved toward her. "What's going on?"

"Mrs. Jones is all checked in." She smoothed back gray hair and looked up a foot toward his face. "You can go sit with her until the doctor comes in." Sympathy glimmered in her eyes. "You look like you need medical attention, too."

"I'm fine." He turned and followed her, his gut clenching. Something was really wrong. He could feel it.

When he reached Audrey's room, he paused at the doorway. She lay in the bed, covered by a white blanket, a bruise on her cheekbone. Fragile and soft, she didn't belong with bruises.

She turned. "Hi."

He forced himself into the room and took a chair by the bed, taking her hands in his. "I'm so sorry, Audrey."

"Nothing is your fault." She took a deep breath. "The

doctors did a physical exam, and I am still bleeding. He went to get an ultrasound machine. I'm so scared."

"Me too." Nate kissed her hands, tears gathering in his eyes. "I was so sure I could rescue you and find out about Jory." Not for a second had he doubted his plan. Idiot. For the first time in his life, he felt true helplessness. There was nothing he could do to save his own baby. As much as he tried to focus and listen for a heartbeat, all he heard was the thunder outside. When would his senses return?

The commander had wondered how to break him. This was it.

A tech rolled a machine into the room, and seconds later a man in a white lab coat followed. He stuck out a hand for Nate. "Dr. Shawnesee."

"Nick Jones." Nate shook the doctor's hand, careful not to bruise it. The doctor stood a foot shorter than Nate and appeared to be all of eighteen years old.

"You look like you need an examination. That must've been some car accident." The doctor moved a rolling seat into position.

Nate swallowed. "I'll get checked out after you're done here." He couldn't even say the word *baby*.

"Okay. Let's take a look, shall we?" The doctor did something with a wand and handed it to Audrey with instructions.

Nate's world fuzzed, and he dropped into the seat, his head in his hands.

All of a sudden, a rhythmic *thump, thump, thump* filled the room.

Nate lifted his head slowly, not wanting to believe. His heart thumped so strongly against his broken ribs he winced. His breath actually stopped.

"Yep. There he is." The doctor pointed to the screen. "Heartbeat is good. Let's check out the amino sac."

Audrey reached out and grabbed Nate's hand. Hard.

Hope. The feeling spread through Nate until his body refused to move an inch. Not one inch.

The doctor pointed out organs one by one and spent several minutes making sure Audrey and the baby were perfectly healthy. Finally, he printed out a 3-D picture of the little guy. "Your son is doing well."

Audrey half sat up. "What about the bleeding?"

"You have two bruised ribs from the car accident. My guess? That caused bleeding." The doctor stood. "You need rest, Mrs. Jones. I recommend you stay here overnight, and then it's bed rest until you don't bleed for two days straight."

Audrey burst into tears.

Nate reached for her with one hand and shook the doctor's with the other. "She's just relieved," Nate said. He couldn't describe his own feelings—they went way beyond relief. His hands shook, and deep inside, emotion welled. The baby. The baby—his baby was all right.

"I know, although I'd like for your wife to take it easy for the next few months. Bed rest isn't strictly necessary, but it's time to take it easy." The doctor shook his hand. "Tell the nurse when you'd like to be examined, Mr. Jones." With a happy wave at Audrey, the doctor skipped out of the room.

Nate hugged her tight, a prayer he hadn't realized he knew tumbling from his lips. "You're all right."

"I know." Audrey wiped off her face. "The baby is okay." Her blue eyes seemed dazed.

"He's fine." Nate eyed the door. "You can't stay here tonight."

Audrey swung her bare legs toward the floor. "We should go. Now."

Matt and Shane instantly appeared at the door.

"Well?" Shane asked.

"Baby is fine," Nate said, a smile welling up. "Audrey needs bed rest."

"Awesome." Shane bounced back on his heels. "Two Humvees just rolled up outside. We need to go. Now."

Nate helped Audrey to stand. "If you saw two, they've already covered the other exits."

Matt nodded. "Get ready to fight, gang."

Audrey cleared her throat. "Why?" She pointed to the window across the room. "We're on the first floor, right? Where's the car?"

Matt eyed her and then the window. "In the parking area over there." He frowned. "Let's go."

Nate opened the window and jumped out first. Audrey tried to swing one leg over, but Matt caught her, lifting her. "Bed rest," Matt said, handing her over to Nate.

Nate held her tight, hunching his body over her to shield her from the blustering wind and rain. He had to get her somewhere warm. Now. Shane and Matt jumped out silently.

They made it through a tangle of shrubs and dying flowers before a bright light descended on them.

Guns cocked and echoed louder than the storm.

Nate's shoulders tensed, yet he gently set Audrey on her feet, pushing her behind him.

Soldiers in black surrounded them.

CHAPTER
34

AUDREY'S BARE TOES squished in the mud. Rain splattered her gown to her body, and she shivered. Thunder bellowed high above, and for a moment, silence ruled.

Then all hell broke loose.

The Dean brothers moved as one: Matt went left, Shane turned right, and Nathan blazed forward. Hard and fast, they punched and kicked, often simultaneously.

A shot fired.

"Alive," one of the men in black yelled. "Unconscious is okay."

Audrey backed away until her butt hit the rough bark of a tree. So the commander wanted them alive. But even so, with the ferocity of the punches being thrown, somebody could be critically hurt.

And Nate was already injured. He had at least two broken ribs and might still be bleeding internally.

Two soldiers took him down, and he grunted as he impacted the ground. Pain filled the noise.

Audrey started forward only to have Matt yell at her to get back. She hesitated, her body trembling, her stomach still cramping. Nate twisted one guy's neck and rolled the other one over to punch him in the face. Hard. The soldier's head clonked a rock and he didn't move. Nate leaped to his feet and one-arm tackled one of several soldiers punching Shane on the ground.

The smell of blood filtered through the falling rain.

A soldier appeared to Audrey's right with a stun gun already crackling, and she screamed.

Faster than humanly possible, Nate lunged for her, curled around her, and rolled her to the ground. Somehow, he kept her from hitting any rocks or shrubs. He tensed and then convulsed. The scent of burned cotton and flesh clogged her nose.

With a growl, Nate released her and charged the soldier, taking him down.

How could Nate even move? Audrey gulped and scrambled to her feet. She needed a weapon.

Suddenly, two headlights swung wildly around as an SUV jumped a curb and skidded across the wet grass, taking out several of the commander's soldiers. Bodies flew in every direction, hitting the building, trees, and shrubbery. The vehicle spun sideways. "Get in," the senator yelled.

Nate kicked his opponent in the head, staggered to his feet, and reached for Audrey.

She tried to fend him off and walk herself, but he lifted her and ran for the SUV, sliding in the back. Matt jumped into the front, and Shane leaped next to Nate.

"Go, go, go," Matt said, pounding the dash.

The senator punched it, and the SUV rammed over several shrubs, barely skirted a tree, and screeched onto the street. The bumps and jumps made the vehicle land hard, but Nate held Audrey tight.

He leaned over and brushed leaves off her face. "Are you all right?"

"Yes." She patted his wet face. "Are you? How much voltage did you take?"

"Not enough." He grinned, his bottom lip bleeding again. "We've trained to take shocks and keep going. Chalk one up for the commander."

"Screw him." Audrey settled back down, shivering. "You okay up there, Senator?"

"Yeehaw!" The senator cut off a Mercedes that honked angrily. "Call me Jim. Grandpop Jim. And just hold on."

Grandpop Jim? Audrey shook her head, trying to relax. The man was having the time of his life.

Matt glanced warily at the senator. "Take back roads to the next grocery store you see, and we'll need to change cars."

"No problem." The senator flipped off a honking trucker.

Shane reached over and plucked a stick from Audrey's hair. "We're gonna have to change cars a few times. You okay, Aud?"

"I'm fine." Her body rioted, but she took several deep breaths.

Nate gave a short nod. "Audrey, lay down the best you can."

She nodded, her body going lax, her head against Nate's chest and her feet on Shane's legs. Touching them both and trusting them to take care of her. Nate and his family would keep watch. Her family, too. Finally. She belonged. Plus, she'd joined the family with a grandpa. Grandpop Jim. They'd all come for her, and they'd protect her. The baby would always need protection, and her new family would provide that.

If they destroyed the chips, the baby would never be alone. The kill chips hung over her head, but for now, she'd rest for the baby.

Nate was a deadly man, but she loved him. All of him. The good and the dangerous...he was all hers and she'd accept him as such. They'd find a way to have peace and safety for their child.

With a soft sigh, she smiled and finally relaxed into the sense of home.

After days of traveling, Audrey finally stretched her legs as she stepped out of the most current SUV. She wore new yoga clothes they'd picked up on the way. It was freaking amazing she hadn't killed one or all of her new family the last day as they'd switched back and driven the wrong way many a time to make sure they weren't followed. Not one of the Dean brothers would let her do a thing or lift a finger, and they were way too worried about making sure she ate.

The senator was even worse—and he'd no longer answer anyone unless they addressed him as Grandpop Jim.

But as she stood in the chilly Montana morning and eyed the great house surrounded by excellent security, she finally relaxed. "Beautiful," she murmured.

The front door burst open, and a tiny blonde barreled out and straight for Shane. He caught her easily, kissing her on the nose. "Hi, angel," he murmured softly. She hugged him tight, burrowing into his chest as if she belonged right here.

At a slower pace, but her smile no less radiant, a tall brunette reached Matt to wipe a finger over a bruise above his eye. "Mattie."

"Laney." He tucked her close, dropping his face onto her shoulder.

Audrey just stared. She'd never seen Matt so, well, at peace.

Nate slipped his hand into hers. "Come inside, sweetheart. You need breakfast."

She'd kill for coffee.

The blonde disengaged herself from Shane and hugged Nate before holding out a hand. "I'm Josie." Her blue eyes sparkled with mischief, and a smile lit up a very pretty face.

Audrey took the hand. "Audrey."

The senator cleared his throat.

Audrey glanced at him. "And this is Sen—I mean, Grandpop Jim."

Josie's face lit up even more, and she lunged for the senator to hug him tight. "Grandpop Jim. Awesome. We've never had a grandpop around."

The senator started and then gingerly hugged the petite woman. His eyes filled. "Glad to be here."

Matt led Laney over to introduce them. Gentle intelligence filled the woman's brown eyes. "How are you feeling, Audrey?"

"Tired of being in a car." Audrey smiled and glanced around. "But very happy to be home." Yeah. This definitely felt like home.

"Good." Laney slipped her hand into Matt's and turned. "We have breakfast ready for everybody, and I wouldn't mind taking your vitals."

Now that sounded like fun.

They all trooped into the sprawling ranch house and into a kitchen with a table big enough to fit everybody and then some. Eggs, bacon, pancakes, and bagels were immediately passed around.

Josie took a sip of orange juice. "We've been working on plans to subdivide and build us each houses. I mean, once we take care of the chips." Clouds covered her face.

Shane slipped an arm around her shoulder. "We have the computer program, and I can duplicate it. Then we'll figure out the codes."

Laney cleared her throat. "Is Jory really alive?"

"Yes." Raw emotion darkened Matt's eyes. "He's alive, and we have to find him. We're going to go through every ounce of data we have to find that other location. Jory has to be there. He just has to be. I'll show you the video later."

Laney rubbed Matt's arm on the table. "We'll get him back, Mattie."

"I know." Matt seemed to force a smile. "In the meantime, Sins Security personnel, ones I trust, confirm a body has been found outside of DC, and the DNA will match one Senator Nash."

The senator grinned and reached for another pancake. "Perfect."

Nate sighed, his fingers tangling through Audrey's as if he couldn't stop touching her. "You understand that it'll be isolated out here? We can get you a new ID, but you can't go gallivanting around town making friends."

The senator eyed the group at the table. "I have everything I need right here. After Ellen passed on, I didn't think I'd find a reason to keep going. Now I have one." He patted Josie's hand. "Pass the syrup, would you?"

Audrey blinked several times and put down her napkin. Man, she was tired.

Nate stood and helped her up. "Come on, sweetheart. Let's get you settled in."

She nodded and followed him through a massive living room and down a hallway lined with gorgeous oil paintings to a bedroom that smelled like Nathan—wild and free. He lifted her as they crossed the doorway to lay her gently on the bed. "The bath is through there, and we have a huge closet."

"That's nice." Not that she'd brought any clothes. "I like it here."

"Me too." He leaned over her, his mouth wandering along her jawline. "I've been dying to touch you the last two days stuck in that car."

Warmth washed over her. "Me too."

He kissed her, slow and deep.

Her entire body dissolved into softness and need.

He lifted his head. "As soon as Laney checks you out, maybe we can continue this."

Audrey tangled both hands in his hair and held tight. "I'm fine. No bleeding for two days, and my ribs feel better. Nobody but you needs to check me out right now." To emphasize her point, she clasped her feet at the small of his back.

Emotion filled his eyes. "I've loved you since the first second you smiled at me on that dismal training field so long ago."

Her heart swelled, and tears pricked her eyes. "I've loved you since the same day—when you took my hand, so careful not to hurt me." She'd been thinking all morning, and now the words deserted her.

"What's spinning through that brilliant head?" he murmured, his eyes darkening.

Brilliant? Yeah, she was smart, and she should use that intelligence for good. "I'm not sure what I can do here." Her gaze dropped to his chin.

One knuckle gently lifted her face back up. "What do you want to do here? Anything you want, I'll make it happen."

She swallowed, forging ahead with plans as if the kill

chips didn't exist. It hurt too badly to think about those right now, and she needed to give hope. "I know everyone works hard here. You guys run Sin Security and will do so after we deactivate the chips. Laney patches you guys up after missions, and Josie does all the books for the security company."

Nate frowned, thoughtfulness quirking his lip. "You can do any part you want. Or if you don't want to help here, I'll try to figure out a way for you to do what you want."

"That's just it." She was making a mess out of this explanation. "I don't want to go and do anything."

He tilted his head. "Okay?"

She shook hers. "No. I mean, I want to have this baby and just love him. Play with him and keep him safe. For a while. I mean, I can get a job—"

"You don't ever have to get a job if you don't want. Honey, we're loaded." Nate grinned.

"But I should. I mean, I should be more than just a mom—"

"Wait a minute." He cupped her face in his big hands. "*Just* a mom? You're kidding, right?"

"Um, no?"

He kissed her gently on the nose. "You're talking to a guy who would've done *anything* to have a mom. We all would have. One who wanted to have us in the first place and who wanted to play with us. Protect us. Do the Band-Aid thing. You know, like on television when the kid falls down and the mom cares. There's no *just* there. It's the most important thing—ever."

She nodded, a tear spilling over. "I might want to work someday."

"Whatever you want, you get." He slid his lips over hers, emotion and love in every movement.

"I want you safe with me forever." God, she needed him.

"Then I'll make it happen."

Nate didn't break promises. For the first time, Audrey relaxed. "We're going to fight our hardest to find Jory and deactivate the kill chips. We just have to."

"We are." He kissed her nose, one hand sweeping down her rib cage. "This little guy will be fine, and we'll get his uncle Jory back. I'll find the code for the chips if it's my last act on earth. We have hope and determination. Then, Audrey, I guarantee you everything you will ever want or need."

"Everything?" A little sister for the boy growing in her would be nice.

"I promise." Nate lowered his mouth to hers. "Forever."

CHAPTER
1

Utah
Present Day

JORY DEAN COUNTED out push-ups rhythmically, keeping his six-and-a-half-foot-plus body aligned for maximum effect. He hit a hundred without breaking a sweat, which energized him further, considering muscle now covered the bones in his body again. Finally. He felt like a healthy adult and not some hospital patient.

At least physically. Mentally? He had some work to do, and he needed to figure out the odd buzz in the area of his parietal lobe.

The cold cement floor scratched his hands, reminding him he was alive.

Somehow, amazingly alive.

In three months, he hadn't had a chance to escape, but now he was strong enough to train and fight, so the bastards holding him would surely let him out to test him, and then he'd take his shot. By his count, he had a week to live, and he needed to start now.

He slowly lifted one hand to twist around his back, not losing the beat. His mind swam with a debilitating combination of despair and frustration, so he shoved all thoughts into the abyss like his brothers had taught him. The thought of them gave him strength, and he stored it deep.

He would escape and get to them, and they had to still be alive. He'd deactivate the kill chips near their spines, and then he'd be finished.

High heels clipped down the hallway toward his cell, so Jory straightened and stood, wiping all expression from his face and emptying his eyes. The computer vestibule fully visible outside his containment area was empty, so he couldn't ask who was coming. It couldn't be—

But it was.

He should probably feel something, anything... but he didn't. Dr. Madison opened the door and came into view, her black hair in a bun and her blue eyes quizzical. She was the closest thing he'd ever had to a mother, and even now, after everything he'd been through, he wondered if he should care, even a little.

As he'd recuperated the last few months, he hadn't seen her, and he'd wondered where she'd gone. Companionship, even hers, was better than being left entirely alone. Except for the techs who dropped off his food and picked up his tray, he'd been alone with his thoughts, and inside his head wasn't a pretty place to be.

The clock counting down on his life and the lives of his brothers had sped up, and death hovered way too close.

He focused on Madison. A purple-yellowish bruise covered her right temple, and as she neared, a limp became evident.

"What happened to you?" Jory asked through a screened

part of the security-glass wall of his container, his mind calculating scenarios of attack and what he needed to do. He had to protect the world he knew until it was time to destroy it. So now, he'd defend her if necessary.

Even though he was nothing but an experiment to her. Not even human. Maybe God felt the same way Dr. Madison did—yet another fucking depressing thought. The cell was making him maudlin.

She fingered the bruise and looked up more than a foot to his face, her forehead furrowing. "Your brother blew up our DC facility, and I was caught underground in an airplane hangar."

That quickly, something quiet and dull in Jory flared awake. Even so, he kept his face stoic and his vitals mellow. He'd kill to see his brothers again. "Which brother?" His voice lowered in a measured move to keep it from fucking trembling.

"Nathan." She pursed her lips in a tight, white line, studying Jory carefully. As usual. "He took my daughter with him."

Jory jolted internally and yet remained preternaturally still, his brain lurching. Nate was still alive. Thank God. "No kidding? Good for Nate." Jory's big brother had never gotten over Audrey Madison, so it wasn't exactly shocking that he'd returned for her. "Was she willing to go?" He wouldn't put it past Nate to toss Audrey over a shoulder as the bombs detonated.

Madison sniffed. "I believe so, but maybe the pregnancy has messed with her intellect."

Jory stilled. Only supreme control kept his heart from thumping hard against his rib cage. He lifted one eyebrow and pierced the doctor with a hard stare. "Audrey is pregnant?"

"Yes. With Nate's baby." Madison reached for a computer tablet in her white doctor's jacket, avoiding his gaze. She'd started doing that the second he'd learned to put a little power into it. "Congratulations; it appears the Gray family can procreate." She smiled, revealing sharp teeth, having control back into place.

Warmth burst through Jory, and he allowed himself a rare moment to ban the ever-present chill. Nate was going to be a father? Oh yeah. He'd make a great father...if he lived after the next week. So they did have a chance to have families of their own. Jory wanted to smile but refused to give the doctor the satisfaction of reading his emotions.

Her gaze dropped to his groin. "I wonder if we could—"

Jory fought the urge to cover his boys and instead stepped closer to the partition. "Don't even think of it, Madison. I'll kill you first." He spoke low and kept eye contact as he gave her the absolute truth. She'd been the one woman as a constant in his life from the beginning, and she'd tended his hurts as he'd trained as a kid. Maybe not with motherly love, but she had stitched him up a time or two while taking copious notes on how fast he healed. So he'd rather not have to snap her neck.

She clucked her tongue. "It's hard to imagine you are the good-natured brother."

"Getting plugged in the chest several times and ending up in a coma for two years tends to piss a guy off." He kept her gaze and stretched his torso, trying not to go crazy in the small cell. He'd awoken three months ago, immediately striving to regain his strength. To get home to his brothers. They had to be worried beyond belief.

He'd also like to remember the day he'd been shot, or more importantly, the identity of the shooter. Who had tried to kill him? He'd definitely like to return the favor.

Dr. Madison licked her lips and eyed his bare torso. "Your workouts and diet regimen have returned you to excellent shape in such a short time. I did a marvelous job with your genetics."

He kept from outwardly reacting to her perusal, his mind quickly calculating scenarios. While he could probably seduce her, based on the speeding up of her pulse alone, what would that gain? Besides his wanting to cut off his nuts afterward. How fucked up was his life that he'd even consider sleeping with Madison to gain freedom? For his brothers, he'd do anything. Even that— although until he figured out how that would gain him freedom, he so wasn't going there. "I care little about genetics," he said.

God only knew what she'd combined with soldier DNA to create him, and even now, he didn't want to know the particulars. He was Jory Dean, he had three brothers, and that was enough family history for him.

He swallowed and forced his body to relax when all he wanted to do was punch through unpunchable glass. When she looked at him like he was steak on a plate, he wanted to puke. "Were Matt and Shane with Nate when he blew up DC?" The more information he could get now, the easier it'd be to make a plan now that he was strong enough.

Time was up, and he needed to strike.

Madison just looked at him.

With a sigh, he gave up the pretense, looking her right in the eye. "Please tell me if they're still alive." Yeah, he could play her game if it earned him information.

She pursed her lips again in her studying, thoughtful, analyzing expression that made him wish he *could* hit a person out of anger and not purposeful intent. He'd never lost control of his temper, and sometimes that was a damn shame.

"You know you've always been the easiest of your brothers to read," she said.

"I know." That's what she thought. Madison was tough to play, but he'd figured out years ago how to manipulate her when necessary. False vulnerability and full truth worked just because she liked to see reactions. So he reacted outwardly while his brain logged internally. For now, she could believe she was smarter than he was, though at this point, she wasn't even close.

"I wonder if your vulnerability is because you're the youngest, or if it's because of your maternal egg donor?" Madison tapped her chin.

"I don't know." Jory shrugged, changing tactics to keep her off balance and not let her see how much he needed an answer about his brothers. "Who was my maternal egg donor?"

She shrugged. "Who cares? We stole eggs from facilities or paid for donations. Either way, the women never wanted the children."

Jory kept his face blank, not even feeling the words that should cut deep. Who the hell really cared about what came before? The Dean brothers shared a paternal donor, and their identical gray eyes served as a genetic marker. They'd given up long ago of finding any information on maternal donors. They didn't have mothers and never would. "My brothers?" he asked.

She smiled. "Shane would've tried to charm me for the answer, while Nathan would've harassed me like a Rottweiler fighting for a bone. Matt? Well, Matt would've played mind games and twisted me up until I gave the information."

"I'm aware of my brothers' talents." Jory preferred

computers to humans, which made mining Madison's brain easier rather than most people's. The woman was almost a computer, completely lacking in emotion. Long ago, he'd given up his soul, so begging didn't mean much to him, even if he had meant it. "Please tell me."

She typed something in on her tablet. "As far as I know, Matt and Shane are alive. They didn't help Nate on the ground in DC, but I have no doubt they assisted in planting explosives."

Electricity sparked down Jory's torso, and his shoulders straightened. Alive. His brothers were all alive. Now he had a short time to keep it that way. "Thank you," he murmured.

She glanced up, and her eyes slowly focused. "There's more."

Man, she loved to see him beg, didn't she? "Oh?" Jory had given her all the satisfaction she'd get this morning. Either she'd give him the rest of the details, or she wouldn't.

"Yes." She frowned, irritation sparking through her blue eyes. "Shane went back for that woman he'd used on a mission once, and Matt kidnapped one of our doctors who'd betrayed us. They've committed themselves to women."

Now Jory did smile. "Bullshit." Whatever game she played, she could roll the dice by herself. He could see Nate rescuing Audrey since they'd gotten together so long ago, but no way would either Shane or Matt drag a woman into the shit storm of their lives. "Nice try, Madison."

She nodded, her forehead smoothing out. "I don't understand, either. Soon we'll have them all back home, and I can figure them out."

Oh, hell no. His brothers were never getting caught again, and Jory needed freedom to deactivate the kill chips near their spines implanted almost five years ago.

He eyed the outside door. So close and yet too damn far. "Why the hell do you want us all here? I just don't get it."

"The commander and the organization are being attacked, and your skills and training are needed." Her voice remained level, but fire lit her eyes. "From several sides. The government is looking at the financials, there are competing firms out there getting stronger, and an organized fundamental group wants the commander shut down."

"Good. Then maybe you'll leave us the hell alone." He'd love to shut down the entire organization. Well, once he got out of the cage.

"That will never happen. Our base inland will be much more appropriate to contain you and yours, as well as retrain you. You'll be transferred within a few days." Madison glanced back down at her tablet.

His head lifted. If he allowed them to transfer him, he might never get loose. "I'm tired of gym shorts and T-shirts. And these tennis shoes are a size too small." He rested broad hands on his hips and glanced around the dismal cell. One cot sat in a corner, and a bare-bones bathroom took residence around a partial wall. "Get me out of here."

"Why?" She arched one fine eyebrow. "That kill chip by your C4 vertebra will detonate in one week and you'll die. Your best chance of survival is staying here."

His eyelids slowly rose, so he flattened his hands on the bullet-proof glass and leaned in. "The chip you screwed up? Yeah. I'm not expecting a rescue there." The bastard scientists had implanted kill chips in all the Dean brothers' spines, and if the right code wasn't entered in the right computer in one week, the chips would activate and sever their spines. Unfortunately, the code changed every thirty seconds, so getting a lock on it from a distance had been all but impossible.

Of course, no damn code worked for Jory. "We both know I'm fucked."

"I do wish you'd watch your language. As a child, you were so well mannered." Dr. Madison typed something into her tablet. "I didn't make a mistake on the chips. When you got yourself shot, a bullet ricocheted off the chip, and it's damaged. It's shocking the device didn't explode then and there." She pursed her lips as if pondering what to have for dinner. "Just shocking."

"Who shot me?"

Madison lifted a slim shoulder. "You have the highest IQ ever recorded, young man. Those memories are in that impressive brain, and you need to access them."

Jory rubbed his eyes. Having no memory of a devastating event was normal, damn it. He might never remember who'd shot him.

But he remembered everything up to that day, including blowing his cover at the scientific facility where he had been gathering information about the commander's organization. He'd scanned the wrong computer system and had set off alarms.

Damn rookie move because he'd been in a hurry and so damn close to finding information about the kill chips. Shit. He'd deserved to get shot for his carelessness.

For now, he was a fucking monkey in a cage, and he had to get out of there before his *impressive* brain melted. So he tried reason. "Madison? I have one week to live. For once in my life, have a heart and let me go live it out." It was the closest he'd come to asking the brilliant scientist for anything after she'd started hitting on him when he'd reached puberty. She had quite the record for playing with cadets, and he'd kept his distance, as had his brothers, he was sure.

She smoothed back her hair. "I didn't raise you to be a quitter. Don't worry. I have a plan."

As usual, he'd have to work against her. He ran a frustrated hand through his hair, which had begun to curl at his nape. "What's the plan?" If he was going to figure out a way to save his brothers, he had to get out of there. Panic broke through his internal calm, and he disintegrated it.

"For one thing, I'd like to get you back into an MRI. Your brain is functioning…abnormally." She stared at his forehead as if she could see into his gray matter, intrigue and suspicion curling her lip. "I'm having a PET scan set up as well for later today."

Fuck, shit, and damn it all to hell. He couldn't let her discover his special abilities, nor those of his brothers. They'd succeeded for years in hiding the very skills that had kept them alive. But ever since the coma, something new percolated in his brain. Something he apparently couldn't hide now. "You've been doing scans for months. Nothing is different."

"The scans from last week are different." She tapped a red fingernail against her lips.

Yeah. His best guess was that new paths had been forged in his brain during the coma, and the weird tingling in his lobe had begun the previous week. Maybe it was just his special abilities increasing in power, or maybe it was something new. Either way, he had to mask the truth.

Two heartbeats echoed from outside the room, so he tilted his head to hear better while trying to appear bored. Dr. Madison had no clue about his heightened senses or his extra abilities, and he needed to keep it that way. Nobody normal would be able to hear the heartbeats. Shit. Nobody normal could even understand some of his gifts, much less use them.

A soldier entered first, followed by a woman in her mid-twenties who slid out from behind him.

Jory's breath caught in his throat. *Exquisite*. For once, that word could be applied accurately. She stood to about five-foot-six in black boots with a matching leather jacket. Light mocha-colored skin, straight black hair, and eyes greener than the most private parts of Ireland.

She took one look at him and stepped back.

He stepped forward and flashed a smile that made her eyes widen. If he had to scare her to get her to leave, he'd do it. Anybody seeing him in captivity would be killed by the commander after serving their purpose. So he allowed sexual tension to filter through the room. How he could do it, he wasn't sure. Maybe pheromones and bodily heat waves, and the ability came easier now than it had before the coma. It was a hell of an advantage to use sometimes, and he ignored Madison's quick intake of breath as he employed it.

"Is she for me?" he asked, forcing his gaze to run over the newcomer's body and surprising himself when he hardened in response. Hell, he hadn't seen a woman except Dr. Madison for more than two years, but at least most of that time he'd been in a coma.

He'd always liked women, although he'd never gotten close to one. Not really. They were either part of a mission or worked as doctors in the facility, and those certainly couldn't be trusted.

This one was petite with delicate bone structure and clear, intelligent eyes. Whatever her purpose, she sure as hell didn't belong in this dismal place. Hopefully she'd turn on her heel and get out since he'd leered at her.

Instead she lifted one eyebrow. Her face flushed. "So that's him."

Well, damn. Another angel with the heart of a demon.

A pang landed squarely in Jory's chest. Beauty should never be evil. "Yeah, that's me," he murmured, dropping the sensual attack. "Who are you?"

She opened her mouth and shut it as Dr. Madison shook her head. "It doesn't matter who she is," Madison muttered. Grasping the woman's arm, Madison led her over to a computer console. "Get to work, and remember the rules."

Jory frowned. Was the woman a prisoner, like him? Maybe he could gain them both freedom, with her help. She *was* outside of the cage, now wasn't she? He smiled.

Dr. Madison glanced back toward Jory, her gaze narrowing. "Leave her alone to work, and I won't have you tranquilized again." With that, she allowed the soldier to escort her from the room, and the door nicked shut behind her.

The woman at the console turned around. "Piper. My name is Piper." She eyed the partition. Her voice was smooth and sexy... feminine. She guarded her expression well. "They didn't give me your name."

Yeah. *They* wouldn't have thought to give his name. "Jory." He really liked the way her tight jeans hugged her curves, and he appreciated the intelligence sizzling in those spectacular eyes. She'd have to be smart to help him escape. "Why are you here, Piper?"

She exhaled slowly and stretched out her fingers. "I'm here to save you, Jory."

Fall in Love with Forever Romance

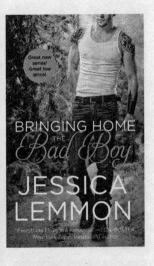

BRINGING HOME THE BAD BOY
by Jessica Lemmon

The boys are back in town! Welcome to Evergreen Cove and the first book in Jessica Lemmon's Second Chance series, sure to appeal to fans of Jaci Burton. These bad boys will leave you weak in the knees and begging for more.

HOT AND BOTHERED
by Kate Meader

Just when you thought it couldn't get any hotter! Best friends Tad and Jules have vowed not to ruin their perfect friendship with romance, but fate has other plans...Fans of Jill Shalvis won't be able to resist the attraction of Kate Meader's Hot in the Kitchen series.

Fall in Love with Forever Romance

"Lovable men and lovable dogs make this series a winner!"
—JILL SHALVIS, *New York Times* bestselling author

FOR KEEPS
by Rachel Lacey

Merry Atwater would do anything to save her dog rescue—even work with the stubborn and sexy TJ Jameson. But can he turn their sparks into something more? Fans of Jill Shalvis and Kristan Higgins will fall in love with the next book in the Love to the Rescue series!

BLIND FAITH
by Rebecca Zanetti

The third book in *New York Times* bestseller Rebecca Zanetti's sexy romantic suspense series features a ruthless, genetically engineered soldier with an expiration date who's determined to save himself and his brothers. But there's only one person who can help them: the very woman who broke his heart years ago...

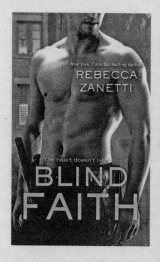

Fall in Love with Forever Romance

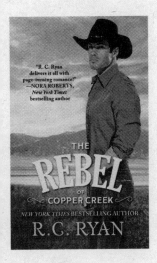

THE REBEL OF COPPER CREEK
by R. C. Ryan

Fans of *New York Times* bestselling authors Linda Lael Miller
and Diana Palmer will love this
second book in R. C. Ryan's west-
ern trilogy about a young widow
whose hands are full until she
meets a sexy and rebellious cowboy. If there's anything she's
learned, it's that love only leads to
heartbreak, but can she resist him?

NEVER SURRENDER
TO A SCOUNDREL
by Lily Dalton

Fans of *New York Times* bestsell-
ers Sabrina Jeffries, Nicole
Jordan, and Jillian Hunter will
want to check out the newest
from Lily Dalton, a novel about a
lady who has engaged in a reck-
less indiscretion leaving her with
two choices: ruin her family with
the scandal of the season, or
marry the notorious scoundrel
mistaken as her lover.

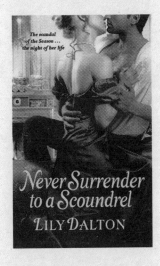

VISIT US ONLINE AT

WWW.HACHETTEBOOKGROUP.COM

FEATURES:

OPENBOOK BROWSE AND
SEARCH EXCERPTS
•
AUDIOBOOK EXCERPTS AND PODCASTS
•
AUTHOR ARTICLES AND INTERVIEWS
•
BESTSELLER AND PUBLISHING
GROUP NEWS
•
SIGN UP FOR E-NEWSLETTERS
•
AUTHOR APPEARANCES AND TOUR
INFORMATION
•
SOCIAL MEDIA FEEDS AND WIDGETS
•
DOWNLOAD FREE APPS

BOOKMARK HACHETTE BOOK GROUP
@ WWW.HACHETTEBOOKGROUP.COM